She was
successful,
accomplished,
on top of
the world—
until
Mr. WRONG
rocked
her world…
again!

GREENE, JENNIFER
THE WOMAN MOST LIKELY TO...

PPB   SB

*She was shook up. That was the thing. That was
why he lost his head and pulled her into a hug.*

The thing was, when he yanked her into that hug
she folded into him as if she belonged in his arms.
Her hair felt all tangled and tickly under his chin,
and the damn woman was *trembling*.

Susan didn't *tremble*. Susan made other people
tremble. It was her life's work, bringing guys to
their knees, orchestrating people's lives. Jon knew
exactly how much trouble she could be, but that still
didn't erase the more critical, immediate issue. For
Susan to tremble in his arms was like asking a cop to
walk away from a crime, a fireman to walk away
from a fire.

His hormones recognized it long before his head
did. She wanted him.

It wasn't his fault.

The kiss, though.

The kiss was definitely his fault.

JENNIFER GREENE

The WOMAN MOST LIKELY TO...

AVON BOOKS

An Imprint of HarperCollinsPublishers

This is a work of fiction. Names, characters, places, and incidents are products of the author's imagination or are used fictitiously and are not to be construed as real. Any resemblance to actual events, locales, organizations, or persons, living or dead, is entirely coincidental.

AVON BOOKS
An Imprint of HarperCollins*Publishers*
10 East 53rd Street
New York, New York 10022-5299

First Avon Books paperback printing: October 2002

Avon Trademark Reg. U.S. Pat. Off. and in Other Countries, Marca Registrada, Hecho en U.S.A.
HarperCollins® is a registered trademark of HarperCollins Publishers Inc.

Printed in the U.S.A.

10 9 8 7 6 5 4 3 2 1

To
my husband and son,
who are inspirations for all my heroes

and my mom and daughter,
who are the sunshine behind
the infamous Sunrise Cake

Chapter 1

Susan Sinclair rubbed her sticky hands on the backs of her jeans. At nine o'clock on a winsomely warm May night, she'd much rather be dancing naked with an unforgettable lover and a rose between her teeth, but that just didn't seem to be an option.

Baking, truth to tell, was never what Susan would willingly call an option, either, but every six months she went through the ritual. Bought four dozen eggs. Unearthed the cake pan. Put on some old CDs on the player and donned her fifteen-year-old lucky U of M sweatshirt.

An outsider wouldn't likely understand the critical importance of the Sinclair Sunrise sponge cake. Cripes, Susan didn't, either. If it were up to her, she'd just buy a cake from the bakery and have done with it. Unfortunately, the sacred family sponge cake was A Tradition. More annoying yet was that Becca and Lydia could both do this. Her daughter had been making the impossible cake since she was a freckle-faced ten-year-old, and her mom . . . her mom could make the cake blindfolded and handcuffed.

Susan wouldn't call herself *competitive*. She just happened to be—occasionally—as stubborn as a goat and more tenacious than a hound. Which meant that every six months, when no witnesses were around, Susan tried making the cake.

So far, it hadn't been going too well.

She pushed up her sleeves—again—took another deep, bracing breath and reached for a fresh egg from the third carton. One of the more ticklish problems with the recipe was needing to separate twelve eggs.

She could separate a white from a yolk, for Pete's sake. She wasn't *helpless* in a kitchen. It was just . . . she'd been at this for two hours already and so far had only successfully separated four eggs. Naturally, having done this before, she'd known enough to buy several spare cartons of eggs, but at this point she was running out of bowls. Every bowl and saucer she owned seemed to be filled with congealing whites and yolks, extending a sticky trail from the counter to the table.

She cracked yet another egg on the counter edge.

The damn thing slipped.

Goo dribbled over the lip of the counter, down the cupboard face and then oozed to the floor. At least the poor thing wasn't lonely. A considerable amount of goo from its sister eggs had already oozed to the floor.

Susan's lips firmed.

Her eyes narrowed.

Her condo—her wonderful, elegant, beautifully decorated and well-loved suburban condo—was normally ultra-clean. Susan liked her stuff tidy. The kitchen decor included a white tile floor, a Corian countertop *and* sink in more of that dazzling toothpaste white and a colorful, original Prateek hung on the breakfast nook wall. Two hours ago, her place could have been photographed for a magazine spread.

Not anymore.

Well, enough was enough. She made $92,500 a year. Had a responsible buyer's job that she'd learned and earned from the ground up. She'd raised a daughter alone, worked her way through a degree at the University of Michigan, paid her bills on time, was a self-supporting, self-reliant tough cookie of a woman. There was a time she'd fiercely wanted love in her life, but there was only one man she'd ever really wanted, and thinking about him just ruffled all her emotional feathers—and annoyed the hell out of her. So forget that. The point was the cake.

She was way too smart to let a #$*#&((* cake beat her. It would be like letting the family down, and Susan didn't let down the people she loved. That was an absolute for her, because if you let down someone you loved, it could haunt your heart forever and ever. So maybe the cake would seem like an itsy-bitsy issue to an outsider—but not to her. And since she had to leave tomorrow for a West Coast business trip, tonight was the last free time she had in a blue moon to conquer this dadblamed recipe.

Resolute, calling on the powerful force of her indomitable spirit—and all baking gods within hearing distance—she scooped up another egg and firmly cracked it on the edge of a stainless steel bowl. For no reason whatsoever, the shell splintered. It happened so fast. Sure, most of the white made it into the bowl, but quicker than a blink, the yolk had plopped in there and broken and blended with the white. Susan gazed at the newest mess, flabbergasted. How could this possibly keep happening?

It had to be the chicken, she thought darkly. None of this was her fault. Somewhere there was a farm where a delinquent chicken—with attitude—had deliberately produced this faulty batch of eggs. It was the chicken with the oppositional defiance problem who needed counseling. Not her.

The more Susan imagined the crazy fantasy, the more she found herself smiling . . . and then outright laughing.

Okay, okay, so she was a complete failure in the kitchen. Always had been, probably always would be. Yeah, she'd try the cake in another few months—and probably fail again. So it cost her sanity and completely destroyed her kitchen. She didn't really care.

When it came down to it, her life was good.

More than good.

She'd struggled for so many years, but finally her life seemed to be on a solid, peaceful track. Becca was thriving in her first teaching job. Her mom seemed quietly happy. A few troubling thorns had poked into Susan's job, but she had huge hopes this West Coast trip would give her the means to fix those. All in all, her life was going as smooth as a baby's bottom.

For once, there was absolutely nothing serious to worry about.

Who could ask for more?

Chapter 2

JUNE

Lydia Sinclair never had an orgasm before she was fifty-five, but that was precisely the point. She'd gotten started so much later than most that she felt obligated to make up for lost time.

When George rolled off her, he was breathing too hard to speak. So was she, yet she still inhaled everything about this moment that she could possibly take in.

Summer sunlight poured through the windows, ribboning cheerful stripes of light on the rumpled bedsheets. The sound of exhausted, heavy breathing contrasted to the innocent coo of a mourning dove. Scents whispered through the windows—the sweet, soft scents of daffodils and lilacs and tulips—contrasting with the distinctive smells of hot, sweaty sex.

The disgrace of it delighted her. Who'd have ever believed it? That she'd be in bed with a man she wasn't married to—or ever planned to be married to. That she'd had sex at noon in broad daylight, on the brightest, sunniest June day in the history of mankind . . . and enjoyed every raunchy, earthy minute of it.

How come no one ever told her that sex was wasted on the young? That being this decadent and wanton was so much fun?

"God."

Lydia turned her head. George showed no signs of recovering. He hadn't opened his eyes, and that single syllable seemed all he could verbally manage yet. Still, it was one of the nicest compliments she'd ever had.

Her gaze softened. Physically George wasn't exactly competition for Mel Gibson—he had a stubborn paunch around the middle and was growing more forehead by the month. But she didn't care about the paunch or the baldness. George had the kindest eyes this side of the Great Lakes. And though he wasn't the best kisser on the planet—certainly nothing on a par with Riff—his enthusiasm certainly earned him an A for exuberance.

The bedroom, she noted, was a complete disaster. George's belt lay in the doorway. So did a shoe. The pants to his postal uniform were crumpled in a puddle by the white wicker rocker, his shirt peeking from behind it.

The male garments looked sinfully shocking in her bedroom. She'd only started redecorating this last fall. It had taken her three years to believe—really believe—that Harold was dead, that she was free, that she no longer had to live and breathe the job of pleasing a husband. She'd gotten rid of all the dark, heavy furniture. Actually, she'd tried to get rid of every practical piece of furniture in the entire house—including the old mattress on this bed.

Once she'd discovered she was orgasmic, the first thing she'd splurged on was a king-sized, serious mattress. Now that she was into sinning and wickedness, she didn't want to be held back by anything as silly as weak box springs.

"Lydia . . . ?"

"Hmm?" Affectionately she reached over to touch and stroke the sun-leathered skin around his neck. It was another new thing. Touching someone—especially a man—for no reason at all except the pleasure of it.

He stroked back. Fingertips traced her cheek, then her brow, then feathered through her thick hair. He must have been more awake than she thought, because suddenly his gentle voice came out with, "It doesn't feel right, stealing these nooners with you."

Hells bells. She should have known there was a tick on every hound. "It feels right to me."

"You're too good a woman to settle for an affair like this, Lydia."

Her eyes narrowed. From somewhere outside she heard a discordant sound—not birdsong, not the distant roar of tractor engines, not the chime clock in the front hall, but the kind of sound that didn't belong. Her mind vaguely registered the slam of a car door, but just then, she focused all her attention on George. "I thought we discussed this before. I told you from the start I wasn't looking for anything serious. I asked you to walk away—right away—if you felt differently."

"I know you did."

"If you're unhappy—"

"I'm happy. I'm happy."

"I'm never getting married again, George. Not to you. Not to anyone. I'd rather dig ditches for a living. Is that clear enough?"

The pad of his thumb caressed her cheek. "Now, I realize some freedom can feel real good, Lydia. But in the long run, I don't think playing around is something you can live with. You're too good a woman. And I'm happy with what we're doing, so don't get your liver in an uproar. I'm just saying, when and if people start talking and you start fretting the immorality of it—"

"I'll never fret the immorality of it. With any luck, I'll never do another moral thing as long as I live." She heard another discordant sound. A clump on the front veranda, as if something heavy had suddenly dropped.

That seemed impossible. Lydia knew when a sound belonged and when it didn't. Copper Creek, Michigan, wasn't that many miles from the bustle and hustle of Traverse City, but strangers rarely intruded on the farms on the Old Mission Peninsula. The shore property was touristy, sure, but this was private land off the beaten path. Bing Matthew had been caretaking the orchards since Harold died, but Lydia recognized every noise that Bing's trucks and tractors made. Neighbors frequently stopped to visit, but that car door slamming wasn't a car she knew. The thudding clump on the front porch wasn't a sound that belonged at 12:26 on a Wednesday afternoon, either.

George, however, was only listening to one drummer—the same one he wanted her to hear. "I'm not pushing you toward marriage, Lydia. I'm in no hurry to do anything. But I want you to know how much I ca—"

"Grandma? Gram! Are you home?"

At the sound of the voice, Lydia instantly froze. There were only two people in the universe she'd kill for—her daughter Susan, and her granddaughter Becca. She loved them both with all her heart, beyond her heart, and it wasn't as if she hadn't seen them in a while. Just like always, they'd been together at Christmas, Easter, the occasional weekend—but not *here*, not home at Copper Creek. And one had never turned up for a visit without the other.

Neither of the girls knew how much her life had recently changed, and Lydia especially hungered to talk with her daughter. She'd raised Susan completely wrong, she realized now. There were things she should have told Suze, about sex and life and men, and more than anything, about the lies women tell themselves—the kinds of lies women think they have to live in order to survive.

Possibly Lydia could have saved Susan a ton of heartache if she'd been more woman-to-woman honest with her. But she'd never had that choice. It took Harold dying to shake her up, to make her see things differently. And she intended to initiate a talk—a serious talk with Susan in a way they'd never tried talking together before.

Only, darn it, she meant tomorrow or next week or next month. Not *now*.

"Grandma!! Yoo-hoo! Are you upstairs?"

Lydia swallowed fast, and then scrambled out of bed faster than a bolt of lightning. She wanted to talk, yes. But she sure as patooties didn't want her daughter or granddaughter to find her in bed, naked at noon with a strange man.

She hissed at George to leave by the back stairs and stay out of sight or she'd never forgive him as long as she lived. Then she grabbed a handful of clothes and yelled loudly, "Why, is that you, Becca? What a wonderful surprise! I'll be down in two shakes of a lamb's tail, honey!"

Becca was still standing on the porch when she heard her grandmother call out. Just hearing Lydia's voice made tears well in her eyes.

Quickly she pushed open the screen door and automatically fell back on childhood habits—slipping off her sandals so she wouldn't track in dirt, hanging her patchwork purse and jacket on the brass tree because Gram liked things neatly put away. She'd left her suitcases in the car—they'd wait. And it sounded as if Gram were in one of the far bedrooms upstairs—she was glad to relax and wait for Gram, too.

Just being here felt like a soothing balm. Last week had been a mountain of hand-wringing and not-sleeping and driving herself crazy. At twenty-two, naturally, she was plenty old enough to handle her own life. She was way too old to be taking every problem to her mom or dad. She was just shook up right now, that was all. But even more, she just couldn't take this to Susan. Her mom had sacrificed for her from the day she was born, was always sacrificing for somebody. She couldn't disappoint Susan. She just couldn't.

But Gram was different. During the tedious long drive from Kalamazoo to Traverse City, Becca kept thinking that she should probably have called ahead rather than impulsively showing up like this—but really, what difference did it make? Gram wouldn't mind. Gram wouldn't ask her any questions; she'd just be thrilled to see her. She always was.

Becca half turned, her gaze expectantly zooming toward the stairs, where she figured to see Lydia any second—when her smile suddenly stalled in uneasy surprise.

If she hadn't already heard her grandmother's voice, she'd have thought she'd accidentally barged into a stranger's house.

Lydia had obviously redecorated. Nothing wrong with that. Cripes, once Gramps died, Becca had been coaxing Gram to overhaul the place in whatever way suited her. It was just . . . well, unconsciously Becca had counted on everything being comfortably, predictably the same.

And nothing was.

Tentatively she ambled around, looking, touching. The old-fashioned parlor had always been stuffed stem to stern with sturdy antiques made of dark, rich woods and big, heavy lamps with fringed lampshades. Now all those things were gone. The carpeting was a plush, pale daffodil-yellow. Daffodil! For a farmhouse carpet! Two chairs and a couch were upholstered in more of that soft, fragile yellow. Instead of Gramps's farming manuals cramming the bookshelves, now there were glass unicorns and romance novels and fancy ceramic eggs. The heavy velvet drapes that always made Becca think of Scarlett O'Hara had been replaced with horizontal linen blinds.

Gram had never even said she liked yellow, for Pete's sake. Gram practically made a religion out of tradition and history and never threw anything away—especially anything that came down from the Sinclair side of the family.

Becca tiptoed into the dining room and found more shocks. The Sacred Sinclair Civil War Table that used to seat sixteen—and creak and groan under the weight of holiday dinners—had disappeared. The room had been converted into a high-tech media center, with a computer set up on one side and a TV the size of Alaska on the other. Her grandmother barely used to watch TV. Now she was doing Surround Sound and the Internet?

Furthermore, a soft blanket of dust covered the surfaces. Dust. In Lydia Sinclair's house. Like Mom would say, it was like walking in a church and finding an angel dancing naked. Some things just couldn't *be*.

For the first time in days, Becca forgot her own

personal life crisis. There was more yellow in the kitchen. In fact, you'd think a madman had gotten loose with gallons and gallons of daffodil-yellow paint before anyone could stop him. The cookie-making, maple-syrup-stirring, Easter-egg-dying, finger-painting kitchen of her childhood had been completely wiped out. Gone was the traditional brick floor, the painted-too-many-times cupboards, the practical Formica counters.

Grandma now had a wine rack. A *wine rack*. And music discs were scattered by a brand-new, state-of-the-art disc player—only not discs of Barry Manilow and Neil Diamond, but discs of R&B and rap and a variety of age music, too.

Rap.

Grandma.

Becca pressed a hand to her heart, but the shocks kept coming. Past the kitchen was an ordinary utility room, only instead of the tidy sight she expected, laundry was heaped on the dryer, unfolded, all wrinkled up. And beyond the utility room was the old Victorian bathroom with the pull-chain toilet—except that the pull chain was gone, and so was the cabbage-rose wallpaper. *Someone* had installed a see-through shower, a new low-water john, and a sleek marble counter with a zillion things on it—brushes and cosmetics and perfumes and creams.

Grandma. Using cosmetics and perfumes and creams.

Grandma. Choosing a see-through shower door.

It was enough to give a twenty-two-year-old granddaughter heart failure.

"Gram!" She roared, this time jogging at a reverse pace back toward the stairs. All right, so she'd come to Copper Creek because she had a crisis ... but when it came down to it, a crisis was just a crisis. No matter what kind of disaster she was in, it wasn't the same thing as discovering something threatening her grandmother. "Gram!"

"I'm coming, I'm coming, darlin'—"

Becca wouldn't have thought anything of a few changes, but this was like a psychopath had absconded with Gram's life, doing things Gram would never do, changing things Gram would never change. She had a fast, frantic impulse to call her dad—God knows, he'd help—but Dad wasn't exactly a favorite in the Sinclair household, and this seemed more like a woman kind of problem besides. Becca couldn't evaluate whether this was a complete psychotic breakdown or menopause—who knew what happened to women when they got in their fifties? But Mom would know. Mom always knew.

Besides which, Susan could fix anything.

From one of the upstairs bedrooms, Becca heard something thump—an odd sound, considering that she heard Grandma's footsteps skittering at the top of the hall. But she swiftly forgot the strange sound. The instant she saw Lydia's bare feet at the stair top, she barreled up the stairs, closing the distance between them faster than a blink.

Again, tears filled her eyes as she wrapped her arms around her grandmother. Silly, emotional tears. She hugged, and then hugged tighter.

"Honey, what on earth are you doing here?"

Knowing Gram would ask, Becca had mentally concocted a story to answer that question, but now she was so scattered and worried that the only thing she could blurt out was pretty much the truth. "I didn't think you'd mind if I came without asking. I couldn't do anything until today because school wasn't over until yesterday, so this was the first I could leave, and then—"

A sturdy hand stroked her hair, her cheek. "Don't be silly, you foolish girl. I'm thrilled you're here. Beyond thrilled. You never have to ask, you know that."

Gram sounded so much like the old Gram—the *real* Gram—that Becca accidentally blurted out more. "I just had to see you. I have a problem. Something I can't tell Mom or Dad, and I can handle it myself . . . but I just needed to get away from the apartment and Douglas and everything. If it's okay, I want to stay for a couple of weeks."

"It's okay, it's okay. Whatever it is, it's okay."

Even though she still felt shaky, Becca forced herself to push back from the hug so she could get a serious look at her grandmother. Only nothing, she thought frantically, was okay.

It was a running joke in the family that the Sinclair women must be clones because they looked so much alike. They all started out with red-gold hair that turned taffy and then to a softer cognac. It was thick, lustrous, unmanageable hair that they whined to each other about constantly. All three of them were five-foot-four on the button. They all had big eyes. They were all allergic to clams, had the same small black mole at the same spot on their spines, and had great skin except for a few days every month when they were zit-prone.

Looking at her grandmother and mom sometimes gave Becca an ooga-booga feeling, because it was like knowing ahead what she'd look like herself down the pike. But just then, her grandmother's appearance scared her for other reasons entirely.

Lydia's cheeks were flushed. She'd lost weight since Becca had last seen her. She was wearing a big T-shirt with a giant sunflower on it, which was fun, except that the T-shirt was inside out, and she was barefoot and wearing mascara.

Gram wasn't afraid of dirt or messes, but she'd always been buttoned up to the nth degree, never unkempt, never one to wear a T-shirt inside out. The mascara was the real shocker, though, because it showed up in smudges under Gram's big brown eyes. Lydia had either been recently sweating or crying.

Something, damn it, was wrong. Really wrong.

The Sinclair women all tended to be strong. But when the problem was the size of Armageddon, there was no question which one they turned to.

Susan.

Jon Laker was stretched out in the hot tub when the cell phone rang. Had anyone discovered him, he'd have claimed to be enjoying a lazy, decadent soak at the end of the day—no way he'd admit that his thirty-eight-year-old muscles were sore as hell. He could still outwork any three teenage pipsqueaks any day of the week. And did.

Only, hell, recovering never used to hurt this much, which was why he glared at the cell phone instead of answering it. He'd *just* gotten settled down. The stresses of the workday were finally easing up, the silence of the night just starting to enfold him in a feeling of peace. He didn't want to let it go.

His place on Traverse Bay was two stories high. Downstairs was the business, the marina office, and he put up with people coming and going all day long, but the second floor was supposed to be his. It'd been a royal bitch to put in the hot tub this high, but the secluded balcony meant he could be naked or surly or whip-tired or anything else and no one would know. He liked people fine, but up here was the only place where he really felt as if he owned himself.

And for a half hour now, he'd been thinking of Susan. He didn't want to. Didn't mean to. But Traverse Bay looked like navy satin on a breathless night like this. Lights shone like jewels in the cottages across the lake. An occasional late boat coming in stirred the water, making other boats slip-slurp in the cradle of the wake—including his own sailboat, the *S-Q*, just below. The lazy slip-slurping sound was the only intrusion on the night's silence, except for laughter sometimes drifting in the air, or the excited whisper of kids walking by, out late, high on being young.

Nights like this, memories seemed to seep and

sneak into his consciousness—memories of scents and sounds and textures. It happened to be a night just like this, exactly like this—silky water, moonlight softer than silver, June smells—that he'd conned Susan Sinclair into going skinny-dipping. They'd both been sixteen. Once he'd conned the pants off her, he'd conned her into making love.

It was that making love business that muggled around in his mind's recollection and wouldn't let go. Sixteen-year-old boys didn't do good sex. Hell, sixteen-year-old boys didn't have a clue what good sex even was. But with Suze—even when he was that young, that dumb, that brash, that hot and ready—they'd actually made love. Lazy, long, liquid love. The kind that clung in a man's mind even years later. Even when he was way too old, and way too smart, to believe that first love was more than illusion.

When his cell phone rang again, Jon quit pretending he was going to be able to ignore it and grabbed the monster.

His daughter's voice was all it took to obliterate the spell. Really, it was only occasionally that those blurry memories sneaked into his mind. There was just a taste of irony that Susan was messing with the peace of his night at the same instant their daughter called—not that he wasn't always glad to talk to Becca.

"Hey, beautiful," he said warmly. "I tried to phone you twice yesterday, but couldn't seem to reach anything but your machine. Nothing new here. I just wanted to wish you congrats."

"Congrats?"

"Yeah, congrats—for making it a whole year teaching. Especially teaching out-of-control animals that age."

When Becca chuckled, Jon could feel a grin forming in the darkness. He loved children—which Becca knew perfectly well. Still, the idea of spending all day, every day, with twenty rowdy kindergartners was the stuff of shudders. He didn't doubt Becca could handle it, because she was a born earth mom. A bitsy one, as far as physical stature, but she had the long red-blond hair, the tendency to dress in easy smocks and jumpers, the whisper of natural freckles on her nose. She wore her emotions right out there, easy to laugh, easy to feel, easy to cry—which made Jon worry about her sometimes—but picturing her with kids was as natural as the sun coming up in the morning.

"Well? Have you made up your mind whether you're going to teach again next year, or quit for good?"

"I won't know if they intend to renew my contract for another month, but I think they will. And I sure loved the school and the kids, so I'm almost sure I'll say yes."

"My God, girl, you have more guts than the Marines. I'm proud of—"

"Dad."

His eyes shot open in the darkness at her sudden change in tone. He and Becca generally chitchatted once a week, and yeah, he'd sensed over the last month that something was off. Becca wasn't the

closed-in type, unlike her mother. Susan could and
did hide any emotion she wanted to, where Becca
showed her whole heart . . . but not lately. Since
she'd reached the mighty advanced age of twenty-
two, Jon figured he owed her the respect of backing
off from the heavy-duty parenting thing. If she
wanted him to know something, she'd tell him. But
now the way she interrupted with that "Dad" rang
the red phone in his paternal white house.

"What's wrong, honey?"

"I'm trying to find Mom. I've called her four
times, left messages, but she still hasn't gotten
back. There isn't any chance you know where she
is, do you?"

Jon had to think before answering that question.
Susan Sinclair would let him know where she was,
maybe, possibly, when hell froze over. They col-
lided fairly frequently over the years, whenever
there was an event affecting their daughter. Ballet
recitals. Graduation. College costs. First dates, first
fender bumps, first period. The time Becca's appen-
dix had ruptured.

No matter what was happening with Becca, he
and Susan had always managed to be civil. Even
when they strongly disagreed, they both loved their
daughter too much to openly clash. Even on the oc-
casions when Jon had wanted to rattle her teeth, Susan hadn't known it and never would.

And for damn sure, neither would his daughter.

"No, honey, I don't know where your mother is.
Is there something I can do?"

"No. Not really. And the thing is . . . she travels a

lot. But she never goes anywhere without leaving me a number or checking in with her machine at home. I can't understand it. And I thought, well, maybe she might have had a reason to call you."

Jon heaved out of the hot tub and grabbed a towel. Forget Susan. Something was wrong here, he could smell it. "Tell me what the problem is," he urged her.

"It's just . . . I'm up here now, Dad. At Copper Creek, with Gram. I just got here this afternoon, and the thing is, I'm not sure Grandma's completely okay. I just want to talk to Mom, that's all."

"You're in Traverse? On the peninsula? Right now?"

He could almost hear her gulp. "Dad, I just *got* here. I was going to call you either today or tomorrow, but this wasn't a trip I planned ahead. I just took off. Because school was out and I just wanted to hang loose for a couple weeks before settling into the summer, you know?"

"Sure," Jon said, but nothing was sounding right to him. Granted, he wasn't Mr. Perception—not about women in general, but especially not about the Sinclair women. But a guy didn't have to have a Ph.D. in sensitivity to know there were holes in his daughter's voice. "You're worried about something. You think your grandmother's sick, is that it?"

"No, no. Yes. Cripes, Dad, I don't know. I just want to talk to Mom. Don't worry about it, okay? I'll keep trying to reach her. And I'm here now, so it's not like Gram's alone if there is a problem. And hey. Since I've got you on the phone now—any chance you've got a couple hours free this week?"

"For my favorite daughter? You name the time, I'll be there."

Two minutes later she hung up. Two minutes after that, Jon had shut off the hot tub, knotted a towel at his waist and headed inside.

But at one that morning, he gave up trying to fall asleep and got up to pace.

The place was perfect for a man alone. He'd always bought the best appliances, whatever made life chores faster and easier. And he could care less about decorating, but he craved a place of peace after a long workday, so everything was either in wood or water color, making it naturally fit in the lakeside environment. The upstairs had two bedrooms, so Becca always had a room of her own when she visited, which she often did. In fact, although she was thick-as-thieves close with her grandmother, it was rare she'd chosen to stay with Lydia instead of him.

He stared out the window, then paced some more. No need for light. Even in the dark apartment, metal gleamed to let him know where furniture and edges were. The deeper the night, the more the lake darkened to a smooth black mirror, all the lights long doused from the cottages and houses. Even the loons were dead asleep. Nothing was stirring outside.

But Jon was roiled up on the inside like a porcupine in a bad mood. He and Becca were close. True, they didn't talk about emotional bologna the way women did, but she knew she could come to him for anything. Maybe he wouldn't feel comfortable with some types of problems. Maybe he'd been known to express his viewpoint a little noisily. But Becca knew damn well he'd climb mountains for her without a blink, so if she wanted his help, she'd surely ask.

So something was off, that was for sure. Becca, coming up to Traverse without even mentioning the trip to him. Asking for Susan when she knew damn well he didn't keep in close contact with her mother. And then there were those "holes" in his daughter's voice.

Somewhere there was trouble.

Jon stopped dead in front of another moonlit window and glowered. He didn't mind trouble. Truth to tell, he was generally fond of it. A little stress got the blood pumping. Gave a man something to do. And a man got stale if he wasn't occasionally tested.

But damnation—he'd had all the trouble involving Susan Sinclair that he needed in this lifetime. Twenty-two years ago she'd twisted a knot on his soul. It was still tied tight. Probably never would loosen up. Hell, there were tons of females in the world—and every single one of them was less heartache than Susan.

He just wanted to keep it that way, that was all.

Chapter 3

Susan Sinclair thunked down her suitcase, impatiently pushed back her rain-soaked hair and dug in her purse for the condo key. It was past seven. Her plane had been four hours late; she'd been on her feet since daybreak Seattle time, and there had been a thunder-and-lightning-and-blinding-rain storm the whole drive home from the Detroit airport.

She wasn't merely tired. She was whipped to the bone and strung tight enough to snap. She had two seconds of energy left, max. If she didn't get to a nice soft surface with a pillow that quickly, she was going to lie down right here, in the middle of the condominium hall, and she didn't give a holy hoot who found her.

She dug deeper. Her wrinkled airline tickets sailed to her floor; then her brush tumbled over the purse edge. Eventually she emerged with the condo key, stabbed it in the lock and pushed at the door . . . only to realize that for some God-unknown reason, the door had been unlocked to start with.

If anything more went wrong, she was going to scream. She was still planning on curling up in a small ball on the carpet right there and falling asleep—she was just slightly altering the plan to include a scream first. A loud, piercing, shrieking, tantrum-sized scream.

She pushed the damn door open. Tugged the damn suitcase and tote inside. Kicked off her damn navy blue heels. Dropped her damned drenched raincoat, yanked at her damned sopping hair again, turned around.

And let out a scream for real.

She was expecting cool, dark and quiet—desperately *needing* cool, dark and quiet—but her condo was hotter than a rain forest in July and emitting all kinds of mind-jarring noises. Televisions blared from her bedroom and the living room. Several buzzers were going off simultaneously from the kitchen. Blinking lights flashed on a half dozen electronic devices, ranging from answering machines to clocks to her oven and VCR.

Before she lost the last of her mind—assuming there was any mind left worth saving—Susan jogged around, switching on lights, turning off TVs, pushing buttons. The problem was obvious. There must have been a major power outage sometime over the last two weeks. God knows when or for how long—but definitely long enough to make some unfortunate smells reek from the refrigerator and goof up all her electronic appliances. Considering the power problem, it was probably best that she hadn't left the air-conditioning on, but now to add insult to injury, the condo was airless and sweltering hot.

Darn it, a headache was already battering at her temples. She sank on the rose-striped couch, startled to realize how close she was to crying.

Sure, she was frazzled—who wouldn't be? Her work schedule over the last two weeks would have stressed an ox. A pit-awful exhausting travel day hadn't helped. And coming home to find the place like this was especially upsetting because it meant that all her answering machine messages were lost—so she had no way of knowing if Becca or her mother had needed to reach her.

Still, it had been a long time—twenty-two years, since Jon Laker, to be precise—since she'd felt this close to bawling her heart out.

Obviously she knew what the trouble was. Her new boss on the West Coast. And going into this trip, she'd sensed there could be a major potential problem brewing, that he'd be nothing like Sebastian to work with—but she knew her job, knew her capabilities, knew her skill at fixing tough situations. When a foundation was that secure, how could it suddenly crack at the seams?

Yet that was exactly how Susan felt. Not only as if her job were suddenly jeopardized, but as if something deep and elemental were cracked inside her. She felt threatened and unsteady.

Aw, hell. Susan pushed off the couch impatiently. A decent night's sleep would undoubtedly make everything look differently. She'd certainly never been a whiner before, and she sure as patooties didn't cry. You could take that to the bank.

But tarnation, when the telephone suddenly

rang, she felt hot, thick tears well in her eyes before she could get a grip. Was a minute of peace and quiet too much to ask? Cripes, *normal* people could surely enjoy a ten-minute nervous breakdown without having to actually schedule one . . . although, come to think of it, she couldn't possibly schedule a nervous breakdown on her calendar for several months. The soonest she could possibly fit one in was late September.

That thought was so loony that she almost laughed. But then the telephone rang again, obliterating any time she had to either laugh or cry. Exasperated, she grabbed the receiver.

"*Mom?* Did I really finally get you? Oh, Mom, I'm so glad you're home. I've been trying to reach you for days, and I was starting to get so worried."

Her daughter's voice immediately shocked some sense into her. She banished the tears, swallowed the clog in her throat and infused her voice with cheerfulness. "Hey, lovebug, I'm so sorry I missed you. I just got home from Seattle, walked in and realized there was a major power outage here. Must have been a big storm or something. Anyway, this is the first I realized that the answering machine wasn't working and I lost any messages. What's wrong, Bec?"

"Oh, Mom."

The two words seemed to tear out of Becca's throat and instantly brought out all of Susan's protective maternal instincts. Becca sucked in some air and tried to talk coherently. Instead, out came a blubbering torrent, just like old times—like when she was twelve and Bill Winchester had told her she was flat-chested, and when she didn't make the cut for cheerleading, and when she made Honors Society but Jacob Osborne *still* didn't ask her to the prom. Becca cried easily, but she only blubbered for the stuff that broke her heart. That stuff that she never seemed to want to tell Susan, but somehow always did.

"Hold on," Susan said gently. "Come on. Just tell me."

"I'm just so shook up. Can you drive up, Mom? To Copper Creek? I'm with Gram and there's something wrong with her. In fact, everything's wrong. Everything. I'm so confused and—"

"Is Grandma sick? Need a doctor?"

"No, no, it's not that kind of physically sick, I'm pretty sure."

"*You're* not sick, are you?"

"Not sick, but . . . no. Not sick like cancer or operations or a medical crisis like that. It's other stuff. I think Gram had some kind of psychotic breakdown. And maybe I have, too. And—"

"Okay, okay, take it easy," Susan said soothingly. Maybe she didn't have the whole story yet, but she'd already heard all she needed to know. Her daughter was seriously upset. Everything else was just details. "I need ten minutes to throw fresh clothes in a suitcase and then I'll be on the road. I can't be there until well after midnight, so just relax, go to sleep. As long as nobody's ill, the problem'll wait until morning, right?"

Two hiccups, then a nose-blow louder than a foghorn. "Right."

"We'll fix it, Becca. I promise. Whatever it is, we'll put our heads together and find a solution. Haven't we always?"

"Oh, Mom." This time the nose-blow came through the phone lines louder than a bellow. "Now I feel like a jerk. Nothing's that bad. I probably worried you for nothing, but I swear, Grandma is really behaving weirdly. I'd just feel better if you saw her for yourself."

"Uh-huh." For Susan, the greater truth was that she didn't have a prayer of resting—no matter how tired she was—until she saw her daughter face-to-face. "I'll be there, baby. Just catch some sleep, and give a hug to Gram."

When she hung up, Susan took a long, bracing breath. If her daughter needed her, that was that. Nothing mattered more than family. Money, work, exhaustion, the crisis in her career—none of that was worth a serious fiddlefaddle by comparison.

But, man. Even after all these years, she always seemed to mentally brace before going home to Copper Creek. She loved her mom. Loved the two hundred years of Sinclair roots.

But Copper Creek was also Jon Laker country, and right now, especially, Susan just didn't want to risk seeing him if there was any other choice.

Seven hours later, Susan stopped at a red light outside Traverse City. In an ideal world, she'd have arrived at Copper Creek long before now, but there'd been no way to just take off. Especially to leave for an unknown period of time; she'd had a zillion things to do, and it had taken more than ten minutes—handling the mail and bills, cleaning up the fridge, unpacking and repacking.

The toughest thing, of course, had been calling Sebastian to arrange for a leave of absence. She'd started working for L'Amour when she was a baby-toting single mom with a fresh college degree, climbed the ladder to the chief buyer position and watched the business grow from one store to eight stores scattered over the country. Sebastian not only depended on her, but knew she was good for seventy-hour weeks.

Naturally he had a cow when she told him she needed time off. And he had a royal cow when she asked for a full month. He'd had to say yes—how could he turn her down when she'd never asked him for anything before? But he'd whined a lot.

Susan hadn't known she was going to ask for a month off, but now she tasted the unfamiliar flavor of relief. As much as she'd always loved her job, she needed this time off, needed some freedom, needed a chance to think about how to handle—and whether she could handle—Sebastian's new part-ner on the West Coast, Brian Weis.

During the darkest night hours, for the long stretches when her Avalon was the only car on the road, pictures flashed in her mind—haunting, up-setting slivers of memory from that one evening with Brian. His private conference room, after everyone was gone and they'd finished a take-out dinner. Brian, peeling off the jacket of his navy suit. Her, peeling off the jacket of her favorite black suit.

His insisting on pouring some wine after a marathon workday. Her wanting to help him cope with his new role of West Coast partner, knowing Sebastian thought the world of him. Her voice bubbling over with enthusiasm on the designer program for spring. Brian, watching her, watching her.

And then suddenly he grabbed, and the wine was spilling all over the elegant drawings, her heart pounding, pounding, a sound coming out of her mouth like a laugh . . . because of course this was funny. It had to be funny. She was too mature, too experienced, too careful to let anything this ridiculous and impossible happen to her, much less in a business setting. She simply had to handle the situation with tact and poise and it would all go away. . . .

The lonely red traffic light turned green. Susan, realizing her palms were slick and her stomach was churning, pushed on the gas.

She simply *had* to get that jerk off her mind. She was almost home. The air was cool and clean, the night soft, and for miles the road cuddled between tall, sweet-smelling woods on both sides. Whatever was wrong—with her, with her life—it wasn't this night, and she needed to be strong for Becca and her mother.

Within minutes, she'd zoomed past the lights of Traverse City, and then it was just a hop and a skip to the turnoff for 37 onto Old Mission Peninsula. Neon lights disappeared fast then. Just as swiftly the busy resort and urban areas disappeared into crystal-quiet orchard country—she turned a last corner, and there it was. The mailbox for Copper Creek was hand-carved to look like a birdhouse, and then came a ridge of huge old bosomy oaks that cloaked the property in privacy.

A few moments later, she cut the lights and the engine. The landscape, bathed in silver moonlight, put a tug in her heartbeat. Five generations of Sinclairs had lived and loved on this land. The two-story house had white siding with a stone foundation, a venerable shake roof, and a comfortable wraparound veranda. It was more sturdy than elegant, an architectural hodgepodge that began as a one-room cabin, then got added on and added on and added on.

It wasn't the house that made her throat suddenly feel so full, though, nor the barns and outbuildings beyond it.

Once upon a time, this had been Hiawatha country, and where man hadn't gobbled it up, the landscape still had that promise of wild beauty. White pines stretched in the distance, with paper birch and quaking aspen hemming the edges of the woods. Copper Creek looked copper-gold in sunlight, but now she looked like a ribbon of liquid silver as she wound her way in and around the wooded banks.

Closer to the house, the land looked more civilized, but also more man-loved. Off to the west, the horse chestnuts were in bloom with zillions of white cone-shaped flowers. Beyond the chestnuts were acres of sugar maples. She and Becca used to drive up from Detroit in late winter to tap the trees for syrup—Becca always complaining that it took too darn much work to get too little, her mom scolding that it wasn't about maple syrup, for Pete's sake, it was for the joy of it.

Susan felt the lump in her throat getting bigger. It was never easy to come home . . . but sometimes it was even harder to stay away.

On the east side of the house were Lydia's prize-winning rose gardens. This early in June, the flowers weren't in bloom yet, but they were the one thing on the land that Lydia Sinclair loved. Nothing got between Lydia and those roses . . . and just beyond the pampered rosebushes, daffodils and lilacs were still in bloom, shadowed now, but their dew-drenched scent was so thick and sweet it made you think—hopelessly—of love. It was the smell of being in love. Of yearning. Of risks so big they opened the heart.

Those were scents she associated with Jon Laker and always would.

Beyond the house, where Copper Creek twisted out of sight, were the two hundred acres of cherry trees. Apples and grapes and cherries grew exuberantly in the middle of the peninsula, nurtured by the temperate winds and moisture affected by the bays, but cherries seemed to love the sandy loam soil and hilly sites the best. By mid-June, the trees were long past bloom, but even in the darkness and distance, she could see that orchards already looked pregnant with the weight of cherries.

Growing up, Susan remembered wanting to escape the farm with a passion . . . but as the years passed, she sometimes wondered how she'd ever become such a hard-core city woman, when she missed the country so much. It seemed especially ironic that her mother stayed, when her mom always claimed she hated the orchards—probably because they were the only thing in life that Dad loved.

The silence folded over her. Even the crickets were asleep this late, and Susan leaned back, thinking she should get out of the car, get in the house, catch some sleep before it was daybreak. Still, she couldn't seem to move. Not yet.

Over the years, the only subject mom and daughter never discussed was Harold Sinclair. No other subject was forbidden, and really, this one wasn't, either. The problem was more than neither ever seemed to have a clue what to say, how to handle anything so impossible or hurtful or confusing to both of them. Still, what mattered now was recognizing how completely different the place was with her father gone.

There was nothing scary in the shadows anymore. Right then, she could only seem to remember the warm, good memories anyway.

Helplessly her gaze wandered to the covey of Norway spruce just off the back veranda. As a little girl, she'd loved to play house under those big old spruces, take her dolls out and nest them in "rooms" made by the tree roots.

She suddenly snugged her arms under her chest, knowing it wasn't childhood memories—or memories of her father—that influenced her feelings about home and family, about men, about the kind of woman she'd wanted to be. Her pulse was suddenly slamming in her chest. No, the man who'd influenced her life most was not her father.

She'd made the best mistakes she ever made in her life with Jon Laker.

She'd made love with Jon Laker under those Norway spruce trees one fall. Rolled under the lilacs with Jon Laker the spring before. Snuck out to her mother's rose garden to whisper secrets in Jon Laker's arms in the heart of a summer night. Damn near suffered frostbite on her tush with Jon Laker one freezing winter morning in the sugar maples.

God, no one could be as naive or wild or impulsive as she'd been at sixteen. Nobody could be as crazy in love. Or as much of a damn fool.

Susan sighed. Through the years, for Becca's sake, she'd gotten along with Jon. But the crisis in her job made her feel vulnerable and unsteady, not herself. Right now she just didn't want to see Jon at all. Yet at the same time she had the crazy, unwanted intuition that the problems confronting her were inexorably related to the mistakes she'd made twenty-two years ago with Jon Laker.

Perhaps coming home would help her find answers. Or maybe coming home was the last thing she should have done, no matter who needed her. But at that moment it didn't matter either way. She felt so exhausted that the simplicity of the night seemed to fold around her and take her in. Moonlight bathed her cheek when she leaned back and closed her eyes. She'd go in the house in a second. But just for one short second she needed to believe—to feel—that she still owned herself.

Chapter 4

"Mom!"

Susan woke with a start at the sound of her daughter's shriek.

It took a groggy second before Susan realized that she was curled up in the car and had never made it in the house the night before. Quickly she pushed the door handle and climbed out—but almost not quickly enough. The screen door slammed open, and suddenly Becca was flying down the porch steps, and typically, chattering a mile a minute.

"I can't believe it, did you really sleep in the car? Oh, I'm so glad you're here! You silly, why didn't you come in the house? How long'd it take you to drive? How long can you stay? Oh, Mom, I'm just so glad you could take off from work to come. I know it had to take you a ton of arrangements. Was Sebastian mad? Are you hungry? Are you tired?"

Susan spliced in answers to a few of the easier questions, but mostly her concentration was on Becca. God, nothing on the planet felt as wonderful as the feel of her arms around her daughter. She was taking in all the information she could from Bec's appearance.

On the surface her baby looked normal—110 pounds of freckles and wildly unkempt hair, wearing a patchwork jumper and cloddy sandals that Susan would have burned rather than wear.

In some ways they looked alike—Becca had the Sinclair hair and big brown eyes and slight build—but in other ways, she was so like Jon. There was that slow curve of a tickle in her smile. The humor that could sneak up at you from behind. The laughter in her soul . . . Becca had always been a life lover the way Susan only wished she could be.

Now, though, she backed away from the hug to take a second studying look. This time she saw the smudges under Becca's eyes, the hint of chalk under the sun-browned cheeks. And she noticed the way her daughter clutched, when Becca hadn't been a clutcher in years—at least not with her mom.

"You told me you were worried about Grandma, not that something was wrong with you. You've been sick," Susan said worriedly.

"No, I'm fine."

"Something is a long way from fine."

"I'm worried about Gram. I told you."

"I know what you said on the phone. But you somehow didn't explain why you suddenly happened to be at Copper Creek instead of in Kalamazoo." And Gram's problems didn't explain the circles, the smudges, the averted eyes . . . much less how Becca had managed to escape her sacred live-in sidekick Douglas and actually do something on her own. "Have you seen your dad?" she asked casually.

"Yeah, of course. I called him the night I got here, and we took a sail on the *S-Q* yesterday afternoon."

"Yet you decided to stay with Grandma instead of your dad?" Susan needed a bathroom and a toothbrush and breakfast and a chance to catch her breath, but that stuff would just have to wait. Something was off here.

On one hand it wasn't odd that Becca and Lydia were together. Grandmother and granddaughter had been coconspirators from the day Becca was born. The two couldn't be trusted. Let loose in a store, alone they'd be cautious buyers; together they'd indulge to their credit card limits. Alone, neither drank. Together they'd voluntarily polish off God knows What and start in with The Giggling. Send the two to a grocery store for milk and they'd come home with fresh lobsters and a surprise puppy and a fortune in ice cream—and likely would have forgotten the milk. They were so close that Susan sometimes felt left out—but really, mostly she loved watching them together.

But just then, that wasn't the point. Because although Becca had *always* found ways to spend time with Lydia, when she was in Traverse she usually stayed with her dad. Jon had room for her. And Jon, damn him, never seemed to fight with Bec the way Susan did.

No matter how much mom and daughter wrangled, though, Susan knew Becca the way no one else

ever would or could. Becca was exuberantly emotional and free-spirited and happy-go-lucky. The
hint of pale unhappiness in her eyes made every
alarm go off in Susan's mom instincts. "You haven't
been sleeping, have you?"

"I'm sleeping just fine."

"Douglas. He's done something."

"Mom, would you quit fussing at me? I don't
want to talk about me. It's Gram. Something . . .
something's strange."

"What?"

"Believe me, you'll see. But even after I called
you . . ." Becca took a breath and then whispered,
"It's not just the house and how she's acting and all
that. Mom . . . I think there are men."

"Men?" What in God's name was that supposed
to mean? But it was already too late to follow
through with that confounding statement, because
suddenly they weren't alone.

"Susan Sinclair!" Again the screen door clapped
open, and this time Lydia clipped down the porch
steps. "Becca told me you were driving up, but I
didn't believe it. You're always so busy with that job,
gallivanting all over the country—and then, what,
you actually slept in that car and didn't come in?"

"I swear, I never meant to fall asleep in the car.
When I finally pulled in, it was just so late. I must
have just dropped off."

"Pshaw. Tell me all that later. Right now, baby,
just give me a hug." That hug was claimed, then a
kiss that stung, then a second hug that smelled like

every comforting memory in her childhood. But then Lydia pulled back and looked her over with suddenly sharp, critical eyes.

"What's wrong?"

"Nothing's wrong."

"There certainly is. Your color's not right. You never said a word about being sick."

"*Mom.*" For Pete's sake, trying to a hide a secret from the women in this family was tougher than getting a politician to tell the truth. "I've just had a rough traveling schedule for a couple weeks. I'm a little tired, but absolutely fine."

"Uh-huh—and that's why you drove all the way from Detroit to see me out of the blue? What about your work?"

"I took a leave of absence." That much was true. "There's some work I can do—that I have to do—on the computer and phone, but basically I argued to get a month off."

"There's no way Sebastian gave you a month off," her mother informed her.

"He didn't *want* to." Again, Susan thought, it was best to tell as much of the truth as she could. "But it's not as if I ever asked for spare time off before, so it's not as if he could say no. The thing is, when I realized Becca was already up here, it just seemed an ideal time to visit. How long has it been since the three of us had a chance to be together besides holidays? I mean, for a serious girl fest. We can pig out on chocolate and chick flicks and gossip."

Behind her grandmother, Becca was making wild

gestures—arching her eyebrows, jerking her head, obviously trying to nonverbally communicate; *"See? See? I told you there were problems, didn't I?*

And Susan saw the changes. The three women started unloading the car—Susan couldn't travel light if her life depended on it, plus she'd thrown everything in the trunk helter-skelter last night. No one said anything, just took in the boxes and suitcases, talking nonstop as luggage was carted upstairs and down. Susan carted things, too, but her gaze sucked in the changes in the house—and in her mother.

Lydia was wearing a T-shirt that said UPPITY WOMEN UNITE. Not only had Lydia never worn T-shirts, but she'd never been an "uppity woman" by anyone's definition. Her toenails, Susan saw, were painted Valentine-red. Her ears were pierced. And although Susan realized full well that she had to be hallucinating, when that T-shirt rode up on her mom's back, Susan kept thinking she was seeing a little bird tattooed on her mom's hip.

She caught glimpses of the media room, the bursts of yellow everywhere. There wasn't a sacred antique in sight—not a single one—but there was dust. And clutter. For years Lydia would have a conniption fit if a spoon sat in the sink, yet now there were pots unwashed on the counter. Lots of cut flowers, but no vegetables in the fridge. Plenty of wine in the brand-new wine racks, but no OJ. The unfolded wash on the dryer included bikini underpants with lace.

Scarlet-red underpants, yet.

Becca had said something about men, but Susan had automatically dismissed the comment. Roses didn't bloom on the moon. Her mom had had the unhappiest marriage this side of the Great Divide. She'd cooked and cleaned and kowtowed to Dad her whole adult life. Men were not *fun*, not to Lydia Sinclair. Sex was "not worth all the fuss women made of it today." And for damn sure, men were not people one wore red bikini underpants with lace for.

"*Mom*," Becca hissed.

"I'm up here." Susan had hauled the last boxes and suitcases to her old bedroom upstairs. And she didn't want to waste time unpacking now, not with so much unsettled between her daughter and mother, but for just a second, she sat down to get her mind together.

Everything kept striking her as off. Yeah, she'd come home expecting problems, but she'd never expected to be dropped into an alternative universe.

Bec was positively right—Lydia had clearly gone through some kind of extraordinary transformation. But whether those were healthy, good changes or worrisome, Susan had no way to know yet. Her mom didn't seem like herself. That was for sure.

But neither did her daughter.

Susan reached for a pillow, snuggling it to her chest, trying to settle herself. She was the doer, the problem-solver in the family. She was supposed to be good with crises—and darn it, she *was*, only she could hardly fix a problem that she couldn't even identify. Right now her family just seemed . . . off focus. Skewed, like a picture that wouldn't hang straight, or the one flower in the vase that rose too high.

Obviously she'd just arrived here. It was time to settle in, be with her mom and her daughter, study the lay of the land before she started fretting. So she tried to just sit still and will some calm into her chugging pulse.

The downstairs had completely changed, but the second floor—at least what Susan had seen—hadn't suffered from the same merciless metamorphosis. There were four other bedrooms and two bathrooms upstairs. Typical of old houses, the bedrooms were smaller than closets, with long skinny windows and alcoves and lots of creaks and groans in the middle of the night. And whatever else Lydia had changed, she hadn't touched Susan's old bedroom.

She only slept in a twin bed when she came to visit and it always reminded her of when she was a little girl. The bitsy bed had a red, white and blue star quilt, plump pillows, a raspberry throw rug on the plank floor. The walls were wainscoted in a polished dark wood, and above that the paint had long faded to a pale soft raspberry. White curtains fluttered in the morning breeze. When she was growing up, the sun had wakened her every morning—infuriating her as a kid—but she'd still loved the east view of the rose gardens and misty orchards. One long radiator had a flat wooden board on it to make a window seat, which was where Becca found her curled up.

Her daughter poked her head in the door, then looked back as if afraid Lydia would find them talking. "So you've seen how crazy this place looks, how much she's changed—do you think Grandma's sick?"

"She doesn't look remotely sick."

"But nobody just *changes*, Mom. Not *really* changes. You can't be neat and tidy all your life and suddenly turn into a slob, can you?"

Susan pushed a hand through her hair. Trust her daughter to ask the tough, impossible questions. A hundred times, growing up, she'd wanted her mother to change. To be different. To be a take-charge woman, strong, self-reliant. Her mom had seemed connected to her father by an invisible leash, always jumping to keep Harold Sinclair happy, always giving in to keep the peace—and expecting her daughter to do the same.

Years ago, she'd sworn to never—ever—become that subservient need-a-man kind of woman. Only now that her mom seemed to have hugely changed—overnight, yet—how come she felt uneasy? Wasn't this the old dream, that her mom would step up and take the reins of her life, be happy?

Only, tarnation, all that wildly soft daffodil-yellow paint didn't exactly seem proof that her mom had suddenly become tough and strong.

"I think," she answered Becca, "that people can change their behavior. But I'm not sure anyone can change their temperaments, their essential nature. Like . . . an alcoholic can change his behavior if he stops drinking. But someone who's born shy and sweet is probably always going to be on the shy, sweet side."

"So you're saying Grandma could maybe change into a slob if she wanted to, because that's, like, just behavior, not who she really is. Okay. I get that. Only Grandma's got some R-rated movie downstairs. And she's still got her Sinatra and Neil Diamond, but she's also got some rap and R&B tapes. Don't you think it's, like, practically cataclysmic to imagine Grandma listening to rap?"

Susan couldn't argue with that. Lydia and rap? It was like putting plaids and stripes together. It just didn't work.

"And I'm telling you, Mom, there are *men*."

Back to that. Susan said patiently, "Exactly what do you mean by 'men'?"

"I mean she's got guy friends. Not just one, but two if not more. And I think . . ."

"You think what?"

Becca whispered, "Mom, I think she's sleeping with *two* of them."

"Oh, come on. I don't know what you may have seen or overheard, but your grandma would never in a hundred, million, zillion years—"

"Girls!" Lydia shrieked from downstairs. "Don't you two dare say a word without me! I don't want to miss anything! Get down here for some breakfast!"

But when they traipsed down to the kitchen, the only breakfast Lydia had started was the coffeemaker.

She'd poured herself a mug thicker than sludge and plunked down on the stool closest to the door. Susan took one glance at the strong coffee and started searching for something else to breakfast with. Instinctively she started a rambling conversation—the kind they always had when they saw each other after an absence—covering health, cosmetics, weather, politics, old friends, how the orchards were doing, jewelry, hairstyles . . . the whole time she stumbled around, trying to find things in her mother's new kitchen.

The back door stood open—a measure of how safe it was to live in Copper Creek. An unfamiliar marmalade cat was hunkered on the back stoop, snoozing. Robins were up, pulling worms from the ground, far more industrious than any of the Sinclair women were on a good morning. A possum had waddled over to the bird feeders to glean leftovers.

Susan could remember breakfasts growing up— Lydia producing eggs, bacon, fresh fruits and likely a still-warm coffee cake on the sideboard— all of which appeared effortless. Now it was a challenge to find cereal. Eventually she discovered some frozen bagels hiding behind the ice cream in the freezer. No cream cheese, but after another intensive search, she emerged from a bottom cupboard with a priceless jar of guava jelly, so old its lid was dusty.

"You two want some toast and guava?" she asked.

"Nothing for me. I don't do breakfast," Lydia said.

As if suddenly realizing that it wasn't yet eight

o'clock, Becca hunched on a stool at the buttercup-yellow counter next to her grandmother. Both of them reached for the toast and jelly as fast as Susan could make it.

She motioned to the orange cat, who'd roused herself long enough to painstakingly clean her paws in the sunlight. "What's the cat's name, Mom?" she asked.

"It doesn't have a name. It's not mine. You know I don't like cats, Susan." As if motivated by the first taste of food, Lydia got up to forage herself. Both members of the younger generation stared at her, aghast, when she started spooning Ben & Jerry's directly from the carton. "She just showed up last winter. Next thing I knew, she was settled in the barn having kittens."

Again Susan glanced out the door, and noted the small empty dishes. "You don't suppose it's because you're feeding her, do you? Fancy canned cat food, yet?"

"That's not my fault," Lydia said defensively.

"No?"

"I *had* to *feed* her. She was so scrawny that I was afraid she was going to die from malnutrition—and then I'd have been stuck with all those kittens."

"Ah." Susan exchanged a wink with her daughter. This was a favorite family sitcom in which they regularly played the reruns. Lydia zealously claimed she had no time for pets, yet invariably a couple of dogs and a half dozen cats were always around somewhere—most of them fat and indolent.

She'd fed orphaned raccoons and squirrels from

bottles, and suffered through rabies shots when she'd tried to save an opossum two years before. Deer ventured as far as her back door in the winter, knowing she was good for a handout of corn day or night. "Well, she looks like she's about forty pounds now, so I don't think you have to worry that she's going to die of malnutrition anymore."

Lydia wound up a kitchen towel, in lieu of any other weapon, and thwacked Susan on the head. "She's *not* my cat."

"I can see that. She looks like she's going to take off any second now." The marmalade monster was so fat she was blocking all egress out the back door.

"Oh, you—"

When the telephone rang, Susan figured she was the only one civil enough to answer it—although God knows who'd be so stupid to call a Sinclair this early on a Saturday morning. It was a man's voice on the phone—a broody tenor of a man's voice who started the conversation with "Morning, there, sexy. It's Riff."

Of course, the caller had no reason to think anyone would answer the telephone in Lydia's house but Lydia.

Susan handed her mother the phone, saying, "It's for you. A man named *Riff*." And then watched her mother grab the receiver to take it out in the hall, her smile suddenly more blinding than sunshine, her step damn near as perky as a polka.

"Was Riff one of those guys you were talking about?" Susan whispered to her daughter.

Becca shook her head, whispering back, "You sure it wasn't George? George calls her every day."

Susan shook her head and then simply waited for Lydia to come back into the kitchen. She did, suddenly all brisk and bright and charged up with energy.

"He sounded like a nice guy," Susan said casually. "In fact, he seemed so familiar that I wondered if I knew him, growing up, but I just couldn't place the name. . . . It was Riff, right?"

"Yup," Lydia said, and turned her back to block the view of her opening a fresh can of cat food—as if they couldn't smell what she was doing from three feet away.

"So . . . this Riff's a friend of yours?"

"He's a lawyer in town."

"Legal trouble? Anything I can help with?" Susan added with an extra dollup of solicitous in her voice.

"No, no. He's just a friend who occasionally calls," Lydia said blithely.

Just a friend, Susan thought. As if "just a friend" would start a conversation with "Morning, there, sexy." She peered at her mother's profile. Lydia had a beautiful face—more beautiful than hers, for sure—but her mom couldn't hide certain emotions for beans. And there it was, that telltale streak of peach dashing across her cheeks.

"So . . . this guy's been in your life how long?" Susan asked amiably.

Lydia had just opened her mouth—undoubtedly

to lie—when Becca suddenly bolted for the bathroom. When the bathroom door slammed, Susan exchanged frowns with her mother.

Lydia whispered, "That happened yesterday, too."

"What happened yesterday?"

"We were talking. Just talking. Not about anything important. And yet suddenly she charged into the bathroom as if a tiger were chasing her. We weren't talking about anything remotely upsetting, so it wasn't anything like that. And it's happened *two mornings* in a row."

Having dropped that bomb, Lydia opened the back door to slip fresh food to the cat-who-wasn't-hers.

Susan forgot about breakfast and the cat. She slumped on one of the kitchen stools, thinking, *Holy kamoly.* That her mom had suddenly turned her house daffodil-yellow and had taken to wearing red bikini underpants—and chitchatting with men who called her "sexy"—was a lot to absorb. But Becca's problem was of another dimension entirely.

Susan had already realized that something was bugging her daughter—something way beyond all the changes in Lydia. And when a girl was twenty-two years old, there was only one subject worth a down-and-out hullabaloo. A man. But now Lydia seemed to be implying something else, and Susan didn't need a blueprint to figure out the layout. Man-trouble coupled with throwing up in the morning could only mean one thing.

"My God," Susan said.

"That's exactly what I thought. In a single word—*eek*," Lydia said.

"She told you? She came up to Copper Creek to tell you?"

Lydia patted her on the shoulder as she pushed past to open the kitchen window another crack. "Now don't get jealous because she came to me first. She came to Copper Creek, yes. But you were out of town and not to be found. And she hasn't *told* me anything. I don't think she wants to talk about it. I think she came here to just ... think things through."

"I understand. And I wouldn't be jealous if she came to you first anyway, Mom." Susan lied, because she wanted that lie to be true. But she *didn't* understand, and hurt clumped in her throat like thick barbed wire. Half the Free World brought her problems, so how come her own daughter didn't feel she could come to her with something as serious as this?

From behind the closed bathroom door, they heard the toilet flush, then water gush, then a moment's silence.

"Now, don't bug her," Lydia whispered. "Just let her be until she's ready to talk."

"What, you think I'd pry?" When the bathroom door opened, Susan smiled brilliantly for her daughter. Becca stumbled back in, perched on a stool, and promptly reached for a bagel and guava jelly.

"You getting hungry for some serious food, dar-lin'?" Lydia asked.

"Starving. God, I forgot how much I love this kind of jelly."

Susan swallowed again. Becca had just thrown up, yet now was trying to gobble down a bagel heaped with two inches of jelly. No rabbit had to die for a woman to interpret those symptoms.

Silently Susan aimed for the refrigerator, forag-ing until she found some canned peaches. She'd barely pried off the lid and dumped the peaches in a bowl before her daughter was reaching for them.

"They were always your favorite," she said.

"I just can't resist peaches," Becca admitted.

"How far along are you, sweet pea?"

Becca's eyes shot up. A peach slice shivered off the spoon and skated down the counter. "What do you mean?"

"I mean, how pregnant are you?"

"I never said . . ." Becca's gaze shot from her mother's to her grandmother's and back again. Her shoulders suddenly sagged, as if realizing how easy it would be to lie to the law or the IRS compared to these two. "All right, all right. Yeah. I'm pregnant. Around four or five weeks along, I think."

"You've been to a doctor? You're okay, healthy?"

"I took a home test, that's how I know. And I'm going to make an appointment with a doctor, but there was no reason to rush into it, because I'm fine." A stubborn note entered her voice. "There's a reason I didn't want to tell you, Mom. I don't know what I'm going to do about the baby. Right now my choices aren't looking real great. And I wanted to think it all out and make up my mind before I said anything to anyone."

"You thought I'd be judgmental, yell at you?" Susan couldn't help sounding wounded.

Becca frowned in confusion. "Of course not. I thought you'd try to help."

"And that's bad?"

"Not *bad*. But whether I make the right or wrong decision, it has to be *my* decision. Besides which, I know you don't like Douglas."

Now, *there* was a subject as comfortable as ticks. Becca had been living with the boy for a year now, since the end of her senior year at college. Susan thought the boy was a complete parasite—a good-looking, worthless, lazy son of a sea dog—but just then it seemed wise to keep her opinions to herself. "What does Douglas think about the pregnancy?"

"I haven't told him." Again Becca's eyes shot up. "Yeah, I *know* I have to tell him. And soon. But that's exactly why I wanted to come up to Copper Creek for a while—so I could think this out by myself. I mean, like, my apartment in Kalamazoo is home now. And where I grew up with you in Detroit is home. But somehow Copper Creek is just . . ."

Susan filled in, "A different kind of home. Our roots are here. That makes it different. This is the home we come back to when we need to feel . . . safe."

Becca nodded gratefully. "Yeah, exactly."

"I understand, because I feel exactly the same way. But I still don't understand at all why you didn't tell me—"

"Now, girls." Lydia surged between them, interrupting as if she sensed an imminent Armageddon. "How about if we all walk out in the rose garden? We can just kind of stroll around. I'll tell you all about the new roses I'm breeding; we'll take in some sunshine, just chill out."

"Chill out? Gram, you're so cool." But Becca was still looking at Susan. "Mom, I don't want to be grilled."

"Since when in your entire life have I grilled you?"

"How about every single time we're together?"

"Becca, that's so unfair." God, that her daughter— the person she loved more than life—could even think such a thing. She'd *never* pry . . . but obviously she had to ask a few questions to understand the situation. "You've told me over and over that you love Douglas. But don't you think—if you really loved him—that you'd have told him immediately about this? That you'd have trusted him with a problem?"

Lydia plopped a straw hat on Susan's head, then Becca's, then held open the back screen door. "The damn cat isn't going to move. You have to step over her. Let's all just go out and—"

"Mom, you don't understand. This has nothing to do with trusting Douglas. It's me I have to trust," Becca said defensively. "Like I said, I just wanted some time to figure out how I feel about this before other people start trying to influence and push me. I don't want to be rushed. I don't want to be talked into doing anything or not doing anything. There's still plenty of time."

"Time for what?"

"Time to decide whether the right thing is to keep the baby or to adopt out the baby or to get an abortion."

"You didn't mention marriage as a choice in there."

"That's right. I didn't. Because that's the only thing I'm sure of—I am *not* marrying Douglas, so don't even try bugging me on that, because it's not going to happen."

When Susan opened her mouth to respond to that, her mother prodded her in the back with a gardening spade. Lydia clearly thought she should shut up, because she suddenly ranted on nonstop about her roses. "Now, see? This rose variety is named Graham Thomas. When it starts to flower, it'll be yellow—a gorgeous rich, deep yellow—and it'll flower all summer long. Like a toddler that can't stop talking—"

"Rebecca," Susan said, "I can't believe you'd think I'd push you into getting married. You know better. But honey, you love children so much, always have. When you were six years old and all the other kids wanted to be old enough to ride a two-wheeler, all you wanted was to be old enough to baby-sit. I'd hate for you to do something you'd regret—"

Lydia jabbed her again in the spine. "There, now," she said loudly, "this particular rose—look, girls!—is called the Jean Kenneally. She's what we call a miniature, so she's not as flashy or sexy as some of the bigger, more voluptuous roses. She doesn't have much scent, either—but her color is this perfect, precious apricot. And she has a perfect figure for a rose, every bloom, every—"

"*Mom*. This isn't about what I'd regret or not regret. It's about figuring what the right thing to do is. Eventually I want a half dozen kids. Maybe even more. And maybe I'll even want them with Douglas. Whether you like him or not, for a long time we got on really well. He was good for me. I was good for him."

Susan had heard all that rock and roll before. "It hasn't occurred to you that if you really loved him, you wouldn't need *space* away from him to make a decision about this?"

Red shot up Becca's throat. "You want this to be about me and Douglas. But the main reason this is so complicated for me is because of you and Grandma."

Lydia dropped both the garden patter and her peacemaker smile. In fact, her jaw dropped as far and fast as Susan's. "*What*? Honey, what does this have to do with me?"

Susan stopped dead, too. "Me and Grandma? I don't understand."

The morning sky still had a faint skirting of sunrise-pink. Mist hung in damp wisps in the low spots, and there was still a silver softness on the leaves in the garden, the verdant smell of dew-drenched grass pervasive and sweet. Yet Susan only had eyes for her daughter, who'd hugged her arms around her chest and looked so unhappy. There were tears in her baby's eyes, huge, crystal tears that filled her eyes and just glistened there without falling.

"Come on. You know exactly what I mean. There's a pattern the Sinclair women all follow. Grandma got pregnant with you before she was married. You got pregnant with me same way. Both of you practically sacrificed your whole lives because of having those babies when you couldn't handle them. Don't you see? I don't want to be part of the pattern."

"Becca, you're not part of any pattern," Susan started to argue, but her daughter rounded on her.

"Yeah, I am, Mom. I was an unwanted baby. Just like you were," Becca said. "I *know* you loved me. I *know* Grandma loved you. But don't you think it's about time we quit doing it all wrong and started getting it right?"

"Rebecca," Susan said gently. How could her daughter believe she was unwanted? But Becca was far too upset to even try to listen.

"I don't want to have a baby—ever—who isn't a million percent sure that I want him and I'm ready for him. I want kids. I *love* kids. But darn it, I'm *not* going to have a baby who thinks he's unwanted or messing up my whole life." She made a gesture with her hands as if her throat were suddenly too thick to speak.

Susan hurled toward her, seeing the hot tears spill from her daughter's eyes, but Becca fiercely shook her head. "I don't want to talk about this anymore. Not now. I just want to be left alone."

She ran in the house, the screen door clattering shut behind her, the marmalade cat immediately taking advantage of this unexpected opportunity by sneaking into the house faster than a jet—but Lydia didn't say anything about the cat and neither did Susan.

Her arms ached to hold her daughter. Ached for the days when a hug and crying together would have solved something, would have mattered, would have helped. Even with the sun starting to beat down, her skin suddenly felt chilled.

She turned around, only to see her mother looking as disturbed and upset as she felt. "Did you know any of that was coming?"

Lydia shook her head. "Like I told you, I guessed she was pregnant, which, God knows, is enough to shake up any young girl. But I had no idea how long she was holding back all those feelings. And just for the record, Susan, you were never, never unwanted."

"Mom, I always knew you loved me. But I thought Becca knew how much I loved *her*." Guilt and confusion danced in her mind. She felt as if scabs had been ripped off places where she'd been unaware there were sores. What had she done to make Becca feel unwanted? That raising her had been a sacrifice for her, for Jon?

The sun slid over the old shake-shingled roof until it was shining directly in her eyes. Damnation. She'd come here raring to fix everything, raring to help her mom and support her daughter, to coddle and pamper and love both of them and make things better.

Instead, life seemed to have gotten impossibly complex in the space of the last hour. To add insult to injury, now it seemed there was no way to avoid her seeing Jon. Not just because he obviously needed to know what was going on with their daughter.

But because—damnation—they had to find some way to stand together to help Becca.

Even if it killed both of them. And knowing how well they communicated, that was a real possibility.

Chapter 5

Jon never thought he'd care about turning gray. Vanity had never been one of his vices. Yet when a handful of gray strands started showing up in his sideburns about three years ago, from then on, iron-ically, females had begun to chase him nonstop.

As far as he could tell, women didn't feel any particular obligation to behave logically. He couldn't imagine why any female would chase him to begin with, but now that he had more gray and less money, you'd think they'd run the other way.

"Mr. Laker?"

"Yeah, I'm here." He stood up from behind the counter, where he'd been trying to hide, pretending he was ultra-busy—God knows, doing what? Rear-ranging sailing supplies? Whatever, it hadn't worked. The girl hadn't left yet and didn't seem re-motely inclined to.

It was well after dinner, had to be past eight, which meant the sun was thinking about dropping and the temperature definitely had. The tiny brunette seemed oblivious. She was—maybe, *maybe*—sixteen. The details were all unnerving.

She'd troweled on a full inch of black mascara. Poured herself into a bikini so small that it gave "inadequacy" a whole new meaning. Ripe, tender breasts spilled over the eensy-weensy top, particularly when the child leaned over the counter and jutted those nubile baby boobs practically in his face.

Jon wanted to ask where the hell her mother was, but that would have hurt her feelings. And although the chicklet was way out of line—and way out of her league—it wasn't that long ago that Becca had been this age.

It wasn't an age that any father forgot. Overnight, Becca had seemed to change from an energetic, playful, athletic girl-child who'd loved to camp and roughhouse and just hang out with him into an instant Lolita. She hadn't even known it, for God's sake. She just seemed to get up one morning, suddenly wearing a bra and batting her eyes at any and all unsuspecting males, terrifying her father 24/7 and being vulnerable the way only sixteen-year-olds can be.

Jon understood more about this tiny brunette than likely she did. And he wasn't going to hurt the child's feelings, but damn, he wished she'd go home.

"I can't find anyone who can give me sailing lessons," she said breathlessly.

"I'm sorry. Really. And I do give sailing lessons, but I'm booked up through the summer. I can't take on more."

"You couldn't make even a little time for me?" She leaned over just a tad further, brushing her long ebony satin hair away from her neck, which—of course—made the boobs shine even closer to the light. "I could learn after dark."

"I don't doubt that."

"It's not like I have to have lessons during normal business hours."

"I have no doubt you'd be accommodating. And I appreciate that you want me. . . ." Jon mentally winced. Some days a guy couldn't get the words right no matter how hard he tried. "The thing is, I love sailing, and that's why I give some lessons. But this is my marina here. This is my living. It's what I do. And in the summer, that's a twenty-hour-a-day job. I can't fit in more."

"Even for me?" The pout was a study in angel-pink lip gloss. Jon heard the bells jangle on the storefront door, which should have elated him, knowing someone was going to save him with an interruption . . . only he couldn't positively swear that the sound wasn't simply the headache belling in his temples.

"I'll tell you what," he said. "I'll find you someone who can teach you sailing—"

"Well, that would be nice, Mr. Laker. But you're the only one I want. You're the only one—"

And then he saw her. Susan. Winging past the nautical ropes, then the aisle with the winches and cleats and tie-downs, then down the aisle with the range of NOAA charts and nautical maps. His business faded out—in fact, the rest of the world turned down its volume, including Ms. Hot-to-Attract-an-Older-Man Boobess.

The last time he'd seen Susan had been at Becca's

college graduation. That time had been like a dozen others. She'd talked to him courteously without looking at him. He'd talked back, even laughed back, without looking too closely at her.

She always dressed a certain way when she knew they were going to see each other. Perfectly. No chips on the nail polish. No scuff marks on the shoes. Her clothes always looked impeccably put together; her hair was coiled so tight it wouldn't dare move in a gale; she was makeup-and-lipstick fresh, perfume fresh, smile fresh. If she'd ever felt anything for him beyond basic friendliness for someone she'd once vaguely known, it never showed.

Now, though, his jaw almost dropped five feet when he saw her. She was all locomotion in commotion. The hair was like Susan's used to when they were kids—wilder than wind and curling precisely how it wanted to—and she wore no makeup beyond a slash of lipstick. God knows where she'd found the clothes, but her usual meticulous attire was absent. The peach linen shirt was wrinkled, big and droopy at the collar, the jeans soft-snug without being tight, the sandals three summers old if they were a day.

Who'd have guessed she could look human? Or that she'd take the incredibly mammoth risk of his seeing her when she wasn't stiff as a statue?

Mostly, though, his gaze riveted on the face. That face. Her face. The small elegant bones, the long straight nose. Her skin was softer than a baby's butt and flawless—except for the splash of tiny freckles on the bridge of her nose. The hair was thick and lustrous and had darkened in the last few years, a color that made her complexion look more fragile than pearls. As pretty as she was, though—and Susan was damn striking—it was her eyes that stunned him, always had, always would. Those huge, deep, dark-chocolate eyes could turn a man upside down and then some.

And tonight, those eyes reflected the Susan he remembered . . . the girl he'd fallen in love with way back when. The girl for whom everything showed in her eyes—hope, dreams, fierce independence, yearnings, passion. Everything that mattered. And tonight something had to matter a ton, because there was worry in those eyes—frantic worry, even fear, and some intense emotion he couldn't begin to guess at. Except that she was here. To see him. And charging toward him with urgent determination. . . .

At least until she saw the nubile teenager hanging over his counter.

Her gaze darted from the girl to him, back to the girl, then she whisked around and charged straight back for the door faster than a soldier at reveille. She called over her shoulder, "Sorry, Jon. I should have phoned first. I don't know what I was thinking of—obviously you're in the middle of business hours. I'll catch you another time when you're not busy."

Hell.

She hurled down all three aisles and back out the door before his lungs could exhale a single gust of air. Damn woman always had, always would, leap to conclusions—wrong conclusions—faster than a teenage boy could get a hard-on, and that was saying something.

It wasn't as if he wanted to talk to her. Volunteering to talk with Susan was like volunteering for a tetanus shot, or maybe a chance to pay double taxes. It wasn't that easy to be enthusiastic when you had every reason to believe the encounter was going to leave you hurt if not emotionally slice-and-diced . . . and probably pissed off as well.

Still, Susan hadn't braved the lion in his den in a long time—which meant that something really had to be wrong for her to seek him out. So his instinct was to charge after her. Which he would have done—except that he abruptly realized the baby brunette was staring wide-eyed at him from behind the counter.

He couldn't leave the marina with a kid alone inside. "Look, I need to close down and lock up, okay?"

"Yeah, I get it. She's, like, important to you, right?"

God. Teenagers. She stirred, but getting her to move fast was like rushing Godot. "Yeah, you got it," he said to placate her.

"I'll come back tomorrow, okay?"

"Okay, okay."

"I could see. She's real pretty and all. And more, like, your age and everything. But that doesn't mean you couldn't still teach me sailing, does it?"

He got her out finally, locked the door, twisted

over the closed sign and chased outside. The sun was at eye level, blinding with that yellow evening light that colored everything with a haze. Kids were shrieking down the sidewalk, adults strolling the beach with ice-cream cones, people of all ages milling on the docks, boats coming in and out . . . but no sign of Susan.

He hiked to the end of the street and searched over heads, trying to spot the wild hair, the peachy blouse. Nothing.

A breeze tucking off the lake shagged his collar, rippled through his nerves. Summer people had every reason to be out on a perfect night like this, and dadblast it, everybody knew him. "Hey, Jon," someone called out, and then "How's it going" and "Jon, been meaning to talk to you." And still he kept hiking, kept searching faces, positive she couldn't have completely disappeared. Not this fast.

Because there were a half dozen fine marinas in Traverse City, he'd needed to create his own niche if he wanted a prayer of making it. So he'd built his place off the beaten path, letting others cater to the fishing and charter trade, concentrating on those more seriously interested in sailing. And that had worked well for a decade now, except that his stretch of beach had only a mite-sized, but bustling shopping area.

That suited Jon, who'd rather suffer flu than shop, but it still made too many places for Susan to duck into. First there was Val's Drugs, then the over-cutesie Koffee Kountry, then a little shop that sold artsy stuff for women: jewelry and bathing suits and scarves and anything else they could price out of sight. Across the street was Moira's Muffins— the only irresistible place in the entire region— nestled between a bunch of art studios. He couldn't spot her in any of the store windows. One of the last places on the block was Flavors of Your Dreams, which naturally was packed, and he stood there, re- membering how much she loved cherry cheesecake and almond crunch ice cream, thinking maybe she'd stopped there . . . but no.

Still, he rounded the corner, mentally swearing at himself. Even after twenty some years, he could still remember crazy things about her like that. Like her loving cherry cheesecake ice cream. Like the way her tongue carved a wave into the ice cream, mak- ing her cone look like an art form. Making his hor- mones salivate just watching her eat one.

When he realized his heart was beating like an overheated jackhammer, he stopped dead, deter- mined to head back home and forget this nonsense. If Susan was in the area, then she was staying at her mother's. He could call her there. And if she'd wanted him for something critically important, she could have—and would have—said something on the spot. It was stupid to think that he had to track her down this second. . . .

But damn, there she was. He'd just backtracked the shopping block, was halfway to the marina again, when he spotted her. Her hands were slugged in her pockets, her hair kicking up in the breeze; she was ambling toward the docks, toward the beach. Walking toward nothing specific, as far as he could see.

He charged toward her until he was within calling distance. "Suze!" An out-of-breath stitch knifed his side. His shop keys were still dangling from his hand. "Susan!"

She turned the instant she recognized his voice. From that angle, the sun slapped her sharply in the eyes, where he was in a position to see clearly how she braced, how careful the smile was. "If I made you run after me, I'm going to shoot myself. I wanted to talk to you, but honestly, it wasn't an emergency."

"I figured it had to be close to one. It's not as if you go to the trouble of tracking me down more than twice a decade. And that was just a kid, Suze. Driving me crazy in the shop." He couldn't imagine needing to explain any further about the teenager. Susan was well capable of leaping to a wrong conclusion, but, even at her meanest and blindest, couldn't really believe he'd have any interest in a girl that age. "What's wrong?"

"Nothing's exactly wrong."

He wasn't opposed to wasting time on bullshit. But not now, and not with her. "You didn't show up at my place to discuss the weather. Is something wrong with Becca?"

"Not wrong, exactly—"

"Yeah, wrong, exactly." A kid whipped past them on a skateboard, threatening both their lives. A golden retriever bounded after the kid, threatening to trip both of them all over again. "I saw her a couple days ago. We went for a sail, had dinner. I know she's freaked about your mother, how Lydia's changed, but if something else was bothering her, she never brought it up with me."

"She probably didn't want to tell you. She sure didn't want to tell me. Jon . . ." She lifted a hand in one of those pure female gestures she had. "There *is* something wrong. And I did come here to talk with you about it—it's just not an easy subject to spring into. I can't just . . ."

"Okay. So. Let's sit somewhere."

"Not your place."

God forbid she should trust him after twenty-two years. As if he'd jump her if he caught her alone . . . well, hell, come to think of it, he had. But only a few times. And only when she'd wanted to be jumped. And that hadn't happened in a while, probably because the outcome was so damn uncomfortable. The instant either turned the heat up, they both spun out of control, then tended to be madder and edgier than fighting cats afterward.

Even the best sex in the universe wasn't worth that.

It came close, though.

They found a protected spot to perch at the end of a dock. The wooden planks were still sun-warmed. Gulls were diving for dinner in the shallows as the sun scooched down. Red-nosed sailors were still coming in, angling in the basin toward their slips, looking sun-soaked and hungry for dinner. People were still running around in bathing suits, freezing their tushes off as the temperature dropped . . . and the temperature always dropped like a stone around this time of evening.

Her blouse was too lightweight; she'd need a jacket if they were going to talk long, but right then Jon wasn't willing to postpone talking until they'd gotten settled in a better place. Susan crouched down on her knees, her posture still all tense and tight, her soft dark eyes all looking the color of worry. Big worry.

"It looks as if your marina is going great guns," she said.

"Couldn't be better. Making more money than I have time to spend."

"Your father still having a stroke that you didn't become a lawyer?"

"Susan. Come on. You didn't come here to talk about my dad."

"I know. I know." Pleading soft eyes.

"So she's pregnant, right?" He hadn't known until he saw those pleading, soft eyes, but suddenly he was back to their own teenage years. Their walking into the woods to have a private place to be alone together, her huddling up on a rock, tenser than wire, eyes blind with anxiety, telling him about another pregnancy then. Hers.

That he guessed about Rebecca made her jaw drop. "You knew? How'd you know?"

"I didn't. It was just a guess. But it wasn't hard to guess that a problem had to be mountain-sized for you to seek me out. And Rebecca would probably have told me herself if it were some other kind of problem." He scraped a hand at his nape, trying to get his mind off their pregnancy and back to the present tense, to the crisis at hand. "She has to be shook up as hell."

"One of the things she's considering is an abortion."

"Yeah?"

Apparently he failed some test when he neglected to respond with horror, because she burst out, "Jon! She's insane for kids! She adores kids!" When he still didn't bite, she said, "How well do you know Douglas?"

That question was easy. "Well enough to want to stake him out on an anthill, buck-naked and painted with honey."

She opened her mouth to make a fast retort, but then she seemed to register what he'd said. When it sank in, she relaxed enough to laugh. "So you know him."

"I know he's sleeping with our daughter. I know I hate that. But come on, Suze. She's over twenty-one."

"He's not going anywhere with his life. He's supposed to have this mighty IQ, but he's had three jobs in a year. He still hasn't finished his degree. He's always going on and on about the next big plan, the next dream, talking real good, but it's our baby who's paying the bills in that place."

"Uh-huh." Her hair got streaks of gold as the sun sank lower. She'd pulled up her knees, wrapped her arms around them. Hadn't gained a pound, he thought. A few wrinkles fanned her eyes. He liked them. A single strand of gold nested around her throat, thin and delicate. He'd bet it cost the moon. He'd also bet she'd bought it for herself, because she always got real wary if someone tried to give her something expensive.

He checked her hands, the way he did half consciously every time he saw her, just in case she was wearing a new ring.

She was. An opal, where last time it had been some kind of blue stone; the time before that a topaz—she must have closets of jewelry. Loved it all. But all these years, she still hadn't worn any man's engagement ring. He didn't know why. Didn't get why. God knows, she could drive any sane man crazy, but he still couldn't imagine her being happy living alone . . . or that there'd be any shortage of men willing to solve that problem for her.

"Jon, for God's sake, are you listening?"

"Of course I'm listening."

"I think she'll tell you herself about the pregnancy. And I'm uncomfortable breaking her confidence— but it just seemed too important to stay quiet about. I thought you and I needed a chance to talk about this together, alone. For one thing . . . she says she isn't going to marry Douglas, but I don't know what she really thinks—and I don't want her pushed into marrying him."

"And you think I'd push her?"

"You pushed me, didn't you? Or you tried to."

Funny how the sun plunked down under the horizon just like that. One minute the gold ball was there, the next the sky was purple and sapphire and the temperature plummeted ten degrees all at once.

He said mildly, "I pushed you to get married because I loved you and I thought you loved me."

"We were children, for God's sake! Sixteen years old!"

"Yeah. I remember." But as he remembered it, the problem with their staying together had nothing to do with their ages. Susan had wanted out. Out of Copper Creek. Out of her parents' house, because her mom and dad fought all the time and were so unhappy. Out of little Traverse City, because she'd wanted city lights and a big life.

He'd wanted a big life, too . . . but his family had a ton of money, so he'd never had to worry about practical issues the way she had. He'd never wanted his parents' life, any more than she wanted to repeat her parents' choices, but the thing was—the baby was his.

There'd been no question about that, because Susan had been a virgin. Actually, so had he. They'd been so in love they couldn't see straight. Couldn't keep away from each other for two seconds out of three. And when the pregnancy happened . . . he wanted the kid. No one believed that. They thought he was young and dumb and had no idea what raising a child meant.

But Jon had known unequivocally that he wanted to be a father to his own child, the right to be a part of the child's life. If they were too young to be married, Jon felt—hell, he *knew*—that they could have worked out some way to be both parents and lovers until they got older.

But they never had a chance to try. The world had contrived to separate them. His parents. Her parents. Teachers, community, everybody. She'd had an aunt in Detroit—Loretta—someone she could stay with during the pregnancy, help put her through college, start her up with a whole new life there. The decisions had really been made before he had a chance to fight. She'd been gone, and though it took years, Jon eventually accepted that they'd never really had a chance.

But sometimes it still bugged him.

Susan hadn't done anything that terrible to him; it was just that he'd been fooled so badly. He'd believed, *really* believed, that they loved each other, the kind of love that was hotter than fire and smoke, deeper than lakes and oceans—the kind of love that could make it. When she'd thrown it away, used the pregnancy to get out of town, to build her different kind of life, it was obvious what mattered to her . . . and it sure as hell hadn't been him.

"Jon, I didn't come here to argue with you."

He looked at her. "That's like saying the sky's blue. You came to tell me about Rebecca. And I'm glad you did. But now, I don't know what to say except that I'd like to think about it. See her again. See how she is, what she says, see how this all plays out." He uncoiled and stood up, extending a hand to her.

"There's more." She took his hand, her slim palm gripping his tightly until he'd hauled her up. When she stood next to him, they may as well have been sixteen again. She wasn't *that* short—but still short enough to make him feel ten feet tall. She painted his whole world with sharp colors just by being in it. Electricity surrounded them in a halo that no one else could see. He could kiss her as easily as he could draw in his next breath—knowing it was stupid, not caring. Knowing there'd be repercussions, not caring.

Jon wanted to let out another gusty, exasperated sigh. The damn woman was more desirable than diamonds—but poison. At least for him.

"What do you mean, 'there's more'?" he asked.

"Becca . . ." That softer-than-crushable-velvet look was back in her eyes again. "Becca seems to be blaming me—and her grandmother—for the problem being extra hard. Not that we're responsible for her getting pregnant. But that we're an influence on what choices she has."

"Say what?"

"She thinks I didn't want her, because she wasn't planned. She thinks my mom didn't want me, because her pregnancy with me wasn't planned, either. She thinks the Sinclair women are in this cycle of messing up their lives, because of getting stuck with a pregnancy before they're ready to handle it."

He fell silent. All around them, the world seemed to have quieted down. The water lapped around the dock, looking like black ink dipped in silver when the moon showed up.

Susan said fiercely, "I wanted her. There wasn't a minute I didn't want her. Not even a second. It was just that when I first found out I was pregnant, I felt . . ."

"Scared?"

"Beyond scared." She gulped down a breath, facing the water. "But how I felt back then doesn't matter. I only wanted to talk about this so you'd know where Becca was coming from. Sooner or later she's going to tell you about the pregnancy. I wanted you to know ahead of time that she had some insecurities about being wanted, so you could tell her—"

"So I could tell her that I love her. But she knows I love her, Sue. She knows you love her, too." He added, "Look. A pregnancy tore up our lives. It's going to tear up hers. There's no hiding from that. A pregnancy's one of those things that doesn't hide well. It's kind of like trying to ignore an elephant in the living room."

"You're sounding pretty damn calm."

Oh, that red hair. She always could fly up over nothing. "You want to fix her," he said quietly. "That's how it is with you. There's a problem, you want to dive in there and fix it. But this is her problem, Susan. You don't have the power to fix her life. It's up to her."

"You make it sound like I'm interfering, and that's not fair! I just don't want her doing something that she could regret for the rest of her life. And for darn sure, I don't want her marrying that good-looking loser—"

"You want to protect her," he said, trying to rephrase what she'd said in a more truthful way. "You want to make a problem disappear, to make things smooth again. But it's too late for that, Suze. She's pregnant. That's a die cast."

"Would you stop sounding so damn reasonable? Or I swear I'll smack you."

"Seems to me nobody goes through life without problems. The choice you've got is to make something good from those problems or to let them destroy you. We came damn close to letting one destroy us."

"You always blamed me!"

"Yup, I did and do."

"I wasn't the only one in the back of that pickup truck bed, Jon Laker. I made the best decisions I knew how to make at the time."

"Yeah, you did. So'd I. And we both flunked that life course big-time, because neither of us ended up happy—"

"I'm happy," she said furiously.

"Uh-huh. Twenty years later, yet we're both still living solo. That's real happy."

"I don't want . . . Oh, hell. I can't talk to you. Not now. I—"

Some instinct made him grab her wrist when she started to spin away. There was nothing new about their ending an encounter in a fight, but that wasn't what motivated him to touching her. Suze seemed rattled all out of proportion to the conversation. Sure, she was upset about Becca, but Susan normally—easily—locked a lid on her emotions. Something had her roiled up tighter than a trigger. When he commented on their both living alone, her color had blanched whiter than almonds. "What's wrong?" he asked quietly.

"For Pete's sake, I *told* you what was wrong. Our daughter's pregnant!"

"I know. And that's big-time serious. I'm as concerned as you are, even if I'm not yelling and stomping my feet." He searched her face, trying to understand what had her so close to coming unglued. It wasn't that dark yet, but the shadows softening her eyes and face made it impossible to catch a clear expression. "Is there something else wrong?" he asked seriously.

She looked at him, and then slowly, fiercely, shook her head. "No, not exactly. It's just that Becca believes that you and I . . ."

She took a breath, then nothing.

"You think Becca believes what?" He prodded her.

She took a breath, tried again. Still nothing. It was as if her tongue were stapled to the roof of her mouth. Her eyes communicated volumes of nerves and anxiety to him, but she couldn't seem to get a specific word out.

"Look. I can't guess what's on your mind. Just say what you're thinking, whatever it is."

"I'm trying, for heaven's sake. It's just . . ."

Maybe she was trying, but once she spit that out, nothing else followed. Again. He lifted his hand in a natural gesture of frustration, but then . . . somehow . . . his hand landed on her shoulder.

Then . . . somehow . . . his other hand landed on her other shoulder.

She was shook up. He wasn't used to seeing her shook up. He was used to seeing her infuriatingly, unshakably cool, as if it would bite her in the butt if she ever dared show a weakness around him. That was the thing. That was why he lost his head and pulled her into a hug. Anybody would have done it. Anybody would have done some panicked, impulsive thing if they saw Susan all messed up like this. Nobody could have just stood there and done nothing.

It wasn't his fault.

The kiss, though.

The kiss was *definitely* his fault.

The thing was, when he yanked her into that hug, she folded into him as if she belonged in his arms. Her skin was chilled from the falling night, maybe from nerves, too. Her hair felt all tangled and tickly under his chin and the damn woman was trembling.

Susan didn't tremble. Susan made other people tremble. It was her life's work, bringing guys to their knees, orchestrating peoples' lives. And God knows, Jon knew exactly how much trouble she could be, but that still didn't erase the more critical immediate issue. For him to resist Susan trembling in his arms was like asking a cop to walk away from a crime, a fireman to walk away from a fire.

She wanted him. His hormones recognized it long before his head did. He just knew there was a hollow spot that suddenly felt full, a sudden champagne high when he'd had nothing to drink. He angled his face, because of all that tickly hair under his chin, so that—by a miracle—when she finally tilted her head, her lips were mere inches from his.

He wasn't precisely sure how his mouth happened to come down and connect with hers. It was probably a force of nature. Maybe he remembered wanting her, but for damn sure he never intended that kiss. It just happened. The way thunder and lightning and other cataclysms just happened. Man wasn't responsible. If you got caught up in a tornado or an avalanche, you didn't stop to analyze; you just did your best to survive.

So that's what he did. Tried his best to hold on and survive.

He'd claimed that mouth before. He knew it like he knew his own heartbeat—God knows, not in a pleasant way. All these years she'd had a hold on him. All these years he still wanted her—and he resented that, furiously, was fed up the wazoo over the whole damn problem. If he could have washed his feelings for Susan out of his mind, he'd have done it—with bleach—a million times over.

And anger might have helped, but just then all that years-old anger seemed to be napping in some mental closet, because it never even surfaced in his consciousness.

Her lips yielded under his, softer than satin. For an instant that trembling of hers increased, and then it was as if the furnace of his body got through, warmed hers that fast. Her hands crawled around his waist, then wrapped tight and clung.

Young. That was the whole damn problem, always had been. She made him feel young. The taste of her, the touch of her, the scent of her took him back to when he believed he owned the world, owned himself, could do anything, be anything, change anything. He was an all-powerful sixteen-year-old again, drunk on her, tougher than a grass-green spring wind, so damned high his head was soaring way, way outside the ozone layer.

Nobody tasted like her. Nobody kissed like her.

A frog bleated under the docks. Sand cooled, chilled. Somewhere in the distance a man's voice yelled for Shakespeare to come—apparently his dog had gotten loose. And in the meantime, while both sane and insane thoughts ping-ponged in his mind, the moonlight came out to shower silver on both of them.

One kiss deepened into two, into twelve. One relatively innocent hug turned into a deliberately dangerous embrace. He felt her thighs brace against his, seeking support. Felt her breasts cushion against his chest, then crush there, warmed, the nipples turning tight and hard as she became as aroused as he was.

A teenage couple whispered, going past. The guy who was pissed at Shakespeare bellowed again. Up and down the shoreline, lights popped on. The water slip-slapped, slip-slapped. Maybe five minutes passed. Maybe five hours.

His neck started to ache, from bending to her shorter height. His mouth started to feel bruised, from the pressure she returned, or the pressure he offered. God knows who was kissing whom by then, but this was always how it had been. They'd never talked well. Even as kids. But he always got honesty from Susan when they touched . . . and she got it back. Raw honesty. The kind of honesty in which you risked everything you were, in which you knew better than to trust anyone this deep, but it was Susan, and he couldn't stop himself. And she couldn't stop herself.

All the stuff she hadn't said got told. She was afraid. Terribly, terribly afraid. She'd been holding something inside her that was burning a hole. And no, she didn't say that in words, didn't say anything at all. But emotions seeped to the surface in every kiss, as clear as truth, as naked as her mouth, as the sheen in her eyes, as the need and heat she whispered to him.

Right then, right there, he could have peeled off that silky blouse, pushed down those old jeans, taken her. Hard. Fast. Now. She'd have let him. He knew there would be consequences, but right then he couldn't think of any—and for damn sure none that mattered. He was hard enough to hammer stone, hot enough to bake fire, and still he kissed her. Softly. Wooingly. With a hunger he didn't want to sate, just to feel, forever, the wonder of it, the power of it, the fierce sweetness of it. Nothing in life was this strong, this pure, this wild. Not for him.

"Jon."

Someone else passed them. Not close. But close enough for her to hear an adult voice, and that was what slammed some reality into her mind, he knew. He knew her.

And damn it, he knew this was insane, too. He'd already suffered that same slap of reality. But he still took one more kiss.

"Jon."

God knows, he was sick of this. Sick of the hold she had on him. Sick that all these years, he still couldn't forget her, couldn't find anyone who stirred him up half as wild or hot as she did. He knew that, felt that, but it didn't seem to matter. . . . All that mattered was holding on to her for every second he could. Kissing her for as long as he could hold his breath. Inhaling her scent, her texture, touching that wild tangly hair, claiming these memories for as long as he was able.

"Jon—" She jerked back her head, which seemed the only way either of them could break free from that last kiss. Her eyes were wild with emotion, pagan with heat, inches from his. *"Listen to me."*

Yeah, well, he had been. She wanted to make love with him. That's what those eyes told him. That's what her hot, stiff little nipples, and the way her pelvis rocked against his erection and that red swollen mouth all told him. But she managed to say the one thing that extremely effectively stopped him dead.

"Jon . . . we *can't* let this happen. This is *exactly* what our daughter thinks. That we still have feelings for each other. That we should be married, a pair. That we belong together."

"Whoa." The idea of marrying Susan wilted Jon faster than a shower in ice. "That's ridiculous."

"Completely ridiculous," Susan agreed.

"Wait a minute. I don't get this." It was like trying to think through a fog. A wilted fog, but nevertheless, he'd been on a slam-dunk track to fantastic sex sixty seconds earlier. No matter how disastrous an idea that had had been, it wasn't that easy to get instantly sane. "How did our kissing suddenly turn into a conversation about Becca?"

"Because that's how she thinks she got pregnant."

Since she wasn't making any sense—and since Jon was feeling decidedly cranky now—he shifted back a step and tried to behave himself, pushing down her blouse, smoothing her hair. Or trying to. "I'll be damned. When I grew up, the birds and the bees were pretty reliable. The only way a person could be pregnant was by doing the kissing with a man. And, well, a little more than kissing. But I had no idea there was a way to get pregnant without the boy and girl directly doing the deed—"

"Shut up, you dolt. That isn't what I meant." But those bruised eyes lightened at his teasing; the sharp anxiety in her face even started to ease into an unwilling smile. Still, she turned swiftly serious again. "She thinks our getting pregnant years ago screwed up any chance of happiness we had. That we'd be together now, married, a family if we hadn't gotten pregnant so young."

"Okay." God knows where this was going. It was like trying to follow the reasoning of a leaf.

"She thinks she doesn't know what it takes to make a happy, healthy relationship with a man. Because she never had a role model for one. I got pregnant with her, never married. My mom got pregnant too young with me, and she *did* marry—but her marriage to my dad was the pits. Becca sees that as a pattern."

"Okay," he repeated, confounded what he was supposed to say to in response to this information.

"The pattern is that the Sinclair women can't seem to have enduring relationships with men. She wants to break that pattern. She says it's about time we figured out what we've been doing wrong and start getting it right. Before it's too late. In fact, I don't *want* her married to Douglas—but I still think that's why she's not even considering it. Because she thinks a pregnancy will mess up any chance she has to build a future with Douglas—because that's what happened to me, to her grandmother. And that's why . . ."

"Why what?" Jon prodded her.

"That's why she thinks you and I should consider getting together. Because we got it wrong the first time. But we never gave it a shot at getting it right."

Jon said kindly, "She's off her rocker."

"I know."

"She's a kid, for God's sake. A baby. She doesn't know anything about our lives. Besides which—I'd climb mountains for her, God knows, but some things are none of her business."

"Jon, I agree."

"She's got a ton on her plate with this pregnancy. And I hear you. She's damn confused. If there's a way I can be there for her—*we* can be there for her—I will."

"Me, too." Susan nodded. "That's why I came to talk to you. So we could make sure we were on the same page. Whoever she talks to, you or me, I just wanted to . . . consult. And make sure you knew where she was coming from."

"Fine."

"Fine," Susan echoed.

"But if that comes up again—about our getting together—just plain tell her. It's bonkers. It won't happen. Ever. Even if hell froze over. End of story."

Again Susan nodded vigorously. "And you tell her the same, if she brings it up to you."

"*No* problem," he assured her.

She sighed, a woosh of a sigh that sounded like pure relief, and then smiled at him—a warm, intimate smile that darn near gave him another hard-on. "I was so uncomfortable about having to talk to you about this. I don't know why I was so worried. Really, I knew we'd agree."

"Completely," he assured her.

He was smiling as he watched her walk away into the night. Smiling as he ambled back to his place. It only occurred to him hours later that he felt as if someone had punched him in the stomach.

That, of course, was nothing new. Encounters with Susan often had him recovering from that reaction. It was just . . . Hell. The crisis with Becca was enough to shamble any father's brain. But that his baby had hopes of him and Susan getting back together was more like a sucker punch coming completely from left field.

It was totally absurd.

No question.

But . . . it wasn't that easy to forget.

Chapter 6

Bonkers. Susan lay wide awake in the too-small twin bed. She'd been chewing on a thumb-nail for hours, scowling at the stucco ceiling, trying to understand how a decent, respectable, responsible woman—such as herself—could suddenly go bonkers.

It was a weighty question. So weighty that she'd first started mulling it when the room was pitch-black. Now night had turned into dawn, and dawn into full-blown daylight. Sunshine now poured through the open east window, dancing and prancing across the plank floor, up the edge of her quilt, onto the pale raspberry sheets, onto her cheek. And still she scowled.

There had been plenty of men in her life since Jon Laker. Plenty. Lots. Zillions.

At least two.

Susan snapped off her thumbnail. It just didn't make sense. She'd played and replayed the scene from last night in her mind, trying to comprehend how in Sam Hill she'd ended up kissing Jon Laker.

How in Sam Hill she'd come a pinch away from making love with him.

Although she didn't like to admit it, she'd fallen off the wagon with Jon a few—an extremely few—times in the very distant past. But that was precisely how she'd learned that passion and Jon were a disastrous mix. And it just made no sense that she'd allowed him to get to her yesterday, not when so many serious things were at stake.

Well. Now she refused to get out of bed—no matter how her kidneys cried, no matter how her stomach growled—until she'd gotten a grip. For heaven's sakes, she had a family who needed her. Her once-sweet, sunny daughter was troubled and pregnant. Her once-warm, comfortable, predictable mom had turned the entire house into a yellow submarine.

Yet instead of concentrating on the things that mattered, a sneaky, subversive memory of that last kiss seeped into the very back of her mind again. The one in which his pelvis was shilly-shallying against her pelvis. The one in which his tongue was halfway down her throat and she'd wound her arms tighter around his neck than a lariat. The one in which she'd have jumped him right on that dock, in full view of the moon and anyone awake on Traverse Bay, as if they didn't have a mountain of unpleasant history between them—and he didn't infuriate the holy hell out of her besides.

Yet for a few minutes, it had happened again. She forgot the rotten history. She forgot how easily he infuriated her. Her eyes closed and suddenly her mind was spinning back twenty-two years. She'd replayed the same memory a hundred million times. There never seemed a particular reason why her mind clung to that particular day, that particular time, yet the reoccurring dream had haunted her for years.

She was back in high school.

Young, vulnerable and scared—and the dream was so real that she could see herself and the scene, clear as day. . . .

She was sixteen . . . the afternoon bell rang, and the once-silent halls suddenly exploded with noise. Teenagers surged out of classrooms with all the grace of stampeding puppies, tripping over each other, a study in uncontrollable energy and zesty hormones. Lockers clanged open. Books slammed. Gum popped. It was fall—but one of those special Indian summer days when the temperature was balmy and the sun tantalizingly bright—so nobody wanted to take home books or even think about homework. The girls shrieked loud enough to shatter china. The boys chased after them wearing loopy grins. The first kid reached the far doors and pushed, letting in a burst of dusty fall sunlight, letting out the first galloping bodies.

Susan, her arms aching from the weight of textbooks, finally managed to escape the chemistry lab. Mr. Weaver, the chem teacher, had always been really nice to her and she hated to be rude, but he drooled when he talked and sometimes looked at her in the way that gave her the willies.

"Hey, Sinclair!" Jessie Wilson lifted a hand to share a high-five, but then noticed the load of books Susan was carrying. "I can't believe you're thinking about studying on a day like today. At least are you goin' to Broadman's this Friday?"

"I'm sure hoping to." She smiled, but the instant Jessie passed by, she remembered all the stuff she had to do tonight. The history project on the Bohemians. The paper on fashion design for French. The calculus test tomorrow. And her mom was counting on her to start dinner.

"Hey, Susan!" Stubber patted her on the butt—something only Stubber would dare try when she had her hands full. Then Billy Peters shuffled by, his face turning brick-red as he waved a hello—God, if she were ever that shy, she'd have to shoot herself. Moira O'Brien yelled from across the hall, did she have the Julius Caesar questions for Thomson's Torture Class? Moira looked like a young version of Mrs. Claus, pink-cheeked and roly-poly, the rare kind of person everybody liked and got along with—although she sure never did her homework until pressed to the wall.

"Susan!"

Aw, shoot. She'd almost managed to pass by the gauntlet door of Mr. Lippert, the journalism teacher. Almost. When he poked a bony finger on her sleeve, obviously determined to snare her attention, she smiled politely. "Hi, Mr. Lippert, how you doing?"

"Just fine, just fine." Mr. Lippert beamed at her. He was always beaming at her. Susan figured she had him fooled by her appearance. She did the model student thing by choice, but in her heart of hearts she yearned to dress cooler. It just wasn't that easy. A ponytail was the easiest way to subdue her wild cinnamon hair; she never had the time or money to wear makeup; and she wore a basic polo and jeans because the hot labels were too expensive. Mr. Lippert just always acted so happy with her that she felt like a guilty imposter.

"Susan, I know you're on the student council and the academic challenge team, but I was really hoping you could spare me a few hours to help with the yearbook."

"Right this minute?" she asked helplessly. God. She really had to get home early tonight.

"No, no, dear. I meant over the next few weeks. I've been getting a crew of kids together, but what I really need is someone like you, someone they'd recognize as a leader. . . ."

There was more of that blah blah blah. Mr. Lippert was a good guy. It was just really hard to get him to stop talking.

". . . And something else, Susan . . ."

"Yes, sir?"

Again he beamed. "I know I shouldn't be telling you this, but I don't think there's any question who's going to be voted the Girl Most Likely to Succeed."

He meant it as a compliment, Susan understood, but by the time she finally broke free, her pulse was thudding and a fierce headache was brewing in her temples.

Lots of days she had after-school commitments, but otherwise her dad expected her home on time or he'd get mad. The problem was that he wouldn't get mad at her. He'd get mad at her mom. That troubled her—all the time—yet when she picked up her pace, ducking bodies right and left, she really knew the sharp, familiar headache wasn't about her being late.

The closer she came to graduating from high school, the more frequently she was bugged by those pressure-cooker headaches.

She knew every kid milling up and down the halls. Even if she hadn't grown up with them, each was easily identifiable by whether they were haves or have-nots. The haves were the ones who had big money. The have-nots came from local farms. Probably the division had started from basic geography. The country around Traverse City had lots of gorgeous spots, but none so special as the Old Mission Peninsula cuddled between the bays. It was so pretty that the rich had migrated from all over the country to build fancy homes up and down the shoreline. In the middle of the peninsula, though, the sweet winds and mild temperatures made for ideal orchard country—especially cherries.

Her family, the Sinclairs, had been successful cherry growers for generations—but that didn't matter. At some point the division had stopped being about money or status. As far as Susan could tell, it was about confidence. The haves—like Jon—

possessed an internal confidence that the have-nots—like her—could never seem to get.

Her mom didn't understand. She was always saying that Susan had everything—looks, smarts, character, personality; she could be anything. But her mom never had the confidence to break loose from the labels. Susan had understood for a long time that it was a tough job. It took being better at everything. It took never making mistakes. It took never screwing up, even once.

Susan wanted to make something of her life, to *be* someone, so bad she could taste it. She wanted to get off the peninsula and away from all its small-town values and labels. She wanted the kind of confidence that the haves took for granted. But sometimes the stress wrapped around her so tight that she couldn't seem to breathe. She had nightmares, about what could happen if she didn't get all A's. Or failed a calculus test and didn't get a college scholarship. Or if she made some horrible mistake that no one would forgive her for, something that would disappoint her mom and her teachers and all the people who were so sure of their expectations of her. . . .

She was charging for the exit door when a hand suddenly reached out and snagged her inside the shadow of a doorway. Her books scattered to the ground, forgotten almost instantly. She recognized the hand even before she saw the face, and faster than lightning she felt a shot of adrenaline zoom through her pulse.

"Hey," she said, "who do you think you are?"

The tall blond guy with the wicked blue eyes trapped her between the closed door and the hall, one hand on each side of her face, his legs splayed—not touching her, but close enough so she couldn't escape without touching him. "The guy who's crazy about you."

It wasn't easy, pretending her heart wasn't galloping at breakneck speed, but Susan managed to raise a cocky eyebrow. "Yeah, well, what makes you think you're so special? Lots of guys chase after me."

"I know. I've watched them," he agreed. "But there's a difference."

"What's the difference?"

"You're just as crazy about me," he informed her, and then dipped his head.

Oh, God, oh, God. One kiss and she was spinning in a kaleidoscope of sensation. Nice girls didn't feel this way, she was almost sure. And they were in a doorway, for Pete's sake. Anybody could see them. They could get in big trouble. She couldn't afford trouble, big or otherwise.

Yet she didn't stop him from kissing her again, and this time his kiss was deep and long. Those wicked blue eyes of his danced, and then the lashes shuttered down when he got into the kiss, into the feeling, into her. His pelvis rocked against hers, forcing her to feel his you-know-what, forcing heat to flush and rush through her bloodstream like a hot, wild river. He angled his head, dove into her mouth with his tongue, yanked off the soft band holding her ponytail and lost his hands in her hair.

She should have cared.

She didn't.

In the beginning, she thought Jon Laker had only come on to her because he was one of the haves. She'd been determined to watch herself. He could easily be playing with one of the have-nots, thinking of her as easy, a country girl who wouldn't say no to him. He wore cool clothes, came from money, could sleep every night knowing he could get into any college he wanted, do anything he wanted with his life.

But it was never that way. The hunger in his eyes, the tenderness, had disarmed her from the start. Jon always made her feel as if no one existed in his world but her. He made her feel . . . dreams. Dreams of being loved. Dreams of the excitement of loving, of giving everything, being everything with him. Dreams of telling secrets and soaring off mountains. Dreams that she could be safe with him, the way she felt with no one else—even herself. Maybe especially herself.

"Jon." A groan escaped her throat, low and achy. His hand had slipped down, was pushing at the hem of her polo shirt. She knew what he wanted to touch. Her breast ached miserably, terribly, wanting to be touched, by him. Only by him.

She wound her arms around his neck, closed her eyes and kissed him back. She knew the risks, all the risks, and simply refused to care. Jon was the one thing right in her life. The one wonderful thing. The only truly wonderful thing.

She couldn't give him up. Not for anyone or any reason. No matter what. Ever.

Abruptly Susan's teeth clipped her thumbnail, creating a razor-sharp edge—but thankfully making that memory disappear into her mind's closet again. It was because Becca had ideas about them being together that that old memory had come back to haunt her—and because that damn man had always made her feel as if she'd betrayed him years ago.

She'd done what she had to do years ago. In fact, her whole life, she'd done her absolute best to do the right thing. It was wonderful to be wildly, romantically in love at sixteen. But life wasn't romantic.

Life was knowing her mother had been stuck in an unbearable marriage and couldn't get out. Life was understanding she never wanted to be trapped that way herself. Maybe being in love was the best thing that ever happened to her—but damnation, love didn't pay the bills. It didn't make a woman *safe*.

Her gaze focused on the stucco ceiling. Over the last hour a tiny spider had been working hard, spinning an intricate web in the corner, the web as delicate as lace but so much more fragile.

What on earth was happening to her? She knew she was tough as an ox and mean as old leather. Yet ever since that problem on the West Coast, she'd felt ridiculously, inexcusably fragile. Breakable. As if all these years she'd believed herself safe and suddenly discovered it was a lie . . . and nearly coming apart in Jon Laker's arms last night made her feel even more scared.

A few kisses from that man and suddenly she'd been sixteen again. Wild. Hot. Uninhibited. Stupid.

She slung deeper under the quilt—deeper under the guilt—thinking, *All right, that's enough of this nonsense.* She was home. She needed to be thinking about her daughter and mom, not herself. She had to find a way to come through for them.

"*Susan?* Are you up?" Her mother's voice came from just outside the bedroom door.

"I'm up. I'm just having a nervous breakdown. Come on in, Mom."

"You're what?" Her mom pushed the door open.

"I was joking. I'm awake, really. I'm just being lazy." She produced an easy warm smile, just to be sure her mom wasn't worried.

Lydia angled closer to the bed. "Becca just woke up. And I know it's still really early, but I want to talk to you both before everybody's gone in different directions for the day." She studied Susan's face. "Were you really joking, or is there something wrong? You haven't mentioned how your job was going in a long time."

"The job's been a little hairy. The Midwest stores are doing fabulous. And you know I love Sebastian, he's wonderful to work for. The West Coast stores are doing okay, too, but the new man I have to work with there isn't quite so easy."

Lydia sat down at the edge of the bed. "In what way is he a problem?"

"He's just a pistol." Susan never meant to mention Brian Weis or the career crisis she was facing. She'd only wanted to duck mentioning anything about Jon. More to the point, once she got a wide-awake look at her mother, her tongue seemed to have loosened from shock. This morning Lydia was wearing Liz C jeans and a spandex top. The spandex top was shown off via a push-up bra and the jeans were downright snug. The outfit was enough to boggle Susan's mind into rattling off more infor-mation. "When I decided to come up here, to be with you and Becca, I took a leave of absence, like I told you. But now I'm thinking maybe I'll make it a permanent leave. Maybe I'm due a job change. Maybe . . ." Her mom suddenly looked alarmed. "And maybe not," Susan said smoothly. "Mostly I was just lazing in bed, daydreaming about wild ideas and silly things."

"It's so crazy. I couldn't wait for you to come home next time so I could talk to you about all kinds of things. Freedom. Choices. I always felt you made choices because you felt you *had* to. And that was my fault, the way I raised you . . . but honey, you *can't* quit your job. I never had to worry about you because of your job. You make all that great money. You don't have to be dependent on anyone or any-thing. You have great benefits and all that security built up—"

"You couldn't be more right. I'd be nuts to quit. I was just talking. Joking. Really, Mom." She wanted to slap herself. She never worried her mom. Never.

But that seemed the jolt she needed to shape up. The instant Lydia left the room, Susan bounded out of bed and into a shower. Ten minutes later she'd pulled on a crisp cotton shirt and shorts, fingered some style into her hair and hurled downstairs. Lydia never willingly chose to get up early, so whatever had inspired her to wake everyone up for an early morning assembly had to be pretty serious.

At first glance, though, it just looked like a girl fest. Warily watching her mom, Susan claimed a mug of coffee from the microwave and then plunked down on the couch in the dining-cum-media room. Becca was already there, curled up on the floor with a body pillow and a box of soda crackers. They shared a mystified glance before the no-name marmalade cat leaped on Susan's lap, circled restlessly and then settled down with a loud purr to watch the proceedings.

Lydia had laid a nest of treasures on the floor. Girl treasures. Specifically Sinclair women treasures. The steel carving knife was four generations old, and had been used to carve every Thanksgiving turkey that Susan could remember. The iron frying pan was just as old and had been cared for just as religiously, because nothing made fried potatoes better than that frying pan. Next to the pan was a cameo pendant, nested on a strip of velvet. The cameo was cracked in one corner, but if you were a Sinclair woman, you knew what it meant. Stories. All the stuff Lydia had spread out on the floor had family stories associated with them, some funny, some sad, some poignant, but all stories related to their personal history.

Lydia pulled up a pale yellow stool. "The three of

us have so few chances to be together that I wanted to take advantage of this one to give you girls some things. Like my great-great-grandmother's carving knife—it's time to pass it on to you, Susan. And Becca, I want you to have the cameo. . . ."

Again, Susan exchanged alarmed glances with Becca. "Mom, this is sacred family stuff. We all love it, but you don't need to give us anything."

"I know that. I just want to. And I want to *do* things, too. Like I found the old antique press in the barn. In another week, the cherries'll be ready. . . . I thought we'd have fun making cherry wine."

"Sounds great," Becca agreed.

"And it's no one's birthday or anything, but I thought we'd have fun making the Sinclair Sunrise sponge cake together. We just have to choose a day when I know I've got a dozen eggs in the house."

"Oh, man. I love that cake and I haven't had it in a blue moon," Becca enthused.

But Susan balked. "Better leave me out of the kitchen. I've tried making Great-Grandma's sponge cake about five times. When you make it, Mom, it turns out about fourteen inches tall. But whenever I make it, it's about two inches tall and heavier than lead. Assuming I end up with a cake at all."

"You know why?" Lydia asked her.

"Sure. Because I'm a major twerp in the kitchen." She waggled a finger at the cat. "You don't have to comment on that."

Becca laughed, but Lydia said quietly, "No, Suze. The reason it fails for you is because women have a rotten habit of forgetting to tell all the ingredients in a recipe. The same way moms tend to tell their daughters things, but often to skip certain details. And that's why I wanted the three of us together this morning. So I could tell you something that I think you both should know. Something I should have told you years ago."

Curious now, Susan gulped down more caffeine. She wasn't sure where her mother was going with this, but there had obviously been a bee in Lydia's bonnet recently. Whatever had inspired the daffodil-yellow house and the red lace panties, Susan wanted a serious look at the whole hive.

Becca scooched closer, too, as Lydia handed them both an old photograph. The picture showed a woman standing alone—a beautiful woman, unsmiling although her expression was thoughtful and bright. She had perfect skin, huge eyes and was wearing a flapper dress with fringe and long pearls, her hair cropped in pin curls.

"That's my mother," Lydia said.

As if this were news. "We know that, Gram," Becca said impatiently.

"I realize you've seen her picture before . . . but I also told you some half-truths about her before." Lydia hunched over the stool, unconsciously reaching over to pet the vagrant cat. "My mother had three kids. First me, the oldest, then Butch—Uncle Griff—and then your Aunt Loretta. What you didn't know before, though, was that my mother got pregnant for a fourth time. And that's how she died. In childbirth."

Susan frowned. "I thought she died in an accident."

Lydia shook her head. "That's what we all said in the family. I don't know why the lie started. I think because my dad didn't want to scare us kids—especially me or Loretta—into thinking having babies was dangerous. But the point isn't the truth of how she died. The point is the lie. How lies get passed on. Once secrets and stories get started, they take on a life of their own. They affect you whether they're true or not."

Susan hesitated. "I sure agree with that . . . but I still don't understand why you suddenly decided to tell us about this now."

"Because . . . well, because I just didn't think about all this before. How that secret—that lie, however well intentioned—affected me so much, and may have ended up affecting you and Becca. My mother dying when I was so young affected my whole life—how I felt about being female, being a woman, being a wife. How I felt about love and sex and men. I never talked to either of you about this stuff. Not really. Not at a gut level."

"So say whatever you want to now, Gram," Becca urged her.

"It's not as if I have something brilliant or insightful to say or anything like that. It's just . . . it just seems to me that the three of us have something critical in common. We all have this drive, to try to do the right thing. It's a good quality. Not a bad one. But somehow it's gotten goofed up for us."

Susan tried to motion the cat away, but the marmalade monster determinedly climbed on her lap and nuzzled herself down. "I don't understand—" she started to say, but the other two were already nose to nose, tuned to each other.

"That's what I've been thinking, too," Becca said. "Like we all keep doing the right thing, but it doesn't work out. There has to be a reason. We keep itching at the same kind of problems, but somehow we're not solving them."

Lydia nodded empathetically. "And I think it goes back to when my mom died. I was just ten, and my dad suddenly seemed to need me so much that I thought the world would end if I wasn't always good. My dad was crazy about Harold. That's why I first went out with your grandfather, maybe even why I . . ." She swallowed that thought. "Anyway, I went into that marriage thinking that I had to keep it together. It wasn't a good marriage, but I still thought that's what a good woman did, stick it out, make the best of it. And then your mother—"

"I'm right here," Susan announced. "No one needs to talk about me as if I were out of town."

"I think she never married my dad because she was trying to do the right thing," Becca said to Lydia, as if Susan were invisible. "They were too young to marry. Or so she thought. She always did the right thing. The sacrificing good-woman thing. But I think the only man she ever really loved was my dad, and they never even had a chance—"

"That's totally ridiculous," Susan tried to interject, but the other two were exuberantly nodding to each other.

"You're getting me," Lydia said to Becca. "I can't pin it all down. Hell, if I could have, I wouldn't have made the choices I did most of my life. But what I'm sure of is that something we're all doing sucks, as they say in your generation. We've got a pattern of trying to be good. Trying to do the right thing. Maybe if we all tried to do the wrong thing for once, things could start turning around. Practice being a little wicked. A little selfish. A little wild—"

"Now, you two just wait a minute!" This time Susan firmly plunked the no-name marmalade cat on the ground so she could stand up. "Mom, I don't believe you're saying this stuff to Becca! And for Pete's sake, what's so wrong with us? Rebecca, you have a major problem on your plate right now, but you're going to survive it, and you've got family behind you a million percent. We'll help you any way we can—"

"Mom." Becca threw up her hands, heaved to her feet. "It's always this way with you."

"Always what way?" Susan asked in bewilderment.

"You have to make things nice. You have to make sure everything's fine. You have to try and fix everything. But I think what Grandma's saying— what I'm saying—is that maybe it's time we all got good and ruffled. Shake things up around here. And one of those things is you and Dad—"

"Don't even think about going there again," Susan snapped. "There's nothing between me and your father. Nothing. I don't know how you got that idea in your head, but get it out right now."

"Mom, I swear, sometimes there's just no talking to you. You're not going to listen no matter what I say. Well, forget it, then." Becca hurled down her soda crackers and stomped out the back door—still in her slippers and sleep shirt.

Susan clawed a hand through her hair. "For heaven's sake. What's going *on* here? What did I say to make her so upset? We never used to have trouble talking. I—"

"She thinks you still love Jon. So do I," Lydia said placidly.

Susan whirled on her mother. "This isn't about *me*. Nothing is about *me*. You're the one who changed the whole house. And Becca, she's struggling with a huge thing like a pregnancy. I'm the only one who's fine!"

"You don't like all the changes I made in the house?" Lydia sounded wounded.

"Sure I do, as long as you're happy with them. I think you just startled Becca, and me, too, because you changed so much so completely. Becca's been worried that you must be unhappy, or you wouldn't have leaped to do all this stuff so fast—"

"Well, the truth is, right now I don't know what I'm happy with. But I'm trying to find out by doing things I never did in my life before. Some of those things are uncomfortable. Even unsettling. But I'm getting better at not hiding my head so deep in the sand. And I think that's what Becca's trying to do.

Get her head out of the sand. Figure out what she really *wants* to do, not just what other people think she should do. Which is to say, I think we're both fine. *You're* the one we're worried about, dear."

"*Me!*" The idea was so ludicrous, Susan wanted to shake her head the way a puppy shook off rain. "I'm the one person no one ever has to worry about. Ever. I've been taking care of myself forever—"

"But you're alone," Lydia said.

"There's nothing wrong with being alone. It's people who can't stand to be alone who end up in sick relationships."

"Oh, that's just psychobabble, dear. Everybody needs somebody. So do you. You give love, Susan, but you don't take it. You never open the door and let anyone in that far. You'd do anything for me, for Becca, for someone you love. But you never let anyone do anything for you. And I feel guilty, because I'm afraid I raised you that way. To be a coward. To hide behind being good, rather than get out there and risk what matters."

"A coward!"

Lydia nodded pensively. "I'm afraid none of us have much courage, but you're the worst. Never facing up to your feelings for Jon. Never being honest with yourself. Never letting love in. . . ."

Susan threw her hands in the air. It was like trying to reason with a cupcake. "I'm *fine*. In fact, I seem to be the only one in this family who has a single sane bone in her entire body. The two of you are the goofy ones. I am not screwed up! I am damned happy! And I'm sure as hell not a coward!"

She couldn't remember ever raising her voice to her mother—except for that one time when she was thirteen and her mom had tried to sell her an idiotic bill of goods about how getting her period was a Womanly Honor. Otherwise, her mom had always seemed stuck with so many unhappy choices that Susan never wanted to add to her problems. It was no different now, so it was absolutely inconceivable that she'd do anything so immature as stomp away and slam out the front door like a child having a temper tantrum.

But it seemed she'd done just that. Outside, her lungs hauled in that first breath of fresh air as if they'd been starved for oxygen.

Her brisk walk turned into a jog, and that turned into a blind run, past the barns, zigzagging through the big old spruce, up through the wooded ridge, then down the spongy earth toward Copper Creek. She'd run the same path a dozen times when she was a girl, always when she was hurt and seeking somewhere to hide and lick her wounds.

She was older now, of course. Mature. It was just . . . her family had always been so close. She'd always felt as if she had a strong nurturing role in both her daughter's and her mother's lives, that they valued her, needed her. So Becca accusing her of not listening hurt like a knife wound. And her mother calling her a coward hurt even worse.

Neither had ever attacked her before. She just didn't understand—what was happening to her family? When they all needed each other the most, why did it seem like they were falling apart?

Jogging toward the creek edge, blinking back a fierce sting of tears, it abruptly occurred to Susan that she was running away from finding out those answers. Which was, specifically, a cowardly thing to do.

And that pissed her off even more.

Chapter 7

Jon lived for the summer months. He thrived on pressure and heat, loved the chaos and crises that came with the busiest season, and this last week had been an exercise in all four.

There was a limit, though. And he had reached it today.

It was about noon when he towed this family—and their crippled cabin cruiser—in to dock. Sweat dripped off his brow as he secured the ropes. He'd been listening to the abrasive voice of the wife for two solid hours. The voices of the three whiny kids were a further insult to his eardrums. A mosquito nailed his neck the instant he leaped onto the dock.

Sometimes Jon marveled at what a man volunteered for. It wasn't as if he'd been forced into this work. He could have had a life as a pretentious, money-grubbing, deal-making lawyer who worked ninety hours a week and screwed around on his wife in his free time. God knows, his father had revered that life. Joseph Laker had never understood why Jon hadn't been panting to follow in those venerable footsteps.

Jon helped the family of five onto dry land, holding on to his amenable smile by a thread. Normally he loved the boat world and everything about it, but this whole morning had been a marina owner's nightmare.

The family had radioed in that their engine had quit. Someone always had an unexpected problem at this time of year—that was exactly what made the work interesting—but in this case the Hollingers had been sitting for two days in the sun, apparently thinking that some miracle was going to start their boat.

The father had taken the boat out without any kind of maintenance check, so, of course, he was hot to blame someone else—such as the wife or kids— for his failure. By the time Jon arrived to tow them in, the guy was yelling, the kids were crying, and the dog—God, why would anyone take a dog for a lake-bound week with no place on a boat to poop?—was howling louder than all of them.

Usually, when Jon reminded himself that he could have given in to all the elegant, hoity-toity family pressure and become a lawyer, he could swallow the bad moments and whistle past them. After two hours with the Hollingers, though, he was fit to be fried. He'd barely gotten rid of them and escaped back to the shop before the phone rang. He grabbed it and barked a *"What?"* into the receiver.

"Dad?"

Faster than a slap, his blood pressure zoomed down a hundred points. "Yeah, it's me, shorty. I didn't mean to snarl. It just happened I spent a morning with the family from hell."

"That's okay. I'll call back another time."

"No, no." He heard it in Becca's voice. A little tremble. Trouble. Undoubtedly the trouble he'd been waiting for all week. "Now's perfect. It's a great day—I just need a root beer and a chance to sit down for two shakes. Everything's going good, great time for you to call."

"You sure?"

"I'm sure."

A short silence followed. Very short, but still long enough for Jon to figure out that he was never going to have nerves of steel. Not where his daughter was concerned.

"The thing is," Becca finally edged out, "I'd like to talk over a problem with you. If you have time. It'll wait and all. No hurry. In fact, if you're busy or you don't want to right now . . ."

This had to be it. The Pregnancy Talk. He'd kept a phone hover-close all week, hoping she'd call and finally come clean. He hadn't wanted to push or force her hand, but it sure scraped his heart that she hadn't trusted him enough to tell him earlier. Before she could vacillate any further, he said immediately, calmly, "How about if we take the *S-Q* out for an hour after lunch? Catch some rays, put our feet up. Be away from everybody. Just the two of us."

She went for it, but God knows how Jon was going to. Fall and winter, his time was all flexible, but June and July were hustle months. Boats always needed fixing; people always needed supplies; tourists were in and out nonstop for sailing lessons and boat rentals and information and parts, a bumped bow here, a nicked windshield there, a potty that didn't work.

For Becca, though, he'd create time or die trying.

He called Marnie in from the shop, told him to man the phone and the fort, to hold his three o'clock if he wasn't back by then and to cancel the insurance guy. Marnie had one of those faces only a mafia mother could love—and that was before he'd quit smoking, when he was still nice. He gave Jon a menacing scowl, stuck in another stick of Juicy Fruit, and took off for the air-conditioned office faster than a bat out of hell.

Marnie was an outstanding mechanic, just a wee bit scary around people, but Jon didn't have lots of spare employees on a second's notice. He hired summer kids, but it's not as if they could be responsible for the whole place. Birch, his true right hand, was out for a couple weeks with a sprained ankle.

The whole time he was scrambling to clear his plate, Jon couldn't help but notice it was the first time in days that Susan hadn't dominated his mind. She'd been plugged into his thoughts like a channel he couldn't change. He kept remembering how those dadblamed kisses had turned wild and wicked on them. How easy it was—even after all these years—to get lost in her. How the two of them seemed to be unfinished business no matter how either of them swore otherwise.

But it was their daughter who came first today, and by five minutes to one, Jon was on the *S-Q*'s deck, stashing iced sodas and juices, checking sunscreen and towels, his gaze darting to the parking lot every few seconds.

By then he'd given himself several mental lectures on precisely how he was going to handle this. He was going to stay cool. He was going to stay calm. He was not going to bring up squeezing Douglas by the balls. He was not going to say a single indelicate word about the immoral, irresponsible, selfish dickhead who'd dared put his daughter at risk. He was not going to mention that one scene from *Armageddon* . . . the great scene, the dad's dream of a scene, where Bruce Willis chased Ben Affleck with a gun all over the oil rig for sleeping with his daughter—one of Jon's favorite movie scenes of all time. But no, he was going to keep a lid on that fantasy completely. He was going to smile. He was going to smile with *sensitivity*. He was going to be the kind of father a daughter knew absolutely she could turn to. He was going to be there for Becca, whatever she needed, whatever she wanted to do.

He'd self-coached himself so well that he was more primed than a springer spaniel in hunting season when he finally saw Becca. She was just climbing out of her car. The worried look in her eyes only pumped him up further.

"Hey, beautiful. Come on board. Great day, isn't it?" He swooped her up in a hug before lifting her on deck. She came just to his chin, like her mother. Same soft eyes, same wild hair catching fire in the sunlight, but unlike Susan, who looked dressed for company even when she had the flu, Becca was ready for serious sailing . . . deck shoes, shorts she could move in, a loose tee.

Slow and easy, he cast off, puttered out to open sea, then raised the sail and let her fly. The breeze cupped the sail like a man claiming a woman's breast, snuggling it tight. The water dancing past them was full of diamonds. They raced for the joy of it, both of them loosening up—who could resist a day like this? The smell of lake and land were headier than champagne, the gulls soaring higher than clouds overhead.

Becca had always loved the water, and once she relaxed enough to crack some real smiles and start laughing, he did, too. He couldn't remember a time he hadn't adored her. Even as a little squirt, she'd taken to sailing, loved the splash of fresh water, the wind in her face. He used to swear that a new freckle popped on her nose every hour they were in the sun.

Eventually he pulled into a familiar cove, where the shoreline curved into a comma on a white stone beach. He dropped anchor, popped the tops on a pair of root beers and sank on the deck with a pillow at his back.

"One of these days we should sail to China together." It was like an old song where only the two of them knew the lyrics.

"Just sail and sail and sail." She knew her lines. "Just see the world and never stop. Live off the sea. Wear necklaces of pearls and shells and eat crab and swim with the dolphins." She pushed the sunglasses to the top of her head to hold back her wildly curling hair. Her smile echoed the bond between them, but then she touched his toe with her toe. "It's going to be really awkward for me to try to say this, Dad."

She'd pushed the exact button to make all his prepared-dad-stuff spill out. "No. There's nothing awkward between us. Don't ever feel that. You know I love you, no matter what. And you know I'll be on your side, no matter what."

"This is a little different."

"That's okay," he assured her. "No matter what it is, it'll be okay. Just tell me."

She hesitated, inhaled a gusty lungful of sea air and then plunged in. "Grandma thinks that Mom is still in love with you."

Root beer sprayed from his mouth when he swallowed the wrong way. "Say what?"

"I do, too. Think that Mom still loves you."

"Say what?"

"I know, I know, it's none of my business," Becca said earnestly. "But it's like you always said . . . we should be able to talk about anything together. Even if it's uncomfortable. And this is like one of those things that has just *got* to come out, Dad."

Jon slapped his chest, hard, to avoid another choking cough. "The problem you wanted to talk about was your *mom*?"

"Not just Mom. The two of you. The you-two that never had a chance to live together. Have you ever thought about it? Living with Mom? Marrying her?"

This just wasn't fair. He was prepared to confront the pregnancy thing. Women didn't have a right to do this. Prime your pump to talk about one thing and then sneak behind your back with another, and yeah, Susan had mentioned something about Rebecca harboring some crazy ideas, but he'd pushed that off his mind for the obvious reason. He couldn't believe she wanted to talk about anything until the Big Thing was handled. "Honey—"

"Just tell me flat out. Do you have any positive feelings for Mom?"

"Well, yes, of course I do. But—"

"There was love on your side. I always knew it. And you told me you were in love with her, besides."

"I told you that when we created you we were way deep in love with each other, true. But, sweetheart, a lot of years have passed since then—"

"I know, I know. But that's just the point. You two got split up because of me. If Mom hadn't gotten pregnant, you two might have ended up married, happy forever. Mom would never have gone off to live with Aunt Loretta in Detroit. She'd have stayed here. You'd have gone to school together and gotten a chance to have the whole relationship develop the way it was supposed to."

"Whoa."

"Please listen to me, Dad. I've felt my whole life like it was my fault that you two never had a chance. And I guess there's nothing I can do about that, but the thing is, *you* can. You could make a chance for the two of you now. If you still have feelings for each other."

"Rebecca . . ." When he called her by her full name, she was supposed to understand that she'd crossed a line. It had worked for the first twenty-one years of her life, but somehow this afternoon his adored daughter plowed on, as stubborn as a blockheaded hound.

"You never married. I thought you were going to a couple times, like that blond lady with the big laugh. She didn't seem to have an IQ much bigger than a door, but she was nice and all, and she sure hung on your every word. I *know* she'd have said yes if you'd asked her, but you didn't, and that seemed the closest you came."

Jon reached up to loosen his shirt collar, then remembered that he wasn't wearing a shirt. "Everyone doesn't need to be married to be happy. And even if they did, that doesn't mean anything related to your mother and me—"

"I think it does." Becca, his sweet, softhearted baby, nailed him with another of those stubbornly earnest looks. "I think you'd have found someone else if you still didn't have feelings for Mom. God knows women chase you all the time. And that's the problem with Mom, too. Guys are always after her—"

"What guys?"

"It doesn't matter what guys. I'm just saying, she goes out. And she could go out lots more, but she always seems to start chilling after a few dates. She doesn't hang in long enough to take a chance and *love* anybody. I think it's because her heart's already taken, because she still loves you. And I think you two should do something about it."

"Holy cow. Holy smokes. Holy shit. Rebecca, you've got to get this nonsense out of your mind."

But when his baby got a bee up her butt, she was just as mule-headed as her mother. "You can pretend it isn't there, Dad. I'm almost sure Mom will never say anything if you don't take the ball. But I wish you would at least *try*. Ask her out, spend a little time together. If you find out there's nothing there, then fine, but what's the harm in giving it a chance? Don't you feel you need closure after all this time? Wouldn't you like to know for sure what you had or could have, before it's all thrown away for good?"

"Becca, honey, I'm just not one of those guys who worries about stuff like 'closure.' "

Tears welled in her eyes. He almost had a heart attack. Hell, what was he supposed to say? Somehow he'd managed to upset her. Only a jerk of a father would upset his vulnerable, pregnant daughter.

This had to be Susan's fault. He wasn't sure how, but damnation, he didn't *do* emotional talks unless he had a ton of time to prepare ahead, and he'd prepared for the pregnancy thing but not for this. How was he supposed to know this was coming? What sane man could have guessed? Becca had never said one thing to him about getting together with Susan in two decades, and before that, she was too damn young to talk.

He sailed back home. Fast. Becca had shopping

to do; he had a three o'clock meeting, so they both had excuses for tabling any further talk. His haste had nothing to do with his business, though.

As soon as they docked, he heartily hugged Becca good-bye and waved until her car was out of sight. Then he jogged into the office and grabbed the telephone.

The Sinclair phone rang fifty million times. No answer.

Because he had to give a sailing lesson, he couldn't try calling Susan again until four-thirty. The line was busy then. Busy again at five. Busy again at five-thirty. With three women in one house, it was no surprise that he had trouble getting through—but he wasn't about to give up trying.

Susan cupped her chin in a palm as she surveyed the kitchen table. The debris left over from dinner was—how could she put it?—impressive.

Unbelievable, but impressive.

All week, she'd been trying to help both her mom and her daughter deal with their problems. She'd initiated all kinds of activities to help raise their spirits. Tonight the plan for dinner had been to make some traditional well-loved Sinclair recipes.

It had been a great plan, except that Sebastian had telephoned with a work crisis around four, and she got drawn into a long conversation—which unfortunately left Lydia and Becca unsupervised in the kitchen.

By the time Susan got off the phone, it was too late. The die had been cast. The two of them had

completely abandoned the original menu. The revised menu contained no traditional Sinclair
recipes. It pretty much lacked all claim to a balanced
diet as well. The platter of finger-tip asparagus was
almost gone, as was the giant bowl of strawberries,
meant to be dipped in brown sugar and sour cream.
Dessert was rhubarb pie.

That was it. The entire dinner menu.

Susan drummed her fingers on the table, feeling
glum. She should have known better than to leave
those two alone together. No problems were getting
discussed, much less resolved. It was always easy
getting those two to bond, only their bonding was
on a par with fellow loonies in the same asylum.
Fellow sex-obsessed loonies.

"A little nutrition never occurred to either of
you?" she asked Becca, who immediately responded with another gale of laughter. Lydia chor-
tled right along with her.

"There's plenty of nutrition, Mom. They just all
happen to be aphrodisiac foods," Becca told her. "I
thought you knew. We got the recipes out of this
book on beefing up your sex life without beef."

"If you just look at the shape of the asparagus—"
Lydia started to say, but Susan pointed a royal finger.

"Don't go there. If you two don't make yourselves sick on the food, you're going to make yourselves sick giggling."

"Mom, loosen up!"

"I'm trying, I'm trying. But I hate asparagus and I
hate rhubarb pie and you two stuck me with both."

"And now you're afraid you're going to attack

the paperboy?" Becca asked demurely—which struck Lydia as so funny that the two went off into another slaphappy giggle fit. When the sputtering eventually died down, Lydia came through with another brainstorm.

"I think the three of us should get a massage."

"Massage?"

"Yeah, you know. Go to a masseur. Strip down naked, get oiled, hear a bunch of new age music, space out." Lydia said to Becca, "My whole life, I was afraid to get one. Partly because I thought it was self-indulgent, but mostly because I was afraid the person doing a massage would be a lesbian. But now I think, I'm fifty-seven, getting wrinkled, getting saggy . . . I mean, only a guy my own age with bifocals could possibly be turned on by this body. No self-respecting lesbian could possibly be interested. Either that or I'm not sure I care anymore. Anyway, we could all go together—"

Susan rolled her eyes to the ceiling. "That's it. I'm not letting the two of you in a room alone together ever again. It's not safe."

"Come on, Mom. Don't you think a massage sounds like fun? Getting oiled and rubbed down?"

It did sound like fun. Adolescent sort of fun, but Becca had been so serious and Lydia so difficult lately. Susan kept thinking that there were serious problems around here, problems that shouldn't be ignored, problems that really, really needed to be worked out . . . but it seemed like she was the only one singing those lyrics. The other two were man-

aging to relax, and maybe that was the most important key to handling the big stuff down the pike.

Susan stood up and started stacking plates. She
was about to agree with this latest harebrained massage idea when Lydia noticed it was time to do
dishes and pushed up from her chair.

"I've got to walk off all this pie! I'll be back in a
few minutes!"

And then Becca saw the dishes, too. "I'll be back!
I just have to go to the bathroom!"

Why, those dogs, Susan thought darkly. The low-
down dirty lazy dogs, abandoning her with a
kitchen that looked like the aftermath of a cyclone.

Naturally, the telephone rang the minute the
women were out of sight. Susan figured it for a nui-
sance telemarketer, but when she grabbed the receiver, it was a young man's tenor on the other end.

She called toward the bathroom, "Rebecca! It's
Douglas on the line!"

Becca showed up in the bathroom doorway too
fast to have been doing anything but hiding out,
but the sparkly eyes and joyful smile had disappeared that fast. She took the phone from Susan
and pulled the cord out into the hall, away from listening ears.

Susan immediately went back to the kitchen and
rattled some dishes, but she tried to listen. Hard. The
distance was just enough to make clear eavesdropping impossible, but she could pick up some things.
Like that neither of them were yelling. Or laughing.
In fact, there were no conversational sounds that in-

dicated strong emotions of any kind—but whether that was a good or bad sign, she had no way of knowing.

Four minutes later, a hand showed up, curving around the doorjamb to hang up the phone—as if the body attached to said hand didn't want to be noticed.

"Hold it," Susan said. "Did you tell him?"

"Did I . . . ?"

That guileless look of confusion hadn't worked since junior high. "You still haven't told Douglas about the pregnancy?"

"Don't start with me. I've had a trying day," Becca said.

"Don't start what with you? You think it's an unreasonable question to ask if you've told the father of your child that you're pregnant?"

"No. I didn't tell him."

Susan, who'd actually been trying to seriously do the dishes by that time, quit when she saw her daughter's face. She heard the no. She also saw the look. The one in which Becca's expression reflected that no one ever in the history of the universe could require as much patience as her mother, because no one could be more stupid, more rigid, more unfair, more demanding, more everything-wrong-that-has-ever-been-wrong-with-a-mother than Susan. Susan tossed down the kitchen towel. "Becca, I *love* you. I'm worried why you haven't told him. I just don't understand how you can think you love this man if you're afraid to tell him something this important."

"Mom. I *will* tell him. He has a right to know. No

matter what I decide to do—or what I end up doing—I'll tell him. This is not about keeping a secret. It's about wanting to get my own head straight before I involve him."

"Why?"

The simple question seemed to throw Becca. "Why what?"

"Why do you feel you need to get your head straight without him? If you love him, if he loves you, wouldn't you want to discuss your choices and confusion and worries about a problem like this together?"

Becca let out an impatient sigh. "Maybe normally, yeah. But maybe our relationship isn't quite as simple as I've made out. Maybe I'm pretty sure he'd push me toward a specific decision that I wouldn't be happy with."

"I don't understand. What do you mean by the relationship not being as simple as you made out? Are you talking about breaking up with him, Bec?" Susan should have known asking further questions was a mistake. She got another of those looks, as if a snake and mongoose had gotten stuck in the same room together.

"*Mom*, do you really think you're the one who should be giving me advice on my love life?"

"Pardon?" Maybe Becca meant an innocuous question, but it still hurt like a blister.

"Come on. I love you. You know that. And you give me great advice and great support. But on a subject like relationships, you don't exactly have a Ph.D., you know? Cripes, I've probably slept with more guys than you have. Apart from which, you're real hot for me to face Douglas, right? When you haven't ever faced Dad."

"Faced your dad? Faced your dad about what?"

Becca threw up her hands. "You don't want to talk about it, fine. But give me a break, Mom. You want to yell at me for not talking to Douglas, when you ran away from Dad when you were pregnant? Beats me how I'm supposed to ask you advice when you did the same darn thing. Aw, screw it."

God knows when the marmalade cat had sneaked in the house, but she was suddenly on the counter, lapping at the melted butter on a plate. When Becca stormed outside, Susan whipped around so fast that she almost knocked over the plate and the cat both.

Her eyes welled up with unwilling tears, but a minute later she realized they were tears of fury, not hurt. She wasn't hurt at Becca's words. She was furious at Jon. She jogged to the phone and punched in his number.

The instant she heard his voice, she snapped, "Damn it, Jon, what did you do to Rebecca?"

"Me? I haven't done anything, for Pete's sake. It's you."

For some confounded reason, he sounded as infuriated and belligerent as she felt. "I know you saw her after lunch, because she said she was going over to see you. You must have said something to upset her up one side and down the other."

"I never said *anything*. She's the one who knocked me for six. And I've been trying to call you all afternoon to figure this out, only, damn it, I couldn't get through that line for love or money. We need to meet."

"Damn right we do," she snarled.

"Soon," he snarled back.

"Tonight," she insisted.

"Immediately," he insisted right back.

"Your place." She poked her finger in the air, in case he failed to get the message who was giving the orders around here.

"Fine. Get over here."

"I sure as hell will." She slammed down the receiver and grabbed her purse and car keys.

Chapter 8

Susan parked the car, grabbed her purse and zoomed up the stairs to Jon's private living quarters above the marina office. She rapped loudly on the door several times before she suddenly had a thoughtful uh-oh.

She never met with Jon alone at his place. Ever. It wasn't as if that were a sacred rule written in blood; it was just that both of them knew they could have an occasional, rare, unusual—catastrophic— problem when they found themselves alone to- gether. And considering that a week ago they'd somehow related on a par with lava and smoke— she was still bewildered about how exactly she'd found herself in his arms—it really seemed a lot wiser to only meet in a public place.

Like most wisdom, though, it was worth gold but came too late. The door was hurled open. The glaring, hulking male on the other side had the sun behind him, so his face was in shadow, but she could see enough to recognize trouble. His skin was sun-toasted, his hair wind-tossed and light as sand after months in the sun. He was just wearing jeans and a tee, but the T-shirt stretched over a sailor's muscled arms and shoulders. The eyes were snapping sexual energy.

She could feel every ounce of estrogen in her body bristling. She told herself it was a testosterone allergy, not attraction.

"Come on in. You want a drink first or you want to start yelling right away?"

That was Jon. Even when she wanted to kill him, he had this sick way of tickling her sense of humor. "I think . . . a drink. If we're going to yell for very long, we'll both get thirsty anyway."

"Good thinking. You want something alcoholic or something lighter?"

"Whatever's easier."

When he strode toward the kitchen, she snugged her arms under her chest, looking around, feeling nervous and edgy. His place was familiar enough; she'd picked up Becca from here countless times. It was just . . .

Somehow she still thought of Jon as the boy she'd known so well. The one who'd raced boats and sky-dived and took his dirt bike into the hills—any activity that would have upset his staid, wealthy parents. The boy she'd known had worn ripped-up T-shirts and chugged beer when he was fifteen. They'd climbed a fire tower for one date, crashed a bar in town for another, sneaked onto private property just for the kick of doing something forbidden. On the inside, he'd been fiercely angry with his parents, who couldn't be pleased, who never looked at *Jon* but only at his grades and his haircut and what college he was going to get into and the standard of living they expected him to aspire to. He was wild. Reckless. Sexy.

And now he had butter-soft leather furniture and smooshy-thick carpet and the place was tidy. Grown-up. The living room had brass lamps, instead of candles dripping wax out of cheap wine bottles. The kitchen had a serious subzero freezer, instead of a creaking model that leaked freon and stored ten kinds of TV dinners.

She wandered to the open glass doors. Outside was an expansive deck, with a hot tub and a breathtaking view of the bay. In his marina basin, dozens of sail masts stuck up like flagpoles. The sky was a baby-blue this late in the day, the sun a soft golden ball. She looked out, but in her mind's eye she was remembering the god-awful apartment he'd rented—somehow, illegally—since he was under eighteen when he found out she was pregnant. The apartment was only part of a whole wild plan he'd concocted. They were supposed to get married—somehow, illegally—and both work to support themselves—somehow, even though both of them were underage, neither skilled at doing anything.

That horrible apartment had had one table—a crate he'd carried home from a dump. The closets were stuffed with at least ten grand in sporting equipment, because those were presents his parents had given him, but the couch was missing a cushion and a leg. He'd brought some of his clothes—shirts with a Saks label, shirts from Jacobson's—but the place had no bed. One pillow. One plate, but according to Jon they could use paper plates most of the time, anyway. No lamps, the only illumination provided by one glaring light bulb overhead and the candles stuck in cheap wine bottles. The gasping refrigerator had two jars of maraschino cherries, a bottle of milk and a box of cereal. They could find a way to make it, he'd said.

Of course, his parents had tracked them down in a matter of hours. And her parents had shown up the instant his parents had called them. The Lakers and Sinclairs normally had nothing in common, but together they made a powerful force against two young kids.

Jon, suddenly coming up behind her now, made her jump. "I was going to make some Long Island iced tea, but then figured we'd better make it plain iced tea when you're driving— Hey, what's wrong?"

"Nothing. Something in my eye. It's gone away." She whirled around, took the glass filled with golden liquid and dancing with ice cubes and gulped fast. "You want to sit outside?"

"That depends on how loud you plan to fight."

"Pretty loud."

"Aw, hell. Let's go outside anyway. Who cares what the neighbors hear?" He opened the screen, and maybe it wasn't intentional, but suddenly she felt him looking her over. Really looking, his gaze taking a slow route from her white sandals to her white jeans and white pullover and resting forever and then some on her face. Awareness charged through her pulse, but he glanced away as fast as she did. "Susan . . . I swear, I didn't mean to yell at you on the phone."

"Well, I didn't mean to jump on you, either. I'm sorry." Outside, there was a nest of comfortable cushioned furniture, but somehow she couldn't sit. She leaned back against the rail instead. "But you *must* have said something to Becca, Jon. Because she was like a broken record, going on and on about how we should be together. She's got everything all confused."

"I *know*. That was the same song she was singing to me, too. But why the hell didn't you straighten her out?"

"*Me?*" Susan's jaw dropped. "How come you think *I* should have been the straightener-outer?"

"Because you're the mom, for Pete's sake. You're the girl."

"Like having a penis absolves you of all responsibility?"

"No. But she was going on and on about this emotional stuff. How was I supposed to talk to her when she wasn't saying anything rational? . . . No. No. Don't get physical, now."

Susan pulled herself up short. Possibly she'd been briefly—briefly—inclined to belt him, but it only took her an instant to get her decorum back. She'd never had a violent bone in her body. Except with Jon. Sometimes he just couldn't seem to help being a sexist heap of testosterone and the thought of punching him was just so tempting.

But she sighed, and sat down on the long cushioned bench, thinking a couple inches away from him would help. And she *did* want to talk. "Becca thinks I ran away from you. That years ago, when I found out I was pregnant, instead of trying to work things out with you, I ran away—that I moved in with Aunt Loretta in Detroit only because I was scared, not because I didn't want to be with you."

"Yeah, well, you did run away." He sank down next to her on the bench—which would have bothered her if his comment didn't startle her so much.

"Come on, Jon, that's not fair or true! I know you thought I left you at the time, but all these years have passed. You *know* we couldn't have made it that young. You know we'd have had no way to raise Bec in any kind of life unless we both got an education, were able to get good jobs."

"You did the right thing," he agreed. "You're damn good at always doing the right thing, Susan."

For an instant she felt stunned into silence. He made the compliment sound like an insult. "You're making out like I hurt you. It was the life circumstance that hurt both of us. I didn't get myself pregnant alone, for Pete's sake."

"You did the right thing," he repeated. "You made the only choices you felt you could."

"Yes! So damn it, quit sounding like you're blaming me!"

He raised both his hands in the universal gesture of surrender. "I'm not blaming you. I just always saw the situation differently. When we were young, I thought we loved each other in a big way. In a real way. In a way that was so strong that we just might have chosen an unconventional answer and made it work."

For the second time she wanted to smack him upside the head. It was sure easy for him to talk—he wasn't the one who'd been sixteen years old and pregnant.

Yet she knew that wasn't exactly fair. Jon had struggled from the time they were sixteen to be an active, involved dad in Becca's life, in spite of distance and everyone's opposition and all odds. He'd made unconventional choices. He'd made a different kind of life work.

"You think I should have believed that love would solve everything?"

"I don't think, Suze. I just wish. That you'd been in love the way I was in love, that you believed you had choices."

Susan could feel a lump in her throat, thicker than sludge, sharper than sadness. Sometimes men were so stupid. It was the core of everything men didn't understand, because they never got pregnant. They never got trapped, not the way a woman got trapped. They always had choices. They always had more freedom. They had no way to understand how cornered a woman could feel, how frightened, how powerless.

God. Memories of her West Coast trip suddenly pounded in her head. Brian Weis had made her feel powerless. She hadn't known she could *be* powerless, at her age, when she had so much more confidence, security and experience than she'd had years ago.

For that matter, even years ago, Jon had never made her feel that kind of trapped—ugly trapped. Panic trapped.

"What's wrong?" he asked.

"I don't know, exactly." She made a helpless gesture. She had no way to explain how or why she felt so confused. That jerk on the West Coast had nothing to do with her daughter's situation, but she felt so judged lately. Judged by Becca. Judged by herself, because her failures as a mom and a woman seemed to be sabotaging her daughter's choices. "I'm just so frustrated at not knowing how to help Becca. And what *really* bothers me is that Bec—and my mother—both seem to think I'm a coward."

"A coward? A coward about what?"

"A coward because I never faced my feelings for you. That I never married—that you never married—because we still have unresolved feelings for each other. But mostly me. That I'm a coward because she thinks I have those feelings and know it and never tried to do anything about it. She's a *baby*. She doesn't understand that a wrong turn can land a woman in quicksand so fast she can't get out. Becca thinks being afraid is wrong, a sign of weakness, when that's just not true, Jon. Sometimes you damn well *better* be afraid."

He set down his drink. Gulls cried in the distance. It wasn't dark yet, she hadn't been here that long, yet the hour had spun to that next stage in the day, the time when the shadows all disappeared and yet there was still light, just not sunlight exactly. It was as if the mute button had been punched on light and sound, softening everything, quieting everything. Except for the intense look in his eyes.

"Exactly who are we talking about being afraid? Becca? Or you?"

"Becca. Of course."

"Of course," Jon echoed faintly. "Well, if we're only talking about Becca, then let's get this straight. Our baby has a right to question. To analyze. To look at the mistakes other people have made, to help her figure out how to handle her own. But our lives—and especially our love life, past or present—is not our daughter's business. Ever."

Susan wasn't sure what was more amazing. That Jon had made such a thoughtful judgment on the situation. Or that he'd referred to their love life in terms of "past or present"—when there was no present. When they both knew there was no present. When there couldn't conceivably be a present.

And then, for some confounded reason, Jon reached out his hand.

She saw his arm extend. Saw his hand. Felt his palm cup her neck, tuck her closer. And yes, of course, he'd kissed her before. They'd fallen off the wagon and made love a few times over the years before, too. But that was sex and lunacy—just like what had happened to them a few nights ago had been disgraceful sex and lunacy.

Only this time the kiss went inexplicably haywire. The sex and lunacy were comfortable, pre-

dictable factors, but this time an amazing surprise
sneaked in. There should have been shame and
speed. Specifically, there should have been an oh-
God-don't-stop speed because that had always
been the excuse—that they'd fallen into madness—
and yeah, they both knew they'd regret it later, but
if they ran headlong fast into each other's bodies, at
least they'd *have* something to regret.

This was slow.

This was his warm palm cupping her neck, and
encouraging her closer to him, inch by inch, until
she couldn't look at his eyes any longer without
feeling dizzy. So her gaze dropped, only then she
was looking at his smooth, narrow mouth. The
pleat of his lips. Coming for her. Aiming for her.
Parting.

She vaguely recalled his saying their love life was
no one else's business. She vaguely remembered
that she wanted to raise her hand to interrupt.

Only then his mouth covered hers, the way stars
blanket a night sky, like sprinkles of light nested on
velvet. That's how she felt. Like he was the light and
she was the velvet. Like her mouth was a cushion
for his. Like his kiss made the daylight blink off and
turn everything into their own private midnight.

A breath of a sigh, and then he came back for
another one. She understood the other kind of
kisses. The slam-bam-crush-me kind of kisses. The
invitation-to-madness kind of kisses. The sweep-her-
under, how-fast-can-we-get-our-clothes-off kind of
kisses.

But this was . . . She didn't know what it was . . .

except that she was thirty-eight years old, and had never felt endangered like this. She didn't know if her heart was beating or bleating. She didn't know if she could ever breathe again. She didn't know if her entire world would ever, could ever, be the same.

His lips found hers for a third time. This kiss was as newborn as the others, like nothing she'd known before. It was soft. Luxurious. As fresh as the dew on one of her mom's prize roses. Fragile. Quivery. Precious.

He took nothing.

He asked for nothing.

He just . . . kissed. Her lips. Her chin. Her eyelids. The line of her jawbone, her throat.

Her awareness of danger accelerated, as if there were a time bomb in her pulse, as if thunder and lightning were imminently threatening, and there was just nothing she could do to protect herself. Where was the sex and lunacy? She knew what to do about that, for Pete's sake. Just do it and then feel guilty for a couple of weeks. Die of shame. Deeply regret it. Promise herself never to do it again.

Being bad was comfortable. Being bad had a whole rule book of emotion and behavior that came with it.

This was different. This was softness that ransomed her common sense. Tenderness that sabotaged her fury—and she knew she was furious. She'd come over here unquestionably furious because of . . . well, because of something about Becca. Something that was Jon's fault. All Jon's fault.

And these kisses were all Jon's fault, too. Each one of them was a wooing wonder, as fragile as starlight, as wild as the scent of roses.

A car horn sounded somewhere in the distance. A breeze tucked around his deck, bringing a cool lake night wind, invisible, whispering over her skin. She didn't care; Jon was warm enough to heat him and her both. A telephone rang from inside his house. Car doors slammed.

He lifted his head, not far, only far enough so she could see his eyes were black as wet ebony and his mouth damp from her taste. He said against her throat, "We're not sixteen anymore."

"No." God, he'd only been dangerous when he'd been sixteen, but now she realized that was like comparing a paper airplane with an SST, a water pistol with an Uzi.

"Suze . . . you know where this is going. Where it could go. Is that what you want?"

That roused her. Her blood had been rushing and gushing down her veins faster than a white-water rapids, but his question put a stop sign in her mind. All the stop signs. They were on his deck, and although people couldn't see them from below, it was still basically public. Their daughter had a serious problem they'd never finished talking about. And Susan's own life wasn't going so hot. She was confused and upset and unsettled . . . and ten times more so because the chemistry between her and Jon wasn't news at all . . . but these kisses were headline news.

"No," she said.

His mouth took a last, long, sipping taste of her neck. He still seemed to be talking to her throat, not to her. "You've said no before and meant maybe."

"Well, this time I'm saying no because I think no is the best idea. For both of us."

For an instant he went completely still, and then, as if he'd been holding his breath, he stiffened and pulled away. She was still trying to get her jangled nerves under control when he stood up, plucked their glasses from the table and strode inside. She heard him mutter a "Hell."

She bounced up, too, disoriented from his sudden change of mood. The inside of his place wasn't pitch-dark, but that spooky gray before total nightfall—too dark for her to make out his expression, only to see him striding with the glasses toward his kitchen. "What's that 'hell' supposed to mean?"

"That you're still running."

"Excuse me?"

"Forget it, Suze."

He sounded disappointed in her. Disappointed! Her nerves roiled up another notch. "You think we should sleep together? You think we should just fall in bed because we suddenly felt in the mood? Our daughter's in trouble because of an unplanned pregnancy, and instead of talking about it, the two of us should risk an unplanned pregnancy of our own? Again?"

"I didn't say any of that."

"But you said I was still running—"

"And I shouldn't have said that. Let's just try talking another time, okay?" He held open the door, which might have struck her as rude, except that she seemed to be charging for it the instant she pushed on her sandals and gathered up her purse and car keys.

She hurled herself out the door, down the stairs and reached her car faster than an Olympic runner. Personally—for a long time, now—she thought there should be a special law allowing women to strangle their ex-lovers. Maybe murder wasn't justifiable, but strangling sure as hell should be.

She climbed in her Avalon, stabbed the key in the lock and peeled toward home, feeling as self-righteous as a deacon. For Pete's sake, what woman in her right mind would have invited sex right then? It would have been crazy. Immoral. Wrong. If they'd slipped into bed before, it was all different now—different because what if Becca found out, with all their daughter was already confused with? Becca already seemed to think the Sinclair women couldn't get their sex lives right to save their lives ... and damnation, maybe the squirt was right. But that was all the more reason not to—never to—have impulsive sex with Jon Laker ever again.

Only she knew that man. Not well anymore—but still, well enough to know when he was disappointed in her. And tarnation, it stung ... that he'd said she was running. That she was a coward.

The same way Becca and her mother had.

* * *

Becca was watching a VCR tape of *The American President*—for what felt like the thirty-ninth time—when she caught the flash of car lights in the window. Her mom was home. Finally.

Even though Becca's favorite scene in the movie had just started—the one in which Annette Bening showed up at the state dinner for her first date with Michael Douglas—she pushed the pause button. If that wasn't a measure of how much she loved her mom, she didn't know what was.

Her mother had just reached the third step of the porch when Becca yanked open the back door. Her mom immediately smiled . . . but Becca was used to her mom putting on a reassuring maternal front through good times and tornadoes. She looked past the smile, took in the mussed hair, the no lipstick, the hectic color in her cheeks. So. She'd been with Dad. And it looked like part of the time they'd gotten on well—maybe way more than well—but Becca figured she'd also pushed both of them enough for now. Deliberately she put a light, teasing tone in her voice.

"Just where have you been out this late, missy?"

Susan's eyebrows lifted. "Just out. Uh-oh. Is it past my curfew?"

"No. But I expect to know where you're going, when you'll be back and I insist on meeting any boys you go out with ahead of time."

"Sheesh. What generation were you born in?" Susan groused . . . and then they both giggled. "You mimicked my voice pretty well, brat."

"Hey, I learned from a pro."

"Where's your grandma?"

"Apparently it's poker night with the girls."

Susan blinked. "Your grandma doesn't play poker."

"That's what I thought." Still trying to unobtrusively study her mom, Becca opened the refrigerator and waved a cardboard container of milk in invitation. "God knows when she plans to be home. It seems to be her new life. Taking up vices. She was wearing white cigarette pants and a black silk top."

"My mother? Your grandmother? In black silk and skinny pants?" Susan put the milk carton back in. "If we're stuck dealing with shocks, I think we both need something stronger to drink." She started foraging, opening the freezer, cupboards, drawers. "How about a root beer float?"

"Man, I haven't had one of those in five months of Sundays, sounds great. The phone's been ringing nonstop. Mostly for Grandma. First that George called, then that Riff guy again. It sounds like George was a little frantic, like maybe Grandma was brushing him off. I'm not sure I'm going to be able to keep up with Gram's men. . . . Oh. Your boss called, too. Twice, in fact."

"Sebastian? Was there a message?"

"Just that he needs to talk to you. He said if you call him tonight, he'll be at the San Francisco Hyatt; otherwise he'll be in the Detroit L'Amour store by tomorrow noon." Since arriving in Traverse, her mom had fielded a bunch of calls from work, no different than any other time she was away from her job. But something was different, Becca had already noted. Her mom had always leaped to call Sebastian back before. Tonight, she simply heard about the message and went on searching for glasses. Becca wasn't sure what that meant, but she couldn't seem to help herself from trying one eensy prying question. "So . . . you were with Dad, huh?"

Susan clunked two huge glasses on the counter at the same time Becca plunked down the root beer. Her mom didn't miss a beat before answering, though. "Actually, I went to a bar to pick up men, but damn, it seems like I'm getting older. I seduced a coupla guys, sure, but that fast I got tired and just wanted to come home. . . ." She backed up, tilting her head to glance at the TV in the dining-cum-media room. "Hoboy, hoboy. You've got *The American President* on? Let's hustle and get these made. That's my favorite scene."

Becca grabbed the ice-cream container before her mother could. "Let me make it. You never put in enough ice cream."

"Do, too."

"Do not."

"Do, too."

"Do not—and you always forget the cherries."

"Because cherries don't go with root beer floats."

"Do, too."

She'd almost forgotten what it was like to play with her mother. Her friends in high school and college seemed to take it for granted that their moms drove them crazy. Susan drove her crazy sometimes, too, but somehow they'd always bantered pretty easily together. The funny thing was, it seemed like her mom actually liked her. Actually liked being with her. Actually liked hearing what she thought about things.

Of course, since Douglas, they'd gotten on as well as a snake and a mongoose. But that was before coming to Copper Creek.

When Becca first got here, she thought that being pregnant was the most traumatic problem a woman could have—particularly when she'd been trying to hold back her real situation with Douglas. But then she realized that her grandma was going through something huge, too, transmuting from the best cookie-making grandmother on earth into Wild Woman—and at her age, yet.

Still, in the last few days, Becca had come to worry the most about her mom. Susan claimed to have no problems at all, but she was starting to really scare Becca. Something wasn't right in Susan's eyes. She kept saying, "I'm fine, I'm fine!" and producing those big, reassuring smiles—but only when she realized someone was looking at her. She was pacing the floor at night, not sleeping.

Tonight, though, things seemed to be more on an even keel. It took a while for her mom to chill, but eventually she really mellowed out. Maybe it just took crashing on the big poofy yellow cushions on the floor, watching Annette Bening dance with the Prez, pigging out on root beer floats . . . but it was as if Douglas didn't exist. As if men didn't exist.

At least for a little while.

Three-quarters of the way into the movie, they

took a potty break. Both raided the kitchen on the way back, carting Oreos, popcorn, marshmallows, and Hershey's caramels in a heaped bowl—the important food groups for movie watching.

"Did Douglas call?" Susan asked idly.

Becca peeled off the top of an Oreo, carefully leaving all of the white inside. Honestly. Sometimes her mom seemed to think she was still a kid. "Actually, I called up a bunch of men I used to sleep with. But I don't know, I seem to be getting older. Having phone sex with six or seven guys isn't the kick it used to be. That's when I turned on the old *American President* flick."

Susan had to choke back laughter. "You brat, is that what's known as payback?"

"Hey, you started it. If you don't want to talk about Dad, I can't think of a reason on earth why I'd talk about Douglas." She reached for more Oreos, changed her mind and went for an open M&M's bag, searching for the orange and yellow ones. "Mom . . . you think Grandma's okay? I mean, I *know* we already talked about this. And on the surface she seems great, like she's having a lot of fun and everything. But I can't seem to quite get what she's doing."

Earlier she'd left a brush on the couch table, because her thick hair had been so tangled and messy after a walk, and she figured she'd give it a good brush while she was watching the movie. But now her mom picked it up and, just like when she'd been a little kid, sat on the couch behind her and started brushing. "I think your grandma's trying to figure out what she wants to do with the rest of her life. So she's experimenting with some things."

"You don't think she's going to keep the whole house yellow forever, do you?" She had to lean back and close her eyes. Her mom started a rhythmic stroke, never pulling, just stroking the brush through Becca's long, thick hair like fingers.

"I doubt it. She's just testing out different things, you know? The way we try on a new style of dress to see if it fits. And I think . . . she was a farmer's wife her whole life, so now she's looking at all the things she never did before. Never could do before."

"Yeah, well, I get that. And I think it's cool. It's just . . . you know. It's eleven o'clock at night and she's playing poker. It's a stretch."

Her mom chuckled softly, then put down the brush and started massaging her scalp, pressing gentle fingertips at her temples, around her ears. "I thought you'd decided that all of our lives needed some shaking up."

"I *do* think this family could use some shaking up. Except . . ." The way her mom was brushing her hair, how good it felt, how shivery and safe, she felt all young again. Like she just wanted to curl up and fall asleep snuggled next to Susan. "Except that I'm sorry about what I said before. About your running away from Dad."

Her mom's brushing slowed. "Maybe you were right, Bec. And maybe that was something that was just really hard for me to face before."

Becca hesitated. For the first time in ages, they were talking pretty well. She didn't want to blow it. "You've pretty much let the pregnancy subject go for the last couple days. I appreciate it."

"I *want* you to talk about it."

"I know you do. So it has to be killing you to try and be quiet. The thing is, Mom, I know you think I'm still really young. But I can handle my life. Try and trust me, okay? You taught me to stand up."

"I know you can stand up, baby. And I'd trust your heart over anyone I know . . . but I still want to be sure you know: Absolutely no matter what you decide to do, I'll do whatever I can to help you. Not judging, just supporting. I—"

"Well, you can stop worrying, because I've about made my decision. I'm going to a doctor tomorrow."

Her mom dropped the brush with a thud.

Chapter 9

It was just starting to rain when Becca turned into the parking lot of the women's clinic. She was nervous, which was probably why she couldn't stop thinking about the argument with her mother the night before.

Cripes, she'd known Susan wasn't going to be thrilled at her decision, but sometimes her mother was just impossible. When she agreed with what you did, then everything was hunky-dory. But if she didn't agree, man, there was no getting her to listen or to see another point of view. Susan had insisted over and over that if Becca was determined to go to this clinic, then she was coming with her.

As if Becca were still a child.

As if she didn't know her own mind or needed a mother to hold her hand.

Becca slammed the car door, hitched up her shoulder bag and ran toward the clinic door—or as close to a run as she could manage in Birk sandals. Even so, her chambray shirt was water-speckled by the time she reached the door, her cheeks shiny from the rain.

Inside, the air-conditioning made her shiver. The neon lights should have come across as lively and bright after the gloomy morning outside, but somehow the room just felt chilly. A handful of other women were already installed in the waiting area.

The place wasn't too bad. The chairs were rainbow-colored. A toy station was set up in the far corner for kids. Before this, Becca had been unaware this women's clinic existed——she'd never been to a doctor anywhere near the Traverse City area, never needed one. But this place was listed in the yellow pages as woman-friendly.

This was going to be tough enough, so that part mattered to her. She really wanted a women's place, hopefully a woman doctor.

She stepped toward the receptionist's glass window, and the freckle-faced redhead smiled as she looked up. "Rebecca Sinclair, nine o'clock, brand-new for us, right?"

"Yes."

"It'll just be a couple of minutes. I need you to fill out these forms. . . ."

Same old yadda-yadda. A young woman across the aisle was so fat she looked as if she were eighteen months pregnant. Another woman walked in, as old as Susan, dressed as if she were a wealthy attorney or something professional like that, but the eyes looked anxious. In the far corner, a plump blond woman—younger than Bec—was nursing a newborn and looked orgasmically happy.

Bec would be happy when this was over.

Naturally, it was a long wait. Two women left.

Four more came in, one hauling an antsy toddler who whined nonstop. The wealthy-looking woman with the anxious eyes was called before Becca; but then, the lady looked like she needed help a lot more than anyone else in here.

A good half hour later, her own name was finally called. First came the urine test, then the peppy little nurse saying, "So what are we here for, dear? And you say you already had a pregnancy test, did you? So let's slip out of our clothes and put on this gown, shall we? I'll be right back with the doctor."

There was something about examining rooms with stirrups. As soon as you got your clothes off, the temperature went down thirty degrees, made your teeth want to chatter. When the door opened, Becca felt as ready as any lamb at a slaughterhouse, but she had her mouth peeled into a responsible, capable smile to greet Dr. Carey.

Only the hunk who walked in couldn't possibly be Dr. Martha Carey. For one thing, the doc was a he.

A capital-*H* He. Six-foot-two. Couldn't be thirty, but late twenties for sure. A brash of Irish black curly hair. Black eyebrows over blue eyes. Shoulders wider than sex. A long, lean build, no butt, the all-guy walk that made any woman think of sex. A sexy, crooked smile and a sexy sigh—come to think of it, everything about him made her think of sex— and the guy probably sighed because he saw her jaw drop.

He was carrying her medical folder, which had a total of one piece of paper in it, the form she'd filled out. He put that down, then stuck out his hand so she could shake it, which wasn't the easiest thing to do when she was using both hands to hold her gown down and closed for dear life.

"Wait a minute," she gulped back.

"I know," he said. "You wanted Dr. Carey. Everyone loves Dr. Carey. I'm Sam—Dr. Sam Cassidy." The rest came across like a practiced recital. "I'm from the U of M, got my M.D. two years ago, specializing in ob/gyn—especially infertility work. When Dr. Carey banged up her car and ended up with a broken leg last week, the clinic apparently tried high and low to get another woman doctor temporarily and just couldn't find one. I swear I won't bite, okay? I'm just on loan for a few weeks. I promise, I'm leaving as fast as they can get Dr. Carey back here."

She wanted to laugh, but damn, he was so adorable. There was a time and a place for an adorable guy, and this wasn't it. This was the place where you wanted either a woman or someone who was old and sweet-looking and kind. Not a guy who you wanted to jump on a Friday night. Not a guy you'd be willing to throw all your principles and morals to the moon for.

Not that Becca would do anything like that, for Pete's sake. It was just . . . he *was* cute.

He also rubbed her wrong. It was the way he meticulously went through her file twice. "You've had a pregnancy test and believe you're about a month along, right? But you haven't formally been to see a doctor until now?"

"Not yet, no." There was attitude in his voice.

She wasn't sure what that attitude was, but there was something that made her heart want to hiccup. He came closer and did the stethoscope thing, which shouldn't have been a big deal—only it was. The instant he clapped that cold metal between her breasts, her pulse started thumping like a revved-up jalopy.

"No reason to be nervous," he said. He looked in her ears, her eyes, her mouth. When he looked at her eyes, he seemed as impersonal as the most careful doctor . . . but just for a flash, their eyes met, and that something was wrong again. The prickly pulse joined her thumping heart. Maybe he saw her as a patient, but there was no way—not in this century—she could impersonally think of him as a doctor.

"Okay, I'm going to do an exam—not a long one, I promise. Just want to do a short check to make sure things are okay—hold on a minute and I'll get the nurse."

Ms. Chirpy came back in and took up her station at the base of the examination table. She stood as still as a statue. He'd told the truth about the exam being short. It wasn't a full pelvic, nothing like that, but if he was belowstairs two minutes, it was two minutes too long for Becca.

"Okay, you can sit up now. Thanks, Norma, that's all we need you for." He turned around, stripped off the gloves and didn't turn back until the chirpy nurse had left the room. By then Becca was sitting up, covered to the neck, her ankles locked together with emotional glue. Her cheeks felt hotter than oven bricks and her stomach was so queasy she was beyond miserable.

"You're about six and a half weeks," he said. "We'll get some vitamins prescribed for you, and are you having any trouble with an upset stomach?"

She couldn't stall any longer. It had to get said. "I won't be needing the vitamins or anything like that. I'm here for an abortion."

Abruptly he stopped moving and silently hunkered down on the black vinyl stool. She felt his gaze on her face as if he were studying her with a laser.

"I can get an abortion at this clinic, right?" she asked.

"Different health care facilities have different types of licenses. This specific clinic is licensed to do first-trimester abortions." His voice was quiet, gentle, but carefully expressed no emotion. "Have you talked to someone?"

"I don't need to talk to anyone."

"If you want a D&C at this facility, you'll have to talk to a counselor first."

"Fine," she said. "I'll set that up immediately, then."

He waited, then asked another quiet, gentle question. "Where's the father in this picture?"

"The father has nothing to do with this."

"By law he does. By blood he does."

"Look. Are you Catholic or something?" Becca asked impatiently.

"No, I'm not Catholic. And if I gave you the impression that I was being critical or judgmental, please don't think that. But this isn't an easy choice for anyone. And I feel real, real wary of signing you up for this procedure unless you're absolutely positive you want it."

"I *am* positive."

"No, you're not."

One more second, and she was either going to walk out that door or punch him. "What the hell makes you think you know me well enough to decide I don't want one?"

His voice softened yet another notch. "Because you're crying, Rebecca."

The hell she was crying. The sanctimonious, self-righteous, know-it-all jerk. She most certainly wasn't crying—when she yanked on her clothes, when she paid her bill, when she set up the counseling appointment, when she walked out the door. It was still raining. The sky was grayer than sludge, the clouds hanging claustrophobically low, rain drooling from the sky and drizzling down her neck.

She looked up and saw a white Avalon parked next to her car. Her mom was standing in front of it, getting wet in the drizzle, but obviously not caring, just standing there, arms crossed, waiting for her.

No matter what that pricey-dicey jerkwater Dr. Cassidy thought or said, she *hadn't* been crying. Until she saw Susan.

Her mom's arms opened and just hung there. Becca didn't know she was running, didn't know she was hurling herself in her mom's arms, but like the explosion of a dam, tears were suddenly gushing out of her eyes, sobs coming in great heaping ugly gulps.

"I can handle this on my *own*!" she gulped out.

"I know you can, baby."

"I didn't ask you to come here! I told you not to!"

"Shut up, Bec. Quit trying to talk. Just let it go."

Her stupid mother didn't even seem to realize it was raining. She just stood there and held her and held her. The ugly gulping sobs finally quieted, making her stupid stomach hurt and her stupid lungs feel air-short, but they petered out eventually to just goddamned tears. Stupid tears. The kind that made your nose run, but at least you knew you were getting it back again. Control.

She'd never prized control as much as her mother did; why the hell shouldn't she cry if she damn well wanted to? Except . . . it could be scary. To cry so hard you weren't sure if you could make it stop. And there were things she was never going to tell Susan—things that weren't a mother's business, for Pete's sake, not once you were a grown woman. But somehow once she started, there seemed no way to turn off the faucet of words.

"It's such a mess, Mom. *Everything* is such a mess, and I just can't seem to figure out how to make anything right. The way it used to be, the girl got pregnant to trap the guy into marrying her, right? Only I'd never do that in a million years. The whole ironic thing is that this is the exact opposite. Douglas tricked *me*. And the thing is, I'd broken up with him."

That snapped her mom to attention like nothing else could have. "You never said you'd split up from him before."

"Because you wanted to hear it so much," Becca said fiercely. "You never liked him. And I realized the relationship was wrong, okay? I wanted out. And I told him. We had it out in an argument. Only it's not like we could physically separate in that instant—one of us had to find an apartment and pack and move out and all that. So we were still stuck living together for at least a little while longer. Only then he wanted to have one last dinner together, some wine, and I was hoping we could stay friends, not be mad at each other, so that dinner seemed a good idea. So we did that. Except that the dinner didn't seem to end with . . . dinner."

"Okay," her mother said, as if she already knew what happened next.

"And . . . well, always before, we used condoms. I mean every single time. Cripes, you *know* I love kids, you think I'd be careless? But this time . . . look, I'm not going into detail. I'm just saying that he said he had them. So I believed him going into this . . . encounter. Only then he didn't have them. And I think he planned it that way because he wanted me to get pregnant. Not because he wants a baby, but because he thought that'd make me marry him. But the point is, by the time I realized he didn't have any protection—"

"It was too late." Her mom gently filled in the blanks.

"So try and understand. I'm *not* marrying him.

No matter what. Because if I go through with this pregnancy and have the baby, I'll never be able to shake him from my life. And I've come to believe that could be bad. *Really* bad. Not just for me, but for the baby. That's the reason I haven't considered adopting the baby out, either. Because Douglas might be able to adopt it, and that's just as scary a thought."

Her mother hesitated. "I'm confused a little. You say you've split up—but it seems as if he's been calling you pretty regularly."

"Yeah. He has." God, her head felt as if it were filled with lead balls, thick and heavy. "That's part of what scares me. He calls and calls and calls. As if we never had an argument. As if we never broke up. He just pretends it never happened. He doesn't want to hear, you get me?"

"He thinks . . ." Her mother came up with a wad of tissue, God knows from where. From wherever mothers produced tissues from thin air.

Becca blew three times before she could seem to breathe again. "He thinks I'm just up here visiting Gram. Because it's summer and he knows I love her and love spending time with her. But the more he calls, the more I get uneasy. I'll tell him about the baby, okay? I mean, I have to. But I'm just saying . . . this isn't as easy as I made you think. He's not the guy I thought he was. Not at all." She jerked her head up. "I can handle it."

"I know you can."

"It's just a problem. I'm an adult woman. I can handle it."

"I know you can," her mom repeated.

"It's just been so awful. I'd never believe Douglas could be . . . scaring me. I can't even explain it."

"That's it," her mom whispered. "That's it, just cry it all out."

"Do you get what I mean now? Do you finally get it? Something's wrong with all of us Sinclair women. And it just gets worse if you have a baby you're not ready for. That's what you did, Mom. Dad's wonderful. He's nothing like Douglas. But it's like your whole life changed and went down a wrong road because of me—"

"Rebecca, you're the best thing that ever happened to me." Her mother pulled back, smoothed back her hair. "How could you not know how loved you are? By both me and your father—"

"But that's not the *point*, Mom. You know what the deal with Douglas was? I thought he was safe. I thought he was nothing like Grandpa, who ruled Gram like some kind of medieval tyrant. And he's not like someone you would have run away from. Like, I don't know what scared you about Dad, but something did, and Douglas—he wasn't scary. That's what I thought. He was easy. That's what I thought. Only, for Pete's sake, that's why I'm in a mess, because I couldn't tell a bad guy from a good one. And you and Gram can't seem to figure that out any better than I can."

After lunch, Lydia took Becca on an antiquing jaunt, which meant they wouldn't be back until dinner—if that soon. Susan paced around the farmhouse, too upset after the morning with Becca to settle down. Finally she gave up and grabbed her car keys.

An hour later, she had a newspaper under her arm and was pushing open the door to Koffee Kountry. Carting a mug of fresh-brewed joe to the farthest café window, she sat down and shook open the paper.

She sipped and read, sipped and read, willing her heart rate to slow down, but it was hard. The next time she talked with Becca, she wanted a calm head, yet right now she was still roiled up as a mother tiger with a threatened cub.

She gulped more coffee. It warmed her throat but completely failed to calm her down.

Damnation. She'd shown up at the darn clinic that morning to be there for her daughter . . . yet she'd left there feeling as if she'd totally failed Becca.

Susan couldn't remember Bec crying that hard in years, if ever. Even thinking about it made Susan's eyes burn all over again.

She'd never liked Douglas, but damn, how could a good mother not know her daughter was in this much trouble? She'd had no idea Becca was afraid of Douglas. Suddenly all their other talks—about Becca thinking her a coward, thinking the Sinclair women couldn't seem to find love or hold on to it, thinking she hadn't dealt with her relationship with Jon—everything took on a different light.

Susan chugged more joe, turning pages in the newspaper, but her mind was still frazzled and shook, mentally still seeing her daughter reaching for her, crying, spilling out her heart in the clinic parking lot.

The minute she'd driven into town, she'd stopped by Jon's marina. God knew she didn't *want* to talk to him—not after their troubling encounter last time—but just because they were juggling emotional dynamite together was no excuse for silence. Their daughter was in trouble, and though it hurt Susan like a bee sting, since she was failing to help their baby, maybe he could.

As it happened, though, Jon hadn't been there. She'd left a message with one of his employees, Marnie, for Jon to call her cell phone whenever he could.

For right now, there was absolutely nothing she could do about Becca or Jon or anything else, except to calm down and try to think.

When she reached for the coffee mug again, she inadvertently glanced up.

And any chance of calming down went out the window.

He was briskly walking with another man. When the morning rain finally stopped, people seemed to burst out of buildings like pent-up children. In spite of the crush of tourists, Jon was taking long strides, carrying long rolls of blueprints over a shoulder, clearly carrying on a concentrated conversation with the other man, yet he suddenly halted. Suddenly glanced through the café window.

Their eyes locked. Only for a millisecond. Only for an itsy-bitsy millisecond.

Swiftly Jon touched the sleeve of his companion,

said something, and when the other man nodded and went on, Jon pushed open the door of Koffee Kountry.

The café was three-quarters full, primarily with boaters and vacationers who loved the ambience. The place smelled of vanilla and luscious fresh coffee beans; the decor was Tiffany lamps hung over artsy tiled tables. Since the place couldn't survive solely on overpriced coffee, they offered snacks as well—especially delectable, cholesterol-choking, impossible-not-to-love pastries.

Jon passed right by the pastry counter, never even looked, just aimed straight for her. He was dressed very strangely—his pants had a crease; his shirt had a tie; and those were real shoes instead of just Birks or Tevas—shocking clothes in a town where no one dressed in anything other than a bathing suit in the summer if they could help it. He'd obviously been doing some kind of serious work, and he had that look. That shoulders-back, I-own-the-world, cocky-guy look. It used to make her hormones curl.

And damn it. Still did.

"I thought it was you," he said. His gaze slid over her face and upper body in one liquid swoop, causing another annoying spiral of hormones. "I got the message that you stopped by the marina. I didn't call you right back, because we probably needed some serious talk time, and I knew I was tied up for a while in a meeting. You were calling about Becca, weren't you? I'd just been thinking the same thing. That we keep throwing the problem on the table, but not really talking it through or coming to any conclusions about how we could help her."

"Yes. It was Bec I wanted to talk about." But she watched him settle his lanky frame across the table from her, leaning the blueprints against the wall, and it wasn't that Becca left her mind. Or that she didn't want to tell him what had happened.

But for an instant . . . they were alone together. Really alone. Didn't matter if the café was filled with people, any more than years ago it mattered when they attended high school dances with a crush of kids. She was alone with him. Her, him and a feeling of longing and belonging so huge that sometimes she couldn't breathe for the wonder of it.

Of course, she didn't believe in that kind of thing now. It was just the memory that hit her suddenly. And even though they had to talk about serious things, it didn't seem unreasonable to just want to *be* with him for a couple minutes—so she motioned to the blueprints. "Are you planning to build something?"

"Yup. Boats. Fancy wooden sailboats for the ultra-rich—not because I give a damn about who's rich, but because only the ultra-rich could conceivably afford them."

"I didn't know you'd gotten into building."

"We're talking aspiring. I've built three now, but it's tough to find a damn fool willing to part with a ton of money just because I'm crazy about wooden boats." The grin was boyishly honest. "Still, I did fool three guys, and I seem to have another one on the hook, so who knows?"

A perky redheaded waitress galloped across the room the instant she spotted Jon. She flashed her eyelashes as she took his order for a coffee, nothing else, no hurry. As soon as she took off, Jon motioned to the newspaper want ads spread in front of her. "Are you actually job hunting?"

She glanced down, startled to realize she'd opened the newspaper to the want ads . . . and that at some subconscious level she'd used a pen to check some of the openings. She'd been thinking about Becca and Jon. Not herself, not her job problems. Yet she heard herself saying, "Yes . . . I guess I am."

"I'll be darned. I thought you were crazy about your job."

She wasn't sure how to answer. The cat was out of the bag—but she hadn't known she had a cat. "I loved my job for years," she agreed. "But I think part of the reason I never looked at other possibilities was because of the sanity issue."

"Sanity?"

"Yeah. It's a great job. I make great money, have super benefits, all the job security I could ask for. A woman would have to be certifiably loony to quit a dream job like that. It's all right. You can say it."

He raised an eyebrow. "I wasn't going to say any of that, much less criticize. I just asked the question because you always seemed to love the work, but how could you think I'd cast stones? I'm the one who refused to be a lawyer, remember? My parents still think I'm out of my mind. So do some friends. They still refer to the marina as my 'little hobby' rather than something I've invested twenty years in. So if you think I don't know what it means to buck the tide—"

"I know you do," she said quietly. Damned if Becca's words didn't come back to haunt her. She'd known Jon was a good guy. Then and now. Maybe Bec had confused what a good guy was; maybe Lydia hadn't picked the best mate, but Susan had trusted Jon from the get-go . . . which had just made it harder when she'd had to walk away from him.

He motioned to the newspaper again. "So what brought this on? The job hunt?"

"A problem with work." The redhead set the coffee mug in front of him and promptly disappeared again. Susan hesitated, then plunged on. "Actually, it's a problem with a man—the guy who's my new West Coast boss. Nothing I'd normally tell you about. I can't imagine you wanting to hear. But trying to advise Becca this last week has thrown me into a tailspin. She's questioning . . . everything . . . all the choices she's seen me make, decisions I thought were good one, values I taught her—or failed to teach her. So much so that I'm afraid to make a move about my job, for fear she'd find out about this and see it as a reason to doubt my judgment, and that would affect my ability to help her—"

"Sheesh. Slow down. I swear, you always did this—throw fifty things on the table at the same time. Back up, okay? Do one problem at a time. Start with the guy and your job problem."

Susan sucked in a breath. "Okay, well . . . Sebastian's always been the head of L'Amour, my primary boss. And he's wonderful. But he's also older now, and he took a partner on the West Coast. When it's West Coast business, I not only need to get along with this man, but I want to, for Sebastian's sake. The first time I met him, I thought maybe I was misunderstanding his ... friendliness. The second time, I thought I could handle his Russian hands and Roman fingers. But it seems I can't. I just can't. And—"

Jon cut in, his voice sharper than a steak knife. "Did this jerk physically hurt you?"

"No." Susan tried to laugh, shook her head. "The problem was more that I hurt myself, apparently by thinking I was above getting myself into that kind of stupid mess—"

Again Jon cut in. "Why the hell haven't you quit already? Or sued the hell out of his ass?"

"Because it's not that simple. Throwing away everything I've worked so hard to build up is hardly an easy choice to make. And suing him for harassment sounds good in theory, but in reality it would hurt Sebastian, who's always been good to me. And then there's our daughter, who—"

"Susan, you're making something complicated that isn't. Get the hell away from the son of a bitch."

"Would you like some coffee spilled in your lap?"

"Huh?"

Finally she'd managed to get his attention. "For *you*, the problem would be easy. For me, it's not. Damn it, Jon. I get so tired of this. You want me to behave the way you would. My parents wanted me to make the choices they would have. Bec would like me to be the mother she wants. I'd love to do it—I've been trying my whole life—to be the person y'all want me to be. *Not* be myself. But I just don't know how to do that."

Jon sucked in a breath. "I made you feel that way?"

"Don't worry about it. So does everybody else," she said impatiently, and pushed on. "That doesn't matter. I didn't bring up the whole darn thing with my job to whine about myself. It's because of Becca. Especially this job problem has really made me think . . . that no matter how much I love her, maybe I'm not the best counselor for her or the best one to give her advice, either."

"That's bullshit. You and I have our differences, Suze. But you're the best mother ever born."

"Damn it. Don't start being nice." The son of a sea dog was going to make her cry. She gulped down enough coffee to shock her throat, then sputtered, waving a hand. "The point isn't me. The point is Bec. She's afraid of him."

"Susan. Try to have a coherent conversation, would you? She's afraid of *who*?"

"She's afraid of Douglas. That's what came out this morning. What I didn't know before. What I couldn't believe she hadn't told any of us—"

"Jesus. Women. Skip all the emotional stuff and get specific, would you? What do you *mean*, 'she's afraid of Douglas'? Did he hit her?"

Jon rarely let his temper completely loose, but she should have realized there were certain subjects that worked like a trigger for him. Anyone harming his daughter was one of them. Damnation, he changed color faster than the flip of a dime. And her voice lowered instinctively to a more calming tone. "I don't know, but I don't think so."

"If he laid a finger on her—"

"Jon, calm down and let me tell you what she said. She thinks he tricked her into the pregnancy. She'd told him she was unhappy, that she wanted to split up. She thought he'd understood, and it was just going to take some time for one of them to find another place to live, but apparently he came on to her one night. I don't know why she said yes, but he told her he had birth control, and that was a lie. She thinks he lied deliberately because he was trying to force her to stay in the relationship, that she'd change her mind, stay with him, get married if she was pregnant." She had to stop for breath, but Jon must have sensed there was more.

"And . . . ?"

"Only, since she came up to Copper Creek, he's been calling all the time, as if she'd never broken up with him, as if they'd never argued. Acting like they're still together. He's spooking her."

"What does *spooking* her mean?"

"It means that this is why she didn't tell Douglas about the pregnancy before. It means this is why she decided to have an abortion . . . because whatever he's doing, whatever he's been saying, he's really been frightening her. She seems to feel as if he's stalking her, obsessive, ignoring anything that implies they're not together anymore."

"What specifically did Bec say the bastard was doing?"

"She didn't get that specific. I don't know. I just know that's what she's feeling. Afraid. Spooked. Some of this didn't come out until this morning, so I had no way to tell you before. But it wasn't details she was telling me; it was feelings."

"Yeah, well, I've got a feeling, too. A feeling I'm going to kill that cretin with my bare hands. Come on." He dug a twenty from his wallet, tossed it on the table and stood up.

"Come where?"

"You and I are going to Copper Creek to talk to Becca. Together. Right now. And *then* I'm going to drive to Kalamazoo to strangle the creep."

Chapter 10

Hoboy. Jon spotted the mailbox for Copper Creek and instinctively winced as he turned into the drive.

He hadn't stepped foot on the property in years. He used to drive Becca back and forth to her grandmother's fairly often, but once Bec turned sixteen and got her driver's license, there was no need for him to go near Copper Creek. More to the immediate point, he wanted to be around the three Sinclair women together like ... well, like his goal in life was to attend a bridal shower. Like he wanted to pay double taxes. Like he wanted to wake up in a rain forest snuggled next to a boa constrictor.

Susan's Avalon had already shot ahead of him minutes before.

Instead of trying to catch up, though, he scraped a hand through his hair and slowed down even further. He'd never disliked Lydia Sinclair ... but she was definitely hard to be around. She wasn't mean. She was just perfect. She'd probably never said a four-letter word in her entire life, never complained or revealed that anything was bothering her. She was always kind, always dressed like a modest, matronly earth mother.

She could really make a guy feel like shit.

Specifically, she could make a guy who lusted after her daughter feel like low-down, worthless, pond-scum shit.

Conceivably that wouldn't matter to a lot of people, but as it happened, the only way Lydia ever knew him was as the creep who'd knocked up her baby girl. Apparently that tended to color a mother's attitude, no matter how many years had passed.

He sighed, heavily and loud, thinking that he hadn't fresh-shaved. Hadn't changed from the clothes he'd been wearing all day. Hadn't had a double shot of scotch.

He hadn't done one sensible thing to prepare for this.

Back in town, coming to Copper Creek had seemed like a great idea. The encounter with Susan had shaken him. He still hadn't weeded through all the endless female emotional analysis, but he grasped certain issues just fine.

Somehow both his daughter and Suze had gotten themselves involved with men they were afraid of. Come to think of it, that's exactly what Lydia had done with that iron-faced general she'd married.

Jon didn't get what the hell that pattern meant, but in the last hour he'd been forced to face certain mind-boggling revelations. The first one regarded Susan. He couldn't be this upset, this riled up, this tight-gut sick that some guy had tried to come on to her ... if he didn't care. Really care. And yeah, he'd known all these years that he had some hang-on feelings, but that wasn't the same—at all—as realizing he was in love with her.

He wasn't sure whether that realization called for celebration or Thorazine. Since that was too immediately difficult to figure out, Jon concentrated on the situation he could do something about.

Becca. Maybe there was nothing a father could do to de-pregnant his daughter, but the way Jon saw it, he had at least two courses of action. The first thing he could do, for damn sure, was protect her. And the second was—as soon as possible—to beat the stuffing out of Douglas.

He rounded the last curve and saw the bevy of vehicles in the yard—not just Susan's and Bec's and Lydia's, but farm vehicles as well, some bunched by the barn, others in the driveway to the house.

He pulled up behind Susan's Avalon, figuring there was no chance of inconveniencing anyone else that way—he'd be leaving long before she could want to go anywhere. For all the vehicles, though, the yard was distinctly sun-speckled silent. When he climbed out of the truck, no one was in sight—including Susan.

He didn't exactly gallop toward the front door.

It wasn't that he was stalling. He just wanted to pause for a second, look around, get his bearings.

The hour neared six, which meant it was still full daylight in June, but the early evening sun was less searing and more a flush of soft light. The cherries were turning red in the far hills. The creek looked like a thick sliver of gold as it wound around the hardwoods and pines. By the house, the last of the lilacs hung heavy, bosomy and sweet.

He loved this place.

Lydia, Susan, Becca—none of them seemed to love the land. Not really. They thought of it as their home base and all; the property had meaning for them.

But Jon's emotional pull to the land was pretty crazy—considering that it had never had been, never would be and never could be his. His family were wealthy city people who'd always been wealthy city people. He loved the outdoors, but he knew nothing about soil or tractors or farming or anything like that. Lakers owned property, but there was no emotional tie to any piece of land; they'd always been men to sit in offices and haul in lots of money.

Still, from the time he was a kid—chasing Susan in the moonlight—he'd felt the magic here. It wasn't just some ... farm. It wasn't just some ... land. There was magic, the way the sun soaked into the hills on an early June evening, turning the cherries into rubies. The way the creek gold-ribboned around the maples and the white woods and the thick elegant blue spruce, as if the creek were a necklace that tied it all together. The way the place stirred his senses—the peek of a fox, the smell of woods and rich, spongy earth, the hundred shades of green.

He heard an odd sound emanating from the east

side of the house and ambled a few steps in that direction out of curiosity.

A woman was in the rose garden. Not Susan or Becca, but someone older than both of them. The woman was crouched down with a basket and gloves on, carrying a spade, wearing a silly exuberant hat that looked bigger than she was. When she pushed off the hat, down cascaded a fall of dusty cinnamon hair, making Jon's jaw drop.

It couldn't be the doyen. It just couldn't be. It wasn't as if he'd ever known Lydia well, but he still couldn't imagine her wearing her hair loose or wearing a hat like that. Lydia wore practical denims or demure skirts with clunky shoes—not a V-neck shirt that dipped to her cleavage and shorts that showed off long tan legs.

She glanced up and then stood up when she recognized him. "Jon Laker? Is that really you?"

The question wasn't exactly hard, but it took him several seconds to respond because he was so stunned. First off, there was none of that pursed-lip stiffness she usually treated him with. And then . . . well, he remembered her as the quiet woman with the relentlessly kind smile who hovered in the background and didn't say anything if Harold was in the same room. Who'd have guessed she could have turned into a . . . well, into a babe?

He hiked forward and stuck out a hand. "It's nice to see you—it's sure been a long time. You look terrific, Lydia. I didn't intend to be an uninvited visitor, but I saw Suze in town and followed her home because I wanted to talk with Becca."

"Uh-huh." She cocked her head. "You didn't recognize me, did you?"

"Sure I did. Right away," he said, and then sucked back the lie. "Hell. I always did have the tact of a tree trunk. No, I didn't recognize you, partly because I'm such a jerk, but partly because you look younge ... um, wonderf ... uh, you just seem to look a little different than you used to."

She laughed at his fumbling, not with that old gentle ladylike smile he remembered, but with one full of mischief. "It's a crazy thing. To feel as if I'm prettier now past fifty than I was in my twenties, but who knows? Maybe being young and feeling pretty is nothing more than a state of mind." She motioned him closer. "We'll go inside in a minute. I'm sure the girls are pulling together something for dinner. Why get pulled into work in the kitchen if you don't have to? Do you know why I raise roses?"

Like her daughter and granddaughter, Lydia could ask two completely unlike questions in a row and apparently expect you to inherently know which one she wanted answered.

"No, why?"

He glanced around the rose garden. His favorite memories there were of Suze and the first time he had her blouse off—it was hard for flowers to compete with memories like that. Still, her roses had always been pretty spectacular and now they were more so. She'd laid out the rosebushes in an elegant sunburst shape, with benches and nooks set up in the V of the sunburst to sit and savor.

Lydia ambled up and down the rows, gesturing

for him to follow as she bent down to check on leaves and buds. "Somewhere around two hundred years ago, gold was discovered in North Carolina. Naturally, white men being white men, they immediately had to drive the Indians out so they could get the gold, and they marched the Cherokee west on a trip called the Trail of Tears. It was said the Cherokee cried the whole way, and everywhere those tears fell, small bushes showed up the following year—full of thorns, but also full of flowers more beautiful than anyone had ever seen."

He didn't have a clue why she'd taken up this long, rambling story. "Um, Lydia? We're a long way from North Carolina."

"It's a legend, you dolt. Supposed to explain how roses got here, but you're not supposed to take it literally."

"Dolt" was quite an impressive insult for a woman who'd always seemed afraid of men. Now Jon wasn't dead positive who was afraid of whom, but he shot a glance at the windows of the farmhouse, hoping Suze would show up to save him. "I hate to disappoint you, but if you're trying to communicate some deep heavy symbolism in that legend, you might want to remember that it's just me."

"Well, hell. I *was* trying to impress you, but the real truth is . . . the only reason I raise my roses is because I love them." Lydia pulled off her cotton gloves, tossed them in the basket along with her spade. "Still, I do love all the lore about roses. I found an old 1827 *Housekeeping Guide* in the barn years ago. It claimed that the mother of the house should spread rose petals in all the rooms, especially when she wants to calm tempers and soothe the family down."

"So . . . have you tried it?"

"Sure have. Doesn't work worth dust. On the other hand, there's another old wives' tale: If you soak a cloth with rosewater, put it on your forehead and close your eyes, it's supposed to ease even the worst headache."

"Does that one work?"

"Nope." Lydia bent down, snipped some unknown thing from a leaf. "And then there are all the love potions associated with roses. A vase holding a single rose is supposed to be a love aid. Or if a girl strings some rose hips together in a necklace, it's supposed to help her attract the boy she wants."

"Any of that stuff work?"

"Absolutely not. It's so annoying—I've believed in fairy tales and legends my whole life, and none of them are worth beans. They're all illusions. And somehow they all seem to be illusions that hurt women." Lydia dusted off her hands, then met his eyes squarely. "Of course, that is exactly the reason I was telling you all that nonsense, Jon. Because I don't want anything else hurting my girls. And just for the record, when you go inside . . . don't you worry too hard about Rebecca. She's got trouble, yes, but she'll be fine. It's Susan. She's the one who bought in to the illusions. I blame myself, but the point is . . . she needs you more than your daughter does."

As a conversation stopper, it worked like a

charm. Gradually Jon's brain processed the startling information that Lydia no longer thought of him as pond scum—in fact, she actually seemed pleased he was there. But her intuition about Susan really jammed his head. He was unsure what Lydia meant about the illusions that hurt women, about the illusions Susan had bought in to, but he got just fine the part that mattered—Lydia was worried that Susan was hurting.

He needed a minute to catch his breath—catch his heart—add up all that stuff and figure out what to do about it. He'd been thrown willy-nilly into chaos. He'd known ahead of time that walking into the house with three Sinclair women would be a test of his sanity, because they all talked at the same time, not just in double questions but in womanese. Man, he really wished he'd had that shot of scotch before agreeing to this.

When he stepped inside, the first thing he saw was yellow everywhere—walls, furniture, cushions, everything. The first thing he heard, though, were screams.

Becca had apparently decided to cook a new recipe for dinner. It was hard to identify the entrée through the char. Some kind of clam spaghetti? An unusual lasagna? Whatever, the pot had some kind of tomato-based sauce that had managed to splatter from one end of the kitchen to the other, including the ceiling, and not counting what had sputtered over in a bubbling hot scorch on the stove.

The girls were at the sink, shrieking at each other, apparently because Becca had burned herself and

Susan was trying to keep her hand under cold running water and both of them were attempting to assert who was in charge.

"Dad!" Becca yelled delightedly when she spotted him.

He wasn't exactly clear how he got roped into cleanup and then staying for dinner. Both of them kept talking at once. He couldn't get a word in—much less a word of protest. Apparently the recipe Becca had been trying to make was some kind of parmigiana, except that there was no veal or eggplant—the lack of which was somehow supposed to be relevant to the red sauce on the ceiling. And then Susan tried to climb on the table to clean the ceiling—which was a joke; letting Susan near a height was like letting a toddler have the car keys. A disaster was inevitable. So he cleaned the ceiling.

Right after that, someone washed and set the table, and then Lydia came in and the crew voted for burgers on the grill. Somehow he ended up sitting down with him. The minute food was served, a marmalade cat showed up on the kitchen counter. The cat purred nonstop. Lydia talked about cherries and roses. Becca talked about some humanitarian problem in Africa and told stories about the kids she'd taught last year. And Susan looked so luminous.

He didn't remember her having that luminous quality before. Mentally he kept trying to wrap his mind about the problems she was struggling with. A career crisis, for sure. And the deal with that guy. And she'd gotten that ridiculous idea about her failing Becca somehow. Yet in the early evening light, those struggles seemed removed. Her eyes looked so soft and her face had this . . . light. A luster. A softness.

A sexiness.

"What's the cat's name?" When he finally got a turn to speak, he thought an innocuous question might be safest, but the three women just looked at him with surprised expressions.

"I don't have cats, dear," Lydia told him. "Never liked the creatures. They're just not like dogs."

He half turned around, thinking maybe he'd hallucinated the fat feline thug hunched on the kitchen counter, clearly ready to pounce on the kitchen table if anyone let her. Nope, she was still there. Purring loud enough to wake the dead. "You don't have a cat," he repeated.

"Certainly not one who's allowed inside," Susan said.

"Sometimes Gram's rescued a wild animal for a short period of time," Becca explained.

"I see," Jon said. "So the cat just got here?"

"There is no cat," Lydia said.

Susan amended, "And it's only been here about four months."

"I see," Jon said again, but all he could think about was kissing her. And worrying about exactly what that son of a bitch on the West Coast had done to her. Very little frightened Susan. She might not have the physical strength of a marshmallow, but she had the stubbornness and determination of a steel wall.

"Now dessert," Becca announced. "Let's see . . .

we have brownies, sundaes, strawberry-rhubarb pie, lemon meringue tarts. . . ."

Again, Jon blinked.

"Dad, we're on vacation. No one should be expected to live without a choice of desserts."

Okay. So trying for a sane conversation with the three of them was doomed. Feeling like a bull in a boudoir, he scraped back his chair. "How about if you grab a dessert and come take a walk with me, Bec?"

They ambled outside, Jon aiming for the creek, hoping to find a spot—any spot—that didn't have memories of Suze attached. That cause was hopeless. It seemed the whole damn place had memories of him and Suze messing around, but walking the creek edge was still a nice, private place to talk.

The clear water gurgled over stones. The air smelled of pine resin and wood violets. Squirrels and rabbits were scampering all over the place, thinking about dinner. So were the mosquitoes.

Jon slapped his neck, nailing the first bloodsucker, knowing he'd stretched his patience as far as it would go. "Come on, Becca. Don't you have something you want to tell me?"

Becca immediately sighed. "So Mom already told you I was pregnant."

"Yeah, and what am I, some kind of scary beast? How come you didn't tell me yourself?"

Becca leaned back against the crusty trunk of an old whitewood. "Dad, I didn't want anyone to know. Not until I was good and ready to talk about it. If I hadn't been throwing up every morning,

Gram wouldn't have figured it out and started telling."

"Okay. But let's get some stuff said. I don't know what you want to do—but you can come live with me, now, later, anytime. You want to raise the kid, we'll make it happen. You don't want that to happen, I'll get on board with you there, too. Money, nannies, security, docs—we can make whatever you want work, Bec."

She lifted her arms, and he bent down, first lifting her up and then just smooshing her in a long, tight hug. Damned if he knew why she started sniffling. He hadn't criticized her. Hadn't talked loud, hadn't yelled, nothing.

"I love you, Dad," she said.

"I love you, too, shortie." Eventually he reached back and dug in his back pocket for tissues. Susan had given him the tip, but really, he'd figured out before Becca was six that he couldn't go anywhere without a way to mop her up. "I don't want you going back to Douglas."

"Mom told you—"

"I don't care who told me what, squirt. If he comes up here and bothers you, I want to know."

"I have to tell him about the baby. It's just not right to keep it from him."

"That's true in principle, but sometimes right isn't black and white. If you're worried about this jerk, afraid of him, then that's the bottom line. I'll deal with him. You don't have to."

"Dad. I'm a grown-up. I made the problem; I'm

part of the problem. You get me? I'm too old to ask you to rescue me. I need to fix this myself."

Hell. There wasn't a Sinclair female born—probably ever—who could just keep things simple. "Honey, I know that. But I'm a dad, so I have some rights in a situation involving my family, too. You can talk to him if you want to. That's your business. Unless he's worrying you or making you afraid."

"Dad—"

"Just listen for one second, okay? In situations like this, right now the only thing I want to do is smash Douglas's face in. Maybe I will, maybe I won't, but what I do isn't your problem. All you need to think about is what you're going to do. But I'm telling you—if you're afraid of him or anyone else, Bec, ever, listen to your own damn instincts. Stay away from him. Call me if he comes in town or does a surprise show-up."

"Dad—"

"Promise me. Or I'm not leaving here until you do."

She wouldn't promise. She just kept saying it wasn't that kind of fear and it was her responsibility to talk to Douglas and she loved him to bits and appreciated the offer but she could handle this. She snuggled up to him on the stroll home, telling him she was relieved the pregnancy issue was out in the open, wishing she'd told him before.

He didn't want to let it go, but the mosquitoes were really taking chunks out of her tender skin, and it wasn't as if going in the house was an answer.

Bec would never open up in front of both her mom and Lydia—not the same way she would alone with him. Jon tried to believe they'd at least opened the subject, gotten some things said, but the real truth was that he felt like a failure and a half.

He was a father. He should be doing something about Douglas. He *needed* to do something about Douglas, but Christ, what? Especially when Becca was so damned opposed.

Feeling glummer than gloom, he walked her back to the house. The sun was just dipping behind the roof, bathing the landscape in purples and golds.

"Quit worrying, Dad," Becca ordered him. She lifted up to kiss him good-bye, just as Lydia pushed open the front door.

"Come on in, Becca. And Jon—Susan's wandered over to the sweet cherries—the west orchard." Lydia smiled meaningfully at him.

Clearly she expected him to track down Susan, when Jon knew that was a bad idea. When he'd screwed up with one female, it was a sign to quit, go home, do guy things, avoid the whole segment of the population who came with estrogen attached. Otherwise either his foot would go in his mouth or he'd just repeat the screw-up pattern some other way.

He specifically didn't want to screw up with Susan. Not now. These last weeks since she'd come home, he felt more and more as if he were facing a mountain pass, with the threat of avalanches in every direction. She'd openly talked with him about subjects that had been forbidden for years. Risked showing him vulnerability that she hadn't in years—if ever.

She cared, he thought.

All these years, he'd never believed they had another shot together. Maybe he'd known he had feelings for her that refused to die. But he hadn't felt this level of risk in more than twenty years—a gut-sure awareness that this was their last chance—but they *had* a chance. Because this time, just conceivably, he wasn't alone in avalanche country.

The point, though, was that it wasn't a good night to step in a snowdrift—so to speak. A guy picked his battles. This wasn't a good night for him. This was a good night to go home, to stay away from Susan so he wouldn't risk doing the wrong thing. Which was undoubtedly why, every step he took closer to the west cherry orchard, he felt crankier than a fistful of prunes.

Three more mosquitoes bit him. More signs this was a terrible idea.

He reached the west sweet cherry orchard and couldn't see her. But then he stood dead still and listened.

The orchard rolled up a high slope, cresting on a ridge where the trees were big and old—climbers, if you were a ten-year-old boy. Or if you were a guy of any age determined to get the sweetest cherries, and the sweetest and biggest were, of course, always at the top of the tree. By the last week in June, there was no better place to be on the planet than a high spot in a cherry orchard by Traverse Bay.

He found Susan by the sound of rustling branches at the south end of the ridge. Her hair was as flaming as the sunset, all gold and brass and fire, her lips and fingers stained cherry-red. Suze, being Suze, had started out in pristine white tennies and white shorts and a red-checked blouse. There was no way to pick cherries and stay prissy, though. The tennies were damp and scuffed, the shorts had bark and berry stains, and her smile, when she whipped around and saw him, was younger than spring.

"Make me go home! I'm going to be sick if I eat any more of these!"

"As if I could stop you."

She chuckled, spit out a pit—just like a country girl—then grinned at him again. "I thought you'd take off after talking to Becca, so I'm extra-glad you stuck around. I'd have worried all night how it went if I didn't have a chance to ask you. Did she tell you about the pregnancy? Or anything about her troubles with Douglas?"

Before she could reel off another dozen questions, he slipped in, "I can't say we got everything covered, but yeah, we got the big issues out of the closet." He had to pluck a sweet cherry, because who the hell could resist the first sweet cherries of the year? Not because it gave him an excuse to be with her.

"I'm glad, Jon. She loves you so much. And she's always been able to talk to you in a different way than she could to me."

He heard the wound in her voice. "Suze, you couldn't be a better mom. Cut it out. If anyone in the universe could get her to talk, it'd be you. Not me."

She shook her head. "I always thought we were close, but lately ... especially about Douglas and this pregnancy ... I just seem to rub her wrong. I'm afraid that she's overwhelmed, that she really needs help. But either I can't say the right things, or I'm not the one she's willing to accept help from."

"Aw, come on—she's twenty-two. Can't you remember being that age? When you're twenty-two, you know all the answers. Your parents are all goofed up; you're not. You love them and all, but you've got too much pride to let on you could need them."

She bent down to wipe her sticky hands on the grass. Somehow, on the way back up, her cheek got a smudge and her mouth another cherry-red stain. That was all it took to click on the glow button he invariably felt around her. It never seemed to matter how tangled their messy history was; some things about Suze had always been as basic as sunset and cherries and the shape of her smile. "God, you're so right. I remember being twenty-two and knowing everything. The line between black and white was so clear, so righteous. How come we can't be twenty-two and that stupid forever?"

But her grin faded too quickly into a sigh. "I understand how strongly she wants to handle her own life. She just scared the wits out of me when she admitted being afraid of Douglas. You know her. She always sees the positive in everyone. I swear, she could find the sweet side in a snake. So when she confessed being afraid, I have to believe there's something terribly wrong about him. Maybe more than even she understands."

"I don't like the tune on his channel, either. In fact, first time I saw him, I thought he was boot dirt."

Another smile, this one winsome and teasing. "The first time you saw him, you guessed he was sleeping with your daughter, so naturally you thought he was boot dirt. You'd have thought any guy was boot dirt."

He looked at her blankly. "Yeah, so?"

She chuckled, and when he scowled at her, she started laughing harder. Not a polite, ladylike laugh, but rolling, gasping chortles of laughter coming straight from her belly.

For Pete's sake, there wasn't a man in the universe who'd blame him for kissing her. She was asking for it every way a woman could possibly ask for it. The way the setting sun put fire in her hair and made her skin look pearled. The way she was laughing at him so hard she was choking on it. The way she teased him. The way her butt looked in those skinny white shorts, the way her hair was all tangled and mussed, the way he'd caught a glimpse of her breasts and couldn't forget them.

What was he supposed to be, a saint?

When he yanked on her wrist, she looked momentarily startled—enough to stop laughing for that instant. By the time he roped his arms around her, though, she'd had ample time to either pull back or punch him. But she did neither. She tilted her head up.

There was a sudden rustle of wind, the whisper of leaves, just before his mouth homed in on hers.

Then there was no sound but the hush of night. No taste but her cherry-sugared lips and the intimate, unforgettable taste of Susan beneath that. Every texture had her signature on it: The thudding of her heart against his. The crushing softness of her breasts against his chest. The thick, rich texture of her hair—and no one's hair was like Susan's; no one groaned like her, no one breathed like her, no one kissed like her.

He wasn't a man to like dancing, but that's how he felt. As if he were spinning with her. Circling inside a cocoon, where on the outside, somewhere, a pale white satin moon was rising, and the scent of ripening cherries was thicker than perfume, and the grass of the orchard was climbing up their ankles, tickling, carpeting their feet, and night was falling like a sapphire-blue blanket, coming fast now. But that was all outside the cocoon.

Inside, his senses were filled with nothing but her. Her lithe, winsome taste softened everything inside him. Her arms looped around his waist, clinging tight. Her throat arched for his kisses, returning his kisses, her tongue wet and hungry, her pelvis rocking against him—and she sure as hell knew it. She'd always liked flirting with danger, loved showing off how wild she could make him. She loved being female, always had.

She could make him crazy in a minute flat. Only it felt more crazy now than it used to. He was older. He'd gotten used to believing he could control his hormones, that he knew how to take his time, that he was long past the callowness of a rushing teenage boy.

All illusions. He was just as callow, just as out of control. He wanted her flat, on the grass, naked, so bad, so desperately, that he could have roared with it. Fire licked at his pulse, need slammed in his groin.

A button gave on her blouse, when he could have sworn he'd never pulled at it. The red-checked blouse snarled around her arms, snagged in his hands, even though he wasn't trying to rip it off her. It was accidental. Her bra straps slipped off her shoulders . . . that was accidental, too. The hook gave, and then the bra flew in the air to grace the limb on a cherry tree . . . that was accidental, too.

But with absolutely clear intent, he took her mouth, her tongue, then grazed a rough, wet path down her throat, lifting her to the cool night air, so his mouth could reach her breasts. First the right one. Then the left.

He wanted to be fair.

Suze had always had a big thing about being fair.

Her breasts had gotten softer after Bec was born. Different. They were fuller, softer, somehow more vulnerable than a young girl's. The nipples were bigger, too, dark as plums, and suckling on her there made Suze growl like a restless cat.

Her hands fisted in his hair then, tugging his head back up, where she took an openmouthed kiss this time, and still they were spinning, spinning, until there was only one thing they could do to ease that dizziness, and that was to lie down.

The grass was cool and tickly and sticky, and she was trembling. Not from cold, because it wasn't that cold, and he twisted around so he was on the ground instead of her to make sure she wasn't chilled. But he felt that tremble, and he saw something flash in her eyes before another dark, wild kiss blinded them both. She was afraid, he thought. Surely not of him?

But there was fear in that trembling, and then an urgency and desperation in the way she responded— her kisses turning harder, hotter, her legs twisting up, trying to hold him tighter, all of her heating up as if she were racing the wind.

He didn't know much, never had. But he knew positively when Susan wanted him. And all evening it had been building in his head—that she was seeing him differently than she had in years. Maybe she didn't want those old doors opened; maybe she'd regret this the way she had a dozen times before. Maybe he never could be what she needed. Right then, though, he only seemed to have one choice. He doubted having sex could change anything—God knows it never had. But her turning to him still set off an unstoppable storm.

His tee skimmed off. Maybe she yanked it, maybe he did, who knew, who cared? But when he was twisting around, he felt her hand at his zipper, groping, pulling, then her trembling hiss of breath when her fingers found him. In the silence of night, there was just her whispered breath and the heavy, juicy scent of cherries and her, touching him in a way that she knew damn well was going to set off lightning.

Or it would be so much easier if he could believe that. He wanted to call it sex. Passion that slipped the leash was such a human problem, one they'd been able to walk away from before.

Yet when they were finally both naked, skin sliding against skin, relentless, merciless kisses giving birth to more relentless, merciless kisses, what he felt was a thousand times hotter than sex. It was need, like a treasure. Love, like a craving that filled him up and over the brim. Emotion so rich it clogged his throat and lungs and head. Her. It all had her name on it.

"Jon," she called him. That aching call whispered in the night air stung his heart, unraveled the last of his conscience.

"You better be ready," he warned her. "There's no way this is going to be a slow ride."

"Shut up and love me."

No matter how thick the grass on the orchard floor, he pushed his jeans, his tee under her. She didn't seem to appreciate the consideration, her hands reaching for him, frenzied, anxious, pulling him onto her, into her. His knee scraped a stone— not that he cared.

Sinking into her was like hot silk sucking him in, wrapping around his mind as well as his cock. It hurt. Wanting her this much, needing her this much. Hurt so good he wanted the pain to go on forever, yet he wanted her to tremble more. Not tremble like before, when she'd seemed afraid, running away from some dragon on her tail—but to tremble for him. With him.

He rode her hard, fast, rocking the night, making the cherries and the stars shake, making the leaves whisper and the smell of earth blend with her scent and her hot, soft skin. He needed release like he needed oxygen, but he waited, waited, taking her as high and as long as he could, taking her until he heard her yell his name as she finally tipped over and let loose.

It wasn't easy, coming back to sanity. Wasn't easy, getting a grip on where the hell they were or how in hell they'd come to be here, nor did he care. Nothing could be more right than pulling her on top of him, letting her use his chest for a bed, resting, cradling her until she could breathe normally again.

Suddenly, though, things changed. He couldn't nail the difference. There just seemed to be a hesitation in the night. Susan went oddly still in his arms, and then she lifted her head. Her eyes looked smoky with passion and confusion. And then she shifted, so that her weight pressed full against him, and her hands reached up to touch his face. Fingertips smoothed the quick frown on his brow. Traced into his hair with tenderness, softness. There was wonder in her voice. The wonder of velvet.

"Why do we keep doing this, Jon?" she whispered. "How come it's so right when we do this? But then not after?"

In a snap, he understood that she wasn't touched. Not the way he'd been. And no, that wasn't news, but it sliced like acid this time. "Why did you want to do this at all, if you were that damn sure you'd regret it afterward?"

"I don't regret it. I didn't mean that at all."

Maybe not, but something wasn't right. There had to be a puzzle piece he was missing. "This was about that guy, wasn't it? The one on the West Coast. You seemed afraid for a while there. Not of me, but still . . . afraid. You needed to be with someone you could trust, is that it?"

She hesitated for a long time, her gaze troubled. "No. At least, not exactly. If I gave you the impression that guy assaulted me—it wasn't anything that bad. It wasn't rape. It wasn't something I couldn't get out of. But I admit that I was frightened, Jon. Also that the situation really shook me up. It made me think about my life—about what I was doing, what I wanted. What I was failing to do."

When he tried to move, she framed his face in her hands. "Jon, I wasn't thinking about him when we made love. But I'm not going to deny that making love with you made me feel . . . helped. Healed. Loved. It's one of the things I've started to realize. That you're the only man I've ever really trusted. I've been trying to—"

She stopped talking when he suddenly shifted free, moving with quick, jerky movements so that he could stand up. He retrieved her blouse, but damned if he could find her bra. It had turned dark that fast, charcoal-dark, and besides that his vision was blurred by emotions slamming at him from every direction. He couldn't see her face clearly—but right then that was just as well. He didn't want to.

"You're angry—what's wrong?"

If her voice was velvet, his was a low, furious bass. "I don't mind your using me, as long as you call a spade a spade. But damn it, Susan. This wasn't about love. Not for you. Do me a favor and don't ever use that word again—not with me—not unless you mean it."

He didn't wait for her to answer, just grabbed his clothes and walked away.

It was her damn orchard. She knew the way home. He only wished that he did.

Chapter 11

Lydia climbed out of her four-year-old Buick,
feeling like a caged lioness who was finally let loose.
For two full weeks now she'd reverted to her old
ways. Trying to be a good mother and grandmother.
Nurturing. Caregiving. Listening. All the crap that
had been natural and important her whole life.

It was easy to be a saint.

That was the whole damn problem.

Being good had never gotten her anything but a
cold-blooded husband, varicose veins, a car suited
to the geriatric set, and a closet full of blouses with
Peter Pan collars. Worse yet, with the girls home,
the old patterns were starting to reemerge. She
guessed it was like the way a recovered alcoholic
would feel if he had to work in a bar, constantly
tempted by the smell of whiskey.

This morning she'd been nearly frantic worrying
about Susan. Something must have happened to her
daughter the night before. Suze couldn't eat, couldn't
even drink coffee; the circles under her eyes were bigger than boats and she was more anxious than a hot
cat—but would she talk? No. French toast the old-

fashioned way, a shopping trip, an appointment with a masseuse, the gift of her great-grandmother's hollow-stemmed champagne glasses—nothing, not even the most powerful bribery, could budge a word out of her.

Lydia had *had* it. She was worried about Susan; she was worried about Becca; but the truth was that all her worrying and nurturing wasn't worth the price of dust bunnies. Instead of spinning more wheels, she'd chosen to do something more intelligent and productive. Escape.

After a blustery morning, the air was rain-cleaned, the sun balmy on her shoulders as she strode up the walk into the offices of Bartholomew, Buchanan, and Evanovich. The lawyers' offices were in downtown Traverse—old Traverse—one of the brick-fronted buildings with lots of character and old, skinny windows. Juggling a sturdy tapestry purse and a cracked leather briefcase, she opened the door.

Inside, silence and taste reigned. Airconditioning immediately blocked out the rude noises of the city, and the carpeting was plush enough to snooze on. Lydia stepped in and stole a deliberate quick glance at herself in the antique mirror off the vestibule. She'd meticulously chosen her clothes for this meeting—clunky shoes, a demure navy skirt that was just an eensy bit too long and a white blouse with a virgin-stiff collar. She'd yanked her hair into a chignon, painted on a thin slash of pink lipstick as her only makeup. She could have starred in a fashion show for postmenopausal matrons.

There was only one other body in sight. Frieda Sullivan, the old battleaxe with the pink hair, had been running the lawyers' offices for nineteen years with an iron hand, viciously pursed lips, and home-made chocolate chip cookies. Somewhere in the mysterious bowels of the building there had to be other office staff, but none were allowed to surface—nor was anyone allowed near the attorneys—without Frieda's knowledge and permission. Even God better not try. When she glanced up from her word processing screen, though, she immediately smiled at Lydia.

"Mrs. Sinclair, how nice you look today! It's always a pleasure to see you. Tell me how we can help you."

Lydia smiled nervously. "I wasn't sure if Mr. Buchanan could catch a few minutes free, but would you just ask him if there's a chance? If he's stuck in meetings, I'll disappear. I should have called first—"

"Now, now, don't you worry. I'll buzz him right away." Frieda glanced at the stately grandfather clock, then punched a phone dial. Her phone system looked more complicated than the cockpit in a jet, but she kept talking in that same soothing voice to Lydia. "I know he's got an appointment at one, but I'm almost sure he's free for a bit right before lunch—especially for a longtime client like you. There's some coffee and cookies over there on the sideboard."

"Thanks, Frieda, but as fantastic as those cookies look, I'm afraid I have to pass. My stomach's a little unsettled. I just don't seem to be a business person, and every time I try to understand this 'trust' stuff, I seem to lose all my appetite."

"Now, none of that. You know Mr. Buchanan'll take care of you! You just relax, dear."

"I'm trying." Lydia cleared her throat. "I heard your grandson was at Purdue?"

"Oh, he is. All A's, two semesters in a row. But finding a job over the summer has been—" She stopped talking, spoke quietly into the receiver and then beamed at Lydia. "There, now. I just knew he'd be able to make an exception for you, Ms. Sinclair. Don't be nervous, now, just go on in ... you haven't forgotten the way, have you? The last door on the—"

"Left." Again smiling a nervous thanks, Lydia sucked in a stalwart breath and gathered her purse and briefcase, then ambled down the hall. The decor deteriorated instead of improved. Lawyers always seemed to think they needed to decorate in dark mahogany and freezer-locker temperatures. Riff Buchanan's door had an antique crystal knob with a dangling brass key.

She knocked hesitantly. "Mr. Buchanan?" Because there was a shy quaver in her voice, she repeated his name a little more loudly, before carefully turning the knob and poking her head in.

Riff Buchanan was fifty-six. The Buchanans had been lawyering almost as long as the Sinclairs had been farming; both names were insufferably inescapable in Traverse history. She'd known Riff forever, even though he'd been a year behind her in school. He'd married the prettiest girl in Traverse, had two children, both of whom were college-graduated and out of the nest now; only then he'd lost his beloved wife seven years ago to uterine cancer. Some thought him the prize catch in Traverse. He had oodles of money, adorable looks, lots of hair . . . and lots of devil in his eyes, which mattered more. Estate law was his specialty, which one could likely tell from the pricey-dicey antiques. His office looked like a showroom—striped wall paper, brocade furniture, Aubusson rug, desk bigger than a planet.

When Lydia carefully closed the door behind her, Riff raised an eyebrow and started to rise from behind his desk.

She waved him back down. "You don't know," she said feelingly, "you can't even imagine what I've been through for the last two weeks."

"Family up the wazoo?"

"I love them. Both of them. I'd give my life for either of them without looking back—but right now, if you don't mind, I don't want to even *think* about family." She turned the key in the door lock, then dropped the briefcase and tapestry purse. Both were just window dressing. In two seconds flat, she'd kicked off her nun shoes and yanked open the first button of her stiff-collared blouse.

Riff didn't blink. He just leaned back in his chair, the speculative gleam in his eyes catching the sunlight behind him. He never said a word when her blouse fluttered to the floor. When she stepped out of her navy poplin skirt. When she sailed around that big old planet-sized desk and hurled herself in his lap.

"What," he said, "am I going to do with you?"

"I have no idea. But you'd better decide pretty fast, because Frieda said you have an appointment at one."

"Did you lock the door?"

"Against my better judgment, yes. Personally I think getting caught would be more fun, but can we talk about this later? I want you to kiss me. Now."

But he didn't. Not right away. He took her in, every sag and wrinkle and flaw shown to perfection by the sunlight streaming in stripes through his wooden blinds. "If you want to play, I'm up for it, Lydia. But I'm not marrying you. I'm not marrying anyone. So if you think this is headed somewhere—"

"Shut up and kiss me."

"Okay."

"Do it right."

"Hell, if you insist."

"I wouldn't marry again if my life depended on it. You want it in writing, I'll sign lickety-split."

"Illicit sex or nothing."

"Illicit sex or nothing," she agreed, and, since he was going so poke-slow, kissed him first. After she surfaced for air, though, she said one more time, "If you ever bring up marriage to me, we're through."

"You can take it to the bank. You'll never get a proposal out of me."

Technically that was exactly what she wanted to hear—in fact, it was the reason she'd jettisoned George recently, and a handful of other guys over the last few months. Every single woman in the country whined that they couldn't find a good man who wasn't afraid of commitment, when, damnation, she seemed to be stuck finding all of them.

Riff, thank God, was still bad . . . but somehow, his promise about never proposing didn't reassure her the way it should have. For some odd reason his promise invoked a strange frisson of sadness this time. But then he kissed her.

She'd only recently become a kissing connoisseur—enough to realize that on a scale of one to ten, she'd been a negative three when she discovered the specific art. It was a lot easier to learn than geometry, though, and a ton easier to enjoy in others. Riff, truth to tell, was only a six . . . but oddly enough, for the last couple of weeks, it seemed to be specifically his kisses she wanted.

Or maybe it wasn't his kisses. She couldn't pin down exactly what kept pulling her more and more toward Riff, but for darn sure, his kissing skills seemed a minor issue because his other talents were so considerable. There was a lot to be said for being involved with a rogue—a bad, bad rogue—who knew how to do all the bad things thrillingly.

When she stumbled out of the office at six minutes to one, her blouse was tidily buttoned and her hair all chignoned again. On the inside, she was a shambles.

Walking like a cowboy back to her Buick, she considered that she simply wasn't limber enough to screw in a chair. It was the kind of thing she should have done when she was young—but unfortunately, she'd never done anything when she was young. That was one of the problems with trying to play catch-up. She wasn't old or even close to it, but some acrobatics were a teensy bit challenging.

Riff challenged her, too—to do about any- and everything she'd never tried before.

She delicately winced when she climbed in the car, turned the key and shot for home. She told herself that she felt renewed, recharged. High. Sinful.

And if that wasn't completely true, it was true enough. She felt a thousand times more prepared to cope . . . at least until she walked in the back door.

The ear-shrieking caterwaul of the vacuum cleaner assaulted her first, but that wasn't the only jangling offense to her nerves. The kitchen reeked of lung-tearing bleach and pine cleaner. There were no dishes in sight. The washing machine was churning. And she hadn't moved two steps before the marmalade cat leaped into her arms, claws out and meowing pitifully, clearly frightened by all the commotion and stinks.

She had to stroke the cat, because what choice did she have? The poor thing was practically having a nervous breakdown, for Pete's sake. But once she'd consoled it and opened some tuna fish and stroked it some more, she settled it on a windowsill and went in search of Susan.

She found her. Butt first. Aiming the skinny vacuum tool under the yellow couch—a place that had never seen a vacuum before.

"Susan?" When her daughter didn't respond, she stalked over to the electric fixture and pulled the vacuum plug. The sudden silence made Susan whip her kerchiefed head up and around.

"What on— Mom, you're home! Oh. Oh, my God." Susan's brilliant welcoming smile faltered when she saw her mother. Really saw her.

Lydia glanced down, trying to see what had caused the sudden expression of shock on Susan's face. "What's wrong? I mean, besides you doing all this crazy cleaning. I've been working for months to cultivate some laziness into my character. It's been harder than quitting smoking, so if you think you're helping by—"

"Mom. I want you to sit down."

Her daughter only used that voice once a decade. It was as much fun as watching lettuce wilt. "Why?" she said warily. "And where's Becca?"

"Becca had to go for another appointment at the clinic. And you and I are going to have some tea and a nice little talk while there's no interruptions." Two mugs of tea emerged from the microwave moments later. Real tea, none of that sissy herbal stuff. Susan carted the mugs as if she were carrying loaded guns, her mouth shot in a determined line, her brow as set as a hound's.

"We've *got* to talk about this," she said firmly.

"Talk about what?"

She sat down at the edge of the couch, more or

less making Lydia feel pinned in the corner chair. "Mom," she said politely, "you just had sex."

"I beg your pardon?"

"Your watch is on the wrong wrist and you're missing an earring and I can see it in your eyes. Now, listen. This is your business. But that's why I started with all the cleaning, to help you deal with the stress."

"What stress?"

"I don't *know* what stress, Mom. Whatever stress made you paint this whole damn house banana-yellow."

"It's not banana. It's way lighter than that. I think of it as daffodil. Or—"

"*Mom.*" Susan clenched her hands together and shot out a foot—as if trying to make sure her mother was fenced in the corner chair and couldn't escape. "Now, I realize that this is a little awkward to talk about, but we can't just avoid talking about things because they're uncomfortable. You know what an STD is, right?"

"Of course I know what an STD is, for heaven's sake—"

"It's not like when you were growing up—or even like when I was growing up. It's more dangerous out there. Everybody thinks of AIDS, but it's not just that one thing. There are all kinds of sexually transmitted diseases—"

"Susan Sinclair! I am not your daughter! I am your *mother*!"

"I know that, darling, and I love you. Now. Are you using condoms? You do know how to protect yourself?" When Lydia sputtered out spitsful of tea, Susan reached over to soothingly pat her knee. "It's okay. I'm not judging. But honestly, I think it's a little dangerous to be playing with multiple partners. I don't know who you were with today, but it couldn't have been George, because George just delivered the mail a half hour ago. Now, I confess, I've never juggled more than one guy. Hells bells, I can't even handle one. The idea of juggling two men is enough to give me nightmares. But if that's what you really think you want to do—"

"Would you quit sounding so dadblasted *understanding*? Or I swear I'll whack you a good one upside the head. And I'm *not* juggling more than one guy. I stopped seeing George. I just still talk to him on the phone. But I never even told you I was ever seeing George or anyone else, for Pete's sake—"

"Now, Mom, calm down. No matter what you ever do, I'm on your side. But that's just the point. If you can't take a problem to family, who can you take it to?"

"I do not have a problem," Lydia enunciated.

"Okay."

"I'm not stressed. And I'm not going to get pregnant, for God's sake. You know perfectly well that I'm past menopause."

"Okay."

"And there's nothing to worry about as far as STDs. I'm not with anyone who plays around. I only wish. Every damned man in this entire town who's courted me since your father died has wanted to marry me—except for one. And he lost his wife. I think he's still in love with her. At least he isn't in love with me." Somehow, talking about Riff, her righteous volume started to lose its oomph. Instead of coming across as strident and sure, a questioning tone seemed to enter her voice. The type of questioning tone only another woman could hear.

"Okay."

"I want to ride on roller coasters. Can you understand that? I want to dance outside naked. I don't want to be safe, Susan. I don't want to do the right thing. I've tried that and tried that and tried that."

"Mom." Susan drew a careful breath, as if she'd waited years to ask this and it was finally coming out. "Did Dad hurt you?"

All the starch seeped out of Lydia's shoulders. "Oh, honey . . . not the way you mean. Your father was a good man. Don't think less of him because I was unhappy. It wasn't his fault. It was mine. I felt . . ." She grappled to explain. "I think I only went out with your father because my dad thought the world of him. Harold loved this land. He was an orphan; I know you knew that. And my dad just saw him as so perfect—someone who'd take care of the land, take care of me, love it, love me. I wanted to make my dad happy, and he wanted me to love Harold so much. I think I even had sex that first time years ago because I was trying to make myself love him. . . ."

"Oh, Mom."

Susan's voice had more sympathy than she'd had in a million years. That was the whole problem with her daughter. No one ever loved her like Susan did, only dagblast it, it made her want to cry. "The point," she said, "is that I didn't love him. And he always knew it. He had a right to be angry with me, Susan. He had a right to be harsh. He got cheated out of the kind of wife he deserved."

"So did you. Get cheated. Feel cheated."

"With me it was different." She threw up her hands, at a loss to put an entire married life into a few words. "I felt as if I didn't exist for twenty-five years. I was his wife and your mother and my father's daughter, but I didn't exist."

"But then why did you stay if you were so unhappy?"

"I don't know." The bewilderment in her voice was more of a surprise to her than to Susan. "To someone else, it always sounds easier to leave. But it never was. I always felt guilty, that I didn't love him the way he wanted me to. And I thought I was responsible for the marriage being successful, so I felt I had to stay. Whether it sounds corny or not, I was trying to be a good woman. To do the right thing." She shot back, "Why didn't you marry Jon?"

"I guess . . . because I saw how unhappy you were. I was scared of marrying too young, being dependent on a man and a marriage for a livelihood, the way I saw you were. You seemed trapped. I was determined to never be trapped. I thought that if I had a good education, a great job, then I could make sure Becca and I both had security and choices."

"Well, that sounds right, Susan. But what I tried to do seemed right to me at the time." Lydia rubbed

Susan's shoulders. "We both got it wrong. The only thing I'm sure of now is that I don't want to repeat the same mistakes again."

"So sleeping with a variety of men is the answer?"

"I never said I was sleeping with a variety of men. But just for the record, in the beginning I *planned* to—I *wanted* to—sleep with every single man in the whole town. I was going to give 'promiscuous' a whole new meaning. I was going to be wild and infamous if it killed me."

"Damn. What interfered with this master plan?" Susan asked delicately.

"I don't know exactly. It still seems like a good plan to me—um . . . this is extremely inappropriate to share with a daughter—"

"To hell with that, Mom. Go for it."

Lydia waved her hands, wishing she could make the gesture communicate because the words were coming so hard. "I never . . . had a satisfactory relationship. Before. So when I finally did, how could I possibly only sleep with one man? I'd never have known. Whether it was that one man who made the difference, or whether it was me, my changing, that made it possible to suddenly have orgasms. I had to know. I deserved to know, dadnabbit. Only it got a little complicated."

"No kidding?"

"None of the guys believed me. About not wanting to be married. About wanting to be immoral. About wanting to live my own life, in my own yellow house, not picking up after anyone ever again, just having sex when I was in the mood. My God.

You wouldn't believe how much work it is to even *try* to be promiscuous—don't you dare look at me that way, Susan Sinclair. I'm serious."

"And I'm serious about loving you." She reached out her arms.

That quickly, Lydia pushed out of her chair and drew her daughter close. Susan might be well over thirty, but she was still her baby. Still smelled like her baby, still snuggled like her baby. No one on earth was as special as her daughter. "Quit worrying about me," Lydia ordered thickly, knowing there was water in her voice that she couldn't seem to help. "I'm perfectly fine."

"I wish I believed you, but I don't think you're all right at all."

"Okay. Then I admit it. I'm all messed up. But it's the first time in my life I've been all messed up, and I'm trying my damnedest to enjoy every minute of it. You know what? I went up to the top of the barn yesterday, so I could bring down the old-fashioned wine press. We were talking about making some cherry wine, remember? I didn't think the cherries were even close to ready yet, but then I tasted the ones you brought home from the south side of the orchard last night. They were perfect, didn't you think so?"

Something crashed in the other room, making Lydia jump. It had to be the cat, pushing a dish or something off the kitchen counter. That bare instant when she glanced away, she almost missed the sudden look of achy strain on Susan's face.

"Susan . . . ?"

"I think making wine from scratch is a great idea," Susan said swiftly. "We can go pick a bunch of cherries right now, clean up the press . . . but let's wait for Becca to get home before starting the wine itself, okay?"

Lydia nodded. "Did something happen between you and Jon last night?"

"Sure," Susan said easily. "We talked about Becca."

"I meant . . . besides that. I thought I heard you prowling the floors last night, as if you couldn't sleep, maybe were upset about something. Like something to do with Jon."

"We're just both worried about Becca, naturally."

Lydia briefly considered sitting on her daughter. Maybe if she put enough weight on her, Susan would have to squeeze out whatever was tearing her up, but temporarily it was obvious that nothing short of torture was going to do it. "So . . . you mentioned Becca went back to the clinic again? What was this appointment for?"

Susan hunched forward. "She's going to see a counselor at this clinic. She said that was their standard procedure—if a woman is considering an abortion, they require the patient to have a session with the counselor first."

Lydia reached out her hands to clasp Susan's, and said quietly, "Honey, you have to leave her alone about this. Whatever you think is right or wrong—whatever I think is right or wrong—Rebecca has to do what's right by her own heart. We've talked about this so many times. . . ."

"I know we have." Susan tented fingers with her. "I'm not judging, Mom. I'd like to think I'd never judge another woman for a decision like this—especially my own daughter. But . . . I'm just so upset. I don't think she really wants to do this. She's afraid of Douglas, afraid of what he might do if he found out she was pregnant. That's not the same thing as actually not wanting a baby. It's making a decision out of fear."

Lydia squeezed her eyes closed for a second. "I know all about making a decision out of fear. And so do you, Susan. It's hard to find a woman who hasn't felt trapped into some kind of . . ." Her eyes popped open. She lost her original train of thought when Susan's words finally registered. "Wait a minute—are you trying to say that our baby is afraid of that boy? Physically afraid? Why the devil didn't anyone tell me about this before?"

When Becca drove in, she found two lunatics in the backyard.

Her appointment at the clinic, with the counselor, had not gone well. She'd headed downtown after that, planning to just hang out until her mood shaped up. She wasn't normally into shopping that much, but her mom and grandma could smell a broody mood at fifty paces, and they never let up with the questions if they sensed something wrong.

The shopping was a good theory, but it just didn't work. By the time she finally headed home, she hadn't bought anything or wanted anything. Her eyes felt painted with salt water and her stomach was rolling. She just wanted to curl up under an old soft blanket and hide somewhere.

The moment she stepped from the car, though, everything changed.

When she left her mother and grandmother that morning, they'd both seemed relatively normal and sane. God knows what happened between breakfast and late afternoon to turn the two of them into lunatics.

The women were in the yard, hovering over some kind of strange metal contraption. Becca identified it as the antique press she'd seen years ago in the loft of the barn. Mom was turning the shallow-handled crank while Gram was feeding it cherries. Buckets of cherries were heaped in the shade. Clearly every bee, mosquito and gnat in the county had come to participate in the party. Both her mom and her grandmother were dressed in old shorts and T-shirts, which may or may not have been white at the beginning of this project. Just then, they were nearly soaked with cherry juice. So was their hair. So were their faces and hands and arms.

There didn't seem to be any problem with their enthusiasm, but production wasn't quite meeting idealistic expectations. The press was cranking merrily enough, but it seemed to be spewing cherry pits all over the yard, and the juice was splashing everywhere except inside the designated bowl. In fact, said designated bowl appeared to be the cleanest thing in the entire yard. That would have been bad enough, except that both women were nearly collapsed in laughter. Gram was holding her stomach.

Mom was bent over, holding hers. Both were gasping and shrieking laughter even as they were
yelling at each other.

Cripes, it was almost as good as Christmas.
"Hey," Becca yelled out. "I'm gone for a couple of
hours, and what in God's name did you two get
into?"

"Becca!" The two women looked up at the same
time, with big goofy grins. "Hurry and join us!
We're making wine! We were going to wait until
you got home, but we decided there was so much to
do, we'd better get started! Come here, darling."

Her jaw dropped when she realized that both her
mother and grandmother intended to hug her.
"Wait a minute, wait a minute, wait a minute—"

Her grandmother's arms wrapped her in a nice,
wet, juicy hug. "See? Now you're as sticky as we
are, so there's no point in worrying about the mess.
Besides, it's really fun, honest," Lydia promised her.

"Besides, we really need the help," her mom
piped in. "We had no problem at all getting the
press to, um, press. But somehow we can't get the
juice to go anywhere near the bowl. If you—"

"Now, come on. This is my good khaki skirt. My
shoes. My—" The bucket that had been pushed in
her arms was dripping cherry juice. Both women
beamed at her.

"Don't be worried about a little mess, dear.
That's what washing machines were made for. And
all we need for the wine recipe is two full gallons of
juice. It should be easy."

"Wine? Why in God's name are we making

cherry wine, when practically no one ever drinks wine around here?" Becca asked, thinking a little reason might get through . . . but no.

"I'm thinking about taking up drinking. Pretty soon. In fact, that's why I bought the wine racks in the kitchen. A girl can't have too many vices."

"Mother, you're not drinking this and neither am I. Unless there's some benefit from all the protein in all the gnats and mosquitoes." Susan grinned. "We're just making it for the fun of it. We were thinking about giving it away as presents. Especially to our enemies."

"What enemies?"

"Well, I don't know, offhand. But maybe we can develop some before Christmas. Now, don't be shy, Bec."

Oh, God. Oh, God. She hadn't seen her mom have a giggle attack in years. Gram, yes, she and her grandmother often had moments when some idiotic thing would strike them both. But seeing the two of them, looking so young and happy and laughing so hard . . .

A soft, sweet lump filled Becca's throat. This was everything she remembered about growing up. How much she'd felt loved. How she could laugh with her mom and grandmother like with no one else, how there was complete acceptance in the circle of women like nowhere else. No matter how much they all bickered from time to time, that's still what family was about. At least her family. Acceptance and love and trust. It was what mattered, past all the crap in life—in spite of all the crap in life.

"You're buying me new shoes," she threatened her mother.

"Anything you want, baby. Just crank."

"And you, Gram. I want a Sinclair Sunrise cake tomorrow."

"You bet, darling. Just keep cranking, girl." Grandma promptly burst into song, some old rock and roll tune about "slip sliding away." The lyrics were so ghastly that Susan boo-hissed in disgust. Obviously Becca had to join in the cheerleading, too.

Eventually they filled a bowl of cherry juice. One measly bowl. It seemed to take five giant buckets of cherries, all to get one measly bowl of juice. This was so appalling that they'd just started laughing again, when Becca vaguely heard the sound of a car. She turned her head, just as a five-year-old black Grand Am pulled in the drive.

Her smile died. Her hand slipped on the crank.

"Hey, Becca," her mom said. "What's wro—" And then Susan whipped her head around, too. All three women stopped in their tracks.

"I'll handle this," Becca told both her mother and her grandmother. And when they both immediately opened their mouths to argue, she said firmly, "Look. You two go inside and start getting cleaned up, okay? There's nothing to worry about. Cripes, it's dinnertime and none of us have even thought about putting anything on the stove. You two go on, go in, let me deal with this."

"Rebecca, I would rather—" Susan started to say.

"Mom. I need to talk to Douglas alone. It's okay. Really. Go."

The man climbing out of the car and heading straight for her was as familiar as her own pulse. In fact, he'd once seemed to own her pulse. The shaggy sweep of brown hair, the crinkly blue eyes, the long, lazy stride—just looking at him, just being with him, once, had made her blood swim. He'd seemed so warm, so caring, so much the loner who just needed the right woman to love him to make a difference.

If Douglas saw her mom and grandmother, he didn't greet or acknowledge them. He was looking at her, just at her, as if she were the only woman in the universe.

Of course, that was the same bullshit she'd believed from the beginning. Douglas always had that gift of making her feel uniquely important to him. No different than ever, he stopped right in front of her, his gaze sweeping over her face, her eyes, as if no one woman could possibly matter to him as much as she did.

"I know. I should have called, Bec. But I missed you so much. I just had to see you." He lifted his arms as if to tug her close.

She stepped back, clutched her arms under her chest. This was exactly what he'd pulled before she left, acting as if they'd never broken up, as if their relationship were still one hundred percent on. And even when she backed away from the embrace, he showed no sign of being upset or frustrated. There was nothing in those wonderful blue eyes but the appearance of loving warmth.

"You're right. You should have called first, Douglas."

As if she'd never spoken, he glanced around the yard and shot her an amused smile. "You look like you're having a great time with your family. And I can see you're busy besides. I'm glad you've having fun, Bec. You deserve a great summer after working so hard all year."

This was how he'd confused her before, being so nice that she didn't know how to respond, what to say. She wasn't even sure when she'd lost all trust in him, only that just being near him now made her palms sweat and her heart start pounding with anxiety. He'd never laid a hand on her, so there was no excuse for feeling fear. Yet it was fear and anxiety she felt and couldn't seem to shake. "The rent's paid up until the end of July. I don't know exactly when I can come and get my stuff, but I really don't think I can do it for at least another ten days—"

"You don't have to move your stuff. Come on. Take a break. Have fun. Then we can talk later."

"Douglas. I'm moving out. We're done. I thought we talked about this. I thought you understood."

"Of course I understood. You were upset. Listen, you want to go out to dinner?"

"No." It was like trying to communicate with a rock. Nothing got through. Besides which, he looked so gentle and caring and kind that she felt like a dimwit for being afraid of him.

"Okay, if you don't want to go to dinner tonight . . . I was thinking about getting a place to stay here for a couple days—"

"I won't see you."

He rolled his eyes, as if she'd said something

slightly exasperating, but nothing that really stressed his patience. "Becca, we never even argued. Nothing was going wrong. Every relationship hits a stall now and then, so did ours, but we have too much going for us to call it quits for nothing. If you don't want to talk right now, we'll just try later."

She thought: *I have to tell him about the pregnancy.* She thought: *I can't.* She thought *I'm going to throw up.* "It was going wrong for me. For me, it wasn't 'nothing.' I'm sorry if I hurt you. I never wanted to. I just can't help how I feel. I don't want to be with you anymore."

It was the most assertive she'd ever managed to be. Her voice had a quaver and her stomach was twisting up. She hated confrontations, which he knew. And he listened with this quiet, gentle smile, as if he were being patient but not hearing a word she said. "Tell me what I can do. I don't know what I did to make you mad."

"You didn't make me mad. My feelings just changed."

"Then maybe they'll change back. Did you think of that? Next week you could care just like you did before—"

"No, Douglas."

He smiled again, just a gentle smile, but in a way that made a shiver worm down her spine. "You remember how it was when we first met? The movie, then the picnic at midnight? Dancing to some silly rock and roll."

"We had some good times," she said shortly, desperately.

"You couldn't keep your hands off me in the beginning. Remember that part? We would have spent twenty-four/seven in bed if we could have." His hand connected with her shoulder before she realized he was reaching for her.

She snapped back another step, feeling more raw, more nervous. "I remember very well. But that's not how I feel now."

"You could. We could get that feeling back. If you'd just give it a chance." He reached for her again. And she stepped back again, avoiding him, deciding that whether she was dimwit or not, she was going in the house. She meant to do exactly that, only she stumbled on an uneven patch of grass and her foot slipped.

Everything went bewilderingly to hell right after that. She threw out a hand to steady herself. Douglas grabbed her arm, possibly to help her regain her balance, but possibly to force her close to him. It wasn't actually a tussle. It might have looked that way, but all she was doing was trying to avoid being touched by him. Whether she was being stupid or not, he was giving her the willies, making her feel awkward and icky and upset, but really, she didn't actually feel in danger.

Still, during that millisecond when there was an almost-tussle, everything changed.

She sensed movement, something moving fast, and then Douglas's face expressed shock when something catapulted onto his shoulders from behind.

My God. It was Gram.

And the force of Gram's weight on his shoulders made Douglas almost slam into her—he undoubtedly would have, with Gram riding on his shoulders, except that, holy kamoly, holy smokes, her mom suddenly showed up from his other side. She barreled at him, to him, with her fists up like little clenched balls. Both women were yelling for Douglas to get his hands off her.

Mom smashed him in the face, then immediately cried out in pain—as if she feared breaking all the bones in her hand. And Douglas was whirling around in a mad circle, trying to shake Gram off his back, and Gram was trying to hit him over the head and hold on at the same time. Mom, still howling, cuddled her hurt hand against her stomach and aimed at him with her head, as if she planned to use her head like a battering ram.

They all slipped in the cherry-sticky grass and went down. For a moment Douglas seemed to be beneath the two women, but then he surfaced, and his arm shot out—possibly just trying to get free? But it looked to Becca as if he were trying to slap her mother. And then Gram punched him again, calling him names and words that Becca could have sworn Lydia couldn't possibly know.

She kept trying to get in the mess of bodies, to stop them, to protect her mom and Gram, but they were rolling and twisting around, all mixed up together. They wouldn't stop and she couldn't make anyone listen. Desperate to do something, anything, she galloped top speed into the house and grabbed the closest phone.

Thank God he answered on the first ring. "Dad! I need you here right away!"

Chapter 12

The weather had been beautiful all day, but by late afternoon, clouds suddenly started fisting together and Jon could smell the tension building in the air. Once the wind started whistling, the boaters hustled in, moored and disappeared into their houses.

Around five, Jon told the staff to take off. There was no point in him paying people to stand around and twiddle their thumbs—and sure, there were maintenance and other chores to be done whether customers piled in or not, but the plummeting barometric pressure affected everyone's mood. His, too. Everyone was too restless to work.

The problem with letting everyone off, though, was that Jon then had all that thumb-twiddling time alone.

Alone wasn't good. Alone made him think of Susan—of making love with her. The sounds she'd made. The look on her face. The night falling, with her soft skin against the carpet of grass, surrounded by the scent of cherries . . . then the sudden slam in the teeth.

She hadn't been thinking about him when they made love. She'd been trying to erase the memory of her boss. Not Sebastian. The new West Coast boss. The turd.

Jon didn't exactly mind erasing the turd from her mind. If she needed someone to help her get over a bad experience, he wanted it to be him.

But everything was different this time. His heart recognized the difference, even if it was difficult to face the whole picture. The thing was . . . they'd had sex before. Used each other before. And he'd survived being the only one carrying a torch before. But there came a time when a guy had to take a stand. Either keep it zipped or go for broke. Either race to win or keep your damned oar completely out of the water.

He wanted love with Susan or nothing.

Funny that it had taken him twenty-two years to put that in black ink, but there it was.

The phone rang before he could think through a plan of action. It was his mother. Much as he loved her, there was no woman on the universe who could quell his libido faster. She asked, "How are the boats, dear?" as if she thought of them as the toys he played with until he got a real job.

"Business is fine," he answered her. "How are you and Dad?"

"I miss you. Miss home. It's too hot on Hilton Head, and all your dad does all day is golf with his friends."

Familiar complaints. His mom had been lonely

as long as he could remember. "If you're miserable there, why don't you just come home?"

"Your dad loves it." His mother sighed. "Have you seen my granddaughter recently?"

"You bet. Becca's been up here for a couple weeks now."

"Has she cut her hair?"

Jon didn't have a clue. "Um, I think so."

"She's been wearing it so long. I was hoping she'd get one of those shorter, more sophisticated styles. She's so beautiful."

"Yeah, I think so, too." But that was an old refrain, too. His mom spoke wistfully of Becca, but where Becca got on with her other grandmother like a house afire, his mother barely knew her. She never called Becca herself, which was standard behavior for her. She never confronted her husband directly, either. She wanted things to be better, but she didn't want to lift her own finger to propel any change.

Still, she *was* lonely. And Jon did love her. So he listened to her natter on until she'd talked all she wanted, then hung up, thinking, no, he wasn't going to think about Susan again. He was going to do something constructive, like prepare the "Building an eighteen-foot Sharpie" course he was scheduled to give in the fall.

Thankfully he was saved from doing any god-awful real work when Artis Newlins charged into his shop. To label Artis a character was a massive understatement. She was a hearty sixty-year-old sailor, built like a brawler with boobs, never spent a day on land if she could help it. He'd always liked her. Before her husband died, though, she'd done the sailing while Lars had done the maintenance, and these last months she'd been grudgingly forced to admit that she needed some education on how to do the boat-belly-work herself.

Artis accepted help the way a small child took to castor oil. Never willingly. Lots of twisty-face and scowly expressions, but this afternoon, probably because the threatening weather eclipsed anything she really wanted to do, she'd felt driven to seek his advice.

"Okay, now, the sequence is to stain first, then epoxy, then varnish. Nothing's gonna take stain if there's epoxy on it."

"What, you think I don't know shit?" Artis said sourly. "I got it." Still, she scribbled down every detail.

"You start by sanding lightly—say, two-twenty-grit sandpaper. Dust that off, but then, what matters, you dampen the areas to be stained with distilled water. Not too much at a time, because you don't want to let it dry."

"Got it," Artis snarled again, and that was when the phone rang.

Becca sounded damn near hysterical. "*Dad!* I need you here right away!" She kept talking, obviously trying to tell him what was happening, but she was crying and hiccupping at the same time.

"Wait a minute, baby. Calm down. I'm having a hard time understanding you."

"It's Grandma and Mom. They're in a fight with

Douglas. I mean, a *real* fight. A physical fight. On the ground. Hurting each other. Dad, for God's sake, I can't get anybody to stop or listen to me. You have to come. *Please.*"

Jon kicked Artis out and locked up the place, but even as he drove toward Copper Creek, he felt exasperated and edgy. There was no question about him going. Becca had asked him to come. That was that. But Jon couldn't imagine either Susan or Lydia involved in any kind of physical confrontation—neither of them could swat a mosquito without guilt. So he didn't know what he was really getting into, except that his interference in something that was none of his business wasn't likely to be needed or appreciated.

He wanted to see Susan. Badly. He'd thought about her nonstop since making love. But damn, he wanted to see her alone. Just the two of them. Nothing to do with Becca or Lydia or some mess that didn't make a lick of sense.

A raindrop the size of a basketball splatted on his windshield. Okay, okay, possibly it was a wee bit smaller than a basketball—but not by much. Suddenly the sky turned darker than smudge, the clouds hanging in heavy pregnant bunches, the atmosphere so thick there seemed no air to breathe.

As he turned at the mailbox entrance, his gaze instinctively zoomed toward the orchards. Cherry harvest had just started this last week. Anyone living near Traverse was tuned to that channel. Certain traditions were inherent to the area. Trucks waddled down the road carrying silver tanks, each holding cold water and a thousand pounds of sloshing cherries. Cherry shakers glinted in and out of orchards, looking like alien metal monsters to anyone who wasn't from the area. Every restaurant served cherry pie and cherry cobbler and cherry ice cream—to do less would have been sacrilege.

And the view was worrisome. A devil wind was hissing through the Sinclair orchards, tossing the leaves like dancers' skirts, causing limb rub and bruising on the cherries—he knew the terms. Everybody did who lived here. Farmers would be moaning all night, hooked up to weather stations, pacing their kitchens, bawling at their kids.

By the time he cut the engine on his truck, the rain was pelting down big-time, looking like cheap silver tinsel that glittered in the dusky gloom. For a second he didn't budge, just stared out his windshield, trying to make sense of the confounding scene in front of him.

Even in the pouring rain, he could see that Lydia's prize landscaped lawn resembled bedlam. An old wine press seemed to be the center of the mess. It glistened in the rain, located on an old wooden bucket. Behind the press, empty wine bottles huddled in a heap, as if the entire county had shown up for a wake. The grass looked more red than green, as if a giant had dumped huge bowls of cherries and then rolled in them. The smell was ripe and fruity, and, God knows, would have been a disaster of gnats and mosquitoes if it hadn't been raining so hard.

The girls had been making wine. That part was obvious. But it didn't begin to explain the rest of the mess.

Scraping a confused hand through his hair, he pushed out of the truck and jogged toward the house. If Douglas had been there, he was apparently gone now. The only vehicles in sight were Susan's and Bec's and Lyd's.

Still, nothing else appeared normal. Lights glowed from every window in the house. Doors and windows stood open, letting rain in, no one seeming to notice and no one answering his knock.

He stepped in, seeing nothing at first, but immediately picking up the sound of voices from the dining room. The voices were projecting at talk-show volume, all three women jabbering at once and sounding mad and upset. Jon considered whipping around and galloping back to his truck. If the women were okay enough to yell, they were sure as hell okay, right? Interrupting the Sinclair women in the middle of another female-squabble-crisis struck Jon as fun on a par with sleeping on a hornet's nest.

Only then it was too late to run, because Becca spotted him.

"Dad!" Cheeks tear-stained, she hurled toward him, wearing a ratty old shirt that stunk of cherries. "I'm so glad you're here! You can't imagine what's been happening—Mom's hurt and Grandma's hurt and no one's listening to me, and outside, holy cow, there's this terrible mess and I think Gram should go to a hospital—"

Susan's voice came from the kitchen, still out of sight. "Rebecca Lindsay Elizabeth, you called your father? I can't believe you told your dad anything about this, much less dragged him out all this way—"

"And in this storm. Jon, you just go right back home."

He searched for the sound of the third voice—Lydia's—and found it when he leaned over the edge of the pale yellow couch. She wasn't on the couch, though, but on the carpet, lying flat on her back with her knees up. As if she'd just had a shower, her wet hair was wrapped in a towel turban and she was only wearing a bathrobe, although it was wrapped securely around her.

"Lydia, why on earth are you—"

Becca answered before he'd even finished the question. "Grandma hurt her back, Dad. Mom and I got her in a hot shower, thinking the heat would help, but once she got out and down on the carpet, then she couldn't seem to get up again."

"I can, too. I just don't want to get up quite yet," Lydia corrected. "And if you don't quit treating me like a batty old woman, I'm going to smack you one. I'm not even sixty, young lady."

"I think she should go to a hospital, Dad. I'm not kidding, I don't think she can move."

"Jon! I've had it with being bullied by these two. Tell my daughter and your daughter that I'm not a doddering idiot yet. I hurt my back, yes. But I can decide for myself if I need a doctor or just need—"

"A snort?" Jon said.

Lydia's smile was wan but grateful. "Finally,

someone who talks some sensible language. Just a shot, okay? Neat, no ice. And it's possible that I am just a little bit stiff. If you could think of anything I could try . . ."

Jon nodded. "Peas."

"Peas?" Becca said disbelievingly. "Look, I'm darn near going out of my mind here. I can't handle another grown adult who won't listen to a lick of reason. Now I need somebody to be serious. Somebody who'll—"

"Jesus," Jon hissed. He heard his baby rant on, but her voice dimmed in his awareness when Susan showed up in the kitchen doorway. She'd obviously just showered, too, but her hair wasn't wrapped in a turban like her mom's; it was wet and wild and already starting to fluff like flames around her face. She'd also pulled on a robe, only it wasn't at all like her mother's but an ivory silk kind of thing, floor-length with a skinny little sash. It looked elegant and sexy and classy.

So did the shiner on her right eye. The bruise was swollen plump and already turning colors. A thin scrape on the soft white skin of her neck was oozing a bit of blood. She was walking with a limp and her forehead was pinched white—which meant she was hurting bad, even if, being Susan, she'd deny it with her hand on a Bible in a court of law.

"See, Dad?" Becca said. "*See?* Now do you believe me? I was scared enough to call 911, but the two of them pulled such a tantrum that I had to hang up. You're the only who can possibly get them to do *anything.*"

Jon wanted to jolt into action, but for two seconds, he couldn't take his eyes off Susan's face. "Suze. Douglas—did he did this to you? Hit you? And your mother?"

"Not exactly," Susan said.

Jon's pulse bucked. "Where the hell is he?"

"Aw, sheesh, not you, too, Dad. Has the whole world gone crazy?" Becca wailed, which made Jon's fury settle down—at least long enough to galvanize him into action.

"Becca. First, get your grandmother some ibuprofen—as much as you can give her for a first dose—then open the freezer and find a bag of frozen peas. Put it behind your grandmother's back wherever it hurts most. Time it. Twenty minutes. Then put a warm Turkish towel on the spot for the next twenty minutes. Then frozen peas again. After an hour, we'll see—by then she'll either be more comfortable and able to move around, or I'll take her to the hospital myself. Lydia, how exactly did you hurt your back?"

"I'm not going to any hospital!" Lydia snapped.

But Becca finally smiled at him as if she meant it. "Thanks, Dad. That's exactly what I'd hoped you do. Make them both behave. But . . . peas?"

"The frozen peas'll mold to the spot, keep it cold, prevent swelling. Ice is the idea, but ice cubes are hard and uncomfortable, so the peas work better. I don't know if she needs an X ray or anything more serious, but—"

"There's nothing serious wrong with me! I just twisted my back a little! Although . . . I admit, I wouldn't mind trying the damn peas," Lydia said from the carpet, "as long as everyone understands I'm not going anywhere near any doctor or hospital."

"Uh-huh." There'd be time for arguing later. Just then, with Becca mobilized into caretaking her grandmother, Jon steered a scowling Susan deliberately into the privacy—or relative privacy—of the kitchen.

"I can't talk, Jon. Both of them are so upset that they're coming apart at the seams."

"And at the moment they're busy taking care of each other. You need some ice on that eye before you take on anything else, tiger. And then I want a report of exactly what the hell happened here."

"I don't need ice."

"Have you looked in a mirror?"

She seemed to take the question seriously, because she padded barefoot into the bathroom near the back door, then almost immediately came back with a stubborn look. "All right, all right. So maybe I could use some frozen peas on there for just a couple of minutes."

"And some first aid for the scrape on the neck. And what are you limping for?"

"I'm not limping."

"Uh-huh." He never did the he-man thing because he wasn't a he-man kind of guy, but just then it felt as natural as breathing to pick her up and plunk her down on the counter, trapping her between his legs. For a good long second she appeared too startled to protest—but then she looked at him. She remembered his being between her legs in other circumstances.

So did he. Hormones skittered between them like hot sparks in a fireplace. That wild hour in the orchard was suddenly there, as if he could smell her skin and the cherries and see the sunset and the color of desire in her eyes. He could feel it again. Longing, so rich, so lonely, so compelling that it was all he could do not to pull her in his arms again. Right then. Right there. And to hell with the consequences.

And he might have—if she hadn't looked freaked enough to bolt if he gave her an inch of freedom. He *had* to stand close. It was the only way to trap her on the counter.

"Where's the first-aid kit?" he asked.

"I don't need any first aid—"

Rather than waste time hearing any more lip, he yelled, *"Rebecca!"* His daughter, being far more of a darling than her mother, immediately galloped into the room, swiftly produced the first-aid kit, then galloped back to her grandmother. Left alone again, Susan eyed him the way she might a prowling panther.

"I can take care of my own cuts and bruises, Jon. I just didn't have a chance before this. By the time Douglas left, all three of us were a mess. I mean, we were all unbelievably filthy. Mom and I took showers first, but I knew her back was hurt and she needed more help than I did, so then—"

Amazing. Put a hand on her thigh, and she talked like an Eveready battery—although, honest to Pete, he was just trying to make sure she didn't run off while he foraged in the first-aid box. When she had to stop for breath, he got in a casual question. "So . . . you attacked Douglas. Got into a brawl?"

"Jon! Of course not!"

"Becca said—"

Put the hand back on her thigh, and out came another flood of words. "Douglas just showed up here, uninvited, unexpected. The three of us were in the yard making wine—or trying to. It was getting really windy and threatening rain, and we really had to get done if— Anyway, Douglas got out of his car, obviously wanting to have a private talk with Becca—"

"I'll be damned, you call that disaster out there 'making wine'?" It seemed a good idea to tease her when he had to clean the scrape on her neck, but as gently as he touched the tender spot with an antiseptic wipe, she winced. And that made him wince in response. It wasn't that bad a scrape, but the mar on the fragile white skin on her neck was like . . . hell, it was like seeing somebody crush a rose. "Get back to telling me what happened."

"Well . . . Becca wanted Mom and I to go inside so she could talk to Douglas alone. So we did—but we left the door open, and my mom hung out by one window and I stood by another. I'd just told my mother about Becca being afraid of Douglas, so neither of us were about to go very far away. Anyway, we couldn't hear the conversation, no matter how quiet we were, but both of us could see that Becca was getting more and more upset the more they talked. And then suddenly we saw him raise his hand. . . ."

Maybe Susan didn't realize it, but her fingers suddenly circled his wrist . . . not communicating fear, but conveying a calming, gentling gesture. He hadn't said anything, but she must have sensed his reaction at the mental picture of Douglas—or any man, anywhere, anytime—touching his daughter in anger.

"Honestly, Jon, I don't know what Douglas intended," she said swiftly. "It may not be fair to assume he meant to hurt Becca. He wasn't acting angry. Rebecca was the one looking rattled, not him, not at all—but when my mother saw him raise his hand, that was it. It was like the trigger on a gun. She happened to be standing at the window closest to the front door, and the next thing I knew, she fired outside faster than a bullet. I couldn't have stopped her if I tried."

He didn't push aside her robe. The silky fabric parted all by itself. By then Susan's hands were fisted in her lap, so it wasn't as if her modesty were compromised, but for him, images immediately flooded his mind of those tanned, slim, bare legs. Wrapped around him. Squeezing tight. Which made the bloody scrape down her calf infuriate him three times worse.

"My mom . . . she just hurled herself on Douglas's back. I couldn't believe it. She held on like a monkey. And Douglas let out this yelp and started to spin around, obviously trying to shake her off—

he couldn't seem to figure out what was going on, for sure didn't understand that my mother was trying to protect Rebecca— *Ouch*, Jon!"

"How the *fuck* did he do this to your leg?"

"Jon!"

"Okay, okay." Miss Priss never could take a little language, and he knew that, but damn it—the scrape on her leg was enough to make him sick. "Just keep telling the story."

"I *am*. The thing is, he was obviously trying to shake Mom off his back, and Mom was trying to hit him and hold on at the same time. It was all so crazy and confusing and fast. Everyone yelling and upset. The point being that suddenly she just plain fell, flat on her back. And when I heard my mom cry out, I . . ."

She stopped talking for an instant, as if catching her breath. He stopped cleaning the ugly scrape on her leg long enough to wait for her to continue. God knows exactly how or when, but the furry orange cat—the one no one claimed to own—suddenly showed up on the counter. The cat nuzzled next to her, blinking at him with golden eyes like a sleepy thirteen-pound protector.

Susan said, "I may have overreacted just a little bit. I really can't swear that Douglas intended to hurt either my mother or Becca. But by then he was definitely mad. And raving about both Bec and my mom being maniacs. I had to do something, you know? So I tried to find a way to nicely tell him to leave."

"Nicely," Jon echoed.

"I can't remember it all that clearly. I may have shoved him a little."

"You may have shoved him a little, but nicely," Jon echoed.

"I'm pretty sure that I suggested he get off the property. Quickly."

"Uh-huh. And then?"

"Well. It was slippery in the yard. Because of all the cherries? And he kind of made this move . . . now that I think about it, he could have been just turning around to leave, only he twisted and slipped because of the slick ground. Only it looked as if he were lifting his hand. Again. And I thought he was going after Becca. Again. So . . ."

"Uh-huh. So . . . ?" He prodded her.

"So I can't remember if this is the exact order of things, but I think that was the time that I kind of gently punched him."

"You kind of gently punched him," Jon echoed.

"I had no idea how much that would hurt my hand, but I'll tell you this. I'm never hitting a man in the face again as long as I live. The next thing I remember, though, was his yelling all these swear words, and he pushed my mother—who was just trying to help me and keep him away from Becca—so it's possible right then that I may have butted my head into his stomach. Because my hand hurt. And because I was trying to stop him from hurting Bec or Mom. And because . . ."

"I get it. Go on." Maybe ten years from now, the retelling of this was going to make him laugh, but right now . . . right now, the more Jon listened, the more he picked up a whole story about Susan that he'd never guessed. God knows she looked shook up and anxious and white and hurting—but something else was going on here. Something in her face. She didn't care about the scrapes and the black eye and the sore hand. She'd managed to fight back. She'd managed to hurt someone who was trying to hurt her loved ones. She'd come up with courage she hadn't known she'd had before, and it mattered to her. "Go on," he repeated.

"I'm just trying to be honest and admit that I could have misread the situation. The thing was, the sun had disappeared and the wind was really wild. The sky had gotten darker and darker. It was obviously going to storm big-time any minute, and besides that the yard was all slippery and squishy because of the cherries. So Douglas may have just slipped and tried to grab on to me for balance and never really intended to smack me in the eye. But right at that second, I just plain didn't know what we were dealing with, except that my mom was hurt and Mom and Becca were both crying and it all seemed to be because of Douglas."

"So you felt you needed to gently punch him again," Jon said.

"Um. Not so gently that time. The other time was gentle. But it was time he took off, you know? There was no way this situation was getting better. He needed to get off the property, not tomorrow, not an hour later, but right then. And I guess I'd have to say that I lost a bit of control—"

"Let's see your hand."

She displayed her hands. The left palm looked like normal—except for being a tad shaky—but her right knuckles looked puffy and red and . . . well, it looked as if she'd been in a fight. He said, "Jesus," and opened the freezer. They were out of peas, but he gave her a bag of corn to hold. "The next time you're in a fight, use your knee."

"Okay."

"You know where to aim."

"Yes."

It seemed safest to lock up any emotions he felt and just go on lecture mode. "You haven't got the physical strength or the skill or the killer instinct to win against anyone in a fight. You just risk hurting yourself. So what you do in a situation where you're stuck getting physical is to get serious. Hit where it counts. Do what you have to do. Don't feel guilty. Don't look back. And for God's sake, don't think like a girl."

"Jon, I swear, I had no idea that I was ever going to . . ." She cocked her head. He was bent down, applying first cream and then a thick bandage to the angry, swollen scrape on her calf, but she must have sensed something because she twisted around until she could see his face. "Why are you looking so mad?"

"Because, goddamn it, I'm pissed off you got to punch him and I didn't."

She blinked. "I would have thought you'd be disgusted that I hit him at all."

"That's how much you know. I'm proud as hell of you. But I admit I'm still confused what Douglas was doing here, where he is right now, a few of the other relevant facts. I mean, it's not as if you Sinclair women regularly get yourselves involved in a brawl. But mostly I keep thinking . . ."

"Mostly you keep thinking what?"

He couldn't answer for that millisecond because he couldn't seem to breathe. It was as if all the talk of punching had punched all the oxygen from his lungs. All he could see were her soft eyes, mere inches from his. The shiner, the cut, the building pile of Band-Aids he was taping all over her body. The white silk robe was now gaping open, revealing an arc almost to her navel, revealing milk-white fragile skin, revealing the throbbing pulse in her throat, revealing the shadow of satin skin hiding under the fabric.

Out of nowhere, an old memory came back to haunt him. Every light in the kitchen was on. The two women were talking in the other room. And if sex had been on his mind, there was nothing sexual about the scene, about the kitchen, about the situation.

Yet, clear as crystal, he suddenly remembered trying to make love to her on the kitchen counter. It was years ago. The counter had been a speckly Formica then, not yellow. They'd just been kids. Carried away by the moment. Unfortunately, because sex was so new to them then, they were both more enthusiastic than skilled. No matter how wild and hot they were, he couldn't seem to figure out how to fit in, and she couldn't figure out how to help him, and then she'd started giggling and he'd lost the erection. He should have been offended and frustrated to death, but Suze had this laugh . . . this wonderful, mesmerizing, sexy peal of a laugh.

That age, no boy could handle a failure. It destroyed his whole sense of prowess. Of manhood. Of coolness. But damned if he didn't fall in love with her, right then, right then, forever, because of that laugh.

She'd never laughed *at* him. She'd laughed in a way that made his whole world brighter. Lighter. Sharper. Changing how he felt and thought, changing who he was and who he could be. Changing who he wanted to be.

A chilled draft of wind whooshed through the window over the sink. Lightning crackled just outside, followed immediately by a house-shaking tremor of thunder. Then came the hiss of rain, a busty, gusty deluge of rain, sluicing down hard. . . .

Almost as hard as his mouth on hers.

This was a different kind of kiss. It was an I-made-love-with-you and things are different now kind of kiss. This was an I-own-you and whether-you-like-it-or-not-you-own-me kind of kiss. It was a kiss that involved pressure and tongues, promises and tenderness. Just because she'd knocked his world cockeyed was no reason to believe she wouldn't hurt him again. He was unsure why she kept kissing him back—what that meant, to her, to them—but he understood unequivocally that this time was their last shot. Either they won each other . . . or they lost each other for good.

Aw, hell. Some of it was easier than that. Some of

it was just knowing that she'd been hurt and confused and upset lately—by life, by her job, by Becca. And he just wanted to be the one she turned to.

He simply had to kiss her. To touch her. To hold her.

And as those first kisses got deeper and richer and darker, her arms swung around him tighter than rope, her fanny scooching closer, thighs splaying wider so she could nest closer to him. So she wanted to be kissed. Touched. Held. By him. Last night in the orchard, maybe she'd wanted oblivion, but this night she knew exactly who she was kissing and what she was inviting.

So did he. This was what it was all about, what it had always been about—him belonging to her, her belonging to him. There was only one Hope diamond, only one Timur ruby, only one Suze. How could he give her up when nothing in his life came close to her?

Rain poured in the window, chilling her back and his hands, yet he made no move to stop these kisses—and neither did she. His mouth pressed, aching hard, probing with his tongue, finding hers, taking hers.

She sighed against him, heavy and low, like the bleat of a sax on a bluesy night, a moan of longing. Of a needing to belong. Of a call to be taken.

The fat orange cat suddenly bounded off the counter.

Her thighs tightened around his waist. Beneath the silk robe, she was bare. Under the fluorescent kitchen light, her hair seemed dusted with fire, like his mood, like his heart. He wanted to sip her up like a sweet long drink. He wanted to bite her. He wanted to breathe her air, sleep her sleep, smile her smiles. He wanted to bury his cock so deep inside her it could never come out, just stay there, held tight, and if he had to die, that's how he wanted to go, dying of desire for her. With her.

A throat cleared. Not his throat, not Susan's throat. Another throat—the sound emanating somewhere from the vicinity of the dining room doorway.

He heard the sound. He just didn't give a damn.

Then came a delicate cough. Then a "Well." Then, after another careful silence, "Um, well, carry on. I just wanted to tell you thanks, Jon, the frozen peas really helped. My back is much better. I'm going upstairs now, and so is Becca—aren't you, Becca?"

"Oh, yes," Becca piped up enthusiastically. "We're both going upstairs immediately now, and we won't be coming back down. Ever."

"But, um, I just have to walk past you two for a second—a very, very fast second—all I want to do is open the freezer and see if there are any more frozen vegetables. The peas are all defrosted now, you know? And the only ibuprofen seems to be in the cupboard here. I'm blinding my eyes, not looking at a thing, so don't even notice I'm here—"

"I'm not looking at anything, either," Becca chirped. "Carry on, carry on! And Mom, I'll take care of Grandma, and we're both just fine, so don't worry about a thing."

The two gigglers hurtled past them. The freezer door opened, then slammed closed, followed by more giggling, until they both disappeared through the dining room door again. One immediately returned, only to turn off the glaring overhead light.

The darkness didn't help. Jon wasn't sure at what precise moment the interlopers had shocked the hell—and hormones—out of him, but his forehead suddenly seemed to be leaning against Susan's forehead. Her mouth was still inches from his, but it wasn't the same.

When he could untangle his tongue long enough to say something coherent, he tried, "Are we related to either of those people?"

"I am. But you're only related to the young one."

"Are we going to be able to live this down?"

"You are. Because you get to leave. But I have to sleep here and face them in the morning."

He winced, as if he were the one who had to wake up to three Sinclair women at a daybreak hour. "All right. You want me to go say something to them?"

"Like what?"

"Hell. I don't know what. Whatever you tell me to say."

"I can't think of one thing to say that could explain what the Sam Hill we were just doing in this kitchen, in a way that would satisfy either my mother or our daughter."

That was true, but Jon had the sudden urge to laugh. They were bantering, not bickering. Having fun together, as impossible as it sounded. She'd eased back, so had he. He brushed her hair away from her brow and cheek. She let him. She tugged her robe closed. He let her. Both sounded light and a little embarrassed, but not really, more like adults who didn't appreciate being caught in an embarrassing situation but knew perfectly well they could survive it.

Only suddenly Jon lost the smile. Maybe the moment called for some careful handling, but he was tired of tact, even more tired of being careful. He couldn't keep getting wound up, wanting Susan Sinclair but not having a clue where or when or how this was going to end—except that his heart was likely to get broken if this went on much further.

He opened his mouth to bark out something real—and something that doubtless would have gotten him in a heap of trouble. But then he noticed her black eye again. The room was shadowed without the overhead light on, but the silver rain clearly reflected her soft, sober profile—and the swelling around her eye. She really *had* been through hell and back already this night.

"We're at a V in the road, Suze. We're going to have to commit to a turn one way or another," he said quietly.

She didn't duck or pretend she didn't know what he was talking about. "Yes. Past time."

"But right now you need rest. You've had a traumatic night. And whether Becca is laughing with her grandmother or not right now, I'm guessing she's not laughing on the inside. She needs to talk about what happened with Douglas."

"Yes."

"I want in on that loop. I want to know exactly where she stands on Douglas. Tomorrow morning. No later. In fact—I can't believe I'm saying this—but I'm inclined to sleep on your mother's couch."

"Good grief. You're willing to face my mother in the morning?"

"Of course not. I'd rather have an out-of-body experience with poison ivy—but I'm not trying to make a joke here, Suze. If you think there's any chance Douglas would come back here tonight—"

She shook her head. "No. Really. I just can't believe that's a worry. I mean, after the fight all three of us went through? He has no possible reason to come back here. I'll lock the doors, keep a phone handy. But if I were nervous, I'd tell you."

"You sure?"

"Totally sure. Honest."

Unwillingly he pushed in a pocket for his truck keys. "You'll come see me in the morning, give me a full report. . . ."

"Yes. I promise," Susan agreed, and out of nowhere—or it seemed out of nowhere—she touched his cheek.

"This is my fault," she said softly. "We're having a problem here—because of me. I'm sorry, Jon."

There was nothing he could say to that. When he hiked out to the truck, there was a thick, angry lump in his throat that made swallowing hard. "Sorry" was the last thing he wanted to hear from Susan, or any other obscure reference to fault, blame or apologies. She'd been home less than a month, tied him up in more knots than she ever had, and he still didn't have a clue in hell what was going on. For him. For her. For them. For Becca, either.

But she wasn't getting away from him this time—not without a fight. Because if he lost her this time, Jon knew it would be for good.

Chapter 13

Past midnight it was still raining, but just dribbling down the windows now. The harsh downpour was done, the thunder and lightning chased off to some other part of the sky. Susan sat curled up in the window seat of her bedroom, unable to sleep, staring at her mother's rose garden below.

She hugged her arms around her knees, so tired she could hardly hold her head up, yet she didn't want to go to bed. Her swollen eye hurt. The long bitter scrape on her leg hurt. Muscles in her body hurt that she'd never known she had.

But her heart hurt the deepest.

She was so in love she couldn't see straight.

Since this was the second time, she should be familiar with the chaos caused by loving Jon Laker. At sixteen, though, loving him had only involved turning her life upside down, having to grow up overnight, being scared out of her mind.

Now she realized what pip-squeak-sized problems those were.

This time she was *really* miserable. And, even miserable, her mind kept wrapping around pictures of him. Pictures of how he kissed. How he leaped in to help, like a knight charging to a damsel's rescue—even though the damsels were three generations of Sinclair women. How he walked, with that loose-limbed, all-guy stride. How he looked at Becca, what a fabulous dad he was and always had been. How he'd once thought he could carry her off and give her a happily-ever-after, screw the odds and forget any rational thinking. It was . . . everything. Everything he said, everything he was.

Susan squeezed her eyes closed. Wasn't love supposed to be an answer? Like a fool, she'd believed that when she was sixteen—only she was older now. Old enough that she had no excuse for repeating the same mistakes.

Jon didn't love her. Then or now. He thought he did then. Maybe he thought he did now—but all these years, she'd known he was carrying a torch . . . for a girl she'd never been.

And all these years she'd kept hoping that he'd see the woman she was, want the woman she was. Be proud of the woman she was.

Instead, it seemed that nothing fundamental had changed—except that she could hurt and be hurt far more deeply, far more irrevocably. And love far more deeply and irrevocably, too.

Her mind was so concentrated on the problem that the sudden sound of the doorknob turning made her jump.

"Mom?" The door pushed open. Susan couldn't distinguish much in the midnight shadows but her daughter's long white nightgown. "I guessed you wouldn't be able to sleep. And no, I won't turn the light on. I can see you over there by the window. And I'll bet the light hurts your sore eye."

"It does, a little."

"Well, I'm glad you're awake, because I couldn't sleep, either."

Another voice piped up behind Becca's. "Me, either."

So much for peace and quiet and a chance to brood in private. Lydia trailed Becca in. Both kidnapped her bed without asking or needing permission, although Lydia still needed to cater to her sore back, so she laid prone with her knees up. Becca took off for a few moments to collect heaps of pillows from the other bedrooms. By the time the two of them had completely destroyed her bed, they were giggling like two girls at a pajama party, and never mind the disaster they'd been through earlier.

Susan stayed braced against the window for a few more minutes, then got up to find hairbrushes.

"Mom! That's a great idea!"

"Uh-huh. You go behind Grandma so she can lean back her head without having to move too much, okay?"

Within minutes they'd formed a hairbrushing train. Susan brushed Becca's hair, and Becca brushed Lydia's, and any other time Lydia would sit in a circle so she could brush Susan's—but tonight, no one wanted Lydia to hurt her back any worse, so they made a train instead of a chain.

Susan couldn't remember when they'd started

the hairbrushing ritual. It just seemed to be something the Sinclair women did, particularly when one of them was in trouble. It didn't matter how it was put together; the essential elements were the same. The stroking. The talking. The taking care of each other, woman-fashion.

Becca didn't let her do much mothering anymore, but she always, always, suckered in for this. Susan took the first long, slow brush, and even in the dark she could see her daughter's eyes close, feel the tension seep out of those slim shoulders. Becca's groans became part of the conversation. So did Lydia's.

Her mom and her daughter were both strong . . . but so bullheaded. Thankfully defenses tended to crumble when their hedonistic tendencies were being seduced. Susan brushed and kept on brushing, just like when Bec was a little girl, letting the long strands shimmer through the brush, then fall like the silken sheen of a waterfall.

"Are you mad at us, Bec?" she got around to asking.

"Mad? About what happened with Douglas? Come on, just the opposite. I think you two are the bravest women I know."

"We really weren't trying to pry or eavesdrop. We were both afraid that he was going to hurt you. And, when he raised his hand, that he intended to hit you."

Becca's voice got quiet. "I'm not positive what he was going to do right then." Silence fell for a moment while they just brushed and stroked, but

Becca eventually let out a chuckle. "God, Grandma, when you launched yourself on his back, you looked like a mad monkey."

"Hey." Lydia's voice sounded wounded.

"Well, you did. And Mom, sheesh. What a slugger."

Susan was still mulling how an ardent pacifist such as herself could have kanoodled another human being so easily. Even brushing her baby's hair made her wrists and palm ache all over again—but really, she didn't care. This was a mom's work. It felt good. "Did you tell Douglas, baby? About the pregnancy?"

Another moment of silence. "I *meant* to tell him the next time I saw him." More silence. "But no, I didn't. And whether you two agree with me or not, I don't want to hear any criticism, okay? Not tonight."

Lydia cleared her throat. "Personally, I think there are a ton of things in life that we women don't tell our men. I also think that there can be a big difference between honesty and integrity. Just because we don't tell someone everything doesn't mean we're less than honest people."

"That's pretty deep for this late at night," said Susan.

"Yeah, well, I was in my first physical fight tonight, and I'm feeling pretty cool." Lydia's eyes were closed, savoring the way her granddaughter was massaging her scalp. "But Becca . . . I want to hear what happened. Not tonight. Before. How this relationship went so wrong for you."

"I don't know," Becca said.

Lydia sounded sleepy—but not so sleepy she was willing to let that pass. The room was dark, the hour was late, and no one was in the room but the three women. Family. "That's not good enough. You need to know. Need to talk it through. When there's a dragon in your living room, there's no way to ignore it. It'll never go away if you don't confront it."

"Dragon." Becca chuckled, but then for a while she just brushed and brushed her gram's hair. Finally she started talking again. "Douglas seemed so great when we were first together. He'd call, he'd pop over, bringing me some little thing, always saying something nice, something personal. He seemed to sense what I wanted to hear most. And that's how it was for a long time. I thought he was good for me. I thought I was good for him."

"And then?" Lydia prodded.

"And then—close your ears, Mom—we had sex. I don't want to hear a bunch of grief. We were in a serious relationship by then, talking about the future. Like setting up in Kalamazoo together after we both graduated, getting jobs, finding an apartment to share, getting married down the pike."

"And then?" Lydia prodded again.

"Then we got the apartment and I got the job . . . but he didn't. He just wanted to take a little break after graduating, he said. Which was fine. Only that's when things seemed to change. I couldn't go to a friend's house without him. If a phone call was for me, he picked it up and joined in. The apartment—like, I have lots of energy?—so I didn't mind cleaning and washing and stuff. It wasn't like work, it was more like playing house. But Douglas was literally just sitting around. There was always a reason he couldn't help. Always a reason he couldn't find a job. Always a reason he couldn't help with the bills."

"When did you realize this was happening, Bec?" Susan asked.

"Over months. It wasn't like one second everything went from wonderful to terrible. It was little stuff that kept happening over weeks and weeks. And then . . . well, it's not like I was afraid of him physically, exactly, but . . ."

When Becca didn't finish that sentence, Susan put down the brush and started massaging Bec's temples. Finally Bec came through with more. "Grandma, do you remember one Christmas? . . . I was really little. Everybody was in the dining room but you and Gramps, and suddenly a plate or something dropped in the kitchen, making a big clattering noise, and Grandpa really yelled. I don't know why he was so mad. I just remember you coming into the dining room, everyone at the table, everyone quiet, and you . . . you were white like a snowflake. And you said something cheery like, 'Grandpa's just having a little rough day; it'll be okay in a bit.'"

"I remember," Susan interrupted. Hell, she should. It was a common scene and chapter in the book of her childhood.

"Well, that's how it was with Douglas. Not at first. It was later he started to get . . . moody. And I kept running to keep him happy, thinking it was my fault he was crabby, things I did or said. If I tried harder, it'd be wonderful like it was in the beginning. I didn't see him as . . . using me. Or leeching off me. I didn't even see how hard he was clinging, like a rope pulling tighter and tighter around my neck."

"Oh, baby," Susan whispered.

"The thing was . . . the thing that really bugged me . . . was that I really believed we were good together in the beginning. So how had I failed this relationship, this man I'd loved so much? And then there was Gramps. Because I remember how we all tiptoed around Gramps, Grandma. As if the women in the family were all responsible for keeping him happy, keeping his temper down. And I was sure, so absolutely sure, that I'd never, never pick a man like that to be with."

"Your grandfather didn't start out that way," Lydia said.

"Yeah—I get that now. Because Douglas didn't start out that way, either. I never saw any bully side to him. I never thought he'd strangle me with how possessive he got. In fact, I thought he was just like me—ecstatic to be graduating, hot to zoom ahead with a job and real life and all. I swear to God, we really *were* good together at the start."

"I believe you, honey."

"So do I, sweetheart," Lydia said.

Becca cleared her throat and then said quietly, "I scheduled a D&C for next Wednesday. Six days from now."

The rain stopped. Just like that. The moon galloped around a cloud and was suddenly there, shining through the window like an innocent white beacon.

Susan found herself holding the sterling-backed hairbrush in midair, until Becca started talking again.

"Maybe you two think I *have* to tell Douglas. Like that I morally or ethically owe him to tell him. And maybe that's true, but I'm afraid he'll go to court to try and stop me—and he can probably do that, hold me up until it's past a safe time to do the procedure."

When neither Susan nor Lydia immediately responded, Becca rushed on. "You know what? This is so ironic it hurts. I just never thought I'd be in this position, because I always wanted babies so much. And I still do. But I'm telling you both, this is different. He's not the man I thought he was. He's not . . . stable. If I tried to keep the child, I'd never be able to completely escape from him. If I tried to give the baby up for adoption, he could adopt it himself. So whether you agree with me about this or not, I'm asking you both to let me alone. Respect that I'm an adult. Respect that I'm doing what I feel I absolutely have to do."

Susan could barely wait to get it out. "I love you, Rebecca. I don't give a damn about what's right or wrong. All I care about is you. And I'll be there for you, any way you want me."

Lydia pushed in, "Same here. I love you, baby. Whatever you do about anything, ever, I'm in your corner."

That made Becca start crying.

Then Lydia started crying.

Susan gathered them up, patting, hugging, holding. The blubbering accelerated. A group cuddle was awkward with Lydia's fragile back and everybody's bruises, and still they hugged, still they held. Susan felt her eyes well with tears that didn't fall, because obviously one of them had to stay strong; one of them had to still be standing so the others could cave in.

She could catch the faint scent of her mom's rose talc, the fruity shampoo her daughter liked, their skin—she could find the two of them in a crowd blindfolded by scents and textures alone. Hugging was good, the bonding was good.

But she couldn't stop worrying that her family was falling apart. No one was sure of anything anymore. All of them seemed to feel as if they were on a raft in a new ocean with no compass.

Maybe her most of all.

Wincing and grumbling, Lydia grated yet another potato into the bowl. The marmalade cat leaped onto the counter, obviously intent on getting closer to the food—any food. It was the last straw for Lyd.

She'd never used an f or s word until she was past fifty, but now she used them all as she scooped up the five-ton feline and dropped her out the back door. "You don't live here, remember? I don't know you. You don't have a name. I don't like cats. You don't like me. Now *go away*."

The cat hunched down on the back porch stoop and blinked sleepily, as if listening to such a tirade were completely beneath her dignity.

Lydia swore some more as she washed her hands and went back to the potato-grating chore. Actually, she was done grating. Now she had to squeeze the moisture out of the potato fragments and make a batter. If this wasn't stupid, she didn't know what was. Here she was, nine o'clock in the morning, making potato pancakes from scratch because the girls needed comfort food.

She plopped a dollop of butter on the griddle. It sizzled and spit. Exactly what she wanted to do.

It had taken years for her to own her life. For months now she'd loved her house, every frivolous daffodil inch of it. She'd taken up laziness, sloth, men. She'd quit cleaning and cooking.

And then the girls came home. Now her back hurt and her conscience hurt and she felt like she had to whisper when a man called. She was turning back into the wimp she used to be, just like that. She was totally disgusted with herself.

"Mom?" Susan sprinted barefoot into the room, followed immediately by Becca. "Holy kamoly, we could smell the pancakes from upstairs. I can't believe this! You should be in bed, with that back! Not doing something special for us!"

Hell, Lydia thought. Damned if her chest didn't swell with a warm fuzzy feeling just like it always had when the girls were happy. She kissed Susan, then Becca, sensing immediately that they were going to drive her crazy with their relentless helping. "Go sit down, go sit down. You know pancakes won't stay warm but a second. You have to be ready to eat when they come off the griddle—get your coffee and settle in."

"I'll do griddle duty," Susan said. "Then you can sit down—Becca, get Grandma a pillow for behind her back."

Susan tried to wrestle the spatula from her—as if she had any intention of giving up control after going to all this damned trouble. "You can wait on me hand and foot after breakfast, but right now . . . Becca, make your mother sit down and get out of my hair."

"Mom. Sit the hell down and get out of Gram's hair."

It was a stunning shock when Susan obeyed. Susan never obeyed. Susan had come out of the womb a perfectly angelic baby, but after that it was downhill. Anytime Susan got an idea in her head, nothing from an avalanche to a hurricane was going to budge her, so Lydia was completely unnerved when her daughter suddenly sat down and meekly started making small talk.

She started serving the potato pancakes, taking in the lavish praise, which was, after all, due her. The two gobbled the pancakes like vultures, which in the past when Lydia was into nurturing would have pleased her no end. She added a bowl of fresh sliced strawberries to the table, then made a second fresh pot of coffee with crushed eggshells, before finally deciding there was nothing else to do.

"I feel like a pampered princess," Susan groaned. "A pampered, spoiled, stuffed princess. That was beyond wonderful, Mom."

"Same here, Gram. Nothing tastes like your pancakes. They're so good it's like . . . like getting a shot of happiness, you know?"

"You sweeties." Lydia bussed Becca's forehead when she settled next to her with a hot mug.

"Feeling okay this morning?" Susan asked.

"A few aches and pains, but a thousand times better than last night."

"Good. Then tell me what's wrong."

Damnation. In the next life she wasn't having any daughters. Or if she was stuck having daughters, she was going to have dumb ones instead of perceptive ones. It was just like Susan to wait until she was all calmed down and then pounce. Lydia scowled across the table at the steady, soothing, stubborn look in her daughter's eyes.

So she pushed it out. "Last night is what's bothering me. Not all the trouble with Douglas, but afterward, what came out when we were talking. I feel that you two are blaming me."

"Blaming you?" Becca asked, looking confused. "Blaming you for what?"

Lydia explained with her hands. "I think you both blame me for your not having happier love lives. Because of how I was with your grandfather. You think I influenced how you felt about men. And it's just not fair."

"Mom, no one's blaming you."

She nodded vigorously. "I think you both are, because you both keep bringing up memories of how I tiptoed around your grandfather. I can't deny doing that, but I'm not tiptoeing now. And I never wanted either of you growing up believing that you had to kowtow to a man. Or suck up."

"Mom!"

"Look, I grew up in a different time for women. The toughest time for me was losing my mom, growing up with my dad always saying, 'I need you to be good or we can't make it.' But it was more than that. I grew up believing that it was a woman's job to hold a family together, a woman's responsibility to keep the men in the family happy. And whether that was true or not, I was raised to believe it."

Becca reached over and covered her hand. "Grandma, no one's mad at you. No one's blaming you for anything."

"Yeah, you are. You both are." She'd been happy for months now—or she'd talked herself into believing that. Only now, dadblast it, that illusion of finally owning her own life seemed fake because she could feel hot, guilty tears well in her eyes. "And maybe you should be. Becca, I almost had a stroke when you described your relationship with Douglas— how you kept trying to accommodate him the same way I did your grandfather. I lived unhappy until the day Harold died. But it's not because I wanted to. It's because I thought I had to."

Susan leaned forward, reaching for her hands, her eyes brimming with love. "Mom, we understand that."

"No, you don't, Susan. And neither do you, Becca. I wanted to be a good woman. I wanted to raise you to be a good woman. But thirty years ago, I thought that meant keeping a marriage together at all costs—that if I did that, I'd have won the grand prize. Only I stayed in my marriage, like a good woman—and there was no prize. Only a husband who came to feel anger and regret and the pain of lost chances because he never had the love he needed in his life. Maybe some of that was his fault, but a lot of it was mine. Times are different, and you two have to decide now what being good means. What being strong is all about. I was wrong, but tarnation, I've paid all the credit card bills for my mistakes, because believe me, they all came due. And I've been trying my damnedest to turn my life in new directions now."

"Mom. I love you so much. Please don't be upset." Again Susan tried to reach for her.

Again Lydia batted her hands away. "What kills me, what really kills me, is that all three of us—I think—are pretty darn great women. You two are so special. You could be anything. Do anything. So maybe all three of us got pregnant when we were too young, but I still don't get it. What keeps holding us back?"

Susan opened her mouth and then closed it. Becca said slowly, "I don't know, Gram. That's exactly what I've been trying to understand. What I do wrong. Not to beat myself up . . . but to figure out why I got messed up with someone like Douglas. So it won't happen again."

"Well, I'll tell you what I think." Her darned hands were trembling. You'd think she was ninety instead of an extremely youthful fifty-seven, but she'd always hated with a passion any kind of confrontation. "I think none of us have actually sat down and figured out what we want. You identify what makes you happy, what you need, and that's half the job. Suze, Bec, neither of you have done that. I haven't done that. How the hell do you hit a home run if you never step up to the bat and swing? You girls—you think about that!"

She stalked toward the back door and pushed. The door wouldn't open and wouldn't open—eventually she realized that the marmalade cat was leaning her full pudgy weight against the screen and was determined not to budge. Throwing up her hands, she stalked past the girls toward the dining room and out the front door.

She didn't want to walk away—she'd walked away from too much in her life—but she needed a few minutes to get a grip.

Truth to tell, her new life wasn't working out quite as well as she'd been trying to sell herself. The yellow was. She just might keep the whole house yellow for the rest of her life. And she liked living alone on her own terms. And then there were the orgasms—no one was going to make her believe that a woman had to settle without those, ever again.

But trying to sleep with both George and Riff had given her conscience an ulcer and her heart a terrible sense of sadness. She'd been lonely in her marriage, so how could she have guessed that trying her best not to care would make her even lonelier?

Still, she'd been doing just fine—until she started seeing how lonely her own daughter was. And then last night she'd had a near heart attack realizing that her own granddaughter had come petrifyingly close to repeating her own history—seeking a man who was safe, instead of a man she could love. Years ago, she should have told Becca that safe men were almost never safe. And she should have told Susan that hiding from risk only trapped you in your own loneliness.

But she'd said all she could manage for right now. Cripes. Her hands were shaking and her nerves were in shreds. It sure took it out of a woman to be tough, after fifty years of cultivating her soft side.

She strode out to the rose garden, determined to cultivate something she knew something about. Her roses.

Susan wedged her Avalon into a tight squeeze on Cherry Street and quickly climbed out. She'd promised to see Jon this morning—to fill in the holes, on what had happened with Douglas and how Becca was. And that was her plan. Just not quite yet.

She was nervous about seeing Jon again—nervous enough to feel as if she were strapped in a cockpit on a plane she had no idea how to fly. The doors were closed. The engines fired up. And there was no other pilot in sight but her.

She needed to have a conclusive risk-all discussion with Jon . . . but there was something else she had to do first.

The blowup at breakfast was still preying on her mind. Her mom had sounded so rattled and upset. Becca was just as depressed. When the Sinclair women were in trouble, Susan had always been the assigned picker-upper in the family, which meant that a shopping jaunt was required. Lyd and Bec needed some loot. Girl loot. Specifically girl loot that was indulgent and personal and useless. And no, stuff like that wasn't going to solve a damn thing, but Susan had to do something to lift everyone's spirits.

She hiked past a cluster of art studios, past Moira's Muffins, heading toward a nest of boutiques—but then hesitated and thoughtfully backed up. Pushing open the glass door to Moira's, she was immediately assaulted with the aphrodisiac scents of sugars and fruit pies and sinfully cholesterol-packed confections. Behind the counter, Moira O'Brien—who'd looked matronly and plump in high school and hadn't aged a day—welcomed her with a round smile.

"Susan Sinclair! Even with those dark glasses on, I'd recognize you anywhere! How great to see you! What can I get you?"

She picked out two happy-face cookies and a pair of napoleons, while Moira talked nonstop. "We've always been so proud of you. The girl who made it out of here. Really made it out. Really, really made something of her life."

"You've done terrific yourself." Susan motioned around the bakery.

"Yeah, the bakery. I'm proud of it. Doing real good. But it's still not the same as a glamorous job like yours."

A shiver chased up her spine when she headed back out, even though the morning was turning picnic-warm. Thankfully the sun gave her a natural excuse to wear dark glasses, because this morning her bruised eye looked like a tie-dyed paisley design in purples and greens.

She ignored the hardware and a shoe store, but then crossed the street to pop into Val's Drugs. The pharmacy had had a recent face-lift, but the real faces hadn't changed. She knew Pete Keller, the pharmacist, and Webster Fisherman at the photography counter and Jane what's-her-name at the checkout. She'd been to school with all of them. After hunkering and stewing at the cosmetics counter, she bought a mud face mask, foot massage cream and then six ounces of Beautiful for her daughter and six ounces of Shalimar for her mom.

Every aisle she walked down, it was, "Well, if it isn't Susan Sinclair!" Followed by some comment on how cool her red and navy outfit was, followed by wistful comments about how great her big-city job sounded.

By the time she left the pharmacy, she had the hiccups. It was hardly the first time she'd strolled these streets. She expected the hi's and the nosy questions and the chance to catch up, but somehow she hadn't noticed before how many people made a point of commenting about her "big-city job."

She popped in a jewelry store called Bab's. The place was new, the owner an outsider, an artsy-craftsy woman who looked like a stick figure with scarves. Becca loved jewelry, but it had to be natural-looking, nothing glitzy. She found a cheerful pendant and clunky bracelet, then searched for something that her mother would like.

Once upon a time Lydia had only worn a wedding ring and occasional pearls. Susan scoured the ring counter and came up with an amber ring—expensive, but it was precisely the kind of frivolous bauble her mom would never have looked at before—and it was almost yellow.

Juggling packages—so many they were starting to shift and slip—she decided she'd done enough of the shopping marathon thing . . . but then she ambled past Roger's Buds and Blossoms. Susan wasn't into plants, but Lydia and Becca sure were.

The place was warm and humid and fragrant. Any other time, dawdling through the nursery would have been pleasant enough, but Susan was already overwarm from all the carrying and hustling around. And then Roger tracked her down before she was halfway through the nursery. Roger Short had been two years behind her in school, but he had the same moony eyes and same saggy butt and same way of talking with a little drool. "Susan Sinclair! The only woman I've ever loved!"

"Roger Short! The only man I can count on to

come up with some new rose root stock for my mother!"

"Well, yeah. But I'd rather talk about love than roses." So he said, but he was already leading her into his private greenhouse—which was hotter than a Brazilian rain forest and choking-humid.

"I'd tell you how much I loved you, but I don't want to poach on Juney's territory." Mentioning his wife brought Roger around. Ten minutes later, she decided all that ghastly humidity was worth it. She spent a near fortune on a scrawny-looking thing that Roger claimed was a fabulous hybrid tea rose named "Honor" that was a sugary white with a tinge of pale yellow. For Becca, she picked out a lavender plant, after which she could no longer walk, breathe or move without dropping something . . . and unfortunately, Roger still wanted to chitchat.

"Juney wouldn't mind my having an affair with you."

"Oh, yeah? You're sure of that?"

"Some women, she'd claw their eyes out. But not you. She always thought the world of you. The Girl Most Likely to Succeed."

Eventually she managed to escape. Outside, she scrambled to juggle the plants and her purse and the jewelry and the odd-shaped package from the drugstore and the box from the bakery. God knows how she was going to make it to her car, much less all the way to Jon's—at least **without** everything crashing on the sidewalk.

Instead of charging for the car to avoid the potential debacle, though, she found herself stopped dead in front of a green WALK light.

Until Roger mentioned it, she'd forgotten all about that Girl Most Likely to Succeed tag from high school. Now it clung in her mind like an inkstain. God, how she'd wanted to be successful. How she'd wanted a career and independence and to Be Somebody. How she'd been afraid of letting her family and friends and the community down if she didn't live up to their expectations.

Sun blazed in her eyes. Pedestrians pushed past her. Her arms ached from the weight and imbalance of the packages, but still she didn't move.

The Girl Most Likely to Succeed seemed to have a job that was tearing her apart—and her mother's lecture from that morning now came back to haunt her. *What do you want?* Lydia had demanded from both her and Becca. Implying that she, Lydia, had never sat down and figured out what she wanted in her life. Implying that Susan hadn't, either.

And suddenly Susan couldn't seem to breathe. She had to see Jon this morning. She had to deal with her job. She had to find a way to help both her daughter and her mother.

But Lydia was right—what *she* wanted and needed from her life never seemed to get on the agenda list. And before going a step farther, for sure before seeing Jon, Susan thought she'd damn well better figure it out. Because the Girl Most Likely to

Succeed had become a woman not succeeding in anything right now.

A woman who felt lost ... maybe because she *was* lost.

Just maybe she'd been lost for a long time.

Chapter 14

Because Jon knew Susan was stopping by that morning, his intention was to lock himself in the office. Theoretically it was a way of killing two birds with one stone—he'd be clean when Susan got there, and something would get done with the mountain of paperwork on his desk. Reality was different. No guy could be expected to sit behind a desk forever, and when the badly listing cruiser was towed in, Jon shot outside faster than a prisoner on parole.

The maintenance bays were located at the far back of the marina, and thankfully that morning there was an open bay for the crippled boat. Five people tried to tell him the story at the same time. Apparently a teenage hotsy-totsy cigar boat had rammed into a big old grandfather-aged cabin cruiser. The damage was visibly bad, but Jon wasn't sure how bad until the boat was hoisted up.

Man. The kids were damn lucky their cigar boat hadn't sunk—even luckier to just plain be alive—but the old darling's dignity hadn't fared so well. The gaping hole at the waterline was as painful as the one in the owners' hearts.

"How much will it cost us to repair, Mr. Laker?" The white-haired gentleman had a hound's jowls and kindly blue eyes.

"I can't give you a detailed estimate this fast, but from the look of this . . . well, sir, there's good news and bad news."

"Tell us both." The missus' hair was as white and thin as her husband's. She even had the same soft blue eyes.

"The good news is, it can be fixed. But I'm afraid the amount will give me a heart attack even if it doesn't you." He bent under the boat, talking, showing, explaining. "I'm afraid there's no shortcut way to do this. There's a ton of structural damage. If you want her back in the water, it's going to cost a bundle."

The couple looked at each other. "We'll never get that kind of investment back out of it, will we?" the gentleman asked.

Jon shook his head. "I think you'd be better off scrapping it and starting over with a new boat. No matter what insurance is willing to give you on the repairs, she's got a lot of age on her. There's a point where you'd be throwing good money after bad."

The missus' bottom lip wanted to tremble. "We've thought about turning her in and buying new a dozen times. But she's like family. She saw all our kids grown. Then our grandkids. We never wanted to put her out to pasture."

"I wouldn't, either. She's beautiful." Well, truthfully she wasn't—she was pretty much just an old, worn-out boat who'd never had that much style or value to start with, but Jon wasn't about to knock their heirloom. Hell, he'd have cried with them if it would have made them feel any better. "I think . . ."

Abruptly he saw a cinnamon head catch the sunlight from the far marina door. His pulse bucked like a frisky colt's. To the couple he said, "You two spend some time thinking over what you want to do, okay? No rush. The only thing I have to know within a day or two is where you want her towed from here."

The instant the couple released him, he strode toward Susan. They met halfway, where the sun was toasting the asphalt. Typically the yard was busier than a beehive, with forklifts chugging around unwieldy storage racks, hoists moving boats in and out of the water, trucks and boats on trailers trying to dodge everybody else. He only saw her.

He'd worried about her last night, all night—and after that fight with Douglas, she should have looked vulnerable and emotionally beat up. Instead, her stride was determined, her cheeks charged with color. She was wearing white slacks with a teensy navy stripe, a navy jersey, straps of red on her feet and dots of red in her ears. She could be in some women's magazine for an ad on the perfect, ideal, beautiful woman. All put together. All contained.

He'd known she couldn't get here earlier than midmorning, but he felt as if he'd been waiting since predawn. He came close enough for his shadow to touch hers, but that wasn't near enough, so he swooped down to touch the real thing.

Her lips molded under his before she could register an "Ooomph"—assuming that was the start of a protest. His tongue found hers, the rascal stealing a little taste, then going back for a deeper, darker sample.

She may not have expected to start their encounter with a belly-dropping, heart-heating kiss, but Jon figured if she was all that furious, she wouldn't have surged up on tiptoe to kiss him back. Naturally, though, he had to call a halt. A busy, sun-baking tarmac was no place to seduce a lady. It just seemed a good place to let her know the gloves were off.

He wanted her. And he wasn't willing to go back to that just-pals bullshit, ever again.

For just then, though, he figured they'd better get back on some kind of even keel or he was going to risk a heart attack. Trying for a lighter tone, he pulled off her sunglasses and squinted at her shiner. "Well, the swelling's down. It's not as showy as yesterday. But damn, it's still worth a photograph."

She opened her mouth, then closed it, a bit like a fish gulping in air. Then said, "You come near me with a camera, you die."

"Well, hey, you're the one who's supposed to be cool with fashion and style and all, but I'm thinking, maybe you should color-coordinate with purple and green for a few days."

"Watch it, Laker. You're cruisin' for a bruisin'."

The old line came from their teenage teasing

years, so she couldn't have been too mad at him about that possessive, bossy kiss. On the other hand, there was a carefulness in her eyes. High color in her cheeks. A real smile. But still, an unquestionable wariness.

He didn't know what that meant, but it worried him.

Marnie laid a palm on the forklift horn, loudly announcing to the world that they were in his way. Jon steered her inside the shop, then gave himself another minute by hiking over to the sink. He smeared some goop on his hands, wiped it off with a cloth, then went for the real soap and water. Although the pull-up doors were open, the shop was still dipped in shade. Cool. Private—for at least two minutes at a time, anyway. "So, did the three of you survive last night?"

"To a point, yes. My mom's back is better, but emotionally she seems really rattled. And Becca . . ."

"Yeah. Where's the jerk?"

"As far as I know, Douglas is back in K'zoo. But Bec keeps leaking little bits of information, Jon. Enough to make me think their relationship was far worse than she ever let on."

He tossed a paper towel in the trash. "Okay. That's settled, then. I'm killing him."

Susan rolled her eyes. "Murder won't help. I only wish. Seriously, though—I do think there's something you could really help her with."

"What?" Truthfully, he didn't care what. Any

course of action was better than standing still and not being able to get his daughter out of this mess.

Susan slugged her hands in her back pockets. "She's still planning to teach in the fall again in Kalamazoo. And she doesn't have an apartment arranged for yet, but she'd still like to move all her things from the place she's got with Douglas. True, her stuff can sit there for a bit since it's paid for, as far as rent goes. But it would sever the tie with him completely."

"Yeah, I agree. Although I don't like the idea of her moving anything if it means her facing Douglas alone."

"I feel the same way. In fact, that's what I hoped you'd say—that you'd either help move her things, or go with her, or, for a third choice, that you and I could do the moving for her. No matter what, though, I don't want her alone with Douglas if there's any other way."

His mind was already wheeling down the mechanical list of options. "I could rent one of those storage sheds so all her furniture could be stashed in Kalamazoo. Makes more sense than to move everything up here, then move it all back at the end of the summer. Free up her time to just concentrate on finding another place."

"Yeah, that sounds like a good plan." Susan added, "I'll go with you."

Jon blinked. "You?"

"Don't look so surprised. Obviously you can't move everything by yourself." When he didn't immediately reply, she said quickly, "Come on, Jon, there's no possible way one person could handle all the lifting and moving on their own."

He couldn't believe she was offering. "Well, yeah, I assumed I'd take one of the employees with me. Somebody with some shoulder muscle."

"But then you'd have two people missing here at the marina at your busiest time. If I go, I can pack up her breakables and girl stuff, things she wouldn't be comfortable with a man handling. And the heaviest thing she has is a futon bed. Even I can help lift things like that."

He considered himself a basically intelligent man, but sometimes a guy had to have the little words spelled out to make dead sure he got it. "You actually want to do this with me?"

"Yup," she said. "So, is it settled?"

"Except for pinning down a time. I assume you want to do this as soon as possible."

"Yeah. In fact, tomorrow, if there's any chance you could free up your schedule that fast. I realize there's no fire. It's just so . . . upsetting. I'd like her things out of there and away from Douglas as soon as we possibly can."

"I agree. And I'll find a way to do it tomorrow."

A blink later, she turned around to leave—which was a good thing, because phones were ringing and horns blaring, people coming and going all over the place and the sun was starting to beat down hotter than a temper.

Still, he watched her hustle toward her car, try-ing to analyze why he felt poleaxed. Something had changed in her attitude since the night before. It was a worrisome something. She had this look, as if she'd plugged into a fresh battery. There was some pure female hell in the sashay of her hips. Danger in the way she tossed her head to whip the bangs out of her eyes. Devil in the way she backed out of the parking space, expecting—and getting—traffic to part like a willing Red Sea in her wake.

He wanted change. He wanted her to see him as a lover and mate in her life, not just as Becca's father. But she was behaving so . . . differently. Jon liked the kind of change that he was in charge of. Instead, he had a feeling somebody had lit a fire in his living room and somehow he couldn't see it.

The next day started out even more confounding. A phone call had set up all the details. He picked her up at daybreak. They'd both agreed that an early start was necessary, because it was an eight-hour round-trip drive to Kalamazoo and back, not counting all the moving time. Both wanted to be back in Traverse rather than spend the night if they could help it. Susan had Becca's apartment key and a list of her belongings. Jon had telephoned Douglas the night before to tell him they were picking up Becca's things—Douglas had responded with complete silence. Jon was prepared for, even expecting, trouble from the jerk.

But not from Suze.

She popped out of the house and climbed in his truck, looking like a hundred and ten percent of trouble. It wasn't anything he could pin down, exactly. Her clothes were predictable enough. Susan's version of grunge started with pristine white tennies, white jeans—without a belt, imagine!—and then a short-sleeved MSU sweatshirt. She carried a cell phone, a purse, a legal pad of lists, and two thermoses of coffee.

"You made me coffee?" he asked.

"Don't you want some?"

He'd kill for coffee. That wasn't the point. The point was that she'd gone to the trouble of bringing a thermos for him. And that she smiled at him. Not a polite hello-good-morning smile. But a Jon-I'm-glad-we're-doing-this-together smile. A smile with energy to it. A smile with personal feeling in it. A smile with sex in it.

A smile that not only didn't make sense, but no man could be prepared to cope with before daybreak.

"Would you like me to drive?"

Obviously she'd forgotten who she was talking to. "If I break my leg, you'll be welcome to drive," he said, which seemed more tactful than answering, *Over my dead body*.

She chuckled, as if he'd said something amusing, and then settled on her side of the truck with her almond mocha cappuccino. She didn't talk. *Really* didn't talk. God knows he bit off anyone's head who tried to talk with him before nine A.M., but for Susan to be quiet this long was like expecting Santa Claus to be real.

Something had to be on her mind. Some secret. The same secret something that gave her that inner, worrisome glow.

The sun seeped over the horizon and pinked up the sky. By the time they'd finished sipping coffee, a watercolor landscape had turned into a bright, sharp day.

And that was the end of the peace and quiet. Their cell phones started ringing—first his, then hers. The first call was from April. April was some kind of Laker relative, but the relationship was one of those new nuclear family relationships that no one could figure out—like his dad's sister's ex-husband's stepbrother's daughter. Whatever, the kid had needed a job for the summer, so Jon had given her one. After discovering she was a total dingbat, he'd revised her responsibilities to include whatever could cause the least harm—like dusting stock—but somehow she'd gotten into the spread-sheet on his computer.

"I know you can handle it, April. In fact, you've done such a terrific job this summer that I'm going to give you a bonus before you start school. But I want you to carefully exit the program and turn off the computer for me, okay? . . . I know you can, I know you can, but . . ."

When he finished that call, Suze was leaning her head back, eyes closed, smiling.

"What's so funny?" he demanded.

"Nothing. I can just see that you're meaner than ever."

Naturally, he was offended. "I *am* mean. But I'm hardly going to beat up on a kid, for Pete's sake."

Again she smiled. "I'll bet you've never fired a kid as long as you've owned the place. In fact, I'll bet—ten bucks—that you wouldn't fire a kid even if you caught them stealing."

He'd have defended himself against this totally unjustified accusation, except that her cell phone rang then. It was Bec, who'd apparently just woken up and started thinking. She was upset that they were moving her stuff. She was an adult and didn't need parents to rescue her anymore. She felt guilty that she hadn't come, that she wasn't doing the work herself.

"You're so silly," Susan said into the phone. "You're the one rescuing me, not the other way around. You'll get stuck making all that cherry jam with Grandma. I'd rather sleep with a porcupine than make jam. You're doing me a favor by letting me do this packing stuff for you. And your dad was whipped from work. He needed the break, too."

When she finished that call, Jon couldn't help but smile.

"What?" she demanded.

"Nothing. I'm just betting you and Bec had that conversation five times over already. And you always come up with stuff when you're talking to her. Stuff that makes her feel better."

The cell phones kept ringing. Marnie called from the shop with an estimate question. Then Jon's father called, not for any reason, just because they traditionally checked in with each other once a week. After that, Susan's cell phone rang.

Jon didn't start out listening—or at least he never meant to. He realized quickly into the call that she had to be talking to Sebastian, her primary boss at L'Amour. When he picked up the content of the conversation, though, he was almost stunned enough to slam on the brakes.

Initially Susan answered some questions about numbers and orders and business details like that. It was after that the conversation took a roller-coaster spin.

Susan suddenly touched two fingers to her temples, obviously troubled by something, and then she said quietly, firmly, "Sebastian, I never wanted to do this over the phone, but hearing you make all these plans . . . I was going to drive in at the end of this week to talk with you. I have to quit. And these last three weeks I'd appreciate your considering as three weeks' notice."

That was when Jon almost jammed on the brakes. Susan's head was turned toward the passenger window, the cell phone pressed to her right ear, as if she were hoping he couldn't hear the conversation. She listened to her boss for a while, then swallowed hard.

"You've been great to me. You already know that. But I have to do this, Sebastian. I'll come in, help with whatever I can help you with, set up, train a new person, whatever would work best for you and L'Amour. . . ."

Another hesitation. More swallows on Susan's part. By then the morning sun was pouring in the passenger window, bathing her skin in soft morning light, but she was paling as if she had a fever.

She plucked at an earring, tried to twist against the window, then twist back.

"No, no, it has nothing to do with money. I've been thrilled with the work all these years, and . . . no, I don't want to be vice president, you dolt. It's nothing like that. You've been so wonderful to me that I can't say enough. But I have to have a change."

More silence. More listening. Susan's eyes squeezed closed, then stared blindly into the sun. "I don't blame you for being angry, but no, I won't reconsider. This is an absolute for sure. Let's talk in a few days, all right? Give yourself time to think about how you want this done. If you want my help, or if you want me to just come in and clean out my office . . . obviously I want to fill you in on some ongoing projects . . ."

When she punched off the cell phone, she said nothing. Just pocketed the telephone and then leaned back with her eyes closed.

Jon figured that he could easily have misinterpreted the conversation because of only hearing her side of it. But one way or another, if Suze thought she was getting away with silence after that tornado news, she was out of her tree.

"So," he said finally, "do we have two apartments that need closing up now? Two apartments that need furniture moved and put in storage? In two different cities, yet?"

She made a small sound, a laugh, but she obviously had to work at it. "It'd seem so. Sheesh. I'm probably not going to make any sense for a few minutes. My mind seems to be running a thousand miles an hour."

"Did I misunderstand? You really just quit your job? I know you talked about it—but I didn't think you'd really do it, Suze."

"Hells bells. Neither did I." She rubbed her face. "Damn. I wanted to quit. I needed to quit. I've been trying to find the courage to quit. But I still had no idea that was going to come out of my mouth until I actually said it. And now I'm wondering if I'm out of my mind. It's not as if I have another job lined up, or like I have a clue what to do with my condo in Detroit, or really considered my whole financial situation."

The Susan he knew would never have quit on an impulsive moment like that. But then, the Susan he knew could never have smiled when her life was suddenly swiveled upside down.

"It feels good?" he asked.

"I realize it sounds certifiable, but yes. It *does* feel good."

He didn't have the right to pry, but damned if he could keep his mouth completely shut. "I'm glad you got away from that guy on the West Coast."

Susan immediately turned toward him. He couldn't really see her expression because he had to concentrate on driving: A hot-rod kid in a souped-up Camero was zooming in and out of lanes.

"I should never have told you about Brian Weis." She tugged at her earring. "He wasn't the real problem, Jon. I thought he was, but the truth is that his scaring me was the best thing that's happened to me in a long time. It made me do some fresh thinking. Some uncomfortable thinking, about who I am and what I want. And as much as I loved the job all these years, I also paid a lot of prices for it. Personal prices. I ran whenever Sebastian called. I gave up weekends, holidays, worked hundreds of nights. I thought it was because I loved it and because I was making good money."

"I thought you did love it. And that you were happy with the money."

Susan shook her head. "I liked the money just fine . . . but mostly I thought the job would make me feel *successful*. I chose a career route to be safe. Because I wanted a feeling of safety and security in my life."

"And the job didn't give you that?"

"No job is going to give me that. I just didn't realize that until recently." Susan fell silent again, and then shook her head with a wry expression. "You're the one who finally made me see that, Jon."

"*Me?* You never talked to me about this stuff before."

Again she looked at him, her voice turning pensive and quiet. "It's funny, but when we were kids together . . . you were the only person in my life who made me feel safe. Yet I ran from you. And now you seem to be the only person in my life who makes me feel dangerous. Reckless. Yet it was only when I was a kid that I was so scared. Go figure."

"Um . . . I'm not sure why you're telling me this, Suze." The country had gone flat, the road an asphalt bridge between endless farm fields. The wildest surprises on the horizon were an occasional barn or silo. At this tedious point in the drive, though, Jon knew they were only a puddle jump from the connection to I-94 and then Kalamazoo . . . and right when he wanted to talk with Susan most.

"I'm telling you . . . because there's a certain level of honesty that's always, always seemed right with you. I always trusted you the way I trusted no one else. Which is something else I didn't realize until recently." She sighed. "It would be so much easier if we were divorced."

He blinked. "Huh?"

She motioned with her hands. "It'd have been so much easier if we'd done it like everyone else—gotten married too young, screwed up, got divorced. Everyone gets divorced these days. People know how to behave if they're divorced. You treat your ex with sarcasm and bitterness. You snap at each other. You bring up old wounds at every opportunity. You talk behind each other's backs."

"Uh, Suze, that would be easier how?" he asked delicately, rather than imply she sounded completely off her rocker.

"Isn't it obvious?"

"Uh, no. Not to me."

"Don't you feel it? Because we were never married and divorced, we've always been stuck in this no-man's-land. We were never enemies—but we were never family together, either. We slept together—but we never really had a chance to be lovers or mates. And I trust you—even though there's no way I can think of you as just a friend. That's what I'm saying. That who we are together is confusing. There's history between us because of Becca, but no clear lines. No rule book for what to *do* with each other."

Well, hell. She'd been talking good stuff with him. Heart stuff. Real stuff. But he was starting to get an uneasy churning in his gut that Susan volunteered for this trip for entirely different reasons than to share the workload of moving Becca's things. And that would be fine, if he could just get a written guarantee that she was talking about belonging together.

But even feeling wary of where she was leading, Jon couldn't let that last comment of hers fly free. "Didn't seem we needed a rule book to know exactly what to *do* with each other a few nights ago."

As he turned on I-94, a half dozen semi tractor-trailers appeared on his tail, again demanding his attention . . . but again, he felt Susan's gaze on his face, studying, assessing. Finally she said, "We've been lovers before. But always . . . accidentally."

"Yeah . . . so?" Her voice was as gentle as a summer breeze, as warm as softness, but he sensed a catch. The way a man can always sense when a woman is going to blast him from here to the Rockies.

"I never thought it was exactly . . . wrong . . . that

we were occasionally lovers. But all these years, I kept thinking we'd quit doing that. Quit falling into bed together. There just seems no purpose when you don't love me."

Fifty cars and semis behind him, all pushing eighty-plus, and he damn near swerved out of his lane. "Say *what*? How in hell did you ever come up with that conclusion? What makes you think I don't love you?"

"Because you don't," she said calmly. "You never did. And at this point, I'm about positive you never will."

"Susan—"

"It's all right, Jon. I accepted it a long time ago. I didn't bring it up to make you feel bad."

"Susan—"

"I was just trying to explain why our relationship has always been so confusing to me. I trust you. I respect your judgment. I value your instincts and your integrity. There are things I can discuss with you that I never tell anyone else. I've slept with you, casually, with no purpose or future in it—which I've never done with anyone else. It just sometimes strikes me as completely bananas—I mean, are we going to be like this when we're sixty-five? Eighty-five? Popping in bed together from time to time?"

Obviously he had to raise his voice because there was no other possible way he could get a word in. "Susan, you have this so backwards that I can't believe it. I'm the one who always loved *you*. You're the one who didn't love *me*."

Her eyebrows arched in surprise for a millisecond, and then she laughed.

Laughed.

The damn woman had things so mixed up that she apparently thought he was joking.

Chapter 15

Susan sank back on her heels, rolling her shoulders to shake out the kinks. Unfortunately, her muscles showed no inclination to dekink. God knows how she'd talked herself into believing this trip would give her some time alone with Jon.

Moving didn't involve alone time. Moving involved bending and twisting and using muscles nobody ever used—or ever wanted to use. For ages now, those muscles had been whining like spoiled prima donnas that they wanted some aspirin, some food, a drink and a nap.

She glanced at her watch. It was already four in the afternoon. Choking-hot sun poured through the tiny bathroom window of Becca's Kalamazoo apartment, and the humidity was heavy. This was a day to spend in a pool, sipping a long, tall drink, not a day to be stuck at the bathroom sink cupboard, prying into your grown daughter's private stuff— the kind of stuff daughters never told their mothers about. The kind of stuff moms were never supposed to know about.

Susan didn't give a holy damn about the K-Y

jelly or the thong bikinis. If she'd found some massage oil or a tape of Ravel's *Bolero* or a pair of toy handcuffs, it wouldn't have bothered her. Or Susan told herself it wouldn't have bothered her. Her daughter was warm and passionate, an emotional lover from the get-go, and she was of an adult age where life finally started to get really interesting—particularly if you were lucky enough to be with a man you trusted.

So far Susan hadn't found anything of an experimental nature, but the medicines were breaking her heart. Becca had one whole shelf devoted to Tums and Maalox, Mylanta and Rolaids—and every other antacid on the market. There was an old prescription for hives. Another more recent prescription for a sleep aid. Susan kept finding things that indicated her loving, giving, laissez-faire, openhearted daughter had been terribly unhappy. Making-herself-sick unhappy. Over-her-head unhappy. And all the while, Douglas kept up a running litany of protests.

"Look, I'm just saying, the couch is mine. If Becca said otherwise, it isn't true. We bought it together, and then afterwards I paid her for her half."

"Uh-huh." It wasn't the first time in the last hour Douglas had decided to interrupt her. But this time, the minute she heard his voice, she dove promptly back into the cupboard. The theory worked for turtles, but it didn't seem to work so well for her. He kept talking.

"And the bed. She gave me the bed. I didn't buy that. She just said she never really liked it and I could have it. Same with the stereo. She said it was, like, getting really dated and there was better stuff out there now."

"Uh-huh."

"If she were here, she'd tell you that."

"So you've claimed, Douglas. Several times." Susan finished filling up one box, then zoomed back in the cave of a cupboard for more. What was it with women? Three cleansers, four shampoos, two conditioners, razors, seventeen lipsticks, three deodorants, perfumes, an entire product range of body lotions, Tampax, six mascaras, cotton balls . . . was it possible that junk-collecting was hereditary? Because the only bathroom that could compete with this much girl stuff was either Lydia's—or hers.

She wanted to smile, but truth to tell, a feeling of heartsickness was stalking her mood. She assumed she'd be able to finish that conversation with Jon, but there just hadn't been time. She knew he'd been unsettled, unprepared for her to throw down that gauntlet—about his never loving her. But wherever they went from here, Susan just couldn't see hiding from the truth. They'd been there, done that, bought the bumper sticker. It didn't work, never had. Not for them, and not for their daughter.

Behind her, a booted foot shifted in the doorway—reminding Susan precisely of what hiding from certain honest trusts had caused Becca. In the closed space of a bathroom with this much heat and humidity, she could smell Douglas's sweat. Hells bells, he could probably smell hers.

"I'm not going to sue for the other night. I could, you know. You can't just go around attacking people. We're talking cut-and-dried assault. I could press charges—but as long as I get the bed and couch and all, I don't want to cause any trouble. We'll just call everybody square."

"That's real nice of you, Douglas." Susan told herself, for the half dozenth time, that she was not going to climb to her feet and punch him. Every time he opened his mouth, though, the prospect became more unbearably tempting.

"And another thing. Like we said. The rent's paid up for another full month. I have no reason to move or to want to move. But if Becca's leaving and taking away all her stuff, then as far as I'm concerned, who lives here is my business. It's not hers after this."

Susan mentally counted to ten. Jon would be back shortly. She wouldn't have to hold on to her temper much longer. But Jon, of course, had no idea Douglas was here, so it wasn't as if he realized she needed him to hustle.

She emptied the last of Becca's toiletries in a third box, then stood up and attempted to move past Douglas toward the bedroom. "I'm going in the bedroom to deal with her clothes now—unless you have a problem with that. Do you have some claim on her jeans and underpants, too?"

"I suppose you think that's funny."

Actually, she didn't think anything about today was turning out even remotely funny. She glanced out the living room window, hoping to see Jon or Jon's truck, but there was no sign of either.

They'd reached the outskirts of Kalamazoo by late morning. Becca had naturally chosen a reasonably priced apartment near the school where she'd been teaching. The front was a fake Tudor, the grounds tidily mowed. Her place was on the second floor, with a kitchen barely big enough to turn around in, a claustrophobic living room, two bedrooms and a bath. The same starter apartment probably reproduced in all fifty states. What gave the place personality were the possessions.

When they'd first walked in, Susan had noticed the same things Jon had. Becca's possessions were no longer in sight. Beer cans decorated the coffee table. Huge, stark black and white prints dominated the walls. Trash was heaped by the door. Someone had attempted to cover a dent in the living room wall with a poster hung too low.

Jon, of course, hadn't seen Becca's personal supply of antacids, or the books she'd hidden in drawers rather than put out on shelves. All Bec's collection of folk art and stencils had been stashed behind coats in the living room closet. There was a black comforter on the bed instead of Becca's colorful quilt, and the sheets looked and smelled unwashed.

Susan swallowed another lump and started taking down hangers. She really didn't want to look at that bed. She also suspected that the instant Jon returned, Douglas would disappear like magic.

God knows the boy had originally shown up like magic. No one was around when they first turned the key and walked in. For several hours they'd dived in and started sorting and packing, but then

Jon left—both to get more boxes and to arrange for the rental of a storage facility.

Naturally, the instant Jon's truck turned the corner, Douglas had shown up—making it obvious that he'd been watching from somewhere close by. It was even more obvious that he hoped not to have to deal with Jon—but had big hopes of intimidating her.

He hadn't lifted a finger to help her—not that Susan expected help. But his attempt to bully and intimidate made her sick, not for herself but for her daughter's sake.

She'd held it together, but she could feel her eyes starting to sting. Tears were sneaking up on her like snipers. She loved Becca so much. So how could she possibly have done such a terrible job of raising her? That her daughter could be taken in by a jerk like this?

"Hey." Bad news had apparently stayed away as long as he could stand it, because suddenly he showed up in the bedroom doorway. "Those tennis rackets are mine. So is that backpack."

Oh, man. If he'd just given her a few more minutes' breathing space, she knew she could have kept it together. As it was, that last comment turned in her stomach like bad meat. She shot to her feet.

"Douglas, you are without question a very, very cute boy. Darling smile." Her finger advanced on him. "Bedroom eyes. Cute little butt." Her finger started wagging closer to his face. "I can easily see what my daughter first saw in you, but I'm a lot older than Becca—and if you think for one second that I've been taken in by your bullshit, you need to get an IQ. Did you think we'd be so stupid as to come here without being prepared? I know exactly what belongs to my daughter. I have a list. I have receipts. I have credit card and check records."

"Yeah, well, that doesn't count for the stuff Becca gave me. Or wanted me to have. See, if she were just here—"

"She isn't here. I'm here. And if you want to have me arrested for assault, believe me, I'll give you a lot better reason than I did the other night. You little piece of dill weed, I'd like to shove your head right down your esophagus—"

"Hey. *Hey*. Like, chill. Where'd all this temper come from?"

"Temper?" She poked him with the forefinger this time. Making him back up. "I don't have a temper. I've never had a temper. My whole life, I've never had the guts to come through with a temper." He backed up as far as the bedroom wall. "You ask anyone, I'm milk toast. But if I ever catch you within miles of my daughter again—"

"Now, Susan." Jon parked a dolly cart just inside the door. The sound of his voice made Susan whirl around and Douglas's head jerk up. Douglas, though, went pale as a sheet.

God knows why. Jon's voice was as cheerful as a summer breeze. "If I were you, Douglas, I wouldn't say another word to Ms. Sinclair. Not if you value your throat. And you might make a note for the future that it's really not a good idea to pick on someone who's so much bigger than you are. You might be over six foot, son, but you are one small human being."

"Jon, I—"

"Now, Suze. You've been working nonstop in this heat. I brought some ice and pop. It's in the kitchen. You don't mind if I have a couple minutes alone with Douglas, do you?"

The question was obviously rhetorical, since he'd already strode in the room and come between her and Douglas. He was still smiling at the boy, but he was also rolling up his sleeves.

Susan took off.

"No, no, everything went fine, Becca. Not to worry." With the motel phone pressed in his ear, Jon pushed off his shoes. "The moving just took us longer than we planned. Your mother is beat. I thought we could manage driving home after dinner—I really need to be back at the marina early tomorrow—but your mom's just too tired to keep going another four, five hours, so we hit a motel. If we crash now, we can get an early start tomorrow, be in Traverse around noon."

Jon listened a few more minutes—naturally Becca had five thousand questions. She was female. She also had some girl conversation to unload. "That's dumb, baby. Your mom and I were glad to do this. Nothing to feel guilty about. . . . Of course you're an adult. Of course you could have done it yourself. . . . Yes . . . yes. . . . Suze, did we get some framed print of a little girl that was in the hall closet?"

There was an almost imperceptible nod from the prone figure on the motel bed.

"Yeah, we got it, Bec. No sweat. . . . Cut it out, baby. I swear it was no trouble. Your mother and I both needed a break. The day was terrific, warm, bright, the drive felt good. You're so grown up there isn't much we can do for you anymore, you know? This was a treat. I'm not kidding. Okay, lovebug. Love you, too. Your mom says she loves you too. See you tomorrow."

When Jon hung up on the phone, the prone figure on the bed still hadn't budged. With the blackout drapes pulled, the only light in the room came from the bedside lamps. The light was cheerful enough— but not adequate to verify a breathing life-form.

"Are you asleep?"

The lips moved, but that was the only sign of animation. "I'm awake. I'm just not moving. I'm never moving again as long as I live."

"This, from the woman who was going to shove Douglas's head down his esophagus? This, from the woman who poked the boy in the chest and called him a dill weed?"

"He is a dill weed."

"You've got that right." Jon hooked a thumb in the back pocket of his jeans, trying to decide what to do with the comatose figure. In general, the motel room wasn't bad. Big TV, lots of ice, and two double beds, both with nice, hard mattresses. So were the pillows, but you never got decent pillows in a motel room, so no point complaining. "Would you like a nice hot shower?"

"No, thanks."

Not even the lips seemed to be moving this time. "You hungry for anything?"

"No, thanks."

"Want to take off those clothes and climb under the covers?"

"No, thanks."

The voice was sounding increasingly pitiful. He decided maybe he'd better test for sure whether she was alive or not. "Do you want to watch the Lifetime channel? A chick flick? Something with a lot of mush and gush?"

"No, thanks."

Okay. She'd failed the test. If she didn't want to watch a chick flick, clearly she was dead. Actually, he'd had a small inkling she was in rough shape when she walked in the room and promptly threw herself crossways on the closest bed, still wearing her shoes.

He sighed, then sank down on the mattress next to her and reached for her neck. "All right, where does it hurt the worst, Suze?"

"Everywhere. My knees, my toes, my neck, my head, my back, my elbows. Oh, cripes. I'm fine, Jon. I just need a minute's rest."

Yeah, sure. When he raised one of her hands, it fell back on the quilted bedspread, completely limp.

He started kneading, not expecting to revive the basket case, only figuring that if she was that whipped, she had to be a bundle of sore muscles. They *had* poured on the coals. How one girl could have accumulated so much stuff astounded him. It looked like such a small apartment.

They'd filled two rental storage units and the complete back end of his truck.

He forgot about their long day, though, as he rubbed her neck, then her shoulders, and then thumbed his way down her vertebrae. An occasional weak groan passed her lips, but that was her sole claim to life or enthusiasm. Eventually he rubbed all the way down to her feet, where he pulled off her tennis shoes. They fell with small thuds to the carpet, the only sound in the room by then.

They'd both worked up a sweat in the heat, both gotten dirty, both kicked up bruises and scrapes here and there. Still, he could smell her perfume, feel the thick, soft texture of her hair slivering through his fingers as he rubbed her scalp. Her face was in shadow, turned away from the bedside lamps, but the rest of her body was shaped in the light's silhouette ... the slim shoulders, the ski slope of her spine, the small butt, the priceless calves, the smelly feet.

There came a point when Jon knew damn well she'd fallen asleep, yet still he kept rubbing and kneading. Not hard. He didn't want to wake her, just wanted the treasure of touching her, and hoped the feel-good rubdown would affect her dreams.

It could be that he'd harbored a few wild hopes of an exotic, erotic night in a motel—but obviously he'd realized several hours ago there was no prayer of that happening. So it seemed especially odd that right then, right at that moment, he realized irrevocably that there was only Susan for him. Yesterday, now, and forever. Smelly feet and all.

More to himself than to her, he whispered under his breath, "What you said earlier—you were so dead wrong, Susan Sinclair. I love you. I always loved you. You were the one who didn't love me."

"Nope."

He jumped at the sound of her voice. The tone was sleepy and faint, but the eyes were still closed, the body still immobile, so he hadn't realized she was remotely conscious. Unsure if she'd really spoken, he stayed silent.

She didn't. "When we were sixteen," she murmured, "you wanted me to do the wildly romantic thing. To run off with you. To pretend that somehow we could do it—make a life, raise a child. You wanted me to make a grand, loving gesture, something that proved I loved you more than any practical consideration in life."

"Yeah, I did," he admitted.

"Well, I desperately, desperately wanted to do that grand, romantic gesture. I adored you. Then and now. I loved you. Then and now. My whole life back then—I was so nervous all the time, so worried about grades, about upsetting my dad, about failing everyone's expectations of me. You were the only wonderful thing in my life. You made everything wonderful. Possible."

He'd lifted his hands from her shoulders when

she started talking. Now he didn't know what to do with them. "Then why—" he started to ask, but she went on.

"Only that's exactly how I knew you didn't love me. The thing is, you were free to make that grand romantic gesture, Jon. You came from piles of money. I came from a background where I was scared of being trapped the way my mom was—scared I'd end up in a marriage as unhappy as hers unless I had an education, could make my own way. It wasn't that I didn't love you. It's that I couldn't shake those fears . . . and I thought you knew me. Really knew me. Only if you wanted a girl who could throw caution to the winds—that wasn't me. I was a girl. A young, scared girl. No more, no less. You either thought I was someone I wasn't—or you wanted someone I couldn't be. And I'm just as tedious and staid now as I ever was. Nothing new. That's how I knew you never loved . . ."

When she never finished the thought, he tried to prod her with a "Susan? Susan?" But she didn't answer.

He bent down. He could see her eyes were closed, but her eyes had been closed before. This time, though, breathy little snores were sneaking out between her lips.

Slowly he climbed to his feet. Her clothes were loose enough to sleep in, but the air-conditioning was coming on strong. He scooched her onto a pillow, then wrapped the quilted spread around her and switched off the lamps.

In the darkness, he yanked off his shirt, peeled off

his jeans. Then pushed a pillow against the headrest and sat up next to her. Since she was still lying primarily kitty-corner, there was no space for both of them—not in a double bed. But he wasn't sleeping then anyway.

He didn't expect he'd sleep for quite a while, no matter how tired he was.

All this time, all these years, he'd harbored the hurt that she'd never loved him. Not as much as he loved her.

It never occurred to him that she'd felt the same way. Loved. But not loved as much as she loved him.

The stunner, though, was that Susan had never felt loved for herself.

He wasn't sure what to do with that information—but it rocked him from here to the Pacific and back. This was it, he knew. The real reason they'd never been together. And it was a reason that needed resolution, serious resolution, if there was even the slimmest chance they ever could be.

Herding donkeys had to be easier than this, Lydia thought. To get either of the girls to move an inch, it took putting up with an endless amount of braying and balking. "For Pete's sake, it's a beautiful Tuesday morning and already ten o'clock besides. You're both moving like you had lead in your keesters. Come on, come on, get in the car. I swear we're going to have *fun* in spite of both of you!"

"Mom, I'm just not sure I'm up for a massage this morning."

"Nonsense." She locked the front door and prodded them both toward her Buick. "It's never too late for a woman to start a life of decadence and indulgence. And our appointment's at ten-fifteen. We're going to be late if you two don't start moving."

"Gram, I always thought the massage was a wonderful idea," Becca said. "It's just that I'm not feeling too good this morning."

Talk about understatements. Becca had thrown up twice that morning, and Susan . . . well, Susan had come back from Kalamazoo two days ago looking as if her world had come to an end. Even last night Lydia had heard her pacing the floor until all hours, finally found her at three in the morning outside on the back veranda, staring at the moonlight like a lovesick calf. Lydia was ready to beat them both with a velvet bat. "That's precisely why we're doing this massage thing, you two. To lift everybody's spirits. And Susan, you bought all those presents the other day, so now it's my turn."

She cranked the engine on the Buick. The car had taken to quitting when it wasn't in the mood to go to town. Just like a man, it seemed to hate to go shopping. "I think I should trade this in for an MG," she muttered, and then waited for the horrified gasps.

But there were none. Susan belted in next to her and Becca climbed in the backseat. Both jammed on sunglasses and fell silent. It was like riding with two sphinxes. Becca, Lydia knew well, had her mind on the appointment with the clinic tomorrow. And Susan . . . well, she didn't know what had happened between Susan and Jon in Kalamazoo, but it had to be something traumatic.

Neither of them would talk.

They weren't the only ones with trouble in their lives, for Pete's sake. Lydia had her heart stuck in a wringer, too. She just hadn't realized it until the girls came home and upset everything.

She propped on shades, since the girls were wearing theirs. "Just for the record, no one has to worry that the masseuse is a lesbian, because I called all over town until I found a masseur."

Well, that at least made them both perk up enough to chuckle, although Susan, being Susan, had to tease. "You think that's somehow better, Mom? To have some strange man's hands all over our bodies instead of a woman's?"

"Well, there's at least a *chance* of a thrill if it's a man, don't you think?" There, now. Finally she'd managed to earn two shocked looks. Not big shock, not shrieks or anything, but at least they were registering some emotion. "This is a hundred and twenty-five dollars, for the record, so don't even be thinking you're not going to enjoy it."

"A hundred twenty-five for all three of us?" Becca asked.

"No. A hundred twenty-five for each."

Becca's jaw dropped five feet. "Gram, that's terribly expensive."

"Uh-huh. So prepare to loll and laze, girls. . . ." Normally it was a twenty-five-minute drive to the spa, but Lydia made it in sixteen. The Buick knew the routes the cops tended to ignore.

The spa was located in a new brick building, built back from the road, secluded with landscaping that Lydia considered fake Feng Shui. The rock garden had such a cool "in" look that her fingers itched to get out there and replant, but obviously they weren't here to get their fingers dirty—much less to interfere in someone else's garden.

Lydia just wanted to interfere in the girls' lives. Where she was entitled.

She shooed them both in ahead of her. Inside were silk walls and silk plants and silk upholstery and a bunch of smoke. Even this early in the day, the whole place was ablaze with candles. The smells were all good—jasmine and freesia and gardenia and vanilla—but the great smells weren't going to be much consolation if they all died from smoke inhalation.

"The Sinclairs," she told the white-uniformed gal behind the desk, who gave her a serene smile.

Serene smiles were clearly the rule around here. The young woman was barefoot—Lydia was impressed; after all, how many jobs would allow you to go to work barefoot, wearing nothing but a bathrobe? They were led into a quiet room down the hall. In another life, the building may have housed a dentist's office, but the smoke and darkness and silk and water fountains diverted the eye from noticing the utilitarian office structure.

"We're obviously supposed to pretend we're in some kind of Chinese garden, right? Or a Shangri-la type of place," Lydia said.

"Isn't it cool, Gram? Close your eyes, and all you hear is the sound of running water. Like waterfalls everywhere."

"Yeah, way cool," Lydia agreed. They'd blocked out so much light that the place seemed darker than midnight, even with all the lit candles and incense. Still, she easily made out three white-cushioned stretchers. The receptionist gal had already told her the protocol. "Okay. Now you can either strip to the buff or leave on your underwear. No one's going to care either way. Whatever makes you comfortable. Then you lay with your head toward the west, cover up with the sheet, close your eyes, and listen to the music for a few minutes."

The music being piped in sounded like medieval harps. Personally Lydia would have preferred hearing Sinatra, but she didn't want to be negative. A little tasteful historical crap wasn't going to hurt any of them. Only neither of the girls, she noticed, had starting taking off a single item of clothes.

"Are you two really that modest?" she demanded.

"No, of course not," Becca said with a laugh, and Susan echoed with a chuckle and, "No."

Still, neither made a move to peel off anything but shoes. Exasperated, Lydia pulled off her sweatshirt, then started tugging off her khakis.

Finally, the others budged off Go. Becca . . . God. She didn't even know how beautiful she was. She slipped off a cotton jumper that could have fit two of her, then a short-sleeved tee. Her hair shimmered down her back when she pulled off a rubber band, then, last, unhooked one of those microfiber bras that only the young could wear . . . and there she was. Peach-skinned, smooth as spring, a glow to her complexion, her hair a riot of life and color and texture. Lydia had no bias whatsoever—her granddaughter was possibly the most beautiful young woman on the planet—but damnation, those eyes were sad.

"Honestly, Becca, I never had boobs as big as yours even when I was your age. Life is so unfair." There was no way Lydia was going to comment on the teensy pouchy tummy.

"Unfair? There's nothing great about big boobs. The guys never leave you alone." Becca climbed under the white cover and sank against the cushions. "All right. I'm getting into this now. This is going to feel great."

"You bet," Lydia agreed, but her gaze zoomed promptly on Susan with the protectiveness of an eagle for her eaglet. "What on earth is that mark on your neck?"

Susan was skimming off a pale pink shirt and shorts. "Nothing. I just got a few bruises yesterday."

"Oh, Mom . . . I knew I should have come and helped you and Dad. That was terrible, leaving you with my whole mess to move."

"We had a blast, I keep telling you. And you got to make jam with Gram. You both know I bruise if I just breathe hard. It's nothing."

"Yeah? Well, you've got another one of those bruises on your breast," Lydia remarked.

"I probably bumped something there, too." Faster than an Olympic diver, Susan hustled under the cover.

So, Lydia thought, she'd found time to mess around with Jon at some point on that moving trip. And they must have been fairly ardently acrobatic, judging from all the love bites. So why didn't her daughter look happier?

Of course, she'd only had a glimpse . . . but at least it had been a telling glimpse. Susan might not have Becca's first flush of youth anymore, but her breasts were smaller—which meant that there was less to sag. Her fanny was still tight, legs trim, hair still glossy and rich, the delicate profile still beautiful. Damn beautiful.

"I'm going to kill him if he hurts you again," Lydia muttered.

"Pardon?"

"Nothing." Everybody was so touchy. Couldn't say anything this whole last week without fretting one of them would take exception. Or cast blame.

Lydia had never doubted the strength of the family before. They'd always turned to each other, always been there for each other. But now it seemed as if each of them had caught a case of heartache so painful that they just couldn't seem to climb out of it. And instead of being able to turn to each other, they were all curled up in their own mental compartments alone.

Still, she had big hopes that the girl day with a masseuse would help. Unlike the two modest ones, Lydia stripped to the buff lickety-split—hells bells, why should she care what anyone thought? But damn. Becca was breathtaking and Susan was really at the peak of her beauty. Whereas she . . .

well ... the nipples were drooping, the fanny falling fast now. The glorious cinnamon hair was fading more every day, and she wasn't heavy, didn't have any spare pounds, but somehow bulges had settled on her hips and tummy that no amount of exercise chased away. And then there were her knees. God. Knees were never pretty, but when a woman got a bit of age on her, they started to wrinkle up worse than a dog's nose.

"Hey, hey, what's wrong, Gram?" When Becca suddenly turned her head, she must have caught some damn fool expression in her face.

"Nothing."

But Becca knew her, had always somehow known her, in spite of their difference in ages. "You're beautiful, you know."

That made Susan's head turn. "Yeah, you are, Mom. More beautiful than both of us put together, and then some."

"Go on with you both. I never heard such foolishness." But suddenly the door opened, and that whole conversation was forgotten. The man who stepped in was smaller than she was. He was maybe five-two. Barefoot. Bitsy. Baldish and gentle-eyed. Pretty hard to get nervous around him, especially when all three women were together in the same room.

Becca drew the first massage, and easily seemed to get into it. She needed this, Lydia thought. Their baby was still young—so young that she still believed that her problem was tragic and nothing would ever get better—but of course it would. Just not today or tomorrow. She was stronger than she knew. She'd get over that son of a dirty low-down slug and go on.

Becca was always the most likely of all of them to find a true soul mate . . . and she would. What woman didn't trip over some ugly frogs along the way?

Susan drew the second massage. She never made any moan-or-groan sounds, but slowly her face lost the lines of stress and anxiety as the man pummeled and prodded her tense muscles. Always, always, Lydia prayed that someone would have the taste and brains and heart to truly know her daughter, because Susan expected such strength from herself. She'd never had anyone she could be truly vulnerable with, and she deserved, so much, to be loved.

By the time it was her turn, Lydia was feeling downright upbeat . . . only, cripes—she'd been so positive that she'd have a great time doing this. Instead, she just plain didn't seem to like a stranger's hands on her body. It wasn't about modesty or prissiness. It was about privacy.

It seemed, in her newfound appreciation for orgasms and men, that joy came with a price. She didn't want just anyone touching her anymore. That had been fun for a couple of months. Not anymore.

Riff's face sneaked into her mind's eye and clung. Damn. How and when had she come to care so much? And to care, specifically, for the one man who repeatedly promised that he'd never, ever marry her?

Chapter 16

Whew. When Becca climbed out of the car, she was attacked by such a sudden attack of wooziness that she had to clutch the door handle to keep from falling.

Thankfully the dizziness disappeared. She figured it must be a leftover reaction from the massage a few hours ago. The masseur had definitely made her feel limp as a dishrag. She still felt like curling up for a nap—but for right now, that had to wait.

She locked the car, then waited until a pickup passed before hustling across the parking lot.

Right after the massage, she'd driven Gram and Mom back to Copper Creek. Seeing how wasted everyone was had given her an idea.

Just inside the grocery store, she grabbed a cart.

It seemed as if Mom and Gram had been doing stuff for her nonstop lately. Like Mom had come home with armloads of presents a few days ago. And she'd done all that moving for her with Dad. And then Gram had sprung for the massages, and she'd gone to the trouble of making potato pancakes from scratch the other day. Besides all that stuff, they'd both tackled Douglas for her—it wasn't like she could ever forget that brawl.

The point, though, was how many ways Mom and Gram had shown they loved her lately. Becca just felt that it was payback time. True, her cooking could be a little unpredictable, but she still knew everybody's favorites.

Mom loved cherry cheesecake ice cream. Gram loved cheddar mashed potatoes. Mom loved fresh mushrooms stir-fried with a good soy sauce. Gram loved a marinated T-bone on the grill. Both of them loved fresh iced shrimp—a treat that was usually reserved for the holidays.

Well, today it was all on her.

It took less than twenty minutes to fill half the grocery cart, but then she turned into the fresh produce aisle and had to pause. Man. Both the smells and sights went straight to her head. Right in front were dazzlingly luscious displays of fresh raspberries and blueberries and, naturally, cherries. Yeah, she could easily get all the cherries she wanted at home, but that didn't stop her mouth from watering, imagining a bowl heaped with giant blues and raspberries. Maybe with a little whipped cream.

She pushed the cart halfway down the aisle, pausing to smile at a little squirt—the little girl was skipping around, a joyful imp with pigtails and a nose full of freckles. She reached over for a quart of blueberries . . . and from nowhere, a knife-sharp pain seemed to slice her abdomen in two.

She fell down with an abrupt thud, partly from the stunning, unexpected power of the pain, but also because her whole body seemed to be going through some kind of shock. Her face flushed with heat. Her whole body seemed to instantaneously turn clammy and damp.

"Hey, Mommy! That lady's sitting on the floor!" said the little girl. In trying to grab the grocery cart, Becca must have pushed it instead, because it went careening down the aisle like a runaway caboose. She tried to get up, only everywhere she looked was green. It didn't make sense. Not the pain, not the green, not the sick-sick flushed feeling.

For one crazy instant, Becca thought that she'd somehow dropped into her mother's life ... because her mom had told the story a zillion times about going into labor in a grocery store, walking down the fruit aisle, going crazy over all the fruit and then suddenly getting labor pains.

Mom, of course, had been alone and scared at the time. She'd been living in Detroit, with Aunt Loretta, and she'd been nine months pregnant ... none of which was true for Becca. Not even remotely true. She was barely pregnant, for heaven's sake. There was nothing inside her bigger than a pencil eraser.

But the pain was sure real.

She sucked in a breath for another shock, when she felt dampness between her legs. Her loose cotton jumper fell below her knees, but she could feel the slippery snake-slide of blood down her thigh, the trickle of it show up on the floor, on her calf, on her jumper. Not tons of it. Just ... unmistakably blood. And then came another cramp.

"There, honey; there, honey. We'll get a doctor. Don't you worry—hey, somebody—"

"Let me get her cart."

"Is this your purse, sweetheart? There, now. Just lay on the ground. Who the hell cares? Nobody here but women all over the store. Don't be scared."

"I'm going to be sick," she said.

"Well, then, you'll be sick. But how about if you just do your best to lay there real still for a minute— god*damn* it, did someone call an ambulance?"

There seemed no end to faces staring at her—a plump-cheeked black face, an Asian face, a couple of plain old Heinz 57 white faces. The one little girl was in sight for a second, but then the child was quickly whisked out of the way. A circle of women protectively surrounded her. Someone put something under her, like a jacket, and they kept *sh-shh*ing her, *there-there*ing her.

"Something is terribly wrong," she said.

"And you'll be at the hospital in a jif."

"I want my mom," she said.

She knew she'd said that, and she knew she said it loudly, but everything blurred for a while. The cramps were like period cramps, only sharper. They hurt—they *really* hurt—but it was more the icky, flushed feeling that frightened her. It just seemed as if the whole world were spinning on a green axis and wouldn't stop and wouldn't stop. She wanted to throw up but felt too sick to throw up, and the last thing on earth she wanted was a ride in a vehicle.

"We'll be there in just a few minutes," the medic on the ambulance said.

"I don't need a hospital. I just need to go home. Can't you just take me home?"

She knew she asked the question, but the world did another fade-out on her. She opened her eyes just a few seconds later—surely no more than a few seconds—only that fast, it seemed she'd been transported into a tiny white cubicle. She knew what an operating room looked like, for Pete's sake. She'd had her tonsils out.

"There, now. I was waiting for you to open your eyes."

Damn. She knew that voice. Not well, but she definitely knew it was the trauma doctor who'd been subbing at the women's clinic. Sam Cassidy, of the thick dark hair and sexy eyes. "Not you," she said.

"Sorry, Rebecca, but I'm afraid you're stuck with me again. Seems the regular trauma medic on call tonight had a sick wife, so they called me in to help out." His voice was softer than melted butter and twice as compassionate, and the minute he realized she was awake, he leaned over her.

"Sam?"

"What?"

God. Her voice was suddenly so thick with tears she couldn't get it out. "Please don't tell me I lost my baby."

He said nothing for a moment, just listened to her heart and took her pulse.

"Please. Do whatever you have to do. I know it's less than two months. I know . . . that I was scheduled for a procedure. But you don't understand. . . ." She had to stop to swallow, only it seemed her throat was clogged with a completely unswallowable lump. She couldn't swallow, couldn't see, couldn't think for the tears swimming through her. Her heart felt the weight of a sadness bigger than she was.

"You don't understand," she tried again. "I've been trying and trying to do the right thing, and I think the right thing is not to have a baby. Not in the circumstances I'm in. But I can't help wanting her. Please. Please. Please don't let me lose her. Please."

"Rebecca." His tone turned gentler yet. "You're healthy and strong. You're going to be able to have a dozen babies."

That was good news. But it still wasn't the news she wanted to hear right then. "Sam . . . it was never that I didn't want a child. It was never that I was irresponsible. It was never that I wanted some easy way out of a problem. I wanted the baby terribly from the instant I knew. But I was scared. The man, the father, he turned into a stranger. What else could I do? I was so afraid that he'd—"

"Rebecca." She felt a calm, soothing hand on her forehead, pushing back a strand of hair. Damn it. He made her want to cry all over again.

"Look. Just help me save the baby, okay? I'll do whatever you want me to do. Whatever you say."

"You already know it's too late. And you're going to sleep for a while, but when you wake up, you're going to feel much better. You'll be going home tomorrow, no question."

"Did I do this? Did I somehow do this to her? Because she thought I didn't want her? I swear, I didn't have any coffee or alcohol. And I came up here to get away from stress. Even though I—look, I swear I was trying to take care of myself and her."

"And you did a great job."

"Then why did I lose her? Are you sure this isn't my fault?"

"What I'm sure of is that nature is one smart cookie. About the only time she sets up a miscarriage is when the fetus isn't strong enough to make a healthy baby, so it's her way of saying, let's just try again next time."

She closed her eyes. "She's gone."

"Yes, she is. By the time you got here, the only thing we could do is clean up with a D&C. But having done that, I'm as sure as I can be that you'll be able to have as many kids as you want down the pike."

"That's good. But it's not the same."

"I know."

"You probably think I'm nuts. I wasn't even two months along. But in my heart, I swear I could feel something. Her. Inside me, part of me. And that feeling's gone now."

"You gonna cry some more?"

"Yeah." She glugged out, "Just go away, would you?"

He said, "No."

"You're a pain, doc."

"You aren't the only woman who's called me that. But your mother and grandmother are on their way. Your mom must have already called a half dozen times. I'm sitting here until they get here. So just go on and cry, if that's what you want to do."

It was exactly what she wanted to do. Cry a river. Weep an ocean.

Mourn a baby that never was.

When Lydia brought out the sacred Kem playing cards, Susan knew her goose was cooked. Cards were a family tradition. When the family was too upset to do anything else, the girls gambled their way through the rough spots.

An hour later, the three of them were still sitting at the kitchen table—Lydia, the cat and her. The marmalade monster hid out of sight on a chair, but every once in a while a paw sneaked onto the table to attack a card—particularly during the deal. Betting, typically, was vicious and competitive.

"All right, Mom, I'll see you the dishes one night, and raise you one week of doing all the laundry. You're bluffing and you know it."

"I am not bluffing. I am outplaying you," Lydia informed her. "But I have to think about the laundry. You know how I hate to fold clothes. I don't want to risk it unless I'm dead positive I can win. . . . Stop that, Susan Sinclair!"

"Stop what?"

"You know what. You get up every two minutes to look out the window. Rebecca is *fine*. You've been hovering over that girl for a solid week—and when you aren't, Jon is. It's time to stop. It's not going to kill Becca to take a walk alone."

"I know that, but I was just going to—"

"Yes. You were just going to run out there and walk with her."

"But she could be crying."

"Yeah, she probably is. That's what you're supposed to do when something sad happens. Cry. Go through some misery. Society today wants to medicate everybody the instant they frown. For Pete's sake, that's what being human is about: Laughing big. Crying big. Experiencing. We're drugging ourselves up—"

"Don't start," Susan begged. She was prepared to grovel. This was one of Lydia's favorite monologues.

"Well, it's true. She bottles the sadness in, that's no good. She has to let it out." Lydia put another two chips in the poker pot—the chips worth foot rubs—and then hesitated. Her voice gentled. "I think when something like this happens, it makes us all think about what really matters. We all waste so much time wringing hands over the wrong things."

Susan nodded, but really she couldn't think. She did something with her pair of queens, but that quickly her eyes were drawn to the window again.

Becca had been gone for an hour, strolling the woods by the creek. She very likely was fine. And very likely did need time alone. It was just hard to know her daughter was hurting and she had no magic mom Band-Aid to make things all right again.

All week, the temperature had been climbing. It rarely got this blistering hot on the peninsula, even in dead summer, but this afternoon all the usual tempering lake breezes had disappeared. It was hotter than a spitting griddle, the sky a bleached-out blue, and the air had an expectant, ominous feeling . . . as if a storm were coming, even if right now there wasn't a single cloud in the sky.

"I just beat the pants off you," Lydia announced. "Two weeks of folding clothes. Hoboy, victory is so sweet. That'll teach you to gamble something that really matters to you."

Susan smiled. And shuffled and dealt. And then picked up a card that the cat's paw swished on the floor.

For a few minutes she was able to get her mind off Becca, but in her heart, she knew she was only going through the motions, not really participating in anything. Lydia was trying so hard to behave as if everything were normal, but nothing was normal for Susan.

Jon hadn't sought her out all week. He'd been there for Becca every single day, seen her every day, too. And since Rebecca was all that mattered right now, that was fine . . . but Susan's heart was slowly feeling eclipsed. She felt as if she'd gambled everything she'd had in the heart kitty, and on a hand she should have known she was going to lose.

She wasn't sure what his silence meant. That he didn't care? Which, of course, was what she'd been afraid of all along—that he didn't really love her, never had. That he really didn't know her, or want to.

All these years, she'd known he blamed her for not being the romantic girl he'd wanted her to be.

All these years, she'd blamed herself for not being that girl, too.

There'd been a half-open door between them for twenty-two years. Maybe she'd been wrong to speak up, but as heartsick as she'd felt in the last week, she knew they both needed to either open that door—or let the damn thing close for good.

If he couldn't love who she was, they had nothing. Before. Or now.

"Susan, for Pete's sake, would you concentrate? You just threw away three kings, you dolt."

Susan put down the cards. What was the point in pretending? This game was history. "Mom, there's something I need to tell you."

"What?"

The cat's paw poised over the edge of the table and then promptly sent a handful of Kem cards skittering. When no one reacted, the cat's head showed up above the tabletop, as if confounded why no one had yelled at her this time.

Susan was braced for criticism, expected it, but still felt good to get this out in the open. "I quit my job. Early last week. We've been so busy with Becca that I just couldn't find a time to tell you."

Lydia responded first with silence. And then she scooped up the cards and put them away, as if finally acknowledging that there was no game in the universe that could help settle them down, not lately, and for sure not today. "Okay. So what are you planning to do now?"

"I'm not sure. I promised Sebastian I'd drive to Detroit sometime within the next couple weeks to fill him in, clean out my office, get some things in order that he asked me to do."

"What about your condo?"

"I'm not sure what I'm going to do about all that, either—it depends on where I find work. And in principle, I have enough savings to take my time job hunting—or even to look at a new career—but not if I'm keeping up the condo and all those city expenses."

"So . . . does that meant you're probably job hunting in Detroit?"

For the tenth time in the last hour, Susan pushed out of her chair and went over to the kitchen window. Becca still wasn't in sight. There was no sign of movement in the woods by the creek. The afternoon heat was still coming, parching the grass, sucking all the color from the leaves and greenery. It was so hot that even the bugs were napping, the birds too listless to fly, the afternoon eerily soundless.

Why hadn't he called her?

"Susan—"

"I don't know, Mom. Technically there's no reason I have to find a job in the Detroit area, except that my condo and things are already there. Mostly, I just have to get *going*. Check out the job market. Get my résumé updated and out there. And I think another week is as long as I can cool my heels on this. Becca isn't likely to be here longer than another week, either. Besides, we've both bugged you enough for one summer."

"You haven't bugged me. Well, a little. But you know I love you two. And you can both stay here forever if it would help—Susan, revisit where you started this conversation. Did you *want* to quit?"

Susan turned around. "Yes. Honestly, I did."

Again her mother fell silent. "The whole time you were growing up, I kept pushing you toward education, toward work and a life in which you could be self-reliant. Not dependent on a man. Safe. I thought that was the right way to raise you."

"Oh, Mom, so did I."

Lydia shook her head. "Everyone needs change sometimes. Yet the first time you brought up quitting, I could hear that old voice tensing in my mind: *Don't give up a good thing! Don't risk your future! Stay safe!* When, damn, that was never what I wanted to say to you, Suze. I never wanted you to be like me. It took me all these years to figure out that hiding behind 'safe' only made sure I'd never discover the possibilities."

"Mom. I'm proud of you in every way. If I turned out half as special as you, I'd be thrilled witless, so quit being such a dolt. You raised me to be strong. What are you criticizing yourself for?"

"Because you're not happy."

"Are you kidding? In a few short weeks, I went from being an overpaid executive to being an unemployed derelict with no sure prospects. How could a woman possibly be happier than that?"

There. She made her mom laugh, although Lydia clearly wasn't completely ready to give up this subject quite yet. "So, really, this could be wonderful for you? Heaven knows, you loved that job for a long time, but if you still don't feel that way, then

I'm glad—so glad—you found the courage to get out and move on."

Susan swallowed. This courage thing seemed to be a new song they'd all learned this summer. None of them had managed to memorize it yet, but every time they tried out the lyrics, the music became more familiar, more comfortable. "Thanks, Mom. For being on my side."

"As if that were ever a question. And if you need some financial help—"

Suze had to cut that one off at the pass. "You silly. With or without a job, it's not as if I'm broke, so quit worrying—"

"I wasn't worrying. But when your father made the unfortunate choice to dive off a tractor head-first, he at least left me the land and some hefty insurance. I couldn't spend what I've got if I lived to be two hundred. I swear, I'm trying to be extravagant. And I'm learning. But even so, I've got it to burn."

"Quit being so damn generous," Susan snapped, and then charged around the table to wrap her mom in a rib-crushing hug.

Lydia prolonged the hug for a good long time, but then she stepped back. "So. Enough of that for now. I hate talking about money." She segued so fast into a different subject that Susan barely felt the sideswipe. "Are you going to tell me what you're doing about Jon or am I supposed to pretend that something huge hasn't happened between you in the last couple weeks?"

That was it. In the next life, she wasn't coming back as a Sinclair woman. She was coming back in a family where nobody gave a damn or asked any nosy questions. "I'm not doing anything about Jon," she said.

"Uh-huh."

"If he chooses to do something, it's up to him." When Susan pivoted around to face the window again, she knew that was true. She'd pitched the ball, but that didn't mean Jon had any interest in swinging the bat.

She'd only told her mom the partial truth. She really didn't have to *race* to job hunt. But Becca was physically recovered from the miscarriage and starting to talk about packing up and getting her life together again.

Bec didn't need her. Heaven knows, her mother didn't need her. And since Jon had chosen to say nothing to her, it seemed obvious to Susan that she needed to—as Gary Cooper used to say—get out of town. Pick up the pieces. Maybe she'd misunderstood what making love these last times had meant. Maybe she'd misunderstood what she and Jon had been sharing together. Maybe her admitting how much she loved him simply didn't matter that much.

When it came down to it—maybe there was no *them.*

Beyond what she'd yearned for in her heart.

"Suze, honey . . ." Something in Lydia's voice made her spin around. Her mom was pouring two glasses of iced tea. "Do you remember a little talk you had with me a couple weeks ago?"

"Which talk? We've been talking nonstop since we all got here."

Lydia plunked both glasses on the table, then scooped up the limp marmalade cat and plopped him outside the screen door in the shade. "I was talking about our sex talk. You know. The one where you explained safe sex to me. And how life was different today and all. I keep thinking about that—because it does strike me that there are a couple of things that never change from generation to generation. Such as that I do believe a woman gets pregnant the same way she always did."

Susan had to smile. "Now, Mom, I never meant to give you such a hard time with that lecture."

"I was charmed. Honest to Pete. At least later I was charmed, even if I was disgusted with you at the time. But I did want to be sure you knew not to wear patent-leather shoes, not to let a boy French-kiss you, never to wear earrings more than an inch long and only skirts below the knee. . . ."

A chuckle bubbled from Susan's mouth, and then another, as Lydia deadpanned all the Catholic girls' school rules of Good-Girl Behavior. They both started laughing then, until Susan suddenly caught an odd choke at the back of her throat—as if a speck of dust had lodged there—just as the telephone rang.

She was closest to a receiver, so hiked to grab it. Still pounding her chest, she garbled out a "Hello."

"Riff here. Could I talk with your mother?"

"Sure, just a second." Covering the mouthpiece, she whispered, "Riff," and for some unknown reason watched the color drain from her mother's face. All the teasing and laughter disappeared faster than lightning. Lydia shook her head frantically to indicate she didn't want to take the call.

"She'll be right there, Riff." Again, Susan covered the phone's mouthpiece and whispered, "Come on, it's too late—he already knows you're here. What's going on? What's the problem?"

At first she thought her mother must simply have misunderstood who the caller was—but Riff was hardly a common name. And Lydia was reluctantly edging toward the phone as if facing a firing squad. "All right, I'll take the call," she said. "But could you ... um ... make sure that no-good, worthless, derelict cat has some fresh water? It's just so hot. I don't want the damn cat getting sick from the heat and then my getting stranded with her."

"Sure, Mom." Clearly her mom was trying to get her out of earshot, so Susan quickly filled the cat bowl with water, and then sat outside on the porch step with her ear glued to the screen.

The cat had never drank water from a bowl in her life and showed no inclination to start now. Finally having garnered a human's attention, though, she snuggled close to Susan, a four-hundred-degree affectionate furball on a day hotter than a furnace—and purring so darn loud that Susan could barely hear.

"I *know* you don't want to marry me," her mother said into the receiver. As far as Susan could tell, they were the first words out of her mother's mouth. "That's how you always start the conversation. And that's always been exactly what I want to hear, so I always laugh. Only . . ."

There was a pause. While her Riff obviously said some things. And then Lydia sank down on one of the daffodil-yellow stools and propped her chin in a palm. "I know I haven't called you all week. And yes, I got your messages. I . . ."

Another pause. Susan gave up with the idiotic eavesdropping and tiptoed back inside. Lydia's eyes were closed, her body stiff, her hand clenching the phone so tightly that her knuckles were white. Susan figured she could clatter pans together and her mother wouldn't notice.

"Yes, I'm upset. And no, it's not your fault. I just . . . Riff, damnation, why *don't* you want to marry me? I *know* what I said! That's not the point. The point is that I'm tired of pretending I don't give a damn. I'm tired of pretending I'm not going to be hurt if you just disappear from my life. I'm tired of pretending I'm having a blast trying to be a fifty-seven-year-old sex kitten. . . . Well, hell. I guess to be truthful, I have to admit I *have* been having fun with that, but . . ."

Susan quit breathing, and wondered, now that she was in a prize hearing position, how she could escape from the room without her mother realizing she'd ever been there. The phrase "sex kitten" completely changed her desire to hear the conversation.

"Call it corny or sentimental or whatever you want," Lydia said unhappily. "But I guess I want to be loved or nothing. I want it all or nothing at all. I understand perfectly that you're still grieving for your wife. I'm not blaming you. I'm just saying that I didn't realize before how short life was. Too short to lie. Too short to not value real love when you find it. I *know* I told you a hundred times I was never going to marry anyone...."

It seemed only seconds later that Lydia clapped down the phone and whirled around. "Susan Sinclair, you know perfectly well I didn't want you to hear that conversation!"

"Mom...if you're in love with a brainless ratfink skunk who doesn't have the taste and honor to marry you, I'll wipe him off the map for you," Susan offered.

"Thank you, dear." Lydia sighed. "I've got all those wine bottles in my new wine rack, getting dustier by the week. Right now I wish I were more of a drinker."

"I'll open one for you."

"No." Lydia pushed up from the chair. "I'm going to feel better about that conversation in a while. Maybe not for a year or two, but I still don't regret getting it done. I wanted to say it. I needed to face it. You and Becca have both taught me a great deal about courage this summer. I didn't love him."

"Riff?"

"No, your father, of course. I never loved Harold. Not the way a woman should love her husband, and he always knew it. That's what turned him mean, Susan."

"You told me this before...."

Lydia nodded. "I know. But talking isn't doing. I didn't accept my responsibility for the bad marriage before. I didn't do anything about *me*. But these last weeks, I've watched you take risks with Jon—put honestly on the line, everywhere in your life, with him, with your job, with Bec. And our Rebecca, maybe she started out making the same kind of mistake I did—talking herself into trying to love someone—but she ended up facing the most painful truths a woman can know. Sometimes a woman just can't win. Sometimes the most you can do is survive—but if you're honest, you can at least survive with your head up. And I'll be damned if I was going to be the only one of us three who didn't own up to some tough truths in my life. Maybe I've lost that darn man by turning around and being honest with him . . . but I had to try."

Lydia leaned over and kissed Susan's cheek. "And hells bells, I can't take any more of this deep talk. I'm going upstairs to soak in a nice cool tub for a little while before dinner."

"Okay. Yell if you want anything."

But when her mother was gone, Susan leaned back against the counter and squeezed her eyes closed. Weeks ago, she'd charged home to Copper Creek to help her family, yet it seemed as if both her mother and daughter had gone through emotional trials of fire and come out on the other side. They were both fine. Hurting, but definitely on the healing side of pain, stronger than they'd ever been before.

She seemed to be the only one with her hand still in the fire. What did it take her to *learn*? For days, she'd been heartsick, trying to accept that Jon didn't love her. But now Lydia had put a new blistering-fresh thought in her mind.

In the heat of battle—and through all the traumas of the summer—she'd never used birth control with Jon.

The chances of conception were unlikely—but there was a chance. She couldn't rule it out completely, or even try a pregnancy test, for at least another week.

Which was exactly when she was planning on leaving Copper Creek.

Chapter 17

"Mom?"

Susan was just pulling on a sweatshirt when she heard Becca's whisper. She hustled to open the bedroom door. "Holy kamoly, are you aware it isn't even seven in the morning yet? Are you ill? Is the world ending? Is this a miracle we need to record for mankind?"

"Very funny." Becca was still wearing a rumpled nightshirt, her hair still tousled from sleep, but she grinned. "I was waiting to hear you move around so I'd know for sure you were up. And I'm going right back to bed. I just wanted to tell you something first."

"Shoot." The last few days had made a difference, Susan thought. Her daughter's cheeks had some real color again, her eyes some life.

"Right after I graduated from college, you remember telling me about an overseas program? You went to a lot of trouble researching all this stuff for me about this cultural exchange program—where they wanted American teachers to work with kindergarten-aged kids."

"Sure, I remember." Damn, but those soft brown

eyes had more than a little life. They weren't sparkling, but there was some downright dance in them. Even at this ungodly early hour.

"I really wanted to do it, you know? Only, by then the Kalamazoo school system had offered me a job, so I just forgot about the whole thing. But then, a few days ago, I got a letter about their program for this fall. They were all set, teachers all lined up, but then one got really sick—so now they're short one teacher. I guess they were going through their records looking for earlier candidates who'd applied and qualified? And they found me. Anyway, I haven't been able to stop thinking about it."

"You want to do it, baby?"

Becca nodded. "They offered me the job, but I'd have to let them know lickety-split, Mom. Like within the next three days. It'd be a lot to put together. This particular group's going to Germany, and they want the teachers to leave by next week. The school system's been slow about getting the contracts together, so it's not like I've actually signed a commitment. I think I could go. . . ."

"Geezle beezle. I think it'd be *wonderful* for you."

"You sure? I wanted to ask you first, before—"

"Are you kidding? I think it'd be a fantastic opportunity!"

They both bubbled on for a few more minutes, after which Susan shooed her back to bed and hustled downstairs. Alone in the kitchen, she found herself standing with hands on hips, caught halfway between a whistle and a frown. She needed coffee. Obviously. But the other two were likely going to sleep at least a couple more hours. Becca's news needed something symbolic to celebrate—Susan couldn't imagine anything better for Rebecca than a year in Europe, a total change and break from where she'd been. Faster than a finger snap, it seemed that Lydia and Becca had both made major, positive changes in their lives.

So if Becca was not only okay, but leaving Traverse quickly, Susan couldn't imagine staying longer herself. If her mom had a shot with the lawyer in town, she certainly didn't need a third wheel around—such as Susan.

All of which meant that Susan figured it was a kiss-or-kill morning. A day to celebrate imminent changes and imminent partings. A day to take risks.

A day to make a Sinclair Sunrise cake.

At nine-thirty, she heard a voice on the other side of the kitchen door. She sent out a box of cereal but insisted that no one was allowed in the kitchen. At ten, there were tentative knocks, pleading for real food, begging for answers. Susan explained what her mission was, but threatened any intruders with dire consequences.

This time, she was going to make that damned cake or die trying.

By eleven, the kitchen looked like a deserted demolition site—a true measure that she'd put her heart and soul into the effort. There were no clean surfaces. No bowls or spoons unused. No cupboard doors or drawers closed. The mixer had helped contribute to the congealing drops of unknown substance on the ceiling.

For the first time in thirty-eight years, she'd managed to get the cake all the way to the oven. Then, though, she was confronted with the next part in the recipe. The marshmallow frosting part. According to the recipe, you were supposed to cook the sugar and water together "until it spins a thread."

This was a myth that had been passed down by the Sinclair women for generations. There was no thread. You could cook that damn sugar and water until the cows came home—even if you didn't have cows—and you'd never get the mixture to "spin a thread."

One did what one could.

When she finally let the women back in the kitchen, she'd yanked off the sweatshirt, peeled down to shorts and a tee, and broken two nails. The Sunrise cake, ideally, was fourteen inches tall, mounded with shiny white marshmallow frosting and dotted with red cherry halves.

Her version was a reasonably respectable eight inches, until she set it on the counter, when for some dadblamed reason it fell another four inches. The frosting had started out looking perky enough—it should, after all that whipping—but somehow it kind of sank on the lopsided cake as soon as she knifed it on.

Lydia and Becca both bounded in the kitchen, circling the cake with nonstop oohs and aahs. "It looks wonderful, Mom," Becca said warmly.

"And it'll taste even better. What a great surprise," Lydia said heartily.

Susan wasn't fooled. But she was also so darn tired she could hardly talk—not to mention that she was sticky from her hair to her toes. "Okay, okay. You don't have to overdo the lies. But this is the first time I've managed to make one start to finish. After all these years. And even though it looks a little weird . . . okay, it looks a lot weird . . . but it should be edible, don't you think?"

Becca exchanged a fast glance with her grandmother, but then exuberantly reassured her, "Mom, we're going to eat this cake if it kills us. Of course it's edible. It'll be delicious."

Outside, they all heard the sudden screech of truck brakes. Bing Matthew, the man who farmed the land for Lydia, had been in the yard all morning with cherry tanks and supplies. Hearing trucks and forklifts and tractor sounds was status quo during the summer—but hearing Bing's normally quiet voice yelp out an "Oh, no!" made all three women sprint toward the door.

Susan pushed through the screen door first. She couldn't immediately see what Bing was crouched over, but the sick feeling in her stomach made it easy to guess.

"Stay here," she ordered Becca and Lydia, who naturally paid no attention and followed right on her heels outside.

"Aw, Ms. Sinclair, I'm so sorry." Bing sprang to his feet when he saw them. Typical of farmers in this neck of the woods, he was dressed in Dockers and Reebocks, his pockets jammed with a calculator and cell phone. Bing had never been pretty in this life, but he loved everything to do with the land, and it showed in the crinkles around his eyes, his patient smile, his nut-brown skin—which right then had turned pale with unhappiness.

On the ground, curled up, was the no-name marmalade cat. Her eyes were open, but she was lying limp, with her back leg bloody and resting at a crooked angle. A sob whooped out of Lydia, almost as fast as Becca gushed out tears. "Oh, no, oh, no, oh, no. . . ."

Susan was just about to burst out crying, too, but obviously that plan was curtailed when she realized the others had beaten her to it. Someone had to bend down to examine the cat. "She's not dead. I know she looks rough, you two, but I honestly can't see anything wrong except for the broken leg." That didn't mean there weren't internal injuries, of course, but it was the most positive she could report.

Bing was beside himself. "I can't tell you how sorry I am, Ms. Sinclair. She was always running all over the yard, and I got to watching for her, but this morning—I swear, she just ran under the truck tire when I pulled out. I wasn't going fast. I just plain never saw her."

"Now, just stop feeling so bad. It could have happened to anyone. She's a completely worthless cat," Lydia said, and then burst out crying all over again.

"Mom, is she going to die?" Becca asked, and then her faucet started leaking again, too.

Susan said the only thing she could say. "Of

course she's not going to die. She's going to be just fine. We're going to take her to the vet. Right now—immediately in fact."

"Mom . . ."

Susan knew better than to allow any more hand-wringing. Both of them needed to get busy doing something, or this was just all going to deteriorate even worse. "Becca, she's going to be just fine. Now hustle in the house and get a big, thick towel to wrap her in, okay? And Mom, would you bring my purse?"

"It's because I never gave her a name," Lydia said. "This is all my fault. She didn't feel loved. I pretended as if I didn't want her."

"Mom. Get my purse. I'll drive, but my wallet's in my purse and I need the car keys. This is not your fault."

"Yes, it is. But I was lying about not loving her, Susan. The thing is, every time I adopt some stray, it's usually so old or sick that nobody else wants it. So then naturally it doesn't live very long. And then I just tear myself up mourning it. So I've been trying and trying not to care."

"I understand."

"I was feeding her tuna fish. You know how expensive tuna fish is? So even though I said I didn't want her, I thought she'd figure out that I really did love her—"

"Mom, at the rate she was going, she was going to be the only two-ton house cat in existence. She knows you love her, now come on!"

My God. It was worse than taking children to the

dentist. Susan drove, because obviously she couldn't trust either of them behind a wheel. Not only were they both sniffling and wailing, but the cat, no matter how hurt, felt a need to express how unhappy she was riding in a car. To add insult to injury, Susan had had no time to clean up since the cake debacle, which meant her khaki shorts and blue top were decorated with various congealing degrees of egg white, sugar and cake batter. None of them had thought to bring a hairbrush.

"Of course she's not going to die," Susan said for the nine millionth time. And then, "Did *anyone* think to bring a handkerchief or some tissues?"

"I've lived in the country my whole life," Lydia sniffed. "You come to accept this kind of thing. Animals live. Animals die. It's the natural cycle of things. Ridiculous to make such a big deal out of it." That said, she burst into tears all over again.

Susan spotted a half-crushed box of tissues on the floor and reached over to grab it. Her eyes were still on the road. One hand still on the steering wheel. She was still strapped in—as were all of them, because she'd made everybody use seat belts.

But the very instant her fingers connected with the tissue box, somehow the tire seemed to bump something in the road. The car swerved. Not a lot. But enough to send the white Avalon careening into the dusty ditch on the right side of the road.

Becca, holding a hand over one ear, clamping the pay phone against the other, said, "Marnie, is that you? Could I talk to my dad?"

It was hard to hear over the cacophony of barks and meows in the vet's waiting room. Possibly it was sex-operation day at the vet's, because almost all the dogs and cats looked healthy and fit. They sounded it, too—they were just whining. A big old St. Bernard was the loudest. He was just sort of yowling, leaning against his owner as if trying to hide his 150-pound body.

On the other hand, a basset hound next to the St. Bernard was baying for all he was worth. The Boston Philharmonic couldn't come up with a louder sound—and nothing the owner did could get the hound to quiet down or obey. And then there were the cats. . . .

"Bec? It's Dad. You aren't sick, are you, sweetheart?"

"Oh, no, not at all." She felt bad that he'd leaped to that conclusion. "It's just . . . I kind of need a favor. We all need a ride. Not this instant, but pretty soon, if there's any way you could come get us."

"We?"

"Yeah. We, as in Mom, Gram and me."

"And you're where?"

"At the vet's. Dr. Lindale, just south of Cherry Bend, you know, on 22?"

"I'll find it. What's the story?"

"Well, Mom's in the office with that cat and the vet, so it's not like we need a ride immediately. But they've been in there twenty minutes, so it can't be much longer. The tow truck driver got us here. I don't know about Mom's car—"

"You were in an accident?"

"Not exactly an accident."

"Are any of you hurt?" her dad asked swiftly.

"No, no. The only thing hurt was the car. It sort of slid in this ditch because we were all crying."

"Crying—"

"Anyway, I don't know what shape Mom's car is in, but it's not like we're short of wheels if and when we can just get back home. I mean, there are the trucks and Grandma's Buick and my car and all. But I started to think—I'm almost sure we can't just call a cab from here. I mean, who knows if a cab would willingly take a cat?"

"The cat?"

"You know. Caramel. Grandma's cat."

"The one she doesn't own?" her dad asked tactfully.

"Dad! We all love the cat!"

"Excuse me. Let's get back to the point."

"Well, the point is, she was hit. Anyway, the thing is, I tried to call Bing because he was at the farm before, but he didn't answer, either, in the barn or the shop. Grandma gave me some neighbors to call, but honestly, Dad, we're all kind of a mess. Mom was baking. I don't have shoes. The cat was a little bloody. If you could just—"

"I'll be there."

Becca hung up. It was amazing how talking to her dad always made her feel better. It was always that way. Dad was just the kind of man who was there for you. Even when he was mad. Even when he didn't get it.

But in the meantime, she tugged fretfully at her

bone necklace, and then slowly made her way toward Gram. Inside, she was squirming. The thing was, about ten minutes ago, this guy had walked in. A lawyer. And since the guy identified himself as Riff, Bec figured that this obviously had to be the man who'd been calling Gram.

Naturally Becca had checked him out, up one side and down the other. He looked okay. A little lawyery. Striped shirt, tie, three-hundred-buck shoes, basic Wall Street haircut—not at all Becca's cup of tea, but then, he was way older. His hair wasn't gray, but you could still tell he had some age, just from the expensive clothes and types of styles. Still, he had a nice face. An extra-nice smile. And he'd come barreling in the door about ten minutes ago, looked around, and zoomed straight for Gram.

How he knew Grandma was here, Becca had no idea. But he wasn't carrying a pet, so it seemed like he was probably here just to see her. He also looked as if he'd come straight from a courtroom. Anyway, he'd spotted Gram, hustled over, and pulled her immediately into his arms.

Just like that.

Man, it was scary what could happen to older people, what they'd do in public and all. Maybe it was menopause with Gram, but who could guess what was wrong with the guy? Unless everybody over fifty had psychotic breakdowns now and then?

Anyway, the point was, she wasn't sure of where to go, what to do. The vet waiting room was

L-shaped, with seating benches under the windows. The cats sat on one side, the dogs on the other, and almost every crook and cranny was filled with yowlers, barkers, meowers or their parents. It's not as if Becca had a choice of places to sit except by Gram—at least until Mom came back out.

She sidled a little closer. Then another few steps. She decided if they were saying dorky stuff to each other, she'd just hightail it outside and give them some privacy. Silent as a mouse—which wasn't easy to be in this place—she sank down on the bench and tried to make herself small. Once she got a close-up of Gram's face, though, she had to roll her eyes.

Gram's maturity wasn't just deteriorating; she was dropping years, just from talking to the guy. He was holding her hand as if they were in grade school. And Gram's cheeks were pink as peaches.

"Look," he said, "I was just waiting for you to come around. I thought you'd run if I told you what I really felt."

"But I thought you couldn't get over your wife."

"I loved her. But Janice has been gone years now, Lyd. I'm not looking to replace her. We had a wonderful marriage, a wonderful life, a wonderful love. But it's not like there's only one diamond on the planet."

"Riff . . . you never let on you thought of me as a diamond."

"Because you were so adamantly against marriage or a serious relationship. I didn't want to say anything to scare you away."

Becca jumped to her feet, thinking, *Okay, that's enough, I'm outa here.* She glanced at the closed door where her mom had gone in with Caramel. There was still no way to know when she was coming out, no way to guess how the cat was doing. On the other hand, she was just going to make herself sick worrying about Caramel, so she pushed open the glass doors and stepped outside.

The vet's office was located at the top of a barren knoll. The only landscaping was some scrubby bushes and four fake red hydrants—obviously put there for dogs to relieve their nerves on. Behind the building were cages for overnight stays. The whole animal hospital took up several acres, which was a good way to make sure no neighbors were bothered by noise, but there sure wasn't much to look at.

She sank down on the cement step, a distance from the door, but in sight if her mom and Gram came out. The sun soaked into her shoulders, warming her face and hair, making her feeling soporific, sleepy. It was happening every once a while, whole minutes when she caught a quiet feeling of peace. Her body seemed fully recovered from the miscarriage, but her heart didn't want to heal up that fast. It was still a revelation, discovering how much she'd wanted the baby, how fiercely her heart seemed to be mourning.

She didn't know if she could have gotten through it without her mom. Susan hadn't said a single word of criticism or judgment. She just kept hugging her now and then. Being there. Loving her. Making it clear she wasn't alone.

It was the first time either her mom or her dad had treated her like a grown-up—a true equal. And that prompted her to do even more soul-searching about Douglas, trying to be merciless and self-truthful, needing to understand how she'd drawn a mental case like him. What was good about her. What wasn't. It was one thing to know your self-esteem was at an all-time low, and another to figure out whether you had any self-esteem worth fighting to get back.

She glanced up when a Lincoln pulled up. A lady in pink climbed out with a boxer. Not a marriage made in heaven. In fact, the dog and owner looked so unmatched together—yet so loving—that she had to smile.

After that, a beat-up—a very, very beat-up—silver Mercedes drove in and parked under the farthest scrub tree. Becca wasn't really paying attention, beyond idly wondering what kind of animal and owner were going to emerge from the old classic car.

The critter that galloped out of the front seat turned out to be a mutt. A leashless mutt. It was almost too silly-looking to be a dog—the legs were long and skinny, the fur as spiky and unkempt as a rock star's, and the swooshy tail exuberantly wagging with enough power to knock over small mountains.

"Damn it, Lurch. You knew damn well you were supposed to sit still until I got your leash on. Now you get back here."

The dog, who could surely star as the biggest,

ugliest mongrel Becca had ever seen, ignored its owner . . . but Becca immediately tensed. She knew that voice.

The Mercedes' car door slammed. A red leash showed up at the end of a long-fingered masculine hand. The hand was attached to a guy in a doc's white coat. She would have recognized Sam Cassidy in her sleep—although he was startled when he suddenly recognized her sitting there. "Rebecca! Hi! . . . I'm—"

Lurch seemed to realize that he'd lost his owner's devoted attention and promptly bounded back to Sam, pranced his front paws on Sam's shoulders and licked his owner's face. It wasn't even a stretch. Becca wondered if the dog could possibly be part horse.

"He's getting f-i-x-e-d today," Sam said. "At least that was the plan. I mean, what else can I do—can you imagine what puppies of his would look like? Only, getting him to cooperate has been a little more challenging than I anticipated. Get down, you big galoot. Show the lady some manners."

Lurch showed no comprehension of the word "manners," but having thoroughly washed Sam's face, he leaped back down and glanced around, as if seeking potential new prey.

"Holy cow. No," Becca said.

The dog had the gait of a racehorse. It was on her in less than four bounds and a leap.

Elephants couldn't have a tongue that big. They just couldn't.

Sam hauled him off and attached the red leash

with an extremely pained expression. "I spend my entire life apologizing for this dog. We tried obedience training. I'm the only one who learned how to obey. He didn't hurt you, did he?"

"Not at all." She hadn't laughed in ages, not really laughed. Now, although her chuckle sounded a little rusty, it seemed right to let a true smile come out of hiding. It was a breathtakingly sun-sweet day; for the first time in forever she felt physically strong again, and darn it, his dog was adorable. Or so impossibly, incomprehensibly ugly that what else could you call him but adorable? "Tell me he's a breed," she said.

"Of course he's not a breed. He's a complete mongrel. I only adopted him because he was on death row at the dog pound. Like they said—who'd be crazy enough to take him? He takes off at a hundred miles an hour—which is another reason we're doing the f-i-x thing. It's one thing to run, another thing to bother all the lady dogs in a ten-mile radius. I had to do something. Damn, you're looking beautiful."

Lurch, as if he'd been brought up by royalty, sat regally between them on the cement. But it took Becca a minute to breathe after catching Sam's last comment. "I beg your pardon, Doc?"

"You heard me." Sam stretched out his long legs. "You're here for . . . ?"

"A cat. Who was hurt in an accident. I'm with my mom and grandmother."

"The cat gonna be okay?"

"We think it's no worse than a broken leg. So we're hoping she will be."

"And are you going to be okay?"

He could have meant in reference to her feelings about the cat, but Becca sensed he was asking a more personal question. She hesitated—not because she was unwilling to answer him honestly, but because the answer coming from her heart surprised her. Since becoming involved with Douglas, she hadn't once felt okay, not on the inside, the outside, anywhere. Not really. Yet she answered with the truth. "Yes. Not this week. Maybe not next week, either, but I'm getting there."

After Sam left, herding Lurch into the vet's office, Becca felt a smile coming from down deep. It really was true. She was looking forward to doing the exchange-teacher thing in Germany. Looking forward to jump-starting her life in new directions. And she couldn't imagine wanting to be involved with a man for a long time, but later, sometime, somewhere, she hoped there'd be someone.

Not every man was like Douglas. And maybe it had taken a trial by fire for her to learn the difference between the turnips and the good guys.

No more turnips for her—and you could take that to the bank.

Susan pushed a hand through her hair, feeling as if she'd survived a war when she finally stepped out of the vet's examining room. Somewhere in her purse she had a checkbook. It seemed ironic that anyone would have to pay for having this much fun. Caramel was going to be fine once her leg healed—at the moment she was stitched and bandaged and looked like a pitiful mummy. But the vet had sworn she'd be fit as a fiddle in a short while— although he did want to keep her overnight.

Susan, on the other hand, felt miles away from fine. She had scratches all over her arms and neck. She didn't precisely mind being used as the cat's pincushion—primarily because Caramel had to be basically healthy and strong to express such pissed-off fury. But right now—between the battle to subdue the cat and wearing clothes covered in dried cake batter—she just wanted to go home and grab a shower and a nap, in that order. As soon as she paid, anyway.

She dug blindly in her purse, seeking and finding the familiar shape of her checkbook, as her gaze whisked the waiting room for Bec and Lydia. With three vets on staff today, the place was predictably packed. A dozen people crowded the bench seats with a menagerie of motley critters, but no Sinclairs were in sight. Could they both have gone to the rest room at the same time? Heaven knows, she'd been gone close to an hour, but it wasn't as if they could have left. They had no car.

Remembering the state of her Avalon made Susan involuntarily wince. What a day. And her poor Avalon liked ditches on a par with how well the cat liked being stitched up.

"How much—" she started to ask the receptionist, when she spotted him.

Jon.

He was just striding in the door, the sun hitting the glass with such dazzling brightness that for an instant she was blinded, not sure if it was him—or if she was imagining him. But the cocky posture and walk were all Jon. The wind-tousled hair and the sun-bronzed face, and the way his eyes honed in on her from ten feet away in the blink of a second and pinned her . . .

Oh, it was definitely Jon.

She'd lost him. She'd been so sure. It was different from when she was sixteen and too damn young to know what they could have—or could be—together. Now it mattered more. Now she understood how powerful love could be. Now she cared enough—loved enough—to know what a broken heart really was.

Jon spotted her in a millisecond, but seeing her was enough to make his heart clutch. She looked . . . ah, hell, he didn't know how she looked. A wreck, by her standards, for damn sure. The thick, lustrous hair was all tangled. The summer shorts and top looked as if she'd been rolling in a clay pile. She had some angry scratches on her wrists and neck, and her face had no makeup. Her skin was so fragile and soft. Her lips were naked. Her eyes vulnerable.

There was no one else in that room. No animals. No people. No anyone. Just her, for him.

"Jon—how on earth did you . . . ?"

It was easy to anticipate the questions. "Becca called me. Said you needed a ride. The funny thing was, I was just about to climb in the truck and drive out to Copper Creek to see you."

She still looked bewildered, and more so when

she glanced around him. "But Mom and Becca—I don't know where they could have gone."

"They're home—or on their way home. I guess the original plan was for me to pick up all three of you, but it seems the tow truck driver—the guy who pulled out your Avalon—called a friend of your mother's. Riff. He came charging over here to take care of your mom. And when I came in, and everyone understood I'd be giving you a ride, Riff offered to take Lydia and Bec home." He was having a real hard time taking his eyes off her. "So it's just you and me. And the cat."

"Not the cat. She has to stay overnight."

"Then it's just you and me, Suze."

For a moment she didn't move—or couldn't seem to move—just looked at him with those liquid brown eyes. But eventually she seemed to remember that she was a responsible, practical woman with a bill to pay. She walked back to the receptionist counter, asked for the amount she owed and started writing a check, although her gaze shot back to him every ten seconds as if unsure if he was really there . . . or why he was really there.

She must have written that first check incorrectly, because she ended up writing two.

In short order, though, he'd hooked a hand under her arm and scooted her outside, away from all those watching eyes and smiles and cacophonous pets. The sun beamed down with a beatific glow, on her hair, her skin, her mouth.

"I've been waiting," he said.

"Waiting for what?"

"Waiting for you. Waiting, trying to figure out what to do. You threw me such a curveball, Susan, when you told me . . . that you believed I didn't love you. That you believed I wanted you to be a wildly impulsive romantic who would throw all caution to the winds. What hurt the most was that you were right, Susan. That's exactly what I wanted when I was a damn fool teenager."

"Oh, Jon, I'm not blaming you—"

He cut past that nonsense. "But it's not what I want now. Only, the problem *now* has been figuring out how to prove that to you. I mean, how the hell can a man do that, prove to a woman that he really, really loves *her*? Do you see the truck?"

"Pardon?" She wasn't sure how a truck had jumped into the conversation.

"The truck, Suze. My plain old red truck." Since he was looking right in her eyes, she seemed more inclined to look right back in his. But eventually her gaze shifted to the red truck behind him. Her jaw dropped in shock.

"What on *earth*?" She laughed, shot another look at the truck, shook her head and then laughed again as she walked toward it.

The truck's windows were open. It was his work truck, of course, the vehicle he used at the marina because it was more practical than a car. Since he'd finally figured out how to approach Susan—and that he couldn't wait any longer than today—he'd had it washed and waxed that morning. Becca's telephone call, though, had created a heck of a dilemma for him, because he assumed he was going to need seating for all three women. And the problem, then and now, was that there was no spare seating.

The cab was stuffed with roses—red roses, white roses, yellow roses, coral roses, pink roses, every-color-under-the-sun roses. They were everywhere, on the floor, on the seat, pushing out the windows, blossoms and blooms sticking out in every direction.

"Jon, what on earth . . ."

"It was your mom who made me think of roses. Weeks ago, she was talking to me, just chatting about her garden, telling me there was all this romantic lore about roses and none of it was true. And that's what hit me." He hooked her wrist, spun her toward him. A car zoomed up the hill to the vet's parking lot, but he paid no attention. He was through looking at anyone or anything else but her.

"What hit you?"

"What hit me is that it's easy, so easy, to make a grand romantic gesture. All it takes is money. I bought out three florists. It took a while to strip the thorns off all those flowers, but basically it was easy." When she started to gape at the flowers again, he turned her face toward his with the gentlest graze of his thumb on her chin. "I always had money, Suze. I always had the kind of security you didn't have, which was why it was easy for me to take it for granted. What I didn't have was you."

He couldn't wait any longer to kiss her, but that first one was soft, a kiss that he wanted to be as silken and smooth as a tender rose petal. Light, not hard. Offering, not demanding. Expressing love, but softly. Wooing soft. Aching soft. Promise soft.

"I love you, Susan Sinclair. I love your cautious and practical side. I love the way you give to people without their even knowing it. I love the way you reach for life, with both fists, always willing to fight for what you want, for what's right. I love your independence and your stubbornness. I love your courage."

"Jon, you're so craz—"

She never could take a compliment. And damned if the woman wasn't just as hard to convince as she always had been. But another kiss silenced her pretty effectively. This one had some wooing and promises and aching hope in it, too, but he closed his eyes this time. And just tried to show her how many years he'd missed her. How many years he'd loved her.

He didn't want to sever that kiss, ever, but there were a few more things he needed to get said. "If *you* need to do something wildly romantic, we'll sail around the world. Or go sleep on all those damn rose petals. I want you to be whoever you want to be, Suze, and that includes 'romantic' if it's important to you. But what matters to me is just being with you. If you change, when you change, if you never change, any way you are . . . and any way you want to be. I'm sorry, so sorry, I didn't value you enough when we were kids—"

"You *did*. I was the one who threw it all away."

He shook his head, briefly and fiercely. "We

didn't have what it took to make it. You always knew that. You were always honest about it, with me and with yourself. I was the one who wasn't strong enough back then."

"Jon, quit being so damned nice. I don't know what to do when you're being this nice. You're scaring me."

"Good," he said, and he didn't have to coax a third kiss because her arms were lifting up, hooking around his neck, pulling him down.

She kissed him that time. Hard and hot. Eyes-closed hot. Lips-parted hard. Love poured from her like a river, running swift and fast and true. "I love you so much. And I thought I'd lost you," she whispered.

"You're never going to lose me, Susan."

"Back in high school . . . I thought it mattered so much. Being the Girl Most Likely to Succeed. I wanted to meet those expectations, be that someone who was strong and self-reliant and didn't need anyone. But I was so wrong, Jon. All I ever really wanted was the same thing my mom and Becca do. The right to be happy. The right to recognize and reach for that happiness. I want the right to be with you. I've never loved anyone else—not remotely like I loved or love you."

He dove for another kiss, and that one didn't end until a lineup of cars in the drive started honking. It *did* seem a crazy place to kiss.

It also seemed like an ideal time to move on— with their kisses, with their lives, with each other.

He'd been thinking and wondering for days now if there was a chance she could be pregnant. He guessed that thought was foolish—it wasn't as if they'd made love enough times to tilt the odds. It was just that the pregnancy before had made them feel trapped, and this time, a baby could seal their future—open up all the freedom that loving each other could bring.

Still, it wasn't as if it mattered that instant. He'd bring it up later. Not now.

Right now all he wanted was to hustle her into the truck and smother her with all those roses and kiss her witless.

So he did.

Six Tips to Planning the Perfect Wedding...

WITH A LITTLE HELP
FROM AVON ROMANCE

Everyone knows that a great love story ends with "happily ever after"... and that means a perfect wedding. But before you get to the Big Day, you have to iron out the details ... picking out a dress, getting the right flowers.

Oh, and there's that little matter of finding the groom.

Now, take a sneak peek as these Avon Romance Superleader heroines ... as created by these talented authors—Cathy Maxwell, Victoria Alexander, Susan Andersen, Jennifer Greene, Judith Ivory and Meggin Cabot—go about finding that husband-to-be.

TIP #1:
IT HELPS IF YOU GET ENGAGED
TO THE RIGHT PERSON TO BEGIN WITH.

*When Anthony Aldercy, the Earl of Burnell, has the bad manners
to fall in love with someone other than his fiancée, he does everything in his power to change his own mind! But pert, pretty
Deborah Percival unexpectedly captures his heart in*

The Lady Is Tempted

BY NEW YORK TIMES BESTSELLING AUTHOR
CATHY MAXWELL

July Avon Romance Superleader

He turned—and for a second, Deborah couldn't think, let
alone speak.

Here was a Corinthian. Even in Ilam they'd heard of these
dashing men about Town. Every young man in the Valley
with a pretense to fashion aped their casual dress. But the
gentleman standing in Miss Chalmers's sitting room was the
real thing.

His coat was of the finest stuff, and the cut fit his form to
perfection . . . as did the doeskin riding breeches. His boots

were so well polished that they reflected the flames in the fire and the nonchalantly careless knot in his tie could only have been achieved by a man who knew what he was doing.

More incredibly, his shoulders beneath the fine marine blue cloth of his jacket appeared broader and stronger than Kevin the cooper's. And his thighs were more muscular than David's, Dame Alodia's groom's. Horseman's thighs. The kind of thighs with the strength and grace from years of riding.

He was also better-looking than both Kevin and David combined.

He wasn't handsome in a classic way. But no one—no *woman*—would not notice him. Dark lashes framed eyes so blue they appeared to be almost black. Slashing brows gave his face character, as did the long, lean line of his jaw. His lips were thin but not unattractive, no, not unattractive at all.

Then, he smiled.

A humming started in her ears. Her heart pounded against her chest . . . and she felt an *unseen* pull toward him, a *connection* the likes of which she'd never experienced before from another human being.

And he sensed the same thing.

She *knew*—without words—that he was as struck by her as she was by him. The signs were there in the arrested interest in his eyes, the sly crookedness of his smile.

Miss Chalmers was speaking, making introductions, but the sound of her voice seemed a long distance away. ". . . Mrs. Percival, a widow from Ilam. This is our other guest, a great favorite of mine, Lor—"

The gentleman interrupted her, "Aldercy. Tony Aldercy."

*Women never said no to Lord Matthew Weston, but he never
met one he'd wanted to say, "I do" ... until he impetuously
married a beautiful woman named Tatiana. So imagine
his shock when he discovered his marriage bed empty,
his bride gone ... and his wife was of royal blood!*

Her Highness, My Wife

BY **VICTORIA ALEXANDER**

August Avon Romance Superleader

"If you are to be my wife you are to be my wife in the fullest sense of the word."

"But surely you cannot expect me to—" Tatiana caught herself and stared. "What do you mean *fullest sense of the word*?"

"I mean my wife has to live on my income." Matthew's grin widened. "It's extremely modest."

"I see." She bit her bottom lip absently. There were benefits to being in close quarters with him. He certainly could not ignore her presence in a—she shuddered to herself—cottage.

"And I have only one horse and he is better suited to pull—"

"A carriage?" she said hopefully.

"It's really a wagon." He shook his head in a regretful manner she didn't believe for a moment. "In truth, more of a cart."

"To go along with the shack, no doubt." She would put up with his living conditions, castle or cottage scarcely mattered as long as she was with him.

"And there will be no servants," he warned.

"Of course not, given your modest income," she said brightly. "Is that it then? Your conditions?"

"Not entirely." He studied the apple in his hand absently.

"Really? Whatever is left? You do not mean—" She widened her eyes in stunned disbelief. "You cannot possibly believe—" She wrung her hands together and paced to the right. "Surely, you do not expect that I—" She swiveled and paced to the left. "That you—that we—" She stopped and turned toward him. "That you think I would— Oh Matthew, how could you?" She let out a wrenching sob, buried her face in her hands, and wept in the manner of any virtuous women presented with such an edict.

"Good Lord! Your Highness. Tatiana." Concern sounded in his voice and she heard him step closer. "I didn't mean—"

"You most certainly did." She dropped her hands and glared at him. "*This* is exactly what you wanted. Was there a moment of regret over your beastly behavior?"

"There is now." He glared down at her but held his ground.

"Ha. I doubt that. Your intentions with this and every other of your ridiculous conditions was to shock me and, furthermore, to put me in my place. These stipulations of yours, especially the last one." She shook her head. "Did you really believe for a moment I would fall to pieces at the idea of sharing your bed? I am not a blushing virgin. I have been married."

"To me." His eyes narrowed dangerously. "Or have I missed another marriage or two?"

"Not yet," she snapped. "But the day is still young."

*Tristan MacLaughlin is sent to protect vulnerable dancer
Amanda Charles from the crazed man who is stalking her.
At first Amanda thinks MacLaughlin is overbearing—
and overwhelming—but she soon discovers
the unleashed passion in his arms.*

Shadow Dance

THE CLASSIC ROMANTIC NOVEL

BY SUSAN ANDERSEN

September Avon Romance Superleader

Tristan yanked her forward and kissed her. And, if before
that instant Amanda had thought he stood aloofly by and
observed life from the sidelines, she discovered then that she
was mistaken. For there was nothing detached about his hungry mouth moving over hers, nothing aloof about the powerful grip of his arms on her back as they pressed her forward
into the heat of his body, or in his blunt fingers, tangled in her

hair, grasping her skull. There was nothing detached at all, and his intensity laid to waste her powers of reasoning.

He had pulled her to him so quickly, she hardly had time to react. Automatically, she raised her hands to push him away. But, for just an instant, she was caught up in the contrast of how things as they appeared to be and as they actually were could be so devastatingly different.

For instance, MacLaughlin's mouth appeared hard and stern, but, Lord help her . . . it was soft. Strong. Hot. But not hard—not hard at all. The only remotely harsh element of his kiss was the heavy morning beard of his unshaven jaw, abrading the tender skin of her face.

Having hesitated for even that brief an instant, she forgot exactly to which it was she had been going to object. Being manhandled again, maybe? Um. Something like that. She didn't remember and she didn't care. Any objection she might have raised was swamped beneath a wave of sensation.

Tristan's mouth kept opening over Amanda's. Restlessly, he slanted his lips over the fullness of hers. When she didn't open to him immediately, he raised his head, stared into her eyes for a moment, and then came at her from another direction, using the hand in her hair to tilt her face to accommodate him. He widened his mouth around her lips and then slowly dragged it closed, tugging at her lips.

She didn't even think twice. Amanda's lips simply parted beneath his, and Tristan made a wordless sound of satisfaction deep in his throat.

His tongue was slow and thorough. It slid along her bottom lip and explored the serrated edges of her teeth. Releasing his grip on her head, Tristan pulled her closer into the heat of his body, moving his pelvis against her with suggestive need. His tongue rubbed along hers. Nerves Amanda hadn't even known she possessed flamed to acute, throbbing life. Her tongue surged up to challenge his and she arched against him, sliding her arms up to wrap tightly around the strong column of his neck, plunging her fingers into his crisp hair. She was aware of every muscle in his body as he pressed against her.

Murmuring soft sounds of excitement, she raised up on tiptoe, lifting her left leg with an agility borne of years of dancing, to hook the back of her knee behind his hard buttock.

Tristan groaned and kissed her harder, aroused nearly to a frenzy. Meaning only to lean her against a support, but misjudging the distance from where they stood, he slammed her up against the wall of the apartment and rocked against her with slow, mindless insistence. One large hand slid slowly up the leg locked around his hip, stroking from knee to thigh, pulling her closer into him before it eased beneath the high-cut leg of her leotard to grip her firm, tights-covered bottom with wide splayed fingers. "Oh, lass," he breathed into her mouth, and then, unable to bear even that slight separation, he kissed her harder, his mouth hungry and a little rough against hers.

Amanda tightened her grip around his neck and kissed him back, following his lead exactly.

He was frustrated by the tights and the one-piece leotard she wore. She looked smashing in it, but it protected her flesh from invasion like a high-security alarm system.

TIP #4:
MAKE SURE YOU AND THE GROOM SHARE
COMPATIBLE HOPES AND DREAMS . . .
REMEMBER, THERE'S MORE TO MARRIAGE
THAN A GOOD CHINA PATTERN!

Susan Sinclair is strong, capable, and can deal with anything—
after all, everyone tells her so a million times a day!
Surely she can handle a man like Jon Laker . . . even if
she melts into a puddle every time he comes around.
After all, she "got over" Jon a long time ago—didn't she?

The Woman Most
Likely To . . .

by JENNIFER GREENE

October Avon Romance Superleader

When Jon realized his heart was beating like an overheated jackhammer, he stopped dead, determined to head back home and forget this nonsense. If Susan was in the area, then she was staying at her mother's. He could call her. And if she'd wanted him for something critically important, she could have—and would have—said something on the spot. It was stupid to think that he had to track her down this second . . .

He was halfway to the marina, when he spotted her. Her hands were in her pockets, her hair kicking up in the breeze; she was ambling near the docks, toward the beach, heading for nothing specific, as far as he could see.

He charged forward until he was within calling distance. "Suze!" An out-of-breath stitch knifed his side. His shop keys were still dangling from his hand. "Susan!"

She turned the moment she recognized his voice. From that angle, the sun slapped her sharply in the eyes, where he was in shadow, so he could clearly see how she braced, how she instinctively stilled. "Honestly, Jon, you didn't have to run after me."

"I figured I did. It's not like you to go to the trouble of tracking me down more than once in a decade. What's wrong?"

"Nothing."

He wasn't opposed to wasting time on nonsense. But not now, and not with her. "You didn't show up at my place to discuss the weather."

"There's definitely something we need to talk about together. But it's not an easy subject to spring into. I can't just . . ."

"Okay. So. Let's sit somewhere."

"Not *your* place."

God forbid she should trust him after twenty-two years. As if he'd jump her if he caught her alone . . . well hell, come to think of it, he had. But only a few times. And only when she'd wanted to be jumped. And that hadn't happened in a blue moon because they'd both spun out of control the instant someone turned the heat up—and then they'd both been madder and edgier than fighting cats afterward.

Even the best sex in the universe wasn't worth that.

It came close, though.

*Stuart Aysgarth might be the Viscount of Mount Villiars—
and he might consider himself extremely important—
but that doesn't mean he is above the law . . . and
Emma Darlington Hotchkiss is determined he honor
his debt to her. And nothing—not even seduction—
will change her mind!*

Untie My Heart

BY JUDITH IVORY

November Avon Romance Superleader

There was nothing innocent in how his finger continued over the curve of her jawbone to her neck, taking the hem of her dress down her tendon all the way to her collarbone. His eyes followed his finger to the hollow of her throat, where at last he hesitated, paused, then—thank goodness—stopped. She shivered involuntarily, tried to speak, but ended up only wetting her lips, dry-mouthed.

The path his finger had traveled left a tiny, traceable impression down her neck to her clavicle, a trail so warm and particular it seemed traced by the sun through a magnifying glass.

"You," he said finally, then paused in that soft, slow way he had that was mildly terrifying now under the circumstance, "are a very hard woman to frighten, do you know that?"

She blinked up at him. "I can assure you, you're doing a good job. You can stop, if that was the goal."

He laughed. A rare sound, genuine, deep, though she definitely didn't like his sense of humor, now that she heard it. For a second more—with him leaning on both arms, his shoulders bunching, pulling at his shirt where they held his weight—he hovered over her, surveying her in that very disarming way again. Then he stood up completely.

Good God, was he tall. From her angle, his head seemed to all but touch the ceiling.

He stared about them, perplexed for a moment, as if he'd lost track of what he was doing, then seemed to remember. And he backed up.

To take a gander at his handiwork, it seemed. Over her knee she watched him withdraw two feet to the window sill and sit his buttocks onto it, his back flattening the lace curtains. There, he crossed his arms over his chest, tilted his head, and viewed her incapacitation from this new angle.

He then said, "Do you know, I think I could do anything to you, absolutely anything, and there would be nothing you could do about it."

"What a cheerful piece of speculation," she said, a little annoyed.

"Save complain. Which you do very well."

She shut her mouth, advising herself to take John's advice and be humble. Or at least quiet.

Mount Villiars laughed again, entertained by his own iniquitous turns of mind. "And whatever I did, afterward, I could hand you over to the sheriff, and, even complaining, he'd just haul you away." The sarcastic jackanapes shook his head as if in earnest sympathy. "Such is our legal system and the power behind the title of viscount. I love being a viscount. Have I mentioned that? Despite all the trouble that arrived with my particular title, I find it's worth fighting for. By the way," he added, "I like those knickers."

She Went All The Way

BY **MEGGIN CABOT**

December Avon Romance Superleader

"Sorry," he said. "I don't really watch movies all that much."

For a moment, Lou forgot she was the victim of an attempted murder and a helicopter crash, and gaped at Jack—Jack, the movie star—as if he'd just done something completely out of keeping with his manly image, such as order a champagne cocktail or burst into a rendition of "I Feel Pretty."

"You're an *actor*," she cried, "and you're telling me you don't really watch movies all that much?"

"Hazard of the trade," Jack said lightly. "The magic of Hollywood doesn't hold much allure when you know all the secrets."

Lou shook her head. Oh, yes. They were definitely in Bizarro World now. No doubt about it.

"Maybe," Jack ventured, as if he hoped to change the subject, "we should build a fire."

"A fire?" If he'd suggested they strip naked and do the hula, Lou could not have been more surprised. "A *fire?* What do you think *that* is?" She pointed at the burning hulk of metal a dozen yards away. "What, you're worried when they start looking for us they won't be able to spot us? Townsend, I don't think they're going to have any problem."

"Actually," he said, in the politely distant tone he reserved, as Lou knew only too well, for incompetent waiters and crazy screenwriters, "I was thinking a fire might warm us up. You're shivering."

She was, of course. Shivering. But she'd hoped he wouldn't notice. Showing weakness in front of Jack Townsend was not exactly something she wanted to do. It was bad enough she'd been unconscious in front of him. The last thing she wanted was for him to think she was afraid . . . or worse, uneasy about their current situation—that she was stuck in the middle of nowhere with one of America's hottest Hollywood idols. She had had more than enough with Hollywood idols. Hadn't she lived with one for eight years? Yeah, and look how *that* had turned out.

She was certainly not going to make that mistake again. Not that she was about to do anything as foolish as fall in love with Jack Townsend. Perish the thought! So what if he seemed to be concerned about her physical comfort, and had saved her life, and oh, yes, looked better in a pair of jeans than any man Lou had ever seen in her life? *Are we having fun yet?* Right there was reason enough not to give him the time of day, let alone her sorely abused heart. Besides, hadn't he had the very bad taste to, until recently, date Greta Woolston? There had to be something wrong with a man who couldn't see through that vapid headcase, as she knew only too well.

It was as she was thinking these deep thoughts that she noticed Jack had stood up and wandered a short distance away. He was picking up sticks that had fallen to the ground, branches that, too heavily laden with snow, had fallen to the earth.

"What . . ." She started as he leaned down and hefted a particularly large branch. The back of his leather jacket came up over his butt, and she was awarded a denim-clad view of the famous Jack Townsend butt, the one women all over America gladly shelled out ten bucks to see on the big screen.

And here she was with that butt all to herself.

In the middle of Alaska.